JEFFERY DEAVER

The Cutting Edge

HODDER &
STOUGHTON

First published in 2018 in the United States of America by Grand Central
First published in Great Britain in 2018 by Hodder & Stoughton
An Hachette UK company

1

Copyright © Gunner Publications LLC 2018

The right of Jeffery Deaver to be identified as the
Author of the Work has been asserted by him in accordance
with the Copyright, Designs and Patents Act 1988.

A CIP catalogue record for this title is available from the British Library

Hardback ISBN 978 1 473 61873 2
Trade Paperback ISBN 978 1 473 61874 9
eBook ISBN 978 1 473 61872 5

Typeset in Sabon MT by Palimpsest Book Production Limited,
Falkirk, Stirlingshire

Printed and bound in Great Britain by Clays Ltd, St Ives plc

Hodder & Stoughton policy is to use papers that are natural, renewable
and recyclable products and made from wood grown in sustainable
forests. The logging and manufacturing processes are expected to
conform to the environmental regulations of the country of origin.

Hodder & Stoughton Ltd
Carmelite House
50 Victoria Embankment
London EC4Y 0DZ

www.hodder.co.uk

To my Texas crew: Dan, Ellen, Wyatt, Bridget, Ingrid, Eric and Brynn, Sabrina and Shea.

I saw the angel in the marble and carved until I set him free.

– Michelangelo

I
PLOTTING

SATURDAY, MARCH 13

CHAPTER 1

'Is it safe?'

He considered this briefly. 'Safe? Why wouldn't it be safe?'

'I'm just saying. It's kind of deserted.' The woman looked around the poorly lit, shabby lobby, the floor ancient linoleum so worn it looked sanded down. They were the only ones here, standing before the elevator. The building was smack in the middle of the Diamond District in Midtown Manhattan. Because it was Saturday, the Jewish Sabbath, many stores and companies were closed. The March wind hissed and moaned.

William, her fiancé, said, 'I think we're good. Only partially haunted.'

She smiled but the expression vanished fast.

Deserted, yes, William thought. And gloomy. Typical of Midtown offices built in the, who knew? Thirties? Forties? But hardly unsafe.

Though not very efficient. Where was the elevator? Damn it.

William said, 'Don't worry. Not like the South Bronx.'

Anna chided gently, 'You've never been to the South Bronx.'

'Went to a Yankees game.' He'd once commuted *through* the South Bronx, and for some years, too. But didn't mention that.

From behind the thick metallic doors, gears ground and pulleys pulled. The soundtrack was creaks and squeals.

The elevator. Now, *that* might not be safe. But the odds of getting Anna to walk up three flights of stairs were nonexistent. His fiancée, broad-shouldered, blond and pert, was in great shape, thanks to the health club and her charming obsession with the devil-red Fitbit. It wasn't the exertion she objected to, with that wonderful wry glance; it was, as she'd once said, that girls don't do stairs in buildings like this.

Even on joyous errands.

Practicality raised its head – yet again. 'Are you sure this is a good idea, Billy?'

He was prepared. 'Of course it is.'

'It's so expensive!'

True, it was. But William had done his homework and knew he was getting quality for the sixteen thousand dollars. The rock that Mr Patel was mounting in the white-gold setting for Anna's pretty finger was a one-point-five-carat princess cut, F, which meant virtually colorless, very close to the ideal D. The stone was graded nearly flawless – IF, meaning there were only some minor flaws (Mr Patel had explained they were called 'inclusions') detectible only to an expert under magnification. It wasn't perfect and it wasn't huge but it was a magnificent piece of carbon that, through Mr Patel's eye loupe, took your breath away.

Most important, Anna loved it.

William came very close to saying, You only get married once. But, thank you, Lord, stopped short. Because while that was true in her case, it was not in his. Anna didn't mind his past, or didn't offer any *evidence* that she minded, but it was best not to bring up the topic (hence, editing out the story about the five years of commuting to Westchester).

Where the hell was that elevator?

William Sloane pressed the button again, though it was already illuminated. And they laughed at the pointless gesture.

Behind them the door to the street opened and a man walked in. At first he was just a shadow, backlit through the greasy glass of the door. William felt a moment's unease.

Is this safe . . . ?

Maybe he'd been a little quick with the reassurance some minutes before. He and Anna would be walking out in ten minutes with a house down payment on her finger. He looked around and was troubled to see there were no security cameras here.

But the man walked closer and offered a pleasant smile and nod, then returned to reading his texts. He had pale skin, was wearing a dark jacket and knit stocking cap, carrying cloth gloves in his phone hand – all necessary accessories on this unusually frosty March day. An attaché case too. He'd work in the building . . .

or maybe was picking up a ring for *his* fiancée at Patel's too. No threat. Still, William – a health-club and Fitbit aficionado himself – was in top form and could take down a guy of this size. A fantasy, he supposed, that every man engaged in from time to time.

Finally, the elevator arrived and the doors squealed open. They got in and the man gestured to the couple to enter first.

'Please.' An accented voice. William couldn't place the nationality.

'Thank you,' Anna said.

A nod.

At the third floor, the door opened and the man again gestured with his palm. William nodded in response and he and Anna continued toward Patel Designs, at the end of the long, dim hallway.

Jatin Patel was an interesting man, an immigrant from Surat, western India, the diamond-polishing center of that country – and of the world, now. When the couple had been here some weeks ago, placing their order, Patel had chatted away, explaining that the vast bulk of gem-quality diamond polishing was done there, in boiler rooms – tiny factories like apartment buildings, hot and filthy, with terrible ventilation. Only the best diamonds were cut in New York or Antwerp or Israel anymore. Because of his skill, he'd risen above the pack of cutters – thousands of them in Surat – and managed to save enough money to come to the United States and open a shop.

He sold jewelry and diamonds retail – to the soon-to-be-Sloanes, for instance – but he was best known for his cutting of high-end diamonds from raw stones.

On that earlier visit William had been fascinated to learn about the diamond trade, fascinated too that Patel would, from time to time, grow coy and steer the conversation away from William's innocent questions. He supposed the diamond world was a shadowy, secretive place in many ways. Look at blood diamonds – those mined in Africa by warlords and terrorists, who used the profits to finance their horrific crimes. (The princess cut William was buying came with a guarantee that it had been ethically mined. William, though, couldn't help but wonder how true that was. After all, was the broccoli he'd steamed last night truly organic, as the placard at their local store promised?)

He was aware that the man who'd accompanied them in the elevator had stopped at a door just before Patel's and was hitting the intercom.

So he was legit.

William chided himself for his concern and pressed the button for Patel Designs. Through the speaker came: 'Yes? Who is there? Mr Sloane?'

'Yes, it's us.'

There was a click of the door and they stepped in.

It was at that moment that a thought struck William Sloane. As in many old-time buildings, the doors to all of the businesses on this floor had transoms above them – horizontal glass panels. Here they were covered with thick bars, for security. The one above Patel's door glowed, revealing lights inside. But the transom next door – the one the man from the elevator had stopped at – was dark.

That business was closed.

No!

A sudden rush of footsteps behind them and, gasping, William turned to see the man, now with his head covered by a ski mask, charge toward them. He shoved them into the small room, where Patel sat behind a counter. The intruder moved so fast that Anna was knocked off her feet and fell hard, screaming. William turned but froze as the man pointed a gun his way – a black pistol.

'Jesus, no! Please!'

Despite his age, and paunchy midsection, Jatin Patel rose fast, going for what must have been a panic button. He didn't get close. The man lunged forward and, reaching over the counter, slammed the pistol into his face. There was a horrific sound. William heard the snap of bone under the impact.

The diamond dealer screamed. Patel, whose complexion was grayish all the time, grew grayer yet.

'Look,' William said, 'I can get you money. You can have our ring.'

'Take it!' Anna said. Then to Patel: 'Give it to him. Give him whatever he wants.'

Drawing back his gloved hand, still holding the gun, he swung it forward into Patel's face again and again. Crying out, begging for him to stop, Patel slumped helpless to the floor, muttering, 'I can get you money! Lots of money! Whatever you want! Please, please stop.'

'Leave him alone,' Anna cried.

'Quiet!' The man was looking around the room. A fast glance to the ceiling. There was a video camera pointing down toward them. Then he was studying the counter, the desk behind it and several dim rooms in the back.

With one hand toward the gunman, palm out, to reassure tht he was no threat, William stepped closer to Anna. His arm went around his fiancée's waist and he helped her up. He could feel her trembling.

The robber ripped a light cord from the wall. He extracted a box cutter – a utility knife – from his pocket and pressed the razor blade out with his thumb. Setting down the gun, he cut the wire into two lengthy pieces. He handed one to Anna. 'Tie his hands.' Nodding at William. That accent again. European? Scandinavian?

'Do it,' William told her gently. 'It's okay.' He added in a whisper, 'He could have shot us. He doesn't want that. Tie my wrists.'

'Tight.'

'Yes, she will.'

With shaking hands, she did.

'Lie down.'

William eased to the floor.

Of course, he'd get the main threat out of the way – him. Then, glancing at Patel, the burglar bound Anna's wrists and shoved her to the floor beside William, back to back.

A chilling thought, cold as a winter stream, cut through him. William realized that the intruder had put the mask on before going into the store, to hide his face from the cameras.

But he hadn't worn it before. Because he needed some customers to get him through the door of Patel's. He'd probably been waiting for a couple to follow to a company that seemed like a good target for a robbery.

The security camera in Patel's would have no recording of his features.

But William and Anna could describe him.

And that meant only one thing: The robber had tied them up so they wouldn't fight back when he killed them.

The man now stepped close, standing over them, looking down.

'Look, please . . . '

'Shhhhh.'

William prayed, If it has to happen, let him shoot us. It'll be fast, painless. He managed a look, twisting his head hard upward. And saw that the man had left the gun on the counter.

The gunman crouched over them, gripping the knife.

William's back was still facing Anna's and, sobbing, he stretched his hand out as far as he could. It found hers. He wondered if it was her left one and if the finger he was caressing now was the one that had come so close to being graced by the princess-cut, one-point-five-carat diamond, only slightly flawed and nearly colorless.

CHAPTER 2

This was his life.

Today was typical. Up at six, a Saturday, can you believe it? Help his mother empty all the pantry and kitchen shelves, for cleaning and laying new contact paper. Then wash the car – on this damp, grim day! Hugging his mother and father goodbye, then taking the train from their home in Queens all the way to Brooklyn, on an errand for Mr Patel.

Yet another train to Manhattan, to start polishing the stones that awaited him. He was on board now, as it swayed its way north.

Saturday. When everyone else was at brunch or plays or movies . . . or museums.

Or galleries.

How unfair was this?

Oh, forget entertainment. Vimal Lahori would be fine – in fact, he'd *prefer* to be – in the damp basement of the family's house in Queens.

But that was not an option.

He pulled his dark-gray wool jacket around him more tightly as he swayed with the gentle motion of the subway. The twenty-two-year-old was thin and not tall. He'd reached his present height of five feet, six inches in grade school and had had about two years' edge over his boy classmates, until others pulled even or eclipsed him. Still, the ethnic bent of his high school, with names more Latino and East or South Asian than black or Anglo, meant he wasn't as diminutive as many. Which wasn't to say that he didn't get bloodied occasionally – though the engine for the most severe torment was that his family had immigrated from Kashmir, the region claimed by the bordering rivals, India and Pakistan. Vimal was, he believed, the only boy to have been beaten up for a border dispute (ironically by two gangly seniors whose religions – one Muslim and one Hindu – should have made *them* sworn enemies).

The wounds were minor, though, and the conflict soon forgotten, largely because Vimal was hardly a Kashmirista (he wasn't even sure where the borders of his ancestral homeland lay). More important, he could move down the soccer pitch the way a honey bee zips from petal to petal; ball control will trump geopolitics any day.

The train approached the stop at 42nd Street. The wheels shrieked and the smoky, salt odor eased into the car. Vimal unfurled and looked into the paper bag he carried. It contained a half-dozen rocks. He removed one, a piece about the size of his fist. It was gray and dark green, striated with crystals. One end was cracked flat and the other rounded. Every piece of stone on earth, big or small, could be turned into something else and, with some thought and patience, the artist could see what it should become. But this one was obvious: a bird, Vimal saw instantly, a bird that was pressing wings to body and keeping its head low to ward off the cold. He could rough out the creature in a day.

But today was not that day.

Today was for work. Mr Patel was a very talented man. A genius, many people said, and Vimal knew it was true. And probably because of his brilliance Mr Patel was also a taskmaster. Vimal had the Abington job to finish. Four pieces of stone, three carats each, more or less. He knew it would take a full eight hours, and the old man – he was fifty-five – would spend agonizing periods of that time examining Vimal's efforts under the glass. Then have him make adjustments. And more after that.

And more and more and more . . .

The doors of the subway opened and Vimal replaced in the paper bag the *Solitary Bird, January* – his name for the sculpture that would never be. He stepped onto the platform and climbed to the street. At least it was Saturday and, with many of the Orthodox stores closed, the Diamond District would be more serene than on weekdays, especially with this nasty March weather. The bustling of the neighborhood sometimes drove him crazy.

Instinctively, the minute he turned onto 47th Street Vimal grew cautious – as did pretty much every one of the hundreds of employees here, a place where many owners were reluctant to advertise too loudly. Yes, there were plenty of 'Jewelers' and 'Diamonds' and 'Gems' in the shop and company names but the higher-end operations and the few important diamond cutters left in the city tended to call themselves by names like 'Elijah Findings,' 'West Side Collateral' and 'Specialties In Style.'

Hundreds of millions' worth of diamonds and gems flowed into and out of these stores and cutting shops every day of the year. And there wasn't a halfway competent burglar or robber in the world who wasn't aware of that fact. And they also knew that the number one way to transport precious gems and gold and platinum and finished jewelry wasn't via armored trucks (too many shipments in and out daily to make a whole truck cost-efficient) or in aluminum attaché cases handcuffed to wrists (far too easy to spot and, as any doctor would tell you, hands can be severed with a hacksaw in less than sixty seconds, even faster if you go electric).

No, the best way to transport valuables was to do just what Vimal was doing now. Dressing down – in jeans, running shoes, a *Keep Weird and Carry On* sweatshirt and wool jacket, while carting a stained paper bag.

So, as Vimal's father – a former cutter himself – insisted, the young man kept his eyes scanning constantly for anyone who might glance a certain way at the bag in his hand or might be moving close while overtly *not* looking.

Still, he wasn't too concerned; even on less-busy days like this, there were guards present, seemingly unarmed but with those little revolvers or automatics tucked into sweaty waistbands. He nodded at one now, as she stood in front of a jewelry store, an African American woman with short purple hair of crinkly texture that Vimal marveled at; he had no idea how she'd managed it. Coming from an ethnic background that offered pretty much one-size-fits-all hair (black, thick and wavy or straight), he was greatly impressed by her do. He wondered how he might render it in stone.

'Hey, Es,' he called, nodding.

'Vimal. Saturday. Boss don't give you no time off? That sucks.'

He shrugged, offering a rueful smile.

She glanced at the bag, which for all she knew held a half-dozen Harry Winston–branded stones worth ten million.

He was tempted to say, It's just peanut butter and jelly. She'd probably laugh. But the idea of making a joke on 47th Street seemed alien. There wasn't a lot of humor in the Diamond District. Something about the value – and, probably more so, the narcotic quality – of diamonds made this an all-too-serious business.

He now entered Mr Patel's building. He never waited for Insufferable Elevator – a fantastical artifact out of Harry Potter, he'd told Adeela, which she'd laughed at – but charged up the stairs, his lithe frame unaffected by gravity, his legs strong and lungs vital from the soccer pitch.

Pushing into the hallway, he noted four of the eight overheads were still dark. He wondered, as he often did, why Mr Patel, who had to have a shitload of money, didn't find a glitzy office elsewhere. Maybe it was sentimental. He had opened his shop here thirty years ago, when this entire floor was cutters. Now his was one of the few fabricators left in the building. Cold on days like this, hot and dusty from June to September. Smelling dank. Mr Patel didn't have a showroom as such and the 'factory' was really just a workshop, the smaller of the three rooms. Given his low-output high-quality work, all he needed was a place big enough for two diamond-polishing scaifes and two cutting machines. He could relocate anywhere.

But Mr Patel had never shared with Vimal his reasoning for staying, because he never shared anything with Vimal, except how to hold the dop stick, how to mount the stones for bruting, how much diamond dust to mix with olive oil for brillianteering.

Halfway to the office, Vimal paused. What was that smell? Fresh paint. The walls on this floor definitely needed a new coat, had for years, but he couldn't see evidence that any workers had been fixing up the place.

During the *week* it was hard enough to get maintenance to do anything. Somebody had actually come in on Friday night or Saturday to paint?

He continued toward the door. The offices here had glass transoms, though they were covered with bars, of course, and he could see shadows of somebody inside Mr Patel's shop. Maybe they were the buyers, the couple who'd come to him for a special engagement ring. William Sloane and Anne Markam – he remembered their names because they'd seemed so nice, actually introducing themselves to Vimal – the hired hand – as he'd left the shop on their last visit. Nice, but naïve: If they'd invested the money they'd spent on their carat-and-a-half diamond, that sum would have grown into a college education for their firstborn. Seduced by the diamond marketing cabal, as he thought of them.

If Vimal and Adeela ever got married – a conversation that hadn't come up yet, nowhere close – but if they did, he'd buy her a hand-carved rocking chair for their engagement. He'd sculpt her something. And if she wanted a ring he'd make something out of lapis, with the head of a fox on it, which was, for some reason, her favorite animal.

He punched in the code for the security lock.

Vimal stepped inside and stopped in mid-stride, gasping.

Three things took his attention immediately. First, the bodies of a man and woman – William and Anna – in a twisted and eerie pose, as if they'd died in agony.

The second was a lake of blood extending outward.

The third was Mr Patel's feet. Vimal couldn't see the rest of the body, just his well-worn shoes, pointing upward. Motionless.

From the workshop to the left of the front room a figure appeared. A ski mask obscured his face but his body language explained that he was startled.

Neither Vimal nor the man moved.

The intruder dropped the briefcase he was holding and pulled a gun from his pocket and aimed. Vimal instinctively spun away, as if he could avoid the bullet, and lifted his hands, as if he could stop it.

A burst of light flowered from the muzzle and the roar deafened Vimal. A searing pain stabbed his belly and side.

He stumbled backward into the dim, dusty corridor, his mind filled with a manic thought: What a sad and ordinary place to die.

CHAPTER 3

He had not returned to the city in time.

To his disappointment.

Lincoln Rhyme directed his Merits Vision wheelchair – gray with red fenders – through the front door of his Central Park West town house. Someone had once remarked that the place brought to mind Sherlock Holmes – in two senses: First, the ancient brownstone would have fit nicely in Victorian England (it dated to that era), and second, the front parlor was filled with enough forensic instruments and equipment to awe the British consulting detective to his core.

Rhyme paused in the entryway to wait for Thom, his trim, muscular caregiver, who'd parked the disabled-accessible Mercedes Sprinter in the cul-de-sac behind the town house. Feeling the cold breeze upon his cheek, Rhyme turned the chair and bumped the door partly closed. It blew back open. A quadriplegic, paralyzed from the neck down, he was quite adept at the high-tech accessories available to those with hampered bodies: the touchpads, eye and voice recognition systems, prosthetics and the like. And surgery and implants had given him some control over his right arm. But many old-fashioned mechanical tasks, from closing doors to – oh, picking a random example – opening bottles of single-malt scotch, remained, literally, out of reach.

Thom arrived a moment later and closed the door. He removed Rhyme's jacket – he refused to 'wear' a blanket for warmth – and peeled off to the kitchen.

'Lunch?'

'No.'

The aide called back, 'Phrased that wrong. I meant, what would you like?'

'Nothing.'

'Not the correct answer.'

'I'm not hungry,' Rhyme muttered. He clumsily picked up the remote for the TV. And turned on the news.

Thom called, 'You need to eat. Soup. Cold day. Soup.'

Rhyme grimaced. His condition was serious, yes, and certain things like pressure on the skin or unrelieved bodily functions could have dangerous consequences. But hunger was not a potential risk factor.

The aide was such a goddamn mother hen.

After a few moments Rhyme smelled something aromatic. Thom did make pretty good soup.

He turned his attention to the television, which he rarely watched. Usually, it was to follow a particular news story, which was what he now wished to do: a story related to the disappointment created by his trip to Washington, DC, the place from which he and Amelia Sachs had just returned.

The station that had crinkled onto the screen wasn't twenty-four-hour news but a documentary network. Airing presently was a true crime show, though dramatized. The villain glared. The detectives looked thoughtful. The music flared. The forensic officer wore a wristwatch *outside* his glove at the scene.

Jesus Christ.

'Were you watching this crap?' he shouted to Thom.

No reply.

Punching buttons, he found a network news channel. At the moment, though, there was no news, only commercials for prescription medicines. He didn't have a clue what the medications did, except turn the actors from somber old grandparents into happy and seemingly less-old grandparents, frolicking with younguns in the final scene, their can't-play-with-the-younguns malady cured.

Then an anchor appeared and after some local news, political in nature, the story he was interested in popped up briefly: It was the account of a trial, presently under way in the Eastern District of New York. A Mexican drug lord, Eduardo Capilla, better known as El Halcón, had made the mistake of coming into the United States to meet with a local organized crime figure in the metro area and set up a narcotics and money-laundering network, along with a bit of underaged prostitution and human smuggling.

The Mexican was pretty sharp. Although he was a billionaire several times over, he'd flown commercial, coach, to Canada, entering legally. He'd then taken a private plane to an airstrip close to the border. From there he'd flown in a helicopter – illegally – to a deserted airport on Long Island, staying – in the literal sense – under the radar. The airport was a few miles from a warehouse complex that he was going to buy and, it was speculated, turn into the headquarters for his U.S. operation.

Police and the FBI had learned of his presence, though, and agents and officers intercepted him there. A shoot-out ensued, resulting in the death of the warehouse owner, along with his bodyguard. A police officer was severely injured and an FBI agent wounded, as well.

El Halcón was arrested but, to the dismay of prosecutors, his American partner, with whom he'd hoped to build a drug empire, wasn't present and his identity was never discovered; the apparent warehouse owner – the man killed in the shoot-out – was a figurehead. No amount of digging could reveal the true U.S. contact.

Lincoln Rhyme had so wanted a piece of the case. He'd hoped to analyze the evidence and provide expert forensic testimony at trial. But he'd committed to meet with a half-dozen senior officials in Washington, DC, so he and Sachs had spent the week down there.

Disappointed, yes. He'd really wanted to help send El Halcón away. But there'd be other cases.

Coincidentally, just at that thought, his phone hummed and displayed a caller ID that suggested there might be one in the offing.

'Lon,' Rhyme said.

'Linc. You back?'

'I'm back. You have something knotty for me? You have something interesting? Something *challenging*?'

Detective First Grade Lon Sellitto had been Rhyme's partner years ago, when Rhyme was NYPD, but they socialized only rarely now and never just called each other up to chat. Phone calls from Sellitto usually happened when he needed help on a case.

'Dunno if it's any of the above. But I got a question.' The detective seemed out of breath. Maybe an urgent mission, maybe he was walking back from the grocery store with a box of pastry.

'And?'

'Whatta you know about diamonds?'

'Diamonds . . . Hm. Let me think. I know they're allotropes.'

'They're what?'

'Allotrope. It's an element – as in chemical element – that exists in more than one form. Carbon is a perfect example. A superstar, in the world of elements, as I think even you know.'

'Even me,' Sellitto grunted.

'Carbon can be graphene, fullerene, graphite or diamond. Depends on how the atoms are bonded. Graphite is a hexagonal lattice, diamonds are tetrahedral lattice. Small thing, it seems. But it makes the difference between a pencil and the Crown Jewels.'

'Linc. I'm sorry I asked. Should've tried this: You ever run a case in the Diamond District?'

Rhyme thought back to his years as detective, as captain running the crime scene operation of the NYPD and, later, as consultant. Some cases had touched on the 47th Street area, Midtown. But none had involved diamond stores or dealers. He told Sellitto as much.

'We could use some help. Robbery gone bad, looks like. Multiple homicides.' A pause. 'Some other shit too.'

Not a term of art in the crime-solving world, Rhyme reflected. He was curious.

'You interested?'

Since the El Halcón case had slipped away from him, the answer was yes. 'How soon can you get here?' Rhyme asked.

'Let me in.'

'What?'

Rhyme heard a pounding from the front hall. Through the phone Sellitto was saying, 'I'm here. I'm outside. I was gonna talk you into the case whether you wanted it or not. Come on, open the goddamn door. It's like January out here.'

'Soup?' Thom asked, taking Lon Sellitto's drab gray overcoat. Hanging it.

'Naw. Wait, what kind?' Sellitto, Rhyme noticed, had lifted his face, as if positioning his nose at a better angle to detect the scent meandering from the kitchen.

'Tomato bisque with shrimp. Lincoln's having some.'

'No, I'm not.'

'Yes, he is.'

'Hm.' Stocky and rumpled – the latter adjective referring to the clothing, not the man – Lon Sellitto had always had weight issues, at least as long as Rhyme had known him. A recent poison attack by an unsub he and Rhyme were pursing had nearly killed him and caused him to shed scores of pounds. A skeletal Lon Sellitto was an alarming sight and he was fighting his way back to his substantial form. Rhyme was pleased when he said, 'Okay.'

Pleased too because it would take the pressure off him. He wasn't hungry.

'Where's Amelia?' Sellitto asked.

'Not here.'

Amelia Sachs was in Brooklyn, where she kept an apartment near her mother's. Rose was recovering well from heart surgery but Sachs looked in on her frequently.

'Not yet?'

'What do you mean?' Rhyme asked.

'She's on her way. Should be soon.'

'Here? You called her.'

'Yeah. That smells good. Does he make soup a lot?'

Rhyme said, 'So you decided we were going to be working the case.'

'Sort of. Rachel and I mostly open cans, Progresso, Campbell's.'

'Lon?'

'Yeah, I decided.'

The soup arrived. Two bowls. Rhyme's went on the small tray attached to his chair; Sellitto's on a table. Rhyme glanced at his.

It *did* smell appealing. Maybe he *was* hungry, after all. Thom was usually right in matters like this, though Rhyme rarely admitted it. The aide offered to feed him but he shook his head, no, and gave it a shot with his right hand and arm. Soup was tricky for the shaky appendage but he managed it without spilling. He was glad he hated sushi; chopsticks were not a utensil option for someone like Lincoln Rhyme.

Another arrival appeared, to Rhyme's surprise, apparently summoned by Lon Sellitto for the Diamond District case: Ron Pulaski. Rhyme thought of him as Rookie and called him that, though he hadn't been one for years. The trim blond uniformed officer was technically with the Patrol Division, though his crime scene skills had brought him to Rhyme's attention and the criminalist had insisted that Sellitto have him informally assigned to Major Cases – Sellitto's and Sachs's outfit.

'Lincoln. Lon.' The latter name was uttered at slightly less volume. The Rookie was, after all, junior in rank, years and bluster to Sellitto.

He also suffered from a condition that had plagued him from the first time he, Rhyme and Sachs had worked together – a head injury. This had sidelined him for a time and, when he had made the tough decision to return to the force, it plagued him with the insecurities and uncertainty that often accompany a trauma to the brain.

When he'd approached Rhyme, mentioning he was thinking of quitting because he felt he wasn't up to the task of policing, the criminalist had snapped, 'It's all in your fucking head.'

The young officer had stared and Rhyme kept a straight face for as long as he could. They had both laughed. 'Ron, everybody's got head injuries, one way or another. Now, I've got a scene I need you to work. You gonna get the CS kit and walk the grid?'

Of course he had.

Now Pulaski doffed his watch coat. Beneath, he was in his long-sleeve, dark-blue NYPD uniform.

Thom offered him food too and Rhyme came close to saying, 'Enough, we're not a soup kitchen' – a clever jab, he thought – but Pulaski declined anyway.

A moment later the low bubble of a powerful car's exhaust thudded through the closed window. Amelia Sachs had arrived. She gave the engine some gas and it then went silent. She walked inside, hung her bomber jacket on a hook and adjusted the belt around her blue jeans, to slip rearward the plastic Glock holster for comfort. She wore a teal high-necked sweater and beneath that, Rhyme had seen this morning as she'd dressed, a black silk T-shirt. They'd listened to the weather report on the radio – today would be unseasonably cold for mid-March, just like the past week. In Washington, DC, they'd witnessed cherry blossoms dying by the thousands.

Sachs nodded to those assembled. Sellitto waved back and noisily finished his soup.

Now that most of the team was in place, and fed – Rhyme reflected with amused cynicism – Sellitto briefed them.

''Bout an hour ago. Robbery and multiple murder. Midtown North. Third floor of Five-Eight West Four-Seven. Patel Designs, owned by Jatin Patel, fifty-five. He's one of the deceased. Diamond cutter and he made and sold jewelry. Was pretty famous, what I hear. I'm not a jewelry kind of guy, so who knows? Major Cases drew it, and they drew me. And I'm drawing you.'

The Major Case Division, overseen by a deputy inspector from the Detective Bureau in One Police Plaza, did not generally run homicides or retail location burglaries.

Lon Sellitto had noted the glance Rhyme and Sachs shared. He now explained why this case was an exception.

'The feeling came down from our friends at City Hall that the last thing we need is a violent robbery in the Diamond District. Especially if he's got more stores in mind. People'll stop shopping. Bad for tourism, bad for the economy.'

'The victims probably aren't too elated either, wouldn't you say, Lon?'

'I'm telling you what I was told is all, Linc. Okay?'

'Proceed away.'

'Now, one other wrinkle *and* this we're keeping a wrap on. The perp tortured Patel. The supervising captain from Midtown North thinks he didn't want to give up the good stuff – open the safe or whatever. So the killer used a box cutter on him till he talked. It was pretty bad.'

Some other shit too . . .

Rhyme said, 'Okay. Let's get to work. Sachs, the scene. I'll get Mel Cooper in. You stay put, Pulaski. Keep you in reserve for the time being.'

Sachs pulled her jacket off the hook, slipped it on, then clipped two spare magazines on her left hip. She headed for the door.

Thom walked into the parlor and smiled at Sachs. 'Oh, Amelia. Didn't see you come in. You hungry?'

'I am. Missed breakfast and lunch.'

'Soup? Perfect for a cold day.'

She gave him a wry smile. Slamming the Torino Cobra, with its 405-horsepower engine and four-speed manual, through Midtown Manhattan made any beverage, let alone hot soup, problematic.

She pulled her keys from her pocket. 'Maybe later.'

CHAPTER 4

The crime scene at Patel Designs on 47th Street presented Amelia Sachs with three questions.

One, since the perp had left hundreds of diamonds behind – just sitting in the open safe – what, in fact, had he stolen? If anything.

Two, why was Patel tortured?

Three, who had placed the anonymous call to report the crime and give a fairly detailed description of the perp? There was a Part B to this question: Was he still alive? When she'd first arrived at the third-floor shop she'd smelled the air and known immediately a weapon had been fired here. She guessed the witness had walked into the robbery, been shot and fled, stopping at the street pay phone from which he'd called 911.

The shop was small and the distance from gun to victim would, at most, have been ten or fifteen feet. Hard to miss with a lethal shot at that range. And there were no stray slugs anywhere in the office or the hallway. The witness had almost certainly been hit.

Sachs, in the crime scene white hooded jumpsuit and booties, stepped around the sizable pool of blood, in the rough shape of Lake Michigan, and laid the numbers for the photographs – the small placards placed where the evidence and significant elements of the crime were located. After shooting the photos, she walked the grid: searching the scene inch by inch. The grid pattern, the only approach she used, as she'd learned from Rhyme, involved walking from one end of the scene to the other, then turning, stepping a foot to the side and returning, the way one mows a lawn. Then you turn perpendicular and search the same scene again, 'against the grain,' as Rhyme described it.

She went through the routine now: gathering trace, taking

footprints, searching for friction ridge prints and swabbing where the perp might have left DNA. Standing momentarily with hands on hips, she surveyed the floor plan of the shop, which embraced, she estimated, only about nine hundred square feet. She glanced out the front door, held open by a rubber wedge, noting a man in a jumpsuit similar to hers. She said to him, 'Computer's in the office. Let's keep our fingers crossed.'

The ECT – evidence collection technician – had specialized training in security cameras and storage devices. He'd extract what he could from the hard drive in Patel's office; a single camera was pointed at the front door from behind the counter. It seemed to be working; a tiny red eye glowed teasingly, and a cable ran from the camera to the man's desktop computer, which sat next to a large printer and, curiously, an ancient fax machine. The camera wasn't connected to a central station, only the computer.

Regarding the security system, though, Sachs was sure that crossing fingers wouldn't be enough. This perp did not seem like a man to forget about erasing security videos. As every cop knew, however, erasing digital media was never permanent. Lots of incriminating data could be unearthed – *if* the data had existed in the first place. A big if.

Sachs now filled out chain-of-custody details on separate cards to be affixed to the evidence itself or the paper or plastic evidence bags it had been stashed in.

Next. The hard part.

She had saved the bodies till the last.

Because, if they didn't need to be processed first, you just put it off for a little bit longer.

The image that immediately seized her attention when she'd first entered and that touched her still was the fingers of the couple whose throats had been slashed. The hands had been tied behind them and at some point they'd moved close – most likely just before the end – and interlaced their fingers. Though they had thrashed in pain from the knifing, their fingers remained intertwined. In their death throes they had found some small comfort in the grip. Or she hoped they had. Sachs had been a street cop, then a detective working Major Cases, for years. The heart hardened, as it must, in this line of work. But details like these could still summon an urge to cry, even if no tears swelled. For some cops this never happened. She thought she was a better officer for it.

The owner of the store, Jatin Patel, had died from a slashed throat too. One difference, though, was the torture. The medical examiner's office tour doctor, a slim Asian American woman, had pointed out the slices on his hands, ear and face. Pistol-whipping too. The wounds were all premortem.

Neither Patel nor the couple seemed to have been personally robbed, though Patel had no phone on him or in the shop. At least, the usual take remained: wallets, purses, jewelry and cash were intact. She photographed the three bodies from all angles, rolled for fibers and other trace and took hair samples for exclusion later. She got fingernail scrapings, though none of the victims had apparently fought the unsub. Alternative light source scans of their skin, near where the lamp cord bound their wrists, revealed no fingerprints. She hadn't expected any; throughout the scene there were so many cloth glove prints, some in blood, that she knew, almost to a certainty, the unsub wouldn't have left his own.

'Sorry,' came the voice from the office.

Sachs walked to the doorway.

The evidence collection technician, whose belly tested the zipper of the overalls, said, 'No hard drive. I mean, he took it. And no backup.'

'He . . . how'd he get it?'

'Must've had tools with him. Easy – Phillips-head screwdriver is all you need.'

She thanked him and walked into the corridor, nodding to the ME doc, who'd been waiting patiently and texting.

'You can take them,' Sachs said.

The woman nodded and radioed down to the bus. Her technicians would bring gurneys and body bags and transport the corpses to the morgue for full autopsies.

'Detective?' A young, compact uniform, out of Midtown

North, approached from the elevator. He stopped well shy of the door.

'Scene's clear, Alvarez. It's okay. What've you got?'

He and his partner, an African American woman in her late twenties, had divided up and begun canvassing for witnesses and looking for other evidence that the perp might have shed as he'd arrived at or left the scene. A search for wits wouldn't have been particularly fruitful, Sachs had guessed. Many of the offices in the building weren't occupied. *For Lease* signs were everywhere. And today being a weekend – and the Jewish Sabbath – the other businesses on this floor were closed. Alvarez said, 'Three offices on the second floor, and two on the floor above us're open. Two people heard a bang about twelve thirty or twelve forty-five but thought it was a backfire or construction. Nobody else saw or heard anything.'

That was probably the case, though Sachs was, as always, a bit skeptical. The crime had happened around lunch hour. Employees coming and going might easily have gotten a glimpse of the perp but it was very common for witnesses to grow deaf – and blind – from that malady known as self-preservation.

'And something here.' Alvarez was pointing into the hall beside the elevator: a security camera mounted to the wall. Sachs hadn't noted it when she'd first arrived. She squinted, gave a brief laugh. 'Painted over?'

He nodded. 'And look at the trail of the spray paint.'

Sachs didn't get it at first, then realized what he meant. The perp – *presumably* the perp – had started spraying paint toward the camera while still behind it, and then hit the lens from directly underneath – to make certain he wasn't recorded for even a second. Smart.

Like taking the hard drive.

'Cameras on the street?'

Alvarez said, 'Maybe good news there. The stores to the right and left of the entrance to this building, they're copying their .MP4 video files for us. I told 'em to preserve the originals.'

Copies were fine for the investigation; the original drives would be needed for trial.

If we get to trial, Sachs thought.

She turned back to the shop, considering the first of the three questions romping through her mind. Number One: What had he taken? She'd done a thorough search, walking the grid, but, of course, that wouldn't necessarily give her any insights into what *wasn't* present any longer.

She scanned the place once more. Patel Designs wasn't a jewelry store like most. There were no display cases for a smash and grab. The operation consisted of three rooms: a front waiting room, an office directly behind and, through a doorway to the left, a workroom filled with equipment, which was used, she guessed, to cut gems and assemble jewelry. This last room was the largest of the three, containing stations for two workers – large turntables, similar to what potters used to turn vases and bowls. Some battered industrial equipment, one piece apparently a small laser. This also served as a storeroom: On shelves and against the wall were piles of empty boxes, shipping and office supplies, cleaning materials. Nothing valuable was kept here, it seemed.

The front room – and waiting area – was a ten-by-fifteen-foot space, dominated by a wooden counter. It also contained a couch and two mismatched chairs. On the counter rested several foot-square velvet pads for viewing customers' jewelry, several eye loupes, stacks of paper (all blank). She guessed Patel did only custom work. He would meet with his customers here and bring out pieces they'd ordered from the workshop or the waist-high safe in the office for examination. An Internet search had revealed that the main business of the company was cutting and polishing large diamonds for other jewelry manufacturers.

Question One . . .

What did you walk out of here with?

She stepped back into the office and looked over the safe and its contents: hundreds of three-by-three-inch white paper squares – folded like Japanese origami. These contained loose diamonds.

The perp's glove prints – both in blood and from residue absorbed by cloth fibers – were on the safe and several of the paper squares. But he hadn't ransacked. She would have thought he either would take all these or, if he wanted something in particular, would have dug through the safe and flung aside the envelopes he didn't want.

There was one way to find out. Sachs had collected what business documents she could find. One would probably contain an inventory of the diamonds Patel had in stock. Evidence technicians at Crime Scene headquarters in Queens, those working in the HVE, the high-value evidence room, would compare the inventory against what was in the safe. Eventually they'd discover what was missing.

It could take months.

Too long. They needed to know as soon as possible what had been taken, so conversations could start with confidential informants who had stolen-jewelry contacts, known fences and money launderers. With robbery, if you don't stop the perps in the act, the investigation will invariably be a long slog through the complicated, wide-flung world of moving stolen merchandise.

But there didn't seem to be any way to short-circuit the process.

Except . . .

Something was wrong about this. Why leave these stones? What was more important than them?

Sachs crouched – carefully; her arthritic knee sometimes complained on these damp days – and looked through the safe more carefully. Some of the envelopes contained only one diamond, some dozens. The gems seemed damn nice to her, plenty perp-worthy. But what did she know? She wasn't a jewelry girl. The only sparkle she wore was her blue diamond engagement ring, which sat modestly beside a thin gold band – now both hidden beneath purple latex.

She guessed there were several hundred thousand dollars' worth of stones in the safe.

There for the taking.

Yet he hadn't.

She rose, feeling a trickle of moisture down her temples. The day was cold but the old building's radiators emitted sweat-lodge heat, which was trapped against her body by the white Tyvek overalls. She remembered the days when one searched a scene wearing only gloves and, sometimes, booties. The protective outfits, a staple of crime scenes around the world, now existed for two reasons: first, because of the risk from dangerous materials at the scene. And, second, defense attorneys. The odds of contaminating a scene by not wearing protective garments were extremely small. But a sharp lawyer could derail the prosecution's case entirely by planting a seed of doubt that it might have happened.

Okay, if not the safe, then what?

As the medical examiner techs removed the bodies – the couple first and then Patel – she gazed over the three rooms once more.

What if, Sachs speculated, it wasn't a robbery at all, but a hit? Had Patel borrowed money from a loan shark and failed to pay it back? Not likely – he owned a successful business and hardly seemed like the kind of man to contact a local gangbanger for a loan at 30 percent vig, the going rate for interest on street borrowing, and that was per *month*.

A romance gone bad? Patel was a widower, she'd learned. And the round, unkempt middle-aged man just didn't seem like the type to become embroiled in a torrid and dangerous affair. If simply killing him was the motive, why the torture? And, for that matter, why break into the shop? Why not just tap him at home or on the street?

Her eyes returned to the workroom. Had Patel or an employee been working on a diamond or piece of jewelry that was particularly valuable?

She walked into the room. The workstations didn't appear to have been used today; all the equipment was arranged neatly on shelves or racks.

However, at one station she noticed another of those sheets of paper folded into an envelope for holding diamonds, like those in the safe. This, however, was empty. Written on it in pen were: GC-1, GC-2, GC-3 and GC-4. The names for the diamonds it had contained, she guessed, since weight in carats was given next to each (they ranged from five to seven point five). There were letters beside each, as well. The designation D, IF was next to three. Beside the last one, smaller, was D, F. Quality ranking, maybe. Also on the sheet was written: *Owner: Grace-Cabot Mining, Ltd., Cape Town, South Africa*. Beside that was the company's phone number.

'Hm,' she muttered aloud when she saw another note, at the bottom. This stated the valuation of each stone. The total worth was sixty-eight million ZAR. She pulled out her phone and Googled, learning that the denomination was, not surprisingly, South African rands.

What *was* surprising was the number she came up with when she ran the currency conversion calculator.

The value in U.S. dollars hovered around five million

Amelia Sachs believed she had found a pretty likely answer to Question Number One.

CHAPTER 5

To confirm that the pricey diamonds were indeed what had been stolen, Amelia Sachs returned to the safe and looked at every one of the hundreds of small folded squares.

No envelopes were marked with the letters *GC* or the company name. A call to Grace-Cabot would confirm that Patel had been in possession of the stones but it was a reasonable assumption that these were what the unsub had taken.

Had he known the gems were here? Or had he simply picked Patel's operation at random and demanded to know where the most valuable stones were?

Only speculation at this point.

Sachs photographed the Grace-Cabot box and receipt, then bagged them.

Now, Question Two: the torture.

Sachs disagreed with Sellitto that Patel had been tortured to give up the combination of the safe or tell where valuable diamonds, like the Grace-Cabot stones, were. In the end, the diamonds were just a commodity. Faced with death, or even the threat of torture, Patel would have given up any or all of his wares. Everything would be insured. No bit of jewelry was worth your life or one second of pain.

No, the unsub was after something else. What?

To find an answer Amelia Sachs did what she often was forced to do at scenes, as harrowing as the process might be: She mentally, emotionally, became the perp. In an instant she was no longer a cop, no longer a woman. She was the man who had created this carnage.

And asking herself – *himself*: Why do I need to hurt him?

Need is the word. I'm feeling an urgency. A desperation.

Why do I have to hurt him and make him talk?

A prickly sensation around her face again, around the base of her neck, above her spine. This wasn't the heat from the stifling air, which she'd felt earlier. And it wasn't the horror she was feeling at the Method Acting role she was playing. No, the symptoms were from the edginess coursing through *his* body.

Something's not right. I need to fix it. What, what, what?

Go back in time, think, imagine, picture . . .

Just after noon, I'm entering the shop. Yes, entering the office behind the couple, William and Anna. These lovers are my entrée through security and they're going to die because they've seen my face. I feel relief at this thought: their death. It's comforting. No loose ends.

When they push through the door, I move in behind them.

I can't control both of them with the knife. No, I'll have that firearm out. But I'm reluctant to use it because of the noise.

Still, I will if I have to, and they know it.

William and Anna and Patel don't move.

They settle.

I settle.

I'm in control.

Good, I'm feeling good now.

I hit Patel – with the weapon, probably. Incapacitate him. The couple gets tied up. They're crying, both of them. Moving close to each other, to feel the other's presence. Because they know what's coming.

I'm not moved by this, not at all.

This thought took her back to herself and her breath grew fast, her teeth ground together, her gut tightened. She dug one gloved index fingernail against a gloved thumb. Felt the pain. Ignored it.

Back. Get back inside him.

And she did.

Now I'm crouching, grabbing the hair of the man and slicing his neck.

Then the woman's.

I hear Patel's cries. But I pay them no mind as I watch the couple thrash and bleed to death. One task done. That's what I think. A task. Done. Good. Tick one thing off the list. That's all the deaths are. A checkmark.

I turn to Patel. He's down, he's no threat. And he's terrified. I ask him for the most valuable stones he's got.

He tells me. He gives the combination to the safe and I get the Grace-Cabot diamonds. But – here's the key. Important. Vital. I want something *else*, something he's *not* giving up.

What?

Now, bending down, I'm cutting differently, cutting to hurt, cutting to let information spill from him, along with the blood. It's satisfying. Again. Another cut. Face and ear and finger.

Then, finally, he tells me.

I relax. The knife finds his throat. Three fast slices.

It's over.

What has Patel told me?

What has he given me?

What am I so desperate to find? What do I so *need* to find?

I have my treasures, five million worth of stones. Why not just leave?

Then she understood.

The one thing I need is to protect myself. I'm obsessed with my own preservation. That's what I could torture someone for. To learn the identity of somebody who's a threat to me. I spray-paint one security camera, I steal the hard drive of the camera I can't paint, I kill two innocent witnesses solely because they've seen my face . . .

I need to make sure no other witnesses will say anything to the police.

There was the man who walked into the robbery, the man I shot, and who called 911 to report the attack. Would I torture Patel to get his name? He didn't see much. Just me in a ski mask, he'd reported. And he probably walked in after Patel was dead. Not much of a threat there. No, more likely I'd have tortured the diamond cutter to find the name of somebody *else* who might have seen my actual face.

Yes, that could be reason enough to torture.

Stepping out of character, Sachs lowered her head and slumped

against the wall, breathing hard and wiping sweat from her eyes
and temples. When she'd recovered from the dark channeling,
she returned to the hallway and browsed through the evidence.
She located Patel's calendar and looked through it. The entries
indicated that 'S' would be here at 11 a.m., 'W and A' – William
and Anna, the murdered couple – at 11:45. 'VL' was written in
the margin on Saturday, not next to any particular time. VL was
likely the answer to Question Number Three – who had called
911. A partial answer only, though, as intitials were not an identification.

She speculated: The unsub could have been in or near the
building when S arrived or left, and he could have been worried
that S had seen his face. He needed Patel to tell him S's name to
find and eliminate him. The same with VL.

She thumbed through other pages of the day planner. Along
with notations of hundreds of meetings and apparent assignments
over the past month, there were two references to appointments
with S in the past ten days. VL appeared regularly, three or four
times a week. So VL was possibly an employee or associate; this
meant he would know the door code and so might walk into the
robbery in progress, surprising the robber, who shot him.

Who are you, both? S? And VL?

And *where* are you?

Then a thought occurred.

If he was the one who'd walked in on the robbery, gotten shot
and fled . . . how had he escaped?

The unsub had shot him. But then he would have chased after
the man immediately. Given five or six seconds to step around
the bodies and avoid slipping in the blood, the killer still would
have had a good chance at catching up with the fleeing witness.

Sachs studied the hall once more. She'd assumed the killer had
entered via the elevator, particularly because he'd spray-painted
the camera just outside it. Or perhaps he'd taken the stairs, next
to the elevator.

But there was another door on this floor, next to Patel's office,
a fire exit. Sachs had noticed it but had noted too the sign that
warned: *Fire Exit. Alarm Will Sound When Opened.*

Since no one in the building had reported an alarm and the door was closed, she assumed the perp hadn't used it. And he wouldn't have thought that VL had escaped that way.

The actual site of the murder, or robbery, is the primary crime scene but there are others, of course. The perp has to get there and then get away and each of the secondary scenes can be a source of delightfully incriminating evidence. In fact, those scenes often yield more helpful clues than the primary scene since the perps might be more cavalier on the way to a job and more careless fleeing afterward.

She walked to the door. Pulling her weapon, Sachs pushed it open. No alarm.

Entering the dim, musty stairwell, Sachs played her flashlight beam upward and then down to the landing below. She paused and listened. There were creaks and grinds, and the wind, this cold ugly March wind, moaned through ancient seams in the building. But she heard no sound of footsteps. Of weapons chambering rounds.

The evidence had not given any indication that the perp had remained behind but there was no evidence suggesting he hadn't.

Crouching, she swept her Maglite beam once more into the darkness.

She continued slowly down the stairs and there, on the landing between the second and third floors, she found a small scattering of objects.

It was similar to what she'd found inside the doorway of Patel's office, chips and grains and dust of dark gray stone. She'd thought it might be gravel tracked in by someone, though none of the victims' shoes revealed similar traces. But apparently not. In addition were shreds of brown paper – the shade of a grocery or lunch bag. And, explaining a lot, there was a bullet. It was deformed and flattened, and on the mushroomed nose were bits of the same gray rock. Several of the shards of stone were bloody, though the slug was not.

A logical scenario presented itself. The unsub breaks in, steals the Grace-Cabot stones, kills the engaged couple, then tortures Patel to get S's name, thinking he might be a witness. He kills

Patel. He's about to leave when VL enters the office, using the door code. The killer's surprised and shoots at him. The vic is carrying a bag containing stones to be carved and polished into jewelry. The bullet hits the stone and he's wounded by some shards. He flees through the fire door, which the killer ignores, thinking he can't have gone that way because of the alarm bar.

So there are two witnesses whom the perp is presumably aware of: S, whose name and address Patel might have given up under torture. And VL, who might have seen only the ski mask but may know something else the unsub does not want to come to light.

Whoever VL is, he'd be at risk too, of course. One concern might be that a stone splinter had lodged in or near a vital organ. He might be bleeding severely.

That risk might or might not be the case.

The other, though, was certain. Sachs assumed that the unsub had looked at Patel's diary and knew that not only S but VL was a potential threat.

Of course, the unsub might flee the area with his spectacular diamond windfall.

But Sachs's few moments of channeling him earlier suggested otherwise. She believed, she *knew* that he was staying put for the time being; a man who would so casually orchestrate a bloody crime scene like this was absolutely not the sort to leave witnesses alive.

CHAPTER 6

The Port Authority, of all things, brought him comfort.

The sprawling, scuffed complex at 42nd Street and Eighth Avenue was, in reality, a massive bus terminal, despite a name that suggested ocean liners from exotic locations were queuing to dock.

The place was a churning tub of harried suburban commuters, of travelers bound for, or journeying from, the region's airports, of tourists. Here you'd also find energized young hopefuls from all over the world, carrying gym bags and backpacks stuffed with jeans, sweats, plush animals, condoms, sheet music, sketchbooks, good-luck theater programs and plenty of dreams sturdy, and dreams fragile.

Here too, hustlers, dealers, scam artists, chicken hawks – not particularly clever ones. But then you didn't need to be a keen tactician when the herd you preyed upon was made up of naïve and enthusiastic kids from Wheaton, Illinois, or Grand Rapids. The Port Authority saw fewer of these sly players than in the past but that wasn't due to a moral surge in looking out for our youth; terrorism had kept the police population on the Deuce high.

Vimal Lahori knew a lot about this – or speculated much upon it – because the Port Authority was a home away from home.

He would slip over here to have some fast food for lunch; it was a short walk from his job at Mr Patel's on 47th. To watch the people, their expressions, their gestures and emotions – to find inspiration he would take home with him and, in his workshop, try to render that vision into three dimensions.

He sat on a waiting area bench and enwrapped his throbbing torso with his arms. He squeezed hard. The pain subsided a bit but then returned. Spread, in fact, as if he'd broken a thin sack of acid and the discomfort now flowed to places where it hadn't been. The worst was in his right side, where, at elbow level, he felt a large lump beneath the skin. As the killer had raised the gun, Vimal had instinctively turned away. Either the bullet or part of it or a fragment of stone had ripped through his clothes and lodged. He'd heard if you went to the emergency room and either told them you'd been shot or they deduced it the medical workers had to call the police.

And that, of course, would not work.

Reaching under his jacket and up under the *Keep Weird* sweatshirt, he probed with his left hand – the only one that could reach the site. He withdrew his fingers and saw blood. A lot of it.

Vimal closed his eyes momentarily. He was at a complete loss, paralyzed. Mr Patel dead – the vision of his feet angling toward the dim ceiling of the shop wouldn't go away. That couple too. William Sloane and his fiancée, Anna. And the man in the mask, walking into the doorway, eyes squinting in surprise to see him. Lifting the gun and the two sounds almost simultaneous: the explosion then the snap of the bullet striking the bag in his hand.

He'd stumbled back and then was sprinting flat-out through the fire door – the alarm hadn't worked for years – and stumbling down the stairs. He'd been terrified the man would follow but no. He must have assumed Vimal had run for the stairwell in the front of the building. Or maybe he'd assumed the bullet would soon be fatal.

And now here was Vimal Lahori.

Finding comfort, to the extent comfort could be found.

His cap pulled low, hunkered down on the bench, Vimal gazed around him. Even now, not a workday, the place was crowded. The Port Authority terminal was near the Theater District. The rush for the Saturday matinees was over. The plays had started or were about to. But there were still a million things to see and do on the weekends, even on a cold March afternoon: the Disneyland of Times Square, movies, brunch, shopping. And his favorites: the Metropolitan and MoMA, the galleries south of 14th Street.

Hundreds streamed past.

Under other circumstances, he would be absorbing the energy.

Under other circumstances, he would be gazing at the electronic departure signs and wondering about the destinations the buses might take him (Vimal had never been out of the metro area). Now, of course, he was looking for the man who was possibly looking for him.

The fire stairs outside Mr Patel's shop had led him to a delivery bay behind the building. He'd sprinted to 46th Street and turned west. And kept on sprinting. Facts are facts and a skinny South Asian speeding from the Diamond District suggested someone on an errand – the way a sprinting black or Latino young man might not. No one had paid him much mind. He'd glanced back frequently and had not seen the killer in pursuit.

He'd stopped only briefly. When he'd hit Sixth Avenue he'd searched for and finally found a pay phone. They were being replaced by the wifi-enabled LinkNYC system, which was highly traceable – the kiosks even video recorded users – but he'd managed to locate an old-fashioned phone, call 911 and report the crime. How helpful the information was, Vimal couldn't say: He'd called primarily to have them send police and an ambulance in case anyone was still alive. The three people in the shop appeared dead but perhaps not. As for a description of the robber, all he could say was it was man of medium build, wearing gloves and ski mask, both black. He seemed to be white. Vimal didn't know the gun. Maybe somebody who was allowed to watch TV and movies more than he was would know what kind it might be. To him it was just a gun.

Then he'd hung up, sprinted another block and plunged into the crowds of Times Square, looking back frequently.

Now he was in his sanctuary, the bustling Port Authority.

He tried to think of anything else that might help the police. But Vimal was sure this had just been a random crime. There'd never been any threats before, never any robberies at the shop. Mr Patel was known throughout the world as a master diamantaire. Sure, he had some amazing stones in the shop, but that wasn't known to the public. His retail operation was very small, and generally customers were referred to him from other retailers when they wanted special fancies.

No one in that circle would rob a fellow cutter, let alone murder anyone. It simply didn't happen in the diamond world.

The pain swelled again.

Another touch to his skin.

More fresh blood.

Had anyone noticed his condition? He scanned the crowds, noting a woman on a nearby chair eating a soft pretzel, a dozen people pulling suitcases behind them like complacent dogs, a clutch of homeless men and women, some filled with the certainty of God, some purely bewildered.

He fished his phone from his pocket, wincing against the pain. He sent one text and was pleased to read the reply.

He sent a silly emoji, then felt like an idiot for doing so under the circumstances.

Then he stared at the screen, debating. And delaying. That he'd had no texts from his father meant that his family hadn't heard the news yet. Even when the story broke, his name probably wouldn't be included. Obviously, he wasn't among the victims at the shop and since Mr Patel paid him cash and Vimal kept none of his personal things at the shop, it would be very unlikely that the police would learn about him.

Still, the instant the story broke about Mr Patel's death, Vimal could expect his phone to begin ringing nonstop.

He continued to look at the scuffed screen. Just send the message, be done with it.

Go ahead.

It wasn't like placing a phone call. It was just a text. Nobody could interact with him verbally, be stern, treat him like a ten-year-old. Just a fucking text.

He typed the message.

You will soon hear there has been a terrible thing. Mr Patel is dead. A robbery. I am fine. But will be away for a time. I will be with a friend. I will contact you soon.

His finger hovered over the arrow of the Send button.

He added:

Love you.

He reached for the Power Down button but before he could press it a reply filled the screen.

WHAT DO YOU MEAN???? WHAT FRIEND ARE YOU TALKING ABOUT??? COME HOME AT ONCE!!!!

As his phone drifted off to sleep, Vimal's heart was pounding almost as fast as when he'd seen the gun pointing his way. A nearly instantaneous reply, he reflected, despite the fact his father had capitalized each word manually.

He noted too that of all the comments he might have made, the man had said nothing about Mr Patel's death or the robbery but had demanded to know the identity of Vimal's friend. There were no friends, of course. He knew no one well enough to stay with, certainly not in this instance. The line was simply a way to put his father – or more, his mother and brother – at ease.

In his mind's eye he was seeing Mr Patel's feet once more. He pressed his lids together tightly, as if that would make the image go away, but it only grew more vivid. More horrific.

He began to cry and he sobbed silently, turning his back to the crowd. Finally he controlled the tears, dabbed his face and inhaled deeply.

Then a thought came to him; he remembered something else about the killer. The man had had that attaché case. An old-fashioned one, the sort you didn't see very much anymore. He had been carrying it as he walked into the front room from the workshop when he saw Vimal. The case, he now reflected, might be the reason he was still alive. The robber had been carrying it in his right hand. He'd had to drop it and pull his gun from his pocket, which gave Vimal a moment – purely a reaction – to turn and raise his hands. When the man fired, the bullet had struck the rocks, not his chest.

A man with a briefcase would be distinctive. Vimal would call 911 once more and let them know. Officers throughout Midtown could look for him.

He rose and walked toward a pay phone. He knew that as soon as he called, somebody in the NYPD would radio officers here – there were a half-dozen that he could see – and report that somebody who knew about the crime was in the Port Authority. He'd have to leave immediately after he hung up.

It was then that he felt, more than saw, somebody approaching.

He turned and observed a man of about thirty-five in a dark raincoat, walking toward him and looking from right to left as he made his way through the foot traffic flowing through the Port Authority hallways. Same height and build as the killer. Somber-faced.

The killer had been in a jacket, hadn't he?

This man had no briefcase.

But a smart thief would have ditched the clothes he wore at the scene of the crime.

Or, hell! What if there were two of them? This was . . . what did they say? The backup.

In any event, this guy was definitely coming his way. He held something small and dark in his hand. It wouldn't be the gun; he wouldn't dare shoot here. It would be the knife he'd used to slash that couple and Mr Patel to death.

Vimal looked for the police. The closest were about two hundred feet away and the man was between them and Vimal.

Besides, the police were the last thing he wanted.

Go! Get away!

He turned and moved fast down the nearest corridor, which was lined with luggage lockers. The pain in his chest and side swelled but he ignored it and kept moving fast.

A T-shaped intersection of passageways was ahead. Left or right? More light from the right one. He slipped around the corner.

Mistake. It was a dead end, continuing for only ten feet and ending at a door on which was stenciled: *Electrical. Maintenance Only. No Entry.*

Try it!

Locked. He saw the shadow of the man as he approached.

I'm going to die, he thought.

Into his mind came not the image of his mother's face, or his brother's. Not the six-carat marquis-cut diamond that he'd completed last week and that Mr Patel had pronounced as 'quite acceptable' – his highest praise.

No, in what was likely to be his last moment on earth Vimal thought of a piece of granite sitting in his studio: a four-sided pyramid. Rich green, with striations of black and just a hint of gold. He pictured every centimeter of it.

The man paused in the intersection and squinted toward him.

Then Vimal thought: No. He took a deep breath and walked forward, standing as tall as he could. He wasn't going to cower. He was going to fight.

Vimal wasn't a large man but his passion was stone and rock; he hefted it and he cut and cracked and smoothed it. His tools were heavy. Sometimes he held a large stone at arm's length, willing the piece to tell him what its soul was so that he could set it free.

These ample muscles now grew taut and he withdrew from his pocket a weapon of his own: the largest rock, the January bird, that had been in the bag when this man – or his associate – had shot him. He kept it hidden behind his back.

Vimal nearly smiled, with grim humor, thinking about the game he'd played with his brother Sunny when they were younger: rock-paper-scissors.

Scissors cut paper.

Paper covers rock.

And rock breaks scissors.

He gripped the stone firmly.

Oh, yes, he'd fight . . . hit the man hard, dodge the knife as best he could, and flee.

From him. And from the police.

The man walked closer. Then he smiled. 'Hey, young man. I was waving at you.'

Vimal stopped, saying nothing, just kneaded the stone. The pleasant face would be a trick to get his guard down.

'You left this on the chair. In the waiting room.'

He held up not a knife but a mobile phone. Vimal squinted

and patted his pockets. Yes, it was his. Each walked toward the other and the man handed it over. 'You okay, son?' He frowned.

'Yeah. I . . . just, busy day. Stupid of me. Sorry.' He slipped the rock back into his pocket; the man didn't seem to notice.

'Hey, happens. I left a new iPhone at the playground when my wife and I took the boys to the park. When I realized it, after we got home, I called the number. A kid – like, a ten-year-old – answered. I said it was my phone and all he said was could he have the password for the App Store?'

The Samaritan laughed and Vimal forced himself to do so too.

'Thanks.' The word was shaky.

The man nodded and walked off toward a queue for a bus going to New Jersey.

Vimal returned to the pay phone. He stood with his head down, breathing slowly, calming. He called 911 again. When he said he was calling about the robbery on 47th Street, the woman tried to keep him on the line but he said simply, 'The man with the gun had a black attaché case. Like businessmen carry.'

He hung up and walked quickly to the exit, casting a last look at the departure board, filled with so many destinations. They all beckoned.

But first things first. Head down, Vimal plunged into the crowds on the sidewalk and turned south, walking as quickly as the pain allowed.

CHAPTER 7

Two tiny *kur* to find.

Two tiny hens to cut up and boil . . .

Two tiny *kur* who knew too much.

Who should have died earlier. But who got away.

Sad, sad, sad. But not everything goes the way it fucking ought to.

Aromatic with tarry cigarette smoke and Old Spice aftershave, Vladimir Rostov now spotted someone who might help him track down his *kur*.

He was in the Diamond District, about a hundred yards from the building that housed Jatin Patel's store, where police stood and yellow tape fluttered. He was, of course, keeping his distance. It was now dusk, closing time in the district, and Rostov was watching his target – either the owner or the manager of a small jewelry store – operate the motor that closed the security gate. He appeared to be South Asian and, Rostov was hoping, would probably know Patel; the diamond community in New York was not as big as you might think.

The man fitted two serious locks into hasps on the door and, with a third, locked the electronic panel that controlled the motor.

The man was slight and looked about, nervously. Ah, good. Rostov loved timid *kur*. They were always so eager to help.

The Russian blended in. New York was the city of dark outer garments, as he was wearing. The city of no eye contact, the city of head down, the city of never respond. Blending in . . . There was little distinctive about him, this compact forty-four-year-old. More muscle than fat, with a long angular, equine face. Former military, he had a military bearing and a military physique, though he did not have – nor had he ever had – a military frame of mind, which meant discipline and the will to follow orders.

Looking normal, but he worked to keep his eyes from zipping a bit too manically around the street. He tried not to mutter to himself. And to anyone nearby. That wouldn't, of course, be a good idea. He was well aware that he was a bit different.

Vladimir Rostov was, as he put it, 'gone to the stone.'

And so he had to force himself to be careful. He could function but sometimes he went right to the edge of sane. And now he was feeling that cringy-crawly sense, as he observed the street, filled with Jews and Indians and Chinese, who sold their cheap crap to the masses.

Proletariat! he thought with a grim silent laugh. Then stanched the, yes, manic grin. Thank you, Lenin. You were a mad fucker too but you understood.

As he glanced into the windows, he could see the gold, the sapphires, the emeralds.

The diamonds.

The earth's blood. Forty-Seventh Street was a hemorrhage. Like the blood on the floor of Patel's shop.

The Indian dealer walked to Fifth Avenue and turned north, oblivious to being followed. Will you help me find my little *kur*? Rostov thought, thumbing the utility razor knife in his pocket, resting right next to the pistol.

His little *kur* . . . In Rostov's universe, the word meant more than 'hens,' the literal translation. By this definition *kuritsa* – the singular – included *blyad*, 'whore,' and *dobycha*, 'prey' and *prez-reniye*, 'contempt,' but always filtered through a sense of amusement.

One *kuritsa* he needed to find was the boy at the diamond dealer's. Name unknown but initials probably VL. And the other one, the Jew who'd met with Patel before the dealer's shop erupted into Stalingrad.

Two *kur*.

On the trail of his prey now.

Rostov lit a cigarette, inhaled deeply a few times and stubbed it out. Collar up, hat pulled down low over his blond crew cut, Rostov kept up his pursuit of the Indian. Where was he going? Was he taking the subway somewhere, a bus? Or did he live on the Upper East Side, the posh area of New York? The man owned a jewelry store, so he'd have money. But Rostov didn't think many Indians lived in that part of town. It seemed exclusive and he assumed they wouldn't be welcome.

Rostov's gut thumped a bit as they passed Harry Winston, the famed jewelry store on Fifth Avenue. The modest gold placard beside the gated doorway read:

Harry Winston Inc.
Rare Jewels of the World.

Now *that*, *kur*, is putting it mildly.

Rostov studied the ornate building, speculating about the quantity and the quality of the gems inside. Unimaginable. Winston, who died in the 1970s, was perhaps the most famous jeweler the world had ever known. The owner of the Hope Diamond and the massive seven-hundred-carat Vargas rough, he was the original jeweler to the stars. (Winston came up with the idea of lending magnificent pieces to actresses to wear at the Academy Awards.)

Rostov thought of a particular diamond the company had acquired a few years ago at a Christie's auction: the Winston Blue, the largest vivid blue diamond ever sold. The stone was in a fancy cut (any diamond shape not a round brilliant is called 'fancy'), pear-shaped. About thirteen carats in weight and, according to the Gemological Institute of America standards, it was flawless. Rostov had only seen pictures of it, of course, and wondered if the stone was presently in the store.

What had struck him about the diamond was that the press stories mentioned only in passing its rarity and its perfection; the focus of the articles was that it had sold for nearly two million dollars per carat, a record for a blue. The world appreciated the diamond not for what it was, but for what it cost.

Fucking media.

Fucking public.

Was it inside these hallowed halls at the moment? he wondered. His heart pounded at the possibility. Even if he hadn't been following the Indian, Rostov would not have been able to go in, of course. Every square inch of his face would be on video. A dozen times. He had even heard that some cameras were of such high definition that they could capture your fingerprints.

That would not do.

A pity.

Rostov endured a coughing fit, trying to keep the noise down. The dealer didn't hear, and the Russian brought it under control. The prey continued north for twenty minutes, then turned east and walked for four more blocks – not so exclusive here. The street was deserted and when he passed a brownstone, with a garden apartment entrance below street level, Rostov moved fast and shoved the man down the stairs, displaying his gun then shoving it back into his pocket.

'No! What—'

Rostov cuffed him on the head, a blow more startling than painful. 'Shhhh.'

The man nodded, cowering.

Always so eager to help . . .

They were in front of the lower-level apartment window and door but the lights were out inside.

'Please, don't hurt me. I have a family.'

'Ah, good. Family. Good. What is name, family man?'

'I . . . I am Nashim.'

'You are Indian?'

'No, no, Persian.'

Shit.

Rostov was angry. 'You mean fucking Iranian.'

His eyes were wide. 'Yes, but my grandfather was a friend of the shah's! I mean it, it's true!'

'Do I give fuck about that?'

This made the mission more difficult. Well, he'd have to make do.

'You have wallet?'

Nashim's voice was stuttering. 'Yes, yes, I have one. Take it. I have a ring too. A nice ring. My watch is not so nice but . . . '

'Just open wallet.'

'I don't have much cash.'

'Shhh. Open.'

With shaking hands, Nashim did.

Rostov plucked the driver's license out and took a picture of
it with his phone. Then he noticed a photo. This too he pulled
out. It depicted Nashim and presumably his wife and two round,
pretty teenage daughters.

'You *are* family man. You are lucky family man.'

'Oh, please.' Tears in his eyes.

Rostov took a picture of the photograph too. He handed it
and the license back to the man. He wasn't able to put them
back into the wallet, his hands were shaking so badly. Rostov did
this himself and tucked the wallet back into the man's breast
pocket. Patted it three times. Hard.

'Now, I am needing to find some person. And why is not your
interest. If you help, all will be good. And I won't have to come
to Fourteen Hundred Twenty-Two First Avenue, apartment five
C, and pay your pretty family a call.'

'Yes.' The man was crying harder now. 'I understand.'

Rostov had not asked if he understood.

'You are knowing Jatin Patel?'

'Are you the man—' His voice stopped cold.

Rostov lowered his head, fixed Nashim with his blue eyes. The
dealer blurted, 'Not well. I met him once. I knew about him.
Everybody knew.'

'There are two peoples he knows. Someone, VL, also Indian,
like him. Younger. May work for Patel. Or *worked* for Patel. And
Jew named Saul Weintraub. He has business in diamond trade
in someplace, Long Island City. But I would like his home place.
Okay? So, easy for you. I make it easy. Who this VL is? And
where I am finding Weintraub?'

'Oh, I would tell you if I could. I promise you! But I don't
know. I swear. We all work in the Diamond District, Jews and
Indians and Chinese and us. But we don't talk among ourselves
so much. We sell to each other, we buy from each other. But
that's all. I don't know who they might be, these people. Please
don't hurt me or my family! I can get you money.'

'I ask for money?'

'I'm sorry.'

Rostov believed him. And, on reflection, he decided it was helpful that the man was Iranian. He'd sell out a Jew in an instant and probably an Indian, as well.

'Nashim, Nashim . . . We are going to be playing game then. You like games?'

He was silent.

'Scavengering hunt. You know this?'

'I know what it is.'

'Here, now, my friend. Here. You are going to start asking questions. Be careful. You should not be obvious. But ask about this VL and this Saul Weintraub. Yes, yes! You are ready to play, my friend?'

'I will. I promise I will.'

'Give me your phone number.'

Rostov punched the number in and then hit dial. Nashim's phone hummed. 'Good, good. You are not fakey man. Okay. You get busy now, Nashim. I will call tomorrow and find out what you can tell me. And I will keep calling until you win scavengering hunt. I am rooting for you! Now I will go home and you go home.' Rostov clapped him on the back. He started away then paused. 'Your daughters. What are their names?'

He suddenly felt the urge, the churning hunger.

Gone to the stone . . .

The Iranian was staring. 'No! I will tell you nothing about them.'

Rostov shrugged. 'Does not matter. I will make up my own. The tall one I think will be Scheherazade. And the younger one, prettier, I am saying, my opinion only . . . she will be Kitten. Good night, Nashim. Good night, my friend.'

CHAPTER 8

As dusk settled outside, those in Rhyme's parlor laboratory were beginning their hunt for the man they'd dubbed Unsub 47, after the street where the robbery and murders had occurred.

He was watching the progress as Sachs and Mel Cooper – his prize NYPD lab man – analyzed what she'd returned with from Patel Designs.

Lon Sellitto was here too, presently on his mobile in the corner, fielding questions from his superiors. The press was having a field day with the story of the box-cutter-wielding killer in the Diamond District, the last thing that City Hall wanted. Like hungry zoo animals, the media would have to be fed something. This was not Rhyme's concern, however. He kept his attention on the progress of the slightly built, admittedly nerdy lab technician and on Sachs as the two labored away.

The uniformed officer Ron Pulaski had been deployed. He was out in the Diamond District, canvassing. And having little success. He'd called in five minutes earlier and reported on his lack of results. Armed with a list of Jatin Patel's clients and business associates, he was canvassing to see if anyone had heard about potential threats (or to assess if they themselves were the unsub).

Yet no one Pulaski or the other canvassing officers spoke to had any thoughts on who 'S' or 'VL' from Patel's calendar were.

This lack of insight was true too of those in the stores and restaurants along 47th Street and nearby. 'Nobody's talking to me, Lincoln,' the young officer had said. 'It's like they're afraid to be seen helping. As if the unsub is nearby, taking notes.'

'Keep at it, Rookie,' Rhyme said and hung up. He wasn't enamored of witnesses in any event – their testimony, he felt, was aggressively unreliable – and was hoping mostly that someone might point Pulaski in the direction of evidence that the fleeing perp had discarded or accidentally shed.

He looked over the four-by-three-foot erasable whiteboard on which Sachs and Cooper were recording their results.

They knew a few things from the anonymous call (assuming it was accurate): The perp was probably white, male, his face obscured by a black cloth ski mask. He wore gloves and was armed. Average height. Another call had been made to 911, reporting that the killer had carried a black briefcase. It hadn't been found at the scene, so he would have it with him possibly, unless he'd ditched it.

Sachs believed that the caller was the employee or associate of Patel's who'd walked into the crime and been shot, VL. A canvass of the Port Authority, where he'd made the most recent phone call, had revealed no sightings of anyone injured. Rhyme had wanted someone to remove the coins from the pay phones from which the man had made the call and fingerprint them.

'You don't need a quarter to call nine one one,' Sellitto had said, amused. 'The city got that worked out in the budget.' Hospitals had been alerted to report anyone injured by what would be rock splinters but the odds that the roughly one thousand emergency room doctors in the New York area would learn of this request and follow through, if they did, were pretty damn slim.

Sachs had called the company that owned the diamonds, Grace-Cabot in Cape Town, South Africa. It was hours later there, early morning, and she'd left a message. There was, after all, a possibility that the stones had been shipped back or were elsewhere, perhaps contracted out to other diamond cutters who worked with Patel.

If that was true the case would become even more confounding, and it would be up to the high-value evidence technicians to run an inventory and learn if anything was in fact missing.

As for physical evidence, there'd been hundreds of friction ridge images – fingerprints – discovered: the shop, the elevator, the handles of the doors to the street, the doors to the stairwell, the railings in the stairwells. But none were in the IAFIS database.

He hadn't expected any hits; the number of cloth glove prints suggested Unsub 47 never took them off.

They never make it easy for us, do they? A rhetorical query that Rhyme didn't bother to express aloud.

Some crimes – sexual in nature and physical fights, for instance – are usually DNA-rich exchanges, and the deoxyribonucleic acid database – CODIS, in America – might reveal an identity in such instances. But a crime like this, by a gloved killer, wearing a long-sleeve outer garment and slacks – as well as the ski mask – would offer little chance for him to leave behind DNA.

Some cloth fibers had been found, none of which matched the clothing worn by the victims. Some were black cotton, most likely from gloves – since they were found on doorknobs and drawers. Also, Sachs had discovered black polyester fibers, which were probably from the ski mask.

No empty cartridge shells from the gunshot; he'd taken the brass with him.

'What do we have there?' Rhyme asked his lab man impatiently. His eyes on the electrostatic footprints from Jatin Patel's shop, now scanned and slapped onto a high-def screen.

Mel Cooper was wearing a white lab coat, cap and gloves, as well as a face mask. And his ever-present Harry Potter glasses. 'Hard to say for certain but our boy's between a ten and an eleven and a half.' Since shoe toes curl upward and heel size varies, it's sometimes difficult to ascertain an exact size. 'And some distinctive wear marks but there's no tread.'

'So businessman footwear.'

'Right.' Much better if the perps wear running shoes. The distinctive tread marks will usually give you brand and model number, and sometimes even color can be ascertained from the model.

'Any small lines in the blood, next to the shoe prints?' Rhyme was looking at an image shot by Sachs on her Sony digital camera.

'Lines?' Cooper asked.

'Wormy lines, *squiggly* lines,' Rhyme muttered. 'I can't tell.' When he noted that both Sellitto and Cooper were glancing his way, perplexed, he started to speak but Sachs, hunched over an examination table, said, 'From dangling shoelaces. They might not show up in the electrostatics but they would in the blood.'

Rhyme smiled. He loved her.

'Ah.' Cooper examined the footprint photos. Sellitto looked once, then checked texts.

'Ah, bored, are we, Lon? Many a case's been closed because of something as trivial as finding out if the perp wears shoes with laces or not.'

'Hey, Linc, you're the squiggly line/bloody shoe-print guru. Not me.' He took another phone call and stepped away.

No squiggles, it turned out. Probably slip-ons.

The witness had reported only one perp present, and footprints confirmed the killer was by himself.

His weapon was most likely a 9mm Glock, like Sachs's, to judge from the polygonal rifling of the slug. Gun barrels for the past 150 years have contained interior indentations to spin the bullet as it leaves the weapon, making it more accurate. Most have lands and grooves – troughs. Glocks, however, have wavy indentations, not sharp edges, which give the bullet more speed and power. They aren't the only guns with this feature – others are Heckler & Koch, Kahr Arms, Magnum Research, Tanfoglio and CZ – but Glocks are by far the most common to feature polygonal rifling.

Sellitto disconnected his phone. 'That was a couple gold shields. Went to Patel's sister's house, delivered the news. His wife had passed away a few years ago and the sister's the only family he's got in the area. They said it was pretty tough for her. She nearly collapsed. They waited till her husband got home to ask her questions. She said she didn't know much about the business. That was a "man thing", she said.

'Patel'd never told her or her husband that he was concerned about security or that anybody'd been casing the shop. But he was really famous as a cutter – here and internationally too. Word could've gotten around that he had some nice shit for somebody to steal. My word, not hers.'

Sachs asked, 'Partners? Employees? She have any idea who that witness was?'

'She didn't really know. He owned the place himself. No full-time employees – he was too cheap and didn't trust anybody else to work on the stones. Except, his sister thought, some young man worked there occasionally, apprenticing to be a diamond cutter. They asked about S and VL. But zip.'

Sachs said, 'Probably paid in cash, off the books, to save money; no payroll information to help us track him down.'

A team from Crime Scene in Queens had searched Patel's modest apartment on the Upper West Side of Manhattan, where he'd lived alone since his wife passed away of cancer some years ago. There was no evidence of a break-in, and – as Rhyme had wondered – the Grace-Cabot diamonds were not there.

Neither was Patel's phone, so their contact at the NYPD Computer Crimes Unit was presently getting a list of numbers, incoming and outgoing, from the provider. They hoped one of these would prove to be a call to or from S or VL.

Sachs stepped away to take a call and, nodding absently as she had a conversation, jotted a few notes. Then gave the caller her email address.

A moment later a computer sounded with an incoming message and she disconnected and called it up.

'Movie time,' she said. 'Security company for the building. This's the security video of the floor this morning.' She down-loaded it and began playing the grainy black-and-white footage.

Rhyme wheeled closer. Patel had arrived for work at about eight thirty this morning. Nothing happened until a few minutes before eleven. A man appeared, bearded and in a black overcoat and a short-brimmed hat, possibly with short dark hair. He pushed a button on the intercom of Patel's shop, was admitted and stayed about twenty minutes.

'Probably S – Patel's eleven o'clock.'

Five minutes after he left, according to the time stamp, some black speckles began to appear in the image and for a fraction of a second you could see a gloved hand and a shape of a head in the ski mask as the unsub sprayed black paint at the lens, while staying largely out of sight. The fuzzy images – literally thirteen frames – revealed nothing.

Rhyme looked to Cooper, who anticipated his question. 'I ran the paint. It's generic. No source.'

The criminalist grunted.

She reminded, 'Patel's security footage is gone. Forty-Seven took it with him but some Midtown North uniforms're collecting video from the street. Most of the stores' cameras are interior but there're a few outside. We'll see what they turn up. They're checking the loading dock on Forty-Six too; that's where the fire exit leads to.'

She asked Cooper for the clearest screenshot of S, from the hallway outside Patel's. He processed the image and sent it to her via email. 'I'll get to the canvassers. See if they can get a name.' She sat down at a nearby terminal, logged in and uploaded the shot for citywide distribution.

Mel Cooper turned to the others. 'I've ID'd the stones that the apprentice, or whoever he was, was carrying – what the bullet hit. Looks like it's in the serpentinite family – it's called that because of the coloring and mottled texture; looks like snakeskin. If it's got garnets or diamonds in it it's kimberlite. That's what this is. I can see little flecks of crystal that could be diamonds. Patel probably cuts and polishes it into necklaces or earrings.'

The parlor landline rang. The caller ID was a country code Rhyme did not recognize.

Sachs glanced at it. 'South Africa.'

She hit Speaker and answered. 'Yes?'

'Yes, hello. I'm trying to reach a Detective Amelia Sachs.' The accent was that melodic blend of Dutch and English.

'This is Detective Sachs.'

The caller identified himself as Llewelyn Croft, the managing director of Grace-Cabot Mining, Ltd., in Cape Town.

'Mr Croft, you're on speakerphone with Lieutenant Lon Sellitto, New York Police, and Lincoln Rhyme, a consultant.'

'I got your message. You said there's been a theft that might involve us?'

'That's right. I didn't leave details on the phone but I'm sorry to tell you the diamond cutter who had the stones, Jatin Patel, was killed in the robbery.'

A pause. They heard a gasp.

'No! Oh, no. I saw him just last week. No, this is terrible.' His voice faded. 'I can't . . . killed?'

'I'm afraid so.'

'We've worked with him for years. He was one of the best diamond cutters in New York. Well, in the world.' His voice cracked. He cleared his throat and continued, 'Are you saying our diamonds were stolen? Are you sure?'

'No, not for certain. One of the reasons I'm calling. I found an empty box with a receipt for a shipment of four items, ID numbers GC-one through -four.'

'Yes,' he said, sounding dismayed. 'Those are ours.'

'In rands they're worth about sixty-eight million?'

A sigh. Then nothing.

'Sir?'

'Yes, that's the insured value. They were rough so when finished they would have sold for much more.'

'This is Detective Lon Sellitto. As far as you know then, Patel had the stones with him? Could he've sent them out to be worked on?'

'No, no. He'd never do that. Only he was talented enough to work on them. My God. Those stones . . . Do you know who did it?'

'We're investigating,' Sachs said.

Sellitto asked, 'Who'd have known that Patel had these diamonds?'

A pause, then Croft said, 'I couldn't say, of course, who Jatin told. But I doubt he mentioned them to anyone. I don't know how familiar you are with the diamond industry but no one talks about jobs. Especially with incomparable stones like these. Security is paramount. And within our company? An inside job, I'm sure you're thinking. Only a few executives knew they were going to Jatin. But we're all partners in the company – and, frankly, we're all fairly well off. As for the line workers and miners? Once the stone is extracted and processed, they have no idea where it goes. Sometimes transport companies sell information to thieves but I flew the rough to New York myself. It was that valuable.' A pause. 'That irreplaceable.'

'The what?' Rhyme interrupted. 'You've said "rough" before. What is that?'

'Sorry. That's what we call uncut diamonds. Rough.' He paused once more. 'My educated guess would be the thief didn't know about our stones in particular. He picked Jatin's store at random then demanded uncut diamonds. Finished stones have laser registration numbers – you can only see them with a loupe. But that makes moving them very difficult. There's a much better illicit market for uncut diamonds. The pros always go for rough.'

Sachs asked, 'Do you know anyone in America the thief'd approach to fence the diamonds to?'

'In America, no. But I can give you the number of our insurer's New York office. I'll have to put them on notice anyway. And they'd have somebody on staff who'd be able to help you.' He gave them the number; Sachs jotted it down.

Croft said, 'I do hope you can bring all your resources to finding this man. This is such a tragedy. Unspeakable.'

Three people slaughtered, one of them tortured. And two witnesses in peril.

But Llewellyn Croft meant something else, it seemed.

'You see, I don't think thief will sell the stones outright. What he'll do is have them cut quickly – he'll *butcher* them and the finished diamonds will disappear into the mass-market trade in Amsterdam or Jerusalem or Surat. Those diamonds were destined for greatness. And now? They'll be ruined.' He repeated, 'Tragic.'

Sellitto's face twisted into a grimace. It was Amelia Sachs who said, 'Well, Mr Croft, we'll do our best to track him down.' She added a cool tone to her voice. 'And make sure no one else loses their life.'

CHAPTER 9

Shivering in the mid-March chill, arms encircling his narrow chest, Vimal Lahori sat in Washington Square Park, that pleasant enclave of peaceful urban greenery in Greenwich Village. Here, on days nicer than this, you saw quite the mix: fringe musicians and nannies, uninspired drug dealers, earnest students, notebook-scribbling poets, thoughtful academics and the businesspeople who *could* walk home from their hedge fund and law offices in Wall Street but generally preferred limos.

Now, early evening, Vimal was in a shadowy, deserted portion of the place, far from the towering, and well-lit, arch, which echoed Paris's Arc de Triomphe. He glanced at the New York University classrooms and residences and the fine *Hamilton*-era town houses, the windows glowing with yellow lights. People would be inside preparing to go out on the town, showering, primping, dressing. Or chopping vegetables and sipping wine for a dinner party soon to be. The sight of these small, inaccessible pleasures made Vimal Lahori want to cry. He played absently with the brown cloth bracelet that Adeela had made for him. His father had wondered if it might interfere with his working the dop stick, so he didn't slip it on until after he'd left the house.

Literally looking over his shoulder frequently on the long, cold walk here, he had made his way via a complicated route from the Port Authority, which was thirty, thirty-five blocks north. He'd been planning to take the train but the shock of that man at the bus station, returning his phone, had shaken him so much that he'd decided to walk.

Not very likely that the killer was prowling the subway, taking train after train in hopes of finding him. He, of course, had seen Vimal, knew exactly what he looked like. But the diamond cutter's apprentice had seen only a mask, gloves and dark clothing.

His paranoia wasn't completely unreasonable though; he'd stopped into a bar to gulp down two Cokes and had watched the news, learning that the man was still loose and believed to be in the city, armed and dangerous. Anyone with knowledge of the crime should come forward immediately. Which sounded like the police spokesperson was adding: for their own safety. Maybe they had information that the killer was in fact looking for him because of what he'd seen. He'd assume that was the case.

Thinking once more of the bloody shop. The shock was gone now, replaced by horror and sorrow. Mr Patel dead. He'd been a taskmaster, stern and rarely satisfied. But reasonable. Kind in his own way. And whatever Vimal thought about the industry Mr Patel had devoted his life to he couldn't say the man was less than a genius. Vimal knew how hard it was to have your hands create what your heart saw.

And that couple, the customers, the young man and woman! What a sad thing they had walked into the crime. William and Anna. Their wedding was to be in six months, he seemed to recall.

He hadn't gotten much of a look at the bodies at the shop, the encounter had been so shocking and so fast. And once the image of the motionless feet of his mentor had seared itself into his memory, he had seen little else. Vimal Lahori believed that image would be with him for the rest of his life.

He looked at his phone – his only source for the time – and noted seven missed calls from his father, twelve texts. As he stared, the muted phone lit up with another call from the man.

He hit Reject and put the unit away.

A grim smile. If only he could also reject the guilt he was feeling.

Mr Patel, that couple . . . An unspeakable tragedy.

And yet . . .

Vimal couldn't deny the warm, if tainted, feeling of relief, a burden lessening. He'd been crushed for a long time by a slow unstoppable pressure like that a hundred miles beneath the earth's surface, pressing, pressing, pressing to form diamonds. Now freedom was possible. There was no way he could have taken this step on his own. Without some cataclysmic occurrence like the robbery and murder, he would have done what he had always done: acquiesced and accepted the life his father has chosen for him. Agreed. Kept mum. Hating himself for it, every minute.

As horrifying as the circumstances were, Vimal Lahori had been given a chance. He'd take it. His life was going in a new direction.

Some motion from across the park. He spotted her now.

First things first . . .

The young woman, with magnificent long, dark hair, walked purposefully into the center of the park, looking from right to left. Despite the horror of what had just happened, despite the pain in his belly and side, he felt that tap within him, that familiar thud.

Every time he saw her – even after all these months of dating – it happened.

Oh, it wasn't the smoothest of relationships. The couple didn't see each other nearly as often as they would have liked. She was a busy medical student at NYU and he worked long and irregular hours for Mr Patel and other diamond cutters his father would 'rent' him out to. And Vimal needed to spend much of his free time in the basement studio at home.

This was typical of many couples, of course, in the metro area in this day and age. These were complications that got sorted out. But in their case there was a stickier problem. Vimal's parents did not know about Adeela Badour, and hers did not know about him.

She wasn't tall but her slim figure offered the impression that she was. Tonight her hair was purely black (occasionally, in defiance of a conservative mother, she would streak the strands blue or green – though hers was a tame rebellion; the tinting was never seen at family gatherings at home).

She now saw Vimal and her long face brightened. At first, that is. But she grew somber then alarmed, perhaps because he looked pale and drawn.

Vimal acknowledged her by lifting his head briefly. He didn't want to wave. He was still thinking of the man in the mask. A look around revealed only a dozen people nearby, all oblivious to him and moving quickly to get somewhere less damp and chill.

She dropped onto the bench and flung her arms around him. 'Vim . . . Oh . . . '

He winced and she released him immediately, then eased back and looked him over. He gazed at her beautiful face. She wore complicated, though subtle, makeup on her rich skin, so carefully applied he couldn't actually say which of her features had been accented.

Vimal gripped her hand and kissed her hard. Her eyes, he now noted, were studying him clinically.

'I saw the news. I'm so sorry. Mr Patel. And those customers. It's all over the TV. But they didn't say anything about anybody else being there.'

He explained to her about walking in and surprising the robber.

'I ran. I think he came after me but I took the back stairs.'

'Your text: You're hurt?'

He explained that the man had shot at him but the bullet missed, hitting the bag he carried. Some pieces of stone or part of the bullet had cut him. 'I need it looked at.'

She said, 'Go to the hospital.'

'I can't. The doctors'd figure out I was shot. They have to report it to the police.'

'Well . . . ' Adeela lifted her perfectly shaped eyebrows. Meaning, That's a *good* thing.

Vimal said simply: 'I can't.' There was no way he was going to explain the reason – no, make that *reasons* – he couldn't go to the cops. 'You brought what I asked for?'

She said nothing.

'Please.'

'Well, where can I look at it?'

'Here, I guess.'

'Here?' She barked a laugh. A medical exam in Washington Square Park on a cold, overcast March evening?

But she would realize that there weren't many other options, as they both lived with their parents.

She glanced about, saw no one nearby and nodded toward his

jacket. He unzipped the garment and tugged up his sweatshirt and undershirt. 'Well,' she said softly. 'Just like a sculptor to get hurt by flying rock. Good thing you don't collect razor blades and knives.'

Adeela then lost her wry smile and went into a different place mentally, a place that would make her a fine doctor someday. He wasn't Vimal Lahori, whose lips she'd kissed and chest she'd tickled as they drowsed after making love. He was a patient. And she, his doctor. That was everything. She squinted, studied him carefully, then reached into her bag. She pulled on blue latex gloves.

'What does it look like?' he asked.

'Shhh. Keep watch.'

He did. But none of the few people nearby paid them any heed.

Her quick hands went to work, with gauze pads and a cold dark-orange liquid, some antiseptic. He felt stinging but nothing too severe.

'Minor lacerations. Bruises.'

'My side. That's what I'm worried about.'

'I see it.'

A burst of stinging pain as she probed the lower right, bottom rib.

'Here's a fragment. Under the skin.' She exhaled, her concern apparent in the sound. 'Vim, a doctor. You have to.'

He saw how that scenario would play out. 'No.'

'I don't have any anesthetic.' Medical students were strictly over-the-counter docs, he supposed.

'Just try.'

'Vim, I study physiology and organic chemistry. Books, computers. We don't even get cadavers for a year.'

'I'd do it myself but I can't reach it. Please.'

She continued, 'And stitches.'

He squeezed her hand. 'Not the hospital. Just get it out. And do what you can. Bandages.'

For an instant, emotion returned to her beautiful face and she grimaced. 'I'll butterfly it. But if the bleeding doesn't stop . . . '

She dug into her purse and extracted a pair of tweezers. 'Here, hold these for me.'

He took them.

'Hand them to me when I ask for them. And hold this.' She handed him her iPhone and switched on the flashlight. 'Point it down, at your side.'

'Do you want the tweezers?'

'Not yet.' He felt her hands touching near the throbbing portion of skin. 'It'll be a minute. But I'll need them fast when I ask.'

She sounded troubled. Was there more of a problem than—

'Ah,' he cried out and reared back as a bolt of pain shot from his side up to his jaw and then vanished to a dull ache.

'Got it,' she said, displaying a bloody shard of kimberlite on a gauze pad. Her strong fingers had squeezed the wound hard to force the splinter out.

'You tricked me,' he whispered, breathing hard.

She took the tweezers back. 'It's called mental anesthetic. Distraction, then you move fast.'

'You learn that in school?'

'Discovery Channel, I think. The Civil War surgeons.'

Adeela set the gauze aside, picked up the bottle of disinfectant – it was called Betadine, he noticed – and squirted some of the cold liquid on the wound. She pressed more gauze on the site and held it there for a minute. Vimal felt an absurd urge to ask how her family was doing and how did her physiology test go?

'Light again,' she said, positioning his hand.

She pulled out some butterfly bandages and secured them over the wound. 'Pain? On a scale of one to ten?' she asked.

'Three and seven-sixteenths. I've always wanted to say that.'

'Here.' Tight-lipped, she handed him a bottle of Tylenol and a Dannon water. He took two of the pills and drank half the water.

'That's the only one that made it under the skin. Just bruises and cuts and scrapes, the rest of them.' She then probed his ribs. This too hurt but, again, it wasn't bad. 'Nothing broken.'

Trying to ignore the throbbing pain, Vimal picked up the

splinter and examined it. The shard wasn't big – about a half inch long and very thin. He put it in his pocket.

'Souvenir?'

He said nothing but pulled his two shirts down.

'Here,' Adeela said, handing him the brown Betadine bottle. 'It'll stain but I don't think that's your biggest worry. Oh. And the sweatshirt.' She took from her bag an NYU purple pullover. Large. Not hers. Maybe she'd bought it for her father. Vimal had asked her for a change of clothing too. His light-gray *Keep Weird* one was dotted with dried blood. He could have bought one but he needed to conserve his money.

Silence flowed between them as they watched a woman walking three French bulldogs on three leashes. They danced in excited harmony and the owner continually swapped the leads from hand to hand to keep them from tangling.

At any other time they would have laughed. Now Vimal and Adeela stared numbly.

She took his hand and leaned her head against his.

'You're not going home, are you?' she asked.

'No.'

'Then, what?'

'Stay out of sight for a while.'

She gave a cool laugh. 'I was going to say, like a witness in a gangster movie. But that's not *like* it. That *is* it. But where, Vim?'

'I'm not sure yet.'

He was, of course, very sure but he didn't want to talk about that just yet. There would be a time. Now he wanted to get inside somewhere. The temperature was growing colder and he was exhausted.

He released her hand. They rose. He put his arm around her, pulling her close and ignoring the pain from his side. 'I'll call you soon. Look, whatever happens, nothing's going to affect us.' He smiled. 'Hell, you've got exams. You won't have any time for me anyway.'

She wasn't amused, he could tell, and he regretted the lame banter. Still, she kissed him hard. They hadn't gotten to the 'love' word yet, but he knew it was now about to be uttered. She was leaning close and putting her lips against his ear. She whispered, 'Go to the police. They'll protect you from him.'

She slung her bag over her shoulder and turned, walking in that slow, sensuous stride of hers, toward the West 4th Street subway station, leaving Vimal Lahori to reflect that the cops could probably protect him from the killer.

But that was hardly enough.

CHAPTER 10

At 8 p.m. Lincoln Rhyme wheeled closer to one of the high-def screens in his parlor. 'Run them.'

Mel Cooper typed and a video appeared.

The footage was from a camera focused on an underground loading dock behind the building where Patel's office was located. The ramp from the dock exited onto 46th Street.

At 12:37 that afternoon, according to the time stamp, that door pushed open and a man with thick dark hair, head down and wearing a dark jacket, was seen walking quickly down the stairs and up the ramp onto the street. His face was not clearly visible but appeared to be Indian – which was logical if he was, in fact, an associate of Patel. He was slim, and short in stature, to judge by a Dumpster he passed. His age was impossible to determine for certain but the impression was that he was young, possibly twenties.

'He's hurt,' Sachs said.

He was clutching his midsection. The freeze frame showed a hint of something light-colored between his fingers, maybe the paper bag that had been hit. Cooper hit Play and the young man moved on, out of the scene.

The tech said, 'And here's the second.'

This tape was of 47th Street, a camera in the window of a jewelry store next to Patel's building. At 12:51, a man in a short black or navy-blue jacket and dark baggy slacks and stocking cap passed the store. It was impossible to see his face; he was looking away. His left hand held a briefcase; his right was in his pocket.

'Holding a weapon?'

'Could be,' Sachs answered Rhyme.

'And one more,' Cooper said. 'Two doors west on Forty-Seven. One minute later.'

The same man had been caught on another jewelry store's camera. His head down and turned away again, he was on his mobile phone.

Sellitto muttered, 'Son of a bitch knew he was on *Candid Camera*. Looking away.'

Sachs said, 'Run it again. Zoom on the phone.'

Cooper did this, to no avail. They could make out no details. 'Check for pings from the cell towers?'

'The Theater District and Times Square on a matinee day?' Sellitto shot him a wry look. 'Drum up fifty officers to check out records and dedicate a week to it, hey, I'm on board with that.'

'Just a thought.'

'We know that the wit's young, male, black hair. Dark-complexioned, probably Indian. Jacket, black or navy. Slacks dark.'

She continued, 'And he's mobile. Whatever damage the rock fragments did, they didn't seem that serious.'

'Our mysterious VL?' Sellitto asked.

'Could be,' she replied.

Could be. Maybe. Not necessarily.

The doorbell rang and Rhyme looked at the intercom.

He and Sachs glanced each other's way. She said, 'Insurance man?'

She'd called the New York representative of the insurance company covering the gems. The cool-hearted Llewellyn Croft had already sent the company a notice of loss and the claims investigator had offered to come over tonight, even though the hour was late.

A five-million-dollar potential loss is a good motivator, Rhyme supposed.

'Let him in,' he instructed Thom.

A moment later the aide directed the man into the parlor. He nodded greetings and blinked in double take as he examined the forensic equipment. 'My,' he said under his breath.

The name was Edward Ackroyd. He was senior claims examiner with Milbank Assurance, on Broad Street, which was in lower Manhattan.

The man exuded medium. Average height, average weight, average amount of neatly trimmed, toffee-colored hair. Even his eyes were hazel, a shade that managed to be both unusual and undistinguished. Appropriately, he was somewhere in the middle of middle age.

'What an abject tragedy this is,' the man said in an accent that might trip from the tongue of a BBC announcer, Rhyme imagined. 'Jatin Patel . . . murdered. And that couple too. Their whole future ahead of them. Destroyed.'

At least Ackroyd's first reaction was loss of life, rather than of the gems.

Thom took Ackroyd's beige overcoat. The man wore a gray suit, with a vest, rare in the United States nowadays. His shirt was starched, and his tie appeared to be as well, though that had to be Rhyme's imagination. Given the nice garb, and the hour, maybe he'd been interrupted at a fancy dinner or a night at the theater. He wore a wedding ring.

Introductions were made. He gave only a minor reaction to Rhyme's condition – he was more surprised by the full-sized gas chromatograph/mass spectrometer in the corner – and when Rhyme offered his working hand, the right, Ackroyd gripped it, though carefully.

'Have a seat?' Sachs offered.

'No, thank you, Detective. I can't stay long. Just wanted to introduce myself.' He looked around. 'I was expecting . . . I suppose, a police station.'

Sellitto said, 'We run some investigations out of here. Lincoln was head of Crime Scene, now he's a consultant.'

'Rather like our own Sherlock Holmes.'

Rhyme gave a weary half smile. He'd heard the simile, oh, about five hundred times.

'I was Metropolitan Police – Scotland Yard – before going private.' Eyes on the equipment once again. 'Quite the setup. And in a private residence.' He strode to the gas chromatograph and looked at it with admiration.

Rhyme said, 'Took a few years to put together. We can do the basics here. Anything more sophisticated, we send the job out.'

'Basics can be all you need sometimes,' Ackroyd said. 'Too many facts, too many clues. Woods-for-the-trees sort of thing, isn't it?'

Rhyme nodded. He felt a hint of camaraderie with the insurance man. Former cop, who'd become somewhat like him, a private investigator.

No, a consulting detective.

As Sherlock Holmes described himself.

Sellitto asked, 'Did you know him? Patel? Or anyone who worked for him?'

'No, but, of course, I knew *of* him. Everyone involved in the diamond industry in any way did. Jatin Patel was a diamantaire – you know the term?'

'No.'

'It means anyone in the stratosphere of the diamond production or cutting world. In his case, it means a *master* diamond cutter. Most diamond processing now occurs in India, some in Antwerp, some in Israel. New York used to be one of the centers. It's much smaller now but the remaining diamantaires here are the best of the best. And Patel was at the top of his game.'

Sachs asked, 'What made him so good?'

'To explain that I should tell you something about the business.'

'Why not?' Sellitto said.

'To turn a rough diamond into a finished piece, there are five stages. Plotting – examining the rough stone to see how to maximize size, quality and profit. The second skill is cleaving – cracking a diamond along its grain with a sharp blow. Cutters will sometimes study a diamond for months before striking the stone. One mishap – and you could lose a million dollars in a tenth of a second.'

'But,' Sellitto interrupted, 'I thought diamonds were unbreakable.'

Ackroyd shook his head. 'Actually that's a misunderstanding, Detective. Diamonds are the hardest natural substance on earth, yes, but "hard" means resistant to *scratching*. In reality they're extremely brittle. You can shatter a diamond with a hammer blow that would have no effect on a piece of quartz. So, as I was saying: first stage, plotting. Second, cleaving. The third task is sawing – that's using a laser or a diamond-encrusted blade to cut the stone *against* the grain into the desired shape. Fourth is bruting – spinning the stone on a lathe against another diamond, or sometimes using a laser, to round it. That's to make the most popular cut: round brilliant diamonds. The last technique is grinding the geometric facets into the stone. That's called faceting or brillianteering.'

Insurance workers, Rhyme guessed, didn't generally exude this level of enthusiasm. But he was beginning to think the diamond industry was a bit different from others, more passionate, more obsessed.

'Now, about Jatin Patel. Nearly all diamond cutters in the world nowadays use computers for ninety percent of their work. Certainly the mass-produced stones for the lower-end consumer market – they're all plotted, cut and polished automatically. That's true too of many, if not most, top-end diamonds. But Mr Patel? He did everything himself, by hand. His diamonds are the best you'll ever find. His death is a huge loss. In terms of art, it's as if Picasso or Renoir had been killed. Now, sir—'

'"Lincoln" is fine. Really.'

'Yes, Lincoln. Of course. Now, Mr Croft has formally put my company on notice of the loss of the Grace-Cabot rough. Under the policy, if the stones are not recovered within thirty days, we will pay the insured value, nearly five million dollars. My company obviously would prefer to recover the gems within that thirty-day period. And I hope we shall. But if not and the claim is paid we would become subrogated. You are aware of that concept?'

Mel Cooper offered, 'I got hit by a runaway grocery cart when I was fifteen. Major stitches and a broken ankle.' His eyes remained on the computer screen. 'Insurance company paid and then they sued the grocery store. They stepped into my shoes.'

This digression grated and Rhyme glared. No one seemed to notice.

'Exactly. And I'm sorry for your trouble.' Ackroyd seemed genuinely sympathetic.

'It was a while ago.'

'Under subrogation, after we pay the claim, Milbank, my company, would continue to try to recover the stolen goods, to sell them. Reimburse ourselves with the proceeds. So, clearly you and my company have a mutual interest in finding the diamonds. And, personally . . . ' He was now speaking with a touch of anger. ' . . . I would like to see the thief put away forever. Diamond heists have a gentlemanly quality. Violence of any sort is very rare. It's not playing fair. And murder? Unimaginable. So I'll help in any way I can. I'm at your service. And to that end I've found one thing that may be helpful.'

A notebook appeared from his inside jacket pocket and his fingers, tipped with closely trimmed nails, flipped through it. 'As soon as Mr Croft called my boss and I was assigned the case I started making calls. A dealer who's helped me out in the past, fellow in Amsterdam, said he had a call from a man in New York a few hours ago, offering some rough to sell. He said about fifteen carats total, which was about the Grace-Cabot weight. The dealer demurred – he wasn't in a position to spend that much money – but he took the number anyway, possibly for the future. Here it is.'

'Mel?' Rhyme asked.

The tech jotted it down from the notebook Ackroyd displayed and made a phone call. He had a conversation with their specialist at the Computer Crimes Unit. Then Cooper was on hold for a moment. After another discussion he disconnected. 'Whoever called your friend in Amsterdam used a burner phone with a New York mobile exchange that's not active now. Could be destroyed or the batteries could be run down. They'll keep it on the alert list if it goes live.'

No probable cause for a warrant, Rhyme reflected. But if it was Unsub 47's phone and he eventually turned it on they could possibly triangulate and pay him a visit.

'Good. Appreciate that,' Sellitto said. 'We were also wondering where the thief might try to fence the diamonds here. I was talking to some detectives and FBI agents who run stolen-jewelry cases – but most of them're low-end and finished pieces. They don't know anyone who could move five million worth of uncut diamonds.'

Ackroyd said, 'No, that's quite the specialized market. I don't know if Mr Croft mentioned it but the thief took the rough because it would be much harder to trace. No serial number, as there would be on finished stones.'

'Yes,' Rhyme said. 'He told us that.'

'Word has spread already about the theft, of course. Everyone in the business is aware of it. I have calls out to contacts here and overseas to let me know if anyone wants to sell the rough . . . or is looking for an underground cutter.'

Rhyme said, 'Croft said that was what he was most afraid of.'

Ackroyd gave a reserved smile. 'Mr Croft . . . he *is* our client, of course, but I think even he would admit he gets a touch too attached to his products. You see, he's part of the old school of diamond production. There's a new trend called "branded" diamonds, often cut with extra facets and in non-traditional sizes and depths. The manufacturers often do this to charge consumers more than the diamond is actually worth, claiming that the buyer is getting something unique – a special brand. But that's spurious. The problem is that many of those companies don't take into account the qualities that make diamonds great. Grace-Cabot would never do that. The rough they sent to Patel for cutting, well, those were going to be exceptional stones when finished. And, if they're cut underground, they'll end up in department stores and high street jewelers.'

'These connections of yours?' Sachs asked. 'Who are they?'

'Oh, diamantaires, brokers, mining executives, jewelry retailers, precious metal and gemstone dealers, transport and security companies, investment companies too – diamonds, like gold, are hedge commodities. I don't want to give the impression they're all a wealth of information, though. Anyone in the trade tends to be distrustful of outsiders. As an insurer, I've worked hard to get one foot in the door, so to speak. I've made some headway over the years but even for me it's an uphill battle, getting people to cooperate.'

Rhyme recalled what Ron Pulaski had told him about the

difficulties in finding merchants to aid in the search for the elusive VL. 'We're finding a lot of resistance to talking to our canvassing officers.'

Ackroyd added, 'And accentuating that natural reclusiveness, there's the violence. I think people are simply afraid.'

Box cutters will do that.

'Well, it's a pity the Amsterdam connection hit a roadblock. But the suspect may turn on his phone once again. We can hope. Now, I'll keep making inquiries and will let you know what I find.'

'If you would, sure,' Sellitto said. 'Thanks.'

Ackroyd took his coat from the rack where Thom had hung it and donned the garment. 'If there's anything I can do, please let me know. I must say at Milbank I have a pretty solid record of recovering the loot for my clients.' Another of his soft laughs. 'Just occurred to me. "Loot" comes from a Hindi word, *lut*. For "pillaged goods." And poor Jatin Patel – that was his ethnicity. Indian. Bit ironic, wouldn't you say? Well then, I'll keep in touch. Good evening.'

'And?' Rhyme asked.

'Might be helpful,' Ron Pulaski said. 'He's the real deal.'

Rhyme sighed at the expression. 'Specifics would be good.'

It had been an hour since Edward Ackroyd had left. Ron Pulaski had returned from his futile canvassing in the Diamond District, seeking leads to the witnesses S and VL and, of course, to Unsub 47 himself. Other officers were continuing the search.

Pulaski, briefed about the insurance investigator, had been given the task of checking him out. He'd gone online and verified that Ackroyd's company, Milbank Assurance, based in London, had offices in New York, San Francisco, Paris and Hong Kong. He'd also asked Fred Dellray, an FBI agent they sometimes worked with, to check with Scotland Yard. Yes, Edward Ackroyd had indeed made a name for himself as a detective in the burglary division before retiring from the force to join Milbank. Pulaski couldn't verify that the company did insure Grace-Cabot – insurance coverage generally wasn't public – but Milbank advertised that its specialty was covering precious metal and gem companies, including mining operations.

So, Ackroyd passed the test . . . and had provided information that might have been useful, and might still be – the Amsterdam dealer. But there was one reservation. Their missions coincided, yes, but only up to a point. Once the diamonds were recovered, Milbank and Grace-Cabot would immediately begin court proceedings to have the rough released from evidence. Rhyme and Sellitto would want them to remain in the custody of the NYPD until the conclusion of Unsub 47's trial, which could be a while. And if the diamonds were recovered and their unsub was not collared, they would have to remain in evidence indefinitely. Neither the insurer nor the mining company would be pleased at that.

But, allowing himself a fragment of a cliché, he thought: We'll cross that bridge when.

For now, the job was to find the killer and if the genteel Brit could help, Rhyme would set aside his reluctance for consultants (a prejudice undiminished by the fact that he himself was one) and sign Ackroyd up.

'Okay, question,' Sellitto said. 'Our Englishman's been vetted. We tell him about the kid in the loading dock and the bearded guy in the hallway, the one who showed up at Patel's for the eleven o'clock?'

They debated and in the end decided not to enlist Ackroyd's help for that mission. Rhyme's thinking was that while he was trustworthy, his contacts might intentionally, or more likely inadvertently, give away facts that Unsub 47 might learn.

'But let's get the kid's picture out for canvassers,' Sachs said.

Rhyme and the others huddled once more around the CCTV videos, and Cooper took screenshots of the young man who was possibly VL. Rhyme said, 'Put them on the citywide wire but have Midtown North and South start a serious canvass. Tell them his initials're probably VL, and that he's young. Indian.'

'Uhm. Think we should say South Asian,' Cooper corrected.

Rhyme muttered, 'List it as South Asian *slash* Indian. And if anybody complains, they can sue the gimp for political incorrectness.'

II
CLEAVING

SUNDAY, MARCH 14

CHAPTER 11

His phone was humming. He didn't recognize the number. But with a sigh and a sinking heart, he answered. 'Yes?'

'Mr Saul Weintraub?'

A hesitation. 'Yes. Who's this, please?'

'NYPD Detective Amelia Sachs.'

'Ah.'

'Sir, did you meet with Jatin Patel on Forty-Seventh Street? Yesterday around eleven a.m.?'

A broch . . .

This was the last thing he'd wanted. Saul Weintraub had so hoped to stay under the radar. The forty-one-year-old stood in the tiny, musty living room of his house in Queens. A cluttered space, but comfortably so, filled with mismatched hand-me-downs from his parents' home and pieces he and his wife had bought over the years. He gripped the phone hard. It was his landline. His heart began to beat fast and nausea churned.

'I . . . ' Can't deny it. 'Yes. I did.'

'Do you know about his death?'

'Yes, yes . . . How did you hear about me?'

'We got your picture from a security camera in Mr Patel's building. We had officers on the street asking about you. A jewelry dealer recognized you.'

A broch . . .

The detective was going to be angry with him for not coming forward. But he just didn't want to get involved. Too many risks – both for his reputation in the diamond business and physical risks from the psychotic robber who'd killed Patel and that poor couple.

'I don't know anything. I would have called right away if there was anything I could have said to help. I was gone long before it happened.'

But the topic of intelligence didn't interest her. 'Now, Mr Weintraub. This is important. We think the man who killed Mr Patel knows your name.'

'*What?*'

'We think he hurt Mr Patel to find out who you were. Have you seen anyone following you or anyone outside your house?'

Hurt? 'No, but . . . '

But he hadn't *looked*. Why would he? He now walked to the window and peered out onto the quiet Sunday-morning street. A boy on a bike. Mrs Cavanaugh, bundled in her beige coat, and that little shit dog of hers.

'I'm sending a car to your house. Just stay inside and keep the door locked. They'll be there in fifteen minutes.'

'I will. But . . . I didn't see anything at Jatin's. I really didn't.'

'We think you may have seen the killer outside, on the street, before he went to Patel's shop. In any event, it's possible that *he* thinks that. We just want to make sure you're okay. We'll bring you in to look over some videotape.'

'But how does he know where I live? Jatin didn't know my home address. I didn't know him well. I've evaluated some of his stones a half-dozen times. That's our only connection. He'd know my office but not my home.'

'Let's hope that's the case. But it might not be too hard to track you down. We'll just play it cautiously. Don't you think?'

He sighed. 'Sure. I suppose.'

Weintraub shifted his weight from foot to foot. Floorboards creaked beneath the decades-old oriental rug that had been a wedding present from Cousin Morris. He thought briefly about his resolve to lose those fifteen pounds and then realized how trivial that mission seemed now.

The woman said, 'The theft was of some very valuable rough diamonds that had just been delivered from Grace-Cabot, the mining company. Did he mention them? Or that anyone might be interested in them?'

'No, he didn't say anything to me.'

'We can go into this later but I want to ask now: A young Indian man, who might've worked with Patel, walked into the robbery, then got away. His initials are VL. Do you have any idea who that might be?'

'I don't know. Honestly. Like I was saying, I do a job for him every few months.'

'That car should be there soon, Mr Weintraub. Do you have a family?'

'My wife's visiting my daughter at college this weekend.'

'I'd make plans to join them or, in any case, leave town for a bit.'

'You think this man is really looking for me?'

'We do, yes.'

'*Gotteniu.*'

'Keep the door locked.'

They disconnected. In the quiet, Weintraub listened to the radiator sputter and hiss. A gaudy wall clock ticked.

A broch . . . Hell and damnation.

Weintraub had heard of the crime, of course. But hadn't gotten many details, as the death had happened on Shabbat and his ability to follow the news was limited. Weintraub was religious and he was, in theory, Orthodox but he played a bit loose with the rule forbidding the thirty-nine types of 'creating' – labors – on Shabbat. He hadn't driven to Jatin Patel's office but hadn't walked either (Queens to Manhattan?); he'd taken the subway. A compromise. And at Patel's, he'd walked up the stairs to the third floor, rather than take the elevator. Watching television was not specifically forbidden, though turning on electricity was and even leaving the set on over Friday night wasn't good, since watching the nonsense of cable news fell into the prohibition against *uvdin d'chol*, mundane, weekday activity. He'd turned the set on well after sundown and learned the horrific news.

Now Shabbat was over and he clicked on TV. The screen blossomed . . . with a commercial. Of course. Nothing about the crime.

He pushed aside heavy, gold-colored drapes and peered outside once more.

No bogeymen. No killers.

Weintraub fetched his overcoat from the rack in the front hall. Ten minutes until the car was here. The area code for the phone of that nice woman officer – nice because she hadn't yelled at him for his reticence – was Manhattan. Was that where her office was? And after the interview, where would he go then? His wife and daughter were at a college mom–daughter weekend. He could hardly go there. Didn't want to, truth be told.

Clenching and unclenching his hands, he thought: Ah, how sad! Jatin Patel. Gone. One of the best diamantaires in the world. The gems that were stolen must have been valuable – he only worked on the best diamonds – but *killing* for stones? That might happen in Africa, Russia, South America, yes. But not here.

He reflected again that she seemed quite nice, Amanda, no Amelia. He couldn't remember her last name but recalled it sounded German. It might have been Jewish. He wondered how old she was, if she was married. Weintraub's twenty-eight-year-old son still had no wife.

He sighed.

His mobile hummed.

Curious. It was the owner of the deli next to his office – about ten blocks away. He and the man were friends but rarely talked via phone.

'Ari. What, is all well?'

'Saul. Just thought you should know. A man was in, having some coffee, and he asked about you. He seemed nice enough. He asked if you were the Weintraub that lived on Ditmars Court. Jenny told him yes. She just told me.'

'When was this?'

'About a half hour ago.'

Weintraub's thoughts leapt quickly: Patel tells the killer my name and my business address – not knowing my home. The killer starts asking about me around my shop, armed with a list of Saul Weintraubs in and around Long Island City. At the deli he asks the counter girl if the Weintraub who owned the shop is the one who lives on Ditmars Court. He's a friend, he says. And Jenny says, yes.

Fucking Internet.

A broch . . .

'I have to go.' He disconnected and summoned the keypad on his phone.

Before he could dial 911, though, a figure stepped forward fast, from behind him, spun him around and ripped the phone from his hand. Weintraub gave a cry of shock and fear. The man's face was obscured by a ski mask. Weintraub thought: Basement window, back bathroom window. He never locked windows the way he should.

'No, no, please! I didn't say anything to them! I promise. I didn't see anything, I'm not a threat!' His heart slammed in his chest.

The intruder glanced at the screen and slipped the phone into his pocket.

Weintraub said desperately, 'Please. I can get you diamonds, gold. Whatever you want! Please! I have a wife, a daughter. Please.'

The man held up one finger to his own lips, shushing him the way he might a babbling child.

CHAPTER 12

One of the *kur* from yesterday morning's excitement at Jatin Patel's shop was dead and gone.

Saul Weintraub.

Goodbye. May your Jew God embrace your soul. Or burn you in hell. Or send you wherever. Vladimir Rostov hadn't been old enough to sample the Soviet Union firsthand but his study of history told him he would have fit right in with USSR state atheism. He didn't believe in second acts for the soul.

Now, one gone. One more *kuritsa* to go: the skinny boy. Rostov was impatiently awaiting word from his little sniffy-cryee Persian friend Nashim, who had better be spending the Day of Rest making calls to his Indian counterparts in the diamond world.

Thinking of those daughters of his: Scheherazade and Kitten.

Pretty girls.

Vladimir Rostov was presently refueling. His residence was in Brighton Beach, the Russian enclave of Brooklyn, but he was in neighboring Sheepshead. He was sitting in what had become one of his favorite restaurants in the world. The famed Roll N Roaster, a landmark in Brooklyn. It was a neighborhood 'joint' – a term he'd heard somebody use but that he didn't quite get, English not being his first language. After he looked the word up, though, it made perfect sense. The man felt right at home in a joint. Especially this one, which served up magnificent roast beef sandwiches – with cheese, always cheese – and Coca-Cola better than in Moscow, no doubt on this.

His only regret was that one could not smoke in the Roll N Roaster, which would have made a meal here an exquisite experience.

A mother with two small boys walked past – the kids, like him, were crowned with blond crew cuts and had broad faces. They stared at his meal, maybe marveling at the quantity. Two and a half sandwiches were sitting before him, a mountain of fries.

Since they were near Little Odessa, the Russian émigré community, Rostov said to them, '*Zdravstvuyte*.'

The boys stared blankly with steel-blue gazes, also matching his. The mother nodded, a faint smile on her overly powdered Slavic face. '*Khoroshego dnya*.'

Rostov's eyes dipped from face to crotch then, as she passed, to ass. She wore a short red jacket and tight black skirt – and he watched her hips sway as she walked out. Rostov debated but decided there was no reasonable scenario that would let his momentary fantasy come to life. Forcing himself on a mother with children in tow could have only bad consequences.

In his appetite for women, like in his appetite for beef (and most other things, for that matter, diamonds among them), he walked a tightrope.

Gone to the stone . . .

Which sounded better in Russian than in English.

He had his parents to thank for the phrase – and the condition itself, which Rostov equated with a form of controlled madness.

It had all begun with his father. One night – not an ounce of vodka in him! – the man had stabbed his wife, Rostov's mother (though only in the face and only with a screwdriver, so hardly a problem). Then he'd stripped his clothes off and run into a nearby forest, where he spent the night, apparently chasing nocturnal animals and howling. At dawn, he'd used a rock to chip away the ice that had formed around him in the stream he'd fallen asleep in and returned home. After forgiving her for the affair, his father began to methodically negotiate the divorce with his soon-to-be-ex. The discussion included a number of real estate, financial and insurance details – but not a word about where little Vladimir would go; the boy had always been an afterthought, at best.

They decided that he would temporarily live with Uncle Gregor and Aunt Ro.

So the twelve-year-old packed a suitcase, not even a wheelie but one you had to heft, and shopping bag and boarded a plane for the picturesque town of Mirny, Russia.

If ever there was a place for a boy to go to the stone, it was Mirny.

Rostov lifted the rest of the sandwich, chewed it down in just a few bites, then vanquished another. Returning to the laptop, which was online, he scrolled. He lived on the device. He watched porn, played games, sent emails, hacked (he was Russian, of course) . . . and followed the news.

This is what he was doing presently, while he chewed and chewed and tried not to think about the Slavic mother's hips. He read several accounts of the incident at poor Mr Patel's.

Nothing new. Nothing to concern him. And so far, Saul Weintraub's killing had not been connected to the events at Patel Designs, not by the press, that is, though the police would know. Weintraub's murder, in fact, didn't take up much space, none in the national news. It was the 'Massacre on 47th Street' (the *New York Post*'s term) that captured everyone's attention.

The suspect was a white male, medium build, in dark clothing, stocking cap.

Hm. Won't find many of *those* in New York.

Last sandwich down. Ah . . .

He turned his attention back to online newspapers and the police's statements to the public. They gave some details but not too many. Nothing about the second *kuritsa*, initials VL on Patel's calendar.

He threw a napkin over his face and stifled a racking bout of coughing. Breathing in, out. Slowly. The urge subsided. He now switched windows to the streaming site of a major cable network and tapped an earbud in, raised the volume. Nothing about the crime for the duration of one Coke and about a dozen fries. Then a segment on the murder and robbery came on, moderated by the network's 'Senior Crime Correspondent,' a job description that amused Rostov no end since she was all of thirty years old.

The blonde (and a very appealing one she was) sat in the studio, remotely interviewing a slim, middle-aged man in a crisp suit jacket, white shirt and tie. His head was adorned with neatly trimmed hair.

'*Joining us now is Dr Arnold Moore, a psychologist at*

Cumberland University in Ohio specializing in criminal behavior. Welcome, Doctor. Now, according to police, the robber who forced his way into the jewelry store on Forty-Seventh Street yesterday took some diamonds but left hundreds of thousands of dollars' more. Is it unusual for a robber to leave such valuable loot behind, like that?'

'Thank you, Cindi. So, professional thieves who target high-end jewelry stores and factories like Mr Patel's are the best of the best. No one would attempt a brazen robbery like this without maximizing their return. That means taking with them every diamond he could lay his hands on.'

'"Maximizing return." You're saying, then, that robbery, well, it's a business?'

Cindi sounded a bit aghast. Rostov liked her boobs, prominent in a yellow dress, though diminished somewhat by a heavy necklace of wooden disks. Why that accessory? he wondered, then turned his attention back.

'Exactly, Cindi. And this wasn't what you might call a typical "transaction."'

Air quotes around the word, of course. Rostov quite disliked this man.

'That's why I think we're dealing with something else here, some other motive.'

'What do you think that could be?' dear Cindi asked.

'I couldn't speculate. Maybe he had a separate reason to kill the diamond cutter and took some of the gems to make the police think it was just a robbery.'

But *isn't* that speculating, Doctor? Rostov thought. Hack.

Cindi jumped in. *'Or are you saying maybe the couple was the target? That would be William Sloane and Anna Markam, of Great Neck, New York.'*

Pictures of them, smiling, appeared briefly on the screen. Rostov washed a mouthful of fries down with Coke.

'That's a possibility, Cindi. But from what I've heard, there was no motive for their deaths. No criminal connections. It appeared they were just bystanders. But you're right, the killer may have picked them on purpose.'

Rostov enjoyed the way they kicked back and forth 'are you saying' and 'you're right' like soldiers lobbing hand grenades. Wanting to make sure the other was responsible for the irresponsible speculation.

'A young couple like that. Any thoughts on why?'

'They were there to pick up their engagement ring. We don't know if their killer knew that but then he could have figured it out.'

'He's targeting engaged couples?'

Hand grenade away.

'All I can say is in my practice I've found it's not uncommon for psychopathic killers to harbor resentment against those who have what they don't.'

Successfully dodged.

'You're thinking maybe he was jilted, left at the altar. Or he suffered because his parents had a difficult marriage.'

The doctor smiled patiently. 'Well, we'd really have to learn more. But it is clear that this doesn't fit the mold for professional diamond larceny.'

A commercial popped up. Rostov tapped the newscast off and sent his Dell to sleep.

He mopped up ketchup with the last of the fries, and – some balance still remaining – used his fingers for the rest of the condiment. After licking, he cleaned the digits by dunking them in his water glass and drying them with a napkin. He rose and bought several more sandwiches, these to go – so he could both eat *and* smoke, like normal people did (his sole gripe with Putin was that he had banned smoking in much of the dear Motherland). Rostov paid and stepped out into the cool gray March morning.

Well, Doctor, you are the fucking clever fellow, aren't you?

We'd like to come visit, my box cutter and me.

Rostov had an image of the pitch and duration of the squealing sounds the doctor might make when he took the razor blade to the bony man's fingers or ears. But like the sweaty bout of sex with the mother whose hips swayed à la an amusement park ride, this was pure imagination.

Coughing gently, Rostov walked steadily down the untidy sidewalk, alternating between bites of the heavenly sandwich and drags on his pungent Russian cigarette. Unable to decide which was the more delicious.

CHAPTER 13

Dismayed at the sight, Amelia Sachs pulled her Torino to the curb on this quiet street in Long Island City, tossed the NYPD sign onto the dash and climbed out.

Four blue-and-whites were there. One unmarked. And an ambulance. Which was now unnecessary, as the polyvinyl tarp covering the body in the front hallway explained.

The body of Saul Weintraub.

Her first thought: What could they have done differently to save his life?

No answers came to her.

The killer would have spent his time since the killing in Midtown tracking down Weintraub. His canvassing had been just a bit better than theirs. The instant they'd learned his name, she'd called. Lock the doors. Don't let any strangers in. And the local precinct, the 114, had gotten a car there as fast as they could.

That Weintraub himself should have called them the minute he learned of Patel's death wasn't a factor. No cop can blame potential witnesses for duck-and-cover.

Her phone hummed. Rhyme.

'I'm here,' she said.

'Got something interesting, Sachs. Text from a burner phone, now dead, of course. It went to a half-dozen TV and radio stations in the area. It's all over the news. I just sent it.'

She minimized the phone screen and went to texts.

The concept of engagement is based on a binding promise to wed by the man to his betrothed. Now I have promise too. I am looking for YOU, I am looking every where. Buy ring, put on pretty finger but I will find you and you will bleed for your love.

—The Promisor

'Jesus, Rhyme. You think it's Forty-Seven? Or just a copycat?'

'I don't know. I'm having somebody from downtown, a linguist, look at it. Not that it'll tell us much, I think. My gut says it's from him. But you know how much I trust that. Well, run the scene there and we'll talk more when you're back.'

She started toward the home, a modest row house, painted white, in need of more paint, and windowsills lined with empty brown flower boxes, like droopy lower eyelids. Instinctively, she tapped her Glock – the Gen4 FS – to orient herself to the weapon's exact position. There was a large crowd. It wasn't impossible for Unsub 47 to be among them – here to learn of the police's progress. Sachs eyed those on the street – fifty or sixty people – and the TV stations vans. Was the unsub among the spectators? Street Crime officers were canvassing. If anybody seemed suspicious or left quickly, they'd pursue the lead. Still, she suspected that the man's business was completed and he'd fled after the murder. A shooting this time, she'd learned. No knife work. The victim had, however, been beaten.

'Hey, Amelia.'

She nodded to Ben Kohl, a gold shield out of the 114. He asked, 'So how come you guys're involved?'

Sachs explained to the detective, a lean balding man in his mid-fifties, 'A wit in the killing at the diamond shop, Four-Seven Street yesterday.'

'Oh, that. Jesus. How'd the perp find him? They know each other?'

'We don't know. How'd you hear?'

'Gunshots reported.'

'Anybody see anything? Get a description?'

'Maybe. But nobody's talking. We've been canvassing but we got nothing so far. I mean, we'll handle it out of our house, you want. But Major Cases want to take it?'

Hope blossomed in his voice.

'If I can borrow some of your people for the canvass. You mind?'

'Mind?' Kohl laughed. 'I'm taking the wife out for our anniversary tonight. All yours. I'll get you three, four uniforms to help out. Just keep our Homicide crew in the loop. This one'll show up as our stat and we'll need to report it out. You understand.'

'Sure.'

Sachs walked close to the scene to make sure it remained clear and to await the Crime Scene bus, so she could get to work.

Mikey O'Brien had a plan and he was unwrapping it in his mind right now.

After the wedding they'd stay in the neighborhood for one year. That was it. Three hundred sixty-five days. Less, if possible. But definitely no more than. By then he'd be a senior floor manager (okay, *teller*) at the bank and be making close to 45K. Emma would be getting thirty from the hospital, more if she worked nights. Enough for a down payment in eastern Nassau somewhere.

Close enough to the in-laws (both sets) to visit. But not *too* close.

The slim redheaded man, twenty-six, strode with hope and a hint of cockiness down Avenue U. Past the tanning salon, the Progressive Medical Center, the deli, the meat market, the pharmacy. Signs in Greek, signs in Italian.

Nothing wrong with this neighborhood, Gravesend. But, it was a place to leave, not a place to stay.

For him at least. Michael P. O'Brien, future district manager of Brooklyn Federal Bank, had places to go.

Another block and he saw her, waiting on the street corner. After errands this morning they'd planned to rendezvous here then proceed to their apartment (the *temporary* apartment – one year, no more, he reminded himself firmly).

He smiled at the sight. Emma Sanders, blond, with stunning green eyes, was beautiful, an inch taller than he was, and round where a woman should be round – perfect for having (and *making*) babies. He smiled to himself as he thought this. There would be three children. Among the names to pick and choose from: Michael III, Edward, Anthony, Meghan, Ellie, Michaela. Emma had signed off on these.

Mikey O'Brien was a happy man.

'Hey, sweet.' They kissed. She smelled of flowers.

He assumed the scent was flowers. That was a subject he wasn't familiar with – no gardening in his genes. But it seemed to be floral. On the other hand, he was soon to be very familiar with the subject. The groom's side was helping contribute to the wedding expenses, and his family – that is, Mikey himself – was picking up the florist's bill.

'How'd it go?' he asked her.

They continued walking in the direction he'd been heading – toward the apartment.

'Oh, honey. She's great. Totally great. She's not trying to talk us into anything we don't want. I thought she was going to and I was going to sic my big, bad Mikey on her. But, uh-uh, she knows the budget—'

Already a shitload of money, Mikey thought but didn't come close to saying.

'—and is sticking to it. I mean, Nora's planner talked her into the eight-piece band, remember.'

Friggin' orchestra.

'But Stacey didn't push me. She's cool with a keyboard, guitarist, bass and drums.'

Had he agreed to a four-piece band? Joey got married with a DJ was all. Worked out great.

Again, keeping mum.

In truth, Mikey O'Brien wasn't even sure why they needed a wedding planner. Wasn't that something you could figure out yourself? He'd put together bachelor parties. And a wake. They'd all gone fine.

But Emma wanted one – because her sister had had one and Nora, her BFF from the hospital, had had one. So, honey, Mikey, pleeeeease.

Oh, hell, sure. She was *so* beautiful . . .

Emma slipped her arm through his and they continued through this interesting neighborhood, where commercial and residential coexisted peacefully. Two blocks farther along, they turned the corner and started toward their apartment. He felt her breast against his biceps.

That low urge unfurled within him, demanding attention, like a horse hoofing the ground.

Maybe just a half hour . . . the bedroom, the couch? The living room floor? Nope, he said to himself. No time. They had to get ready to meet her parents out on Long Island.

The wind shook branches overhead and speckled the couple with icy water. Mikey brushed it off his shoulders and happened to look back. He noted someone behind, about thirty feet away, in dark coat, gloves and stocking cap. Gravesend, despite the name, wasn't particularly dangerous. But this *was* New York. You had to keep an eye out. This guy, though, was by himself. So no gang action. He was looking down at the screen of his phone as he walked. Innocent as could be.

Soon they were home. The block was a little scuffed, a little worn, in need of a sidewalk sweeping and repair and couldn't the damn super at 368 get that moldy green couch off the effing sidewalk until trash day?

But it was a pleasant enough place.

Good for a year.

The plan.

They climbed the five steps to the front door of their building, a dark, battered four-story walk-up brownstone. Here, they paused, as he fished for keys. He felt Emma tug him closer, with a certain, unmissable message. He turned and they kissed again, lingering. Okay, the horse was done hoofing; he was out, trotting through the fields.

The wedding was two weeks from today. Who – aside from his mother – would note that a baby was born exactly eight months and fifteen days after?

He could handle Mom.

'Hey,' he whispered to her. 'What do you think about—'

Then, in an instant, the man behind them, the *innocent* man, charged forward. He'd pulled the stocking cap into a ski mask. Shit, shit, shit. He held a gun in cloth-gloved hands and was pointing it at Emma's head. 'Scream, and you die.'

Which led, of course, to a scream of sorts.

From Mikey, not his fiancée.

Gasping, he said, 'Here, here! Take my wallet. You can have it.'

'Shhh. Shhh. We go inside.' The voice was accented. He couldn't tell what country or neighborhood he might be from. Like he was covering up his real accent, trying to sound American.

'Honey,' Emma whispered.

'No, no, little chicken!' the man barked and grabbed her arm, which had been lingering behind her back. Her phone fell to the concrete. The gun still aimed their way, he crouched and picked it up. The dialing app was on the screen and she'd punched in 9 and 1 and 1 but had not hit Send. He powered it down.

He leaned close and Mikey smelled garlic and onion and meat on his breath and aftershave on his skin. 'You are being smarter, *will* you?'

Heart racing, as his jaw quivered, Mikey said, 'Yes. We will. Now listen, please. I'll go inside. Let her go.'

The man laughed and he seemed genuinely amused. 'Now.'

With shaking hands, Mikey unlocked the front door and they walked inside and up the stairs to their apartment on the second floor.

CHAPTER 14

'Look, please, man. You don't want to do this.'

'Hm.' The intruder seemed to be sniffing the air as he looked around their small apartment. He turned his eyes to Emma, who sobbed and held the fingers of one hand over her mouth. At first Mikey thought the intruder was looking at his fiancée's chest or legs but, no, he was concentrating on her hands. No, just *one* hand. Her left.

What could he possibly want? They had nothing. *Less* than nothing; they were in debt already from the wedding plans.

He said, 'My uncle's a cop in Syosset. He's a ball breaker. Just take what you want and walk out the door. I won't say anything to him.'

'A cop? Your uncle is cop.'

Mikey wished he hadn't said that. He hoped he wouldn't pee his pants. He stared at the gun.

'Honey, honey,' Emma gasped.

'It's okay, sweet.' Then to the intruder: 'Come on, man. What do you want? I don't have money here. We can get you some. A couple thousand.'

Though he knew that wasn't what this guy wanted. He sure wasn't going to get a ton of loot from a couple like them, in Gravesend, Brooklyn. What he wanted was to kill Mikey and rape Emma.

But Mikey would make sure that the second part of that wasn't going to happen, whatever it took. The man had a gun and he looked like he'd have no trouble in the world using it. But he wasn't huge. Oh, Mikey was probably going to die but he had rage and that fucking Irish madness on his side. The rage that, on the rare times it kicked in, kicked in huge. He'd lunge and grapple and do enough damage so that Emma could get out the window or the front door. And when the bullet got fired into Mikey's brain or gut or heart, the sound of the shot would scare the man off.

Or, who knew? Maybe he'd take the guy by surprise and get the gun away from him and shoot him in the balls and the elbow and knee and then – after a time – call the police. Keep the agony going, for ten, fifteen minutes.

Mikey shivered with fury. He hadn't been in a fight for eight years, when he'd beat the crap out of the fucking asshole who'd made fun of Mikey's kid sister, who had Down syndrome. The guy had outweighed him by thirty pounds but had gone down like a cardboard box. Broken jaw and dislocated shoulder.

Now, move now . . . Surprise the son of a bitch, while he's not looking at you!

The man cut his eyes to the left, in an instant, and slammed the gun into Mikey's cheek. A searing pain, a flash of yellow. He staggered back, tripping over the ottoman that had been his parents' and that he and his brother had played aircraft carrier on two decades ago.

Emma cried out and ran to him, hugging hard.

'Prick,' she shouted.

'Listen here, little hen,' he muttered at Mikey. 'I know what people going to do before they are trying it. I am psychic, don't you know? You had hero vibrations.'

The intruder rose and pulled a utility knife from his pocket. Emma gasped. The man thumbed the blade out and yanked a lamp cord from the socket and cut it. He shoved Emma to the floor and rolled Mikey onto his belly and bound his hands behind him. He tied Emma's hands too, though in front of her.

He muscled them each into a sitting position. He himself sat on the ottoman.

'Please, please!' Emma cried. 'Take our money and leave!'

His cold blue eyes swept over Mikey and his fiancée. 'You.' He pointed the knife at Emma. 'Give me hands. Now!'

She looked toward Mikey, who shook his head no. But she offered her hands anyway. Her right was on top.

'Why would I want that hand? You stupid hen.'

She began to sob harder.

'Left. I want *left* hand.'

He took her fingers, staring at her ring.

That's what he'd been looking at earlier.

Mikey understood. 'You're that killer. You're that one on the news! The Promisor. You killed that couple, the engaged couple in Midtown! Please, mister. Come on. We didn't do anything to you.'

'The Promisor,' the man whispered. He seemed to relish the word.

Emma's head dropped and tears poured, moisture oozed from her nose and mouth.

'You want it, take it,' Emma muttered. 'It's worth a lot.'

'*Was* worth lot,' he said. He tapped the stone with the back of the knife. His face revealed contempt. 'Not worth lot now.'

Mikey now understood that he'd been staking out the wedding planner storefront, waiting for an engaged couple. Like he'd followed that couple into the jewelry store in Midtown yesterday. He'd followed Emma back here. He wanted to kill engaged couples. That's what the news said.

Mikey began, 'Please— '

'Shhh. Tired of you saying that.' He fell silent for a moment. 'Do you know what this was?' he asked, his voice low, manic. Holding up her hands and tapping the ring once more. Harder.

Wincing from the impact, Emma gasped, 'What . . . what do you mean?'

This wasn't the answer he wanted.

He shouted this time. 'You are having any idea?'

Emma looked down.

'Billion years . . . You are *listening*?'

Mikey whispered quickly, 'We're listening. Yes.'

Emma nodded. Tears still streamed. The assailant continued to hold her hands.

'Billion years ago there is piece of carbon. Like charcoal. Just like charcoal. Nothing. It was nothing. Just pieces of blackness hundred miles underground. Buried there. Ah – ' His eyes shone. 'But then something miracle happened. Like baby happens. Two thousand degrees centigrade. Huge, huge pressure, hundreds thousands pounds in one inch. And over those billions years, what happens? Most perfect thing in world is created. Diamond. Heart of earth. Diamonds are heart of earth. You know Jesus?'

Emma nodded. 'We're Catholic.'

'Jesus is redeemer,' he said.

'Yes,' Mikey said.

'Diamonds redeem sins of earth.' He eased back, pointing the triangular blade of the knife from one of his captives to the other slowly.

A fucking psycho.

Though he was sitting, with hands tied behind him, Mikey was judging angles. More carefully this time.

The assailant said, 'Now, is raped, is destroyed. Heart of earth is piece of crap on your finger.'

'I'm sorry. I didn't . . . we didn't mean anything.'

He yanked her hand into a shaft of sunlight. 'Do you see?'

There was a burst of colored lights refracted from the stone, like you'd see from a prism.

He whispered, '"Fire" it's called. That fire is God's anger you have taken miracle and cut it up into little teeth for your finger.'

'I'm so sorry.' Emma undoubtedly was trying to think of something to say to convince him that they were innocent of this crime.

It would do no good. This man was a plane crash, a propane tank explosion, a heart attack. There'd be no reasoning with him.

Then he grew calm and leaned back, looking, it seemed, self-satisfied. 'I am just doing mission. Justice to God, justice to earth. Yesterday I saved big diamonds before they was cut. *And* I kill this terrible man so he could not defile stones anymore. In India – where diamonds first discovered – it was sin to cut them. He should know that. He betrayed his people. He paid for that.'

'You're hurting me!'

'Oh, poor chickee . . . ' The sarcastic words drooled from his lips. The madman eyed the ring as he caressed her finger. 'Tell you story, you lovebirds. I tell you story. After Depression and war, nobody was buying engagement rings. No money, no time for engagements! Just get married, bang the babies out, move to suburbs. Happy, happy. Ach, but De Beers, the diamond company, they had most famous advertising of all time. "A Diamond Is Forever." And business came back. Everybody bought diamonds! You *had* to have diamond or your husband was asshole and you got laughed at. And all those stones, beautiful stones, got cut and cut and cut.' His eyes grew angry and a demonic grin spread across his face. 'Am thinking something else is forever too.'

He pulled her ring finger straight and pressed the blade against the base.

Oh, Mary, Mother of Jesus . . . He's going to cut her finger off before he kills us!

He gripped the knife with his right hand and tightened his hold on Emma's digit with his left. As he eased forward, though, Emma let out a fierce scream and twisted away. He lost his grip and she fell back. He lunged with the knife and missed her.

It was then that Mikey, braced on the floor, kicked the man with both feet, as hard as he could, using every ounce of energy in his strong legs. The man tumbled off the ottoman and into a bookcase. He hit his head and lay stunned, squinting in pain.

Emma, with her hands in front of her, easily rose to her feet.

'Run! Now, go!' And Mikey struggled to stand.

He meant her alone. His improvised plan was to pile onto the madman and use his teeth to rip flesh or break fingers. He'd die but at least his love would escape.

Emma didn't hesitate. But she didn't make for the door. She grabbed Mikey by the shoulder and yanked her fiancé to his feet.

'No!'

'Yes!' she shouted.

Mikey noted that the assailant was wiping tears of pain from his eyes and gripping his battered head. They'd have only a few seconds to escape before the man could focus. Together they sprinted toward the door, Emma in the lead, and she pulled it open fast. Then they pushed into the hall, just as the stunningly loud gunshot sounded behind them and a bullet, missing Mikey's head by less than a foot, cracked into the wall across the hall.

They fled toward the stairs at the end of the hallway, which would lead them straight down to the entryway and the street.

Of course, if the man followed them into the hall, he'd have a perfect shot into their backs as they descended the stairs. But there was nothing else to do. At least here, at this moment, Mikey thought hysterically, they were less dead than in their apartment.

He positioned himself directly behind Emma as they took the steps two at a time downward to the lobby.

She got to the ground first and leapt to the front door, pulling it open.

Which was when he fell.

On the third step from the bottom, he lost his balance and, not having use of his hands, he went down hard, first on his side, then onto his belly, the wood taking skin from throbbing cheek and chin.

Emma cried, 'No, honey!'

'Keep going!' he called.

But once again she ignored him. She stepped forward and crouched to help Mikey up.

Above them, a door slammed and the floor creaked – he knew the exact spot, just outside their apartment, where the loose board made that noise. The sound meant the killer would be approaching the top of the stairs now.

He'd be aiming.

With a fierce lunge, Mikey rose to his full height. He stepped behind her and shouted, 'Run!'

He prayed that his body would shield the bullets, stopping them, and give his love – his beautiful girl – a chance to make it, unhurt, into the street.

CHAPTER 15

The murder of Saul Weintraub had taken place within a four-by-four-foot square of the entrance alcove in his house.

Unsub 47 had come in through an unlocked basement window, walked straight up the stairs, shot Weintraub three times, once to the face and a double-tap to the chest, and then fled though the front door. She knew it had happened this way since the killer had left moist footprints – from the drizzle outside – in a direct path from entry to exit.

Although Weintraub hadn't been tortured with the knife, he had been beaten – pistol-whipped, it seemed, since there were no blunt objects in his house that might have caused the wounds; nothing Sachs found held blood or tissue. She guessed the blows were to force him to reveal what Weintraub had told the police or who VL was. There was another possibility, too: that the killer had demanded something. Weintraub's coat lay beside him and one of the pockets was turned out, as if the killer had asked that he produce something.

Or was it simply because Weintraub, in anticipation of walking out to the police car, had pulled his gloves from the pocket? They lay nearby too.

Dressed in her white overalls, booties, hood and cornflower-blue gloves, she walked the grid in the house while two crime scene evidence techs, whom she knew from the main headquarters, ran the secondary scenes – the backyard and alley and the sidewalk on which he'd, possibly, entered and later fled. Sachs was optimistic about finding evidence in the back – near the window where he'd entered – but the odds were slim that she would find any relevant clues on the sidewalk in front of the house; heavy foot traffic would have deposited thousands of bits of trace, dirt, mud, trash, animal crap and pee.

She sent several of the uniforms whom Ben Kohl had assigned to her to canvass for wits and search for evidence for three or four blocks in the direction the unsub had fled. She knew the escape route since a woman, a dog walker, had seen him jogging from Weintraub's house, just after the shots. He'd pulled off a cap or mask and the woman had seen that he was white with short light-colored hair.

Sachs assembled what she'd found. No single bit of evidence seemed particularly helpful. The shoe prints seemed the same, the fibers too – from the gloves and the ski mask.

Three spent brass shells. Fiocchi 9mm – probably what had been fired in Midtown at the witness, though there he'd collected the spent round. The fact he'd left them here meant he was in a hurry, probably because of the noise of the shots. The brass also had been ejected some distance, the ones she found, under furniture.

A Motorola radio crackled from the belt of an officer nearby. She couldn't hear the transmission but he sent a reply from his shoulder mike and walked up to Sachs. 'Detective? One of the uniforms canvassing? Found something in a storm drain. Two blocks that way.' He pointed in the direction that the perp had fled. 'She didn't want to touch it. Clothing or something.'

Sachs picked up some collection gear and headed along the sidewalk, nodding to the curious and concerned bystanders and deflecting questions. One woman asked, 'Was it a hate crime?'

'We're investigating,' Sachs told her and walked on. After two blocks she slowed, seeing no other cops. Had she misheard? But then she looked down a side street and saw a patrol officer, a Latina in her late twenties, waving. Sachs turned and joined the woman.

'Officer.'

'Detective.' The solidly built woman had a beautiful face, round. And she had applied makeup with care that morning. Sachs was pleased to see that Officer M. López was able to balance her personal inclinations with her profession. This small thing told Sachs she'd have a long career in blue. 'I was going south, like you sent us, but thought I'd try this way. It's a shortcut to the subway, up a block. Nobody heard any tires squealing away after the shots so I thought he might've done an MTA.'

Jumping on a Metropolitan Transportation Authority subway car could put distance between a criminal and a crime scene faster than a Ferrari.

López continued, 'And since he got spotted by that wit – the woman with the dog – I was thinking, it'd been me, I would've lost the jacket. I've been checking trash cans and' – she pointed to the grate at her feet – 'storm drains. Looks like some clothing in there. Didn't touch it.'

'Good.' Sachs laid a number next to the grating and photographed it herself with her phone. 'Did you—'

'I canvassed apartments. Nobody saw him.'

Sachs smiled in reply. She bent down and flashed her Maglite into the opening. It was a wad of dark cloth and it didn't appear wet, which meant it hadn't been there for very long. Drizzle had been the order of the day.

Pulling on gloves, she fished out the garment. It was a wool jacket and fairly new. Unsub 47 had worn a similar one, according to the anonymous 911 report and the video from the store on 47th Street, near Patel's building.

López added, 'Don't know for certain it's his. Maybe you can get gunshot residue off the sleeve to make sure.'

Which was on the program. Sachs bagged the jacket and fished in the drain but could find nothing else.

'Which subway?'

López told her and she jotted the numbers of the train lines.

'Thanks, Officer. Good work.'

'I'll keep on with the canvass.'

'Thanks. I'm sending an ECT crew out. You can help 'em. And I'll send a note to your file.'

The woman tried not to beam. ''Preciate it.'

Sachs encircled the area with yellow tape. She placed a call to the CSU's main office, asking for an evidence collection tech she knew. She told the man the location of the storm drain and asked for a more thorough examination. A team would use fiber-optic cameras and lights to peer into the drain and see if the unsub

– if it was indeed him – had thrown out the mask or anything else.

She returned to the scene at Saul Weintraub's home to find that the crowds had largely dissipated. She stripped out of the overalls and gloves and wrote chain-of-custody notations on the cards.

Her phone buzzed. She glanced at the caller ID.

'Rhyme. We're finished here. I'll bring the evidence—'

'Sachs.'

The tone of his voice made clear that there was a problem.

'What is it?'

'Have the techs bring the stuff to me. You need to get down to Gravesend.'

'Brooklyn?'

'Yeah. Our unsub's not wasting any time, Sachs. You've got another scene to run.'

CHAPTER 16

Lincoln Rhyme loved cloth.

When stitched into garments, the complex substance reveals the size of the perp, possibly age and maybe site of storage and, often, the source of purchase. It can shed fibers faster than a golden retriever blows his coat. And even better, cloth captures and retains wonderful trace evidence and in some rare instances fingerprints. Not to mention it can serve as a sponge to soak up and store that most wonderful of substances, deoxyribonucleic acid. Also known as DNA. Three letters that, Rhyme would theatrically tell his criminalistics students, spelled bad news for perps.

Rhyme was presently watching Mel Cooper process the jacket discarded by Unsub 47 in the storm drain in Queens.

They knew the garment was his because it contained traces of gunshot residue that was nearly identical in composition to residue on Weintraub's body and found at the crime scenes in Patel's building in the Diamond District. Cooper also discovered traces of the same rock dust near Weintraub's body that was found at Patel's: that kimberlite. The substance was proving helpful. The bullet striking the stone had blown a significant amount of rock dust and tiny chips throughout Patel's shop, some settling on the unsub. It was acting like a marker to link him to locations and contacts.

Locard's Principle, after Edmond Locard, the French criminalist, holds that in every exchange between criminal and victim, or criminal and crime scene, there is a transfer of matter. ('Every contact leaves a trace.') If the forensic scientist is diligent enough, and clever enough, he or she can find that substance and determine what it is. That doesn't mean, of course, that it will lead you to the perp's door, but it can start you on the path.

This kimberlite, a perfect example of Locard's matter, had become a helpful partner in their hunt for the unsub.

Rhyme called, 'Prints?'

'Negative,' Cooper replied. He'd been over every inch of the jacket with an alternative light source then tried gold and zinc vacuum metal deposition, which can sometimes raise fingerprints on cloth. Well, that was always a long shot with garments.

Rhyme told him, 'Get samples to Queens for DNA and TDNA.'

'Already ordered,' Cooper said. There was likely a DNA sample somewhere on the coat. Sweat or spit or tears or – it wasn't unheard of with outer garments – semen adhere plentifully. If this was the case here, the DNA profile might have a positive hit in the CODIS or an international database and reveal the suspect's identity. Even if no significant amounts of fluid or tissue were found, though, there would certainly be skin cells, which might be used for a Touch DNA analysis. This technique is less accurate than a full DNA workup – it requires only a half-dozen skin cells – and can result in false positive results. But this would not be for a criminal trial, merely direction in getting the unsub's identity.

Cooper slipped the jacket into an evidence bag and, since he hadn't done so earlier, added his name to the chain-of-custody card. He left it inside the front door to await pickup by a team from the DNA analysis unit in Queens.

The brand labels had been cut from the jacket – clever. It was roughly a medium size, man's. The stitching suggested mass manufacturing in a third-world country. Probably sold in a thousand stores around the country. There would be no leads from this angle.

In evidence bags Cooper assembled samples of fibers he'd taken from the jacket, along with fibers found inside the pockets – they were black cotton, very similar to those found at Patel's, from the gloves, and polyester fibers, from the mask.

Patrolman Ron Pulaski called in. He explained he was still having no luck tracking down the mysterious VL. Rhyme recalled what their insurance investigator had warned of: the reluctance of those in the diamond community to talk to outsiders. As well as a natural tendency not to get involved in a case in which the perp was fast to use a razor knife and gun.

'Keep at it,' he told the Rookie and they disconnected.

VL's refusal to contact the police was perplexing. Yes, he'd be scared of being targeted by the killer, but generally a witness would come forward immediately and ask for protection – and help catch the perp. It was also curious that no friends or family had contacted the police – surely he'd told someone about his run-in with the perp. He was a young man and must have a family.

Of course, it was possible he'd died of the wounds from the rock fragments. They hadn't seemed serious but Rhyme had known victims of bad gunshot wounds to walk and act normally for hours before keeling over and dying.

Possible too that the unsub had found him, like he had Weintraub, killed him and disposed of the body. But in either of those cases he would have expected a missing-persons report. And Cooper's survey of the precincts – admittedly quick – had found none.

The tech was peering into a microscope. 'Trace on the jacket: more kimberlite. And some plant material. Two types. One is from leaves and grass similar to the control samples Amelia took from around the storm drain. What you'd expect. But there's some flecks that're unique.'

'And they're what?'

'Hold on.' He was flipping through cellular-level images in the horticultural database that Rhyme had created at the NYPD years ago and that he still helped maintain. He loved plants as forensic markers.

'Something called . . . Yes, I'm pretty sure it's something called *Coleonema pulchellum*. Aka confetti bush. Not indigenous to the area – it comes from Africa – but common here as a deodorizer and in potpourri.'

The perp had been to a gift shop lately, possibly. Or did he live in an apartment where pungent smells were a problem?

'The brass,' Rhyme called.

Cooper, who was certified by the AFTE, the Association of Firearm and Tool Mark Examiners, turned to the two spent 9mm shells that Sachs had collected. The slugs themselves, all of which had lodged in Weintraub's body, would be sent from the Medical Examiner's Office, after the autopsy. Given the urgency of the case, the doctor performing the postmortem had photographed one slug and sent the image to Cooper. The preliminary analysis was that it had been fired from the same weapon that was used at the shooting at Patel's. No surprise since the gunshot residue was almost identical; the powder in all the rounds would have come from the manufacturer's same lot.

'Prints on the brass?' Rhyme asked.

Cooper shook his head.

No surprise here either.

Cooper then ran through the list of trace and minute substances that Sachs had collected.

'Sawdust, diesel fuel, metals consistent with welding. Heating oil, air-conditioner coolant. Then trichlorobenzene. I don't know what that is.'

'Used as a pesticide, I think. Or used to be. Nasty stuff. Look it up.'

Cooper read from a government environmental alert: '"Trichlorobenzene has several uses. It is an intermediate – a building block – to make herbicides, substances that destroy or prevent the growth of weeds. It is also used as a solvent to dissolve waxes, grease, rubber and certain plastics and a dielectric fluid (a liquid that conducts little or no electricity)." And, yeah, you're right, used to be used for termite control.'

This trace suggested that their unsub had been in or near a factory, old buildings, a basement, a service station or a construction site. Something to note but there was nothing particularly helpful in these finds to aid them in locating him.

Cooper got a call and had a brief conversation, then walked to the computer just as the screen switched to email. He said, into his phone, 'Got it.' He disconnected.

'What's that?'

'Amelia had an EC team prowl around the storm drain where she found the jacket. They hit gold.'

'And that would be?'

'A MetroCard.'

'Well. But is it his?'

'I'd say yes. It wasn't there very long,' Cooper said. 'Wet but not too wet. Like the jacket.'

In 2003 the Metropolitan Transportation Authority's MetroCard had replaced the token for payment in city buses and subways. Rhyme loved them because each one had a unique identifier, so the point of departure of every subway rider could be established. Couple that with the MTA's extensive CCTV and facial recognition algorithms and you could occasionally come up with a reasonable estimation of where and when that rider disembarked.

'They're scanning the data and sending it separately.'

Unsub 47 would not, of course, have used his own credit card for the purchase but – if he'd used the fare card for travel – they might get some good facial images of him swiping it at a station.

Rhyme asked, 'Prints, DNA on the card?'

'Negative. Evidence of cloth glove impressions.'

A sigh. 'Anything else in the storm drain?'

'Nope.'

Rhyme gazed at the evidence chart. The facts written upon it – and facts that were absent – proved what Rhyme already knew: Unsub 47 was uncommonly clever, never leaving prints, disabling video cameras, ditching his jacket after being spotted, wearing a ski mask or looking away from security cameras, making determined efforts to eliminate witnesses and tidy up after the theft.

But Lincoln Rhyme was used to being challenged by smart perps. He thought about the most brilliant one he'd been up against: Charles Vespasian Hale, known by the nickname 'the Watchmaker.' The name came from both his obsession with timepieces and the fact that his crimes were planned with the precision of a clock's mechanism. The man was a superstore of criminal services, available to anyone who could pay his substantial fee – from terrorist attacks to murder to kidnapping to mundane larceny, and everything in between. (Including jail-breaks, Rhyme reflected, with the pique he always felt when he thought of Hale; the man was still on the lam, having escaped from the prison Rhyme had put him in.)

Rhyme now heard Thom let someone into the town house, and Lon Sellitto ambled into the parlor, shedding his jacket.

'Too effing cold out there. Ridiculous. March. You ever see a March like this?'

Rhyme usually ignored conversations regarding climate. He did this now and briefed the detective on their incremental progress.

Sellitto grimaced. 'City Hall won't be happy. We've gotta move faster.'

'Tell Forty-Seven to be more cooperative.'

'Linc. We held off telling that Brit about S and VL. And one of 'em's dead. Let's get him canvassing for the protégé. Whatta you think?'

Rhyme shrugged. This was one of the few gestures his body was capable of. 'At this point, sure.'

Sellitto called the number on Ackroyd's card and asked him if he could come in. The detective disconnected. 'Be here soon.'

Cooper's computer sang with the sound of incoming email.

'Transit. The CCTV.'

Rhyme explained to Sellitto about the MetroCard.

'Damn. That's good.'

The New York City transit system is overseen by two separate police forces. The Metropolitan Transportation Authority Police takes care of law enforcement for much of the surface transportation in the region, including some outlying counties. The NYPD's Transit Bureau guards the subways.

The message, from an officer at Transit's Brooklyn headquarters on Schermerhorn Street, reported that it was a one-ride card, bought with cash. He'd used it two days ago. 'He got on the train in Brooklyn, the stop near Cadman Plaza. They don't know if or where he transferred or got off, but he started out heading toward Manhattan. And those trains would get him to Forty-Second Street pretty fast.'

Sellitto muttered, 'Walking distance to Patel's.'

The day before the killing. Maybe casing it, checking out security.

Cooper read some more. 'The RTCC folks say there's some-thing odd we should look at.'

The NYPD was part of the Domain Awareness System. It was a surveillance system that included a network of close to seven thousand CCTV cameras throughout the city, about two-thirds of them owned by private companies and individuals, who had given the police access. Scores of detectives staffed camera moni-tors at the Real Time Crime Center, located at One Police Plaza. The software was so sophisticated that it could automatically flag a 'suspicious package' or identify and track potential suspects with as little input as 'six-foot, medium build, light-blue jacket.'

The RTCC had pulled the video from the subway station when and before the fare card was swiped.

'Odd?' Rhyme murmured.

Cooper typed and video appeared on the screen, in color and of pretty good resolution. Medium definition.

'Here's the rider.' The tech pointed to a figure on the monitor.

He appeared similar to their other image of the unsub, on 47th Street, just after the killings. The jacket appeared identical to the one they'd just analyzed. He wore a black stocking cap that could be a rolled-up ski mask. And, of course, he kept his head down as he swept the fare card through the reader.

'Now here's the MTA camera facing the street outside the subway entrance. Five minutes earlier, as he's approaching the station.'

Cooper ran the tape several times.

'What's he doing?' Sellitto muttered. 'I don't get it.'

Odd . . .

It appeared that Forty-Seven was approaching the subway in a straight line from across the street but then he stopped abruptly, turned around and walked back toward where he'd just come from. Then he reversed direction once more, continuing into the station.

Rhyme said, 'There's a trash bin there. He turns around to throw something out. What is it? Yellow. He was holding some-thing yellow. And orange. I can see orange too. But what? Again.'

Cooper played the tape once more.

It was Sellitto who said, 'Got it.'

'What?' Rhyme asked.

'Look what's behind him.'

Ah, Rhyme thought, nodding. He too understood. On the other side of the street was a construction site. Several workers wore orange safety vests and yellow hard hats. The same shade as what was in Forty-Seven's hand.

Sellitto said, 'He exits the jobsite, swaps the hard hat for his stocking cap. He's going to pitch out the hat and vest but can't find a trash bin in front of the subway. He turns around and finds a bin. Then goes to catch his train.'

'He's not a worker – he's in street clothes and nobody on a job would throw out a hard hat.'

'I'd vote he stole the hat and vest to get into the site. Why?'

Rhyme offered, 'Meeting somebody who works there. One possibility.'

Sellitto said, 'Another one: That station's near the government buildings, right?'

'Cadman Plaza,' Cooper said. 'The streets're loaded with CCTVs – the police, the federal buildings, courts, administrative offices. To get to the station entrance any other way, aside from the jobsite, he'd have to go past a dozen cameras.'

Sellitto offered, 'He *lives* south of the construction site?'

'No, he can't steal hard hats and trespass,' Rhyme said, 'every time he wants to take the train. I'd go with he was meeting somebody in the site. Maybe he was picking up his weapon? Talking to somebody about fencing the rough?'

Although less so than in the past, the New York City's construction industry was populated with men who had organized crime connections.

Sellitto called the RTCC supervisor and gave him the ID information about the video. He would have officers check street cameras in the surrounding blocks for an hour before the unsub swiped the card. The search criteria would be a man fitting the general description, filtered by 'wearing or in possession of yellow hard hat and orange vest.'

As Rhyme watched Mel Cooper add the latest details of

the case to a whiteboard, he thought: Why? Why're you doing this?

'Easy answer,' called a woman's melodious voice.

Rhyme turned. He hadn't been aware Amelia Sachs had returned from Brooklyn. Or that he'd just spoken the questions aloud. He asked, 'Which is?'

'He's just plain crazy.'

CHAPTER 17

He'd spent the night at the airport. LaGuardia – two bus journeys away.

Vimal Lahori had huddled in the backs of both vehicles, wincing as the rough ride punched his wounds.

He'd found a waiting area chair, near the ticket counters, as if planning to check in for an early flight, after a cancellation. He was one of a dozen displaced travelers. No one paid him any mind.

Lahori would have preferred his beloved Port Authority but he suspected that the place would be watched by the police. And there was also the killer, who might continue to be prowling the streets of Midtown. He'd dreamed much, mostly nightmares, though he couldn't recall the specific images. He'd woken to the memory of Mr Patel's feet. Tears had streamed for a few minutes. But then he forced himself to rise and wash up in the bathroom. There, in a stall, he checked the wound once more. It stung and was surrounded by a huge bruise but wasn't puffy with infection. He clumsily changed the dressing – the wound was hard to reach – and squirted some more of the chilly Betadine on it.

Now, after another bus ride, he was moving with his head down along a sidewalk in Flushing, Queens. He found the place he sought, a retail and wholesale jewelry shop on a busy street. He entered N&B Jewelers and walked to the clerk, a young, round South Asian woman.

'Is Mr Nouri in yet?'

'He's in a meeting.'

'Could you tell him Vimal Lahori would like to see him?'

She glanced at his rumpled, dusty clothes and made a call. She disconnected. 'He'll be down in five minutes.'

He thanked her and wandered around the store. It had just

opened – noon on Sunday – and there were no customers yet, just an armed guard, staring blankly at the ceiling.

Vimal looked at the displays in the windows, behind thick glass. The jewelry pieces Mr Nouri had placed there were of a number of various styles and sizes and prices, intended to snare potential buyers with many different tastes and budgets.

Some would come to N&B to buy that very *special* stone. The engagement rock being paramount in this category, of course.

But there were many other markets that De Beers or other mines tapped: the anniversary ring, the daughter-having-a-baby charm, the sweet-sixteen or quinceañera earrings, the prom tiara, the grandmother pin. The diamond industry was constantly coming up with new excuses to sell you its wares – like greeting card companies – and to make sure you felt pretty damn guilty if you lapsed. With weary cynicism, Vimal would look through the direct-mail material Mr Patel received from branded diamond companies, suggesting to retailers new approaches to reach buyers, like gay engagements. 'Old norms are "out the window,"' one brochure enthused. 'Suggest that *both* partners can wear diamonds to signify their upcoming union . . . and double your revenue with each nuptial!'

Or the 'Degree Diamond': 'She made you proud with that diploma; show her how much her achievement means to you!'

He'd once joked to Adeela that the industry might soon come up with a 'funeral diamond' to be buried with you, though after the events of the past day, that idea was no longer funny.

He saw a door open at the back of the showroom and Dev Nouri walked out. He was a bald, fat man of about fifty-five. A loupe sat on his head – the familiar ten-power magnifier that was standard in the industry. The lens was pointed upward. He waddled forward and they shook hands.

The shop owner looked about with a concerned expression, and Vimal realized that he was maybe worried that the Promisor might have followed him.

Ridiculous. But Vimal too gazed out the window.

He saw no one who might be the killer in Mr Patel's. But was relieved when Mr Nouri said, 'Let's go upstairs.'

They walked into a hallway and Mr Nouri used a thumbprint pad to open a thick steel door. They passed through this and climbed to the second floor, where the dealer's office and cutting and polishing factory was located. Vimal's father had once told him that the cutters in Surat, India, made Hondas; Mr Patel made Rolls-Royces. Nouri's stones would be squarely in the BMW category.

They stepped into Nouri's cluttered office and sat. 'Now, tell me. You were there? When Jatin was killed?'

'I was, yes. Though I got away.'

'How terrible! Jatin's sister . . . his children. How sad they must be!'

'Yeah. It's terrible. Just awful.' Vimal spun Adeela's cloth bracelet nervously. 'Mr Nouri. I need some help.'

'From me?'

'Yes. My parents and I think it's best for me to leave the city for a while. They gave me what money they could. But I need some more. I'm hoping you can help me.'

Nouri did not catch the lie. He was more troubled, it seemed, about impending financial requests. 'Me? I don't have—'

'I'm not asking to borrow. I have something to sell.'

'Inventory from Patel's?' He looked suspicious.

This was one reason that Vimal had not gone to the police. The rocks were technically Mr Patel's. They would have confiscated them as evidence, and he needed them desperately. They might even have arrested him for theft.

But Vimal said, truthfully, 'It's not a customer's. It was Mr Patel's, yes. But he owed me for the month. I'll never see that money now.' Vimal produced one of the rocks in the bag that he'd been carrying when he was shot. It was the January bird.

'But what is this? Kimberlite?'

'Yes.'

Nouri took the stone from Vimal's hand. He flipped down the loupe and studied the stone. 'I've never seen any.'

Kimberlite was the raw ore from which the majority of diamonds around the world were extracted. The mineral was named after the town of Kimberley in South Africa, where in the late 1800s the famed Star of South Africa, an eighty-four-carat stone, was found embedded in a vein of kimberlite, setting off the world's first diamond rush.

But diamond rough was usually extracted at the mines, and the kimberlite discarded, so those further down the gem manufacturing chain rarely, if ever, saw the rock that gave birth to the diamonds they worked on.

Up went the loupe. 'You want to sell it?'

'Yes. Please.'

'But what would I do with it?'

Vimal held the stone under a lamp. 'Look. You can see crystals. They'd be diamonds. Extract them. Then cut and sell those. There could be some big rough inside. Look at that one.' He pointed out a shimmery dot on the side of the stone. 'It could be worth thousands.'

Nouri laughed. 'Do you know how diamonds are extracted from kimberlite?'

'I understand it's complicated.' The rock was first crushed – with enough pressure to break up the kimberlite but not the diamonds. Then the resulting diamond-laden bits were tumbled in water-filled drums and treated with ferrosilicon sand. It was a long process.

'It is. And I don't have the equipment. Don't know anyone who does. I'd have to send it to Canada. But no mine would take a small rock like this. They handle tons at a time.'

He was pierced with disappointment and desperation. 'But—'

'Vimal, I'm sorry. I could lend you a hundred dollars.'

Vimal closed his eyes briefly. His shoulders slumped. He stared at the stone, turning it over and over in his hand. There were tiny flashes, rough diamonds. He supposed Mr Nouri was right: The extraction process was only profitable on a mass scale.

'No, I don't want a loan. Thank you.' He shoved the stone into his pocket.

He started to turn but Mr Nouri, looking at him with sympathy, said, 'Wait. I'll tell you what. Do a cut for me. I'll pay you a thousand.'

That wouldn't go very far in starting a new life. But he was desperate. 'Yes, please. But I don't have much time.'

'This won't take long. Some people, yes. You? No. Come with me.'

CHAPTER 18

'I thought they were dead, Rhyme.'

'Who?'

Sachs said, 'Mikey O'Brien. Emma Sanders.'

'Again, who?'

'The couple in Gravesend.'

'Dead?'

She'd just returned from the two crime scenes: Weintraub's house in Queens and the attack in Brooklyn. 'You said victims.'

'I only heard from the precinct that there was a shooting. Two vics, the captain was telling me. Something about the perp following them from a jewelry store.'

'No, from a wedding planner.'

'Ah.'

Sellitto nodded her way. He was on the phone with the officers canvassing in Gravesend for witnesses who had seen the perp. The detective held the mobile in one hand and a Danish in his other. He'd cut the pastry in half and eaten the first portion, then, it seemed, given in to temptation and started nibbling on the remainder.

Rhyme had little interest in psychological profiling. Sachs, on the other hand, was more a self-proclaimed people cop and felt the mental mechanism of perps was helpful in tracking them down. He didn't fully agree but he respected her. And was curious about the diagnosis.

Crazy . . .

She explained to Rhyme and Cooper what the couple had said about their escape, how their hands had been bound but not their legs. Mikey had kicked the perp and they'd fled. He'd fired one shot but missed. By the time he started after them, the woman was outside, screaming. Forty-Seven didn't stay around and got out the back door.

'It was our boy, for sure?' Rhyme asked.

'Oh, yeah. No doubt about it: Unsub Forty-Seven and the Promisor one and the same. Just before he tried to cut that girl's finger off, he explained why he killed the couple at Patel's.'

Disconnecting his phone, Sellitto looked up. 'Got away in Gravesend. Canvass reports nothing.'

Rhyme shrugged at the discouraging news, then told the detective that Sachs had confirmed their unsub was in fact the Promisor.

The doorbell rang and Thom went to get it. He returned with Edward Ackroyd, the insurance adjuster. Thom took his beige overcoat – because the man was Brit, Rhyme thought of it as a greatcoat, though he had no idea if the English used that expression, or ever had. 'Tea?' the aide asked.

The man smiled – perhaps at the aide's assumption of beverage choice – and declined, but asked for coffee.

'Filtered? Cappuccino?'

Ackroyd asked for the latter.

The aide hung the man's coat up and retreated to the kitchen.

'Thanks for coming in,' Sellitto said.

'Of course.'

'Don't know if you saw the news. Our unsub got to a witness. His name was Saul Weintraub. He was shot.'

'Oh, no.' Ackroyd sighed. 'Did he get a chance to tell you anything before he died?'

Sachs said, 'Not much. Just that he didn't know Patel well. I sent a car to bring him in, interview him some more. But . . .' Her grim face acknowledged how this plan had so badly failed.

'How did the suspect find him?' Ackroyd wondered.

Sellitto said, 'We think he got his name by torturing Patel. But not his address. There are a lot of Saul Weintraubs in the city. He did some detective work and tracked him down. Now there's a second witness we're sure he's after too. His initials, we think, are VL. He's young, Indian, maybe Patel's assistant or protégé. We're hoping you can help us find him. Before the unsub does.'

Sachs said to Cooper, 'Call up the picture.'

'Security footage. Just after he got away.'

Ackroyd looked over the fuzzy image from the loading dock, squinting closely. 'Early, mid-twenties. Not tall. Five six, eight. Slim. South Asian.'

'I'm thinking,' Rhyme said, 'you'll have to be discreet. Maybe not mention the initials, when you call. Just ask about protégés of Patel.'

The Englishman nodded. 'Yes, of course, in case the suspect gets in touch with one of my contacts.'

'Another thing you should know,' Sachs said. 'He just assaulted another engaged couple – in Gravesend. A neighborhood of Brooklyn.'

'Good Lord, he did?' Ackroyd asked, clearly surprised. 'So soon after Weintraub? Are they dead?'

'No. They survived. Not badly injured.'

'Really?' The Englishman's face narrowed. 'Ah, very good. For them, of course. And for us, as well. What did they have to say?'

Rhyme glanced toward Sachs, who said, 'That brings me to my diagnosis: crazy. I think we have his motive. And it has nothing to do with stealing the rough to sell it. He's saving it.'

Ackroyd nodded. 'Saving? Not uncommon. Diamonds are a solid investment and an inflation hedge.'

'No, no. I mean, like saving an endangered species: keeping diamonds out of the hands of the engagement ring mill. He stole the rough to keep it pure. They said he rambled on about how diamonds are the heart of the earth and that cutting them is like raping or murdering them.'

Crazy . . .

Thom appeared with a cup and Ackroyd took it. He sipped and complimented the aide on the beverage. Then the man shook his head. 'Saving diamonds. "Heart of the earth." That's one for the ages. There are certainly some nutters who hoard diamonds but that's always for the value. They think if there's a nuclear war or rebellion they'll have the diamonds to barter. As if after an atomic holocaust the first thing people will want is baubles.'

Sachs added, 'And it looks like he was intentionally targeting Patel too. He referred to the "Indian" he killed yesterday. He'd betrayed his people, he said.' Sachs flipped through her notes. 'Something about diamonds being sacred.'

'In ancient India, yes, that was true. For them it was a mortal sin to cut diamonds. The Greeks and Roman began cutting them and turning them into jewelry although it wasn't long until the Indians got on board. As one might expect, the spiritual nature of the stones took second place to commerce and vanity.' Ackroyd seemed to grow thoughtful . . . and then perplexed. He asked, 'Did he give any indication of where the rough was? Where he lived? Anything else about him?'

'Nothing. Just threats and ranting. They gave me some details. He has light-blue eyes. And a foreign accent but it was as though he was trying to obscure it, speaking American-accented English. His grammar was, I'm quoting, "messed up." He's a smoker. They could smell it. And he's got a new, or a second, weapon. A revolver. Mikey knows guns. And I dug the slug out of the wall. Damaged but not bad. It's a thirty-eight, I'm sure.'

Sellitto said, 'He pitched out his jacket after the Weintraub killing. He probably tossed the Glock into a Dumpster somewhere. Or another storm drain.'

'I'll get an EC team from Queens to check out the other drains,' Sachs said and called Crime Scene headquarters to arrange it.

Sachs and Cooper turned to analyzing the evidence from the Gravesend assault.

The results of the fingerprints were negative. The floors were carpeted, so she hadn't been able to take electrostatic footprints. Cooper did a gunshot residue profile from furniture near where the unsub had been standing when he fired. Sachs had also collected a few items that were more likely associated with the perp, rather than Mikey or Emma, or recent visitors to the place: black cotton fibers, some scraps of cooked ground beef and two blond hairs. The hairs and swabs of surfaces the unsub had been near were sent to the main lab for DNA testing.

The analysis on the Promisor's text had come in. It was impossible to trace the call and the burner had been bought with cash. Some fast research had revealed that the first sentence was from a knowledge base like Wikipedia.

The concept of engagement is based on a binding promise
to wed by the man to his betrothed. Now I have promise
too. I am looking for YOU, I am looking every where. Buy
ring, put on pretty finger but I will find you and you will
bleed for your love.

—The Promisor

*Since he had quoted that first sentence, the words and phrasing
revealed nothing about him.* The rest, presumably generated by
their unsub, provided some minor insights, basically what Sachs
had discovered: that English was probably not his first language
– the sparsity of articles or modifiers (not 'buy *the* ring') was
typical of a number of foreign tongues. The splitting of 'everywhere' into two words supported this as well, as did the absence
of contractions – as with 'I am' and 'I will.'

And there was nothing in the NCIC crime database, or any
other they had access to, that profiled anyone fitting the behavior
of the unsub.

'Promisor,' Ackroyd muttered. He looked as though he wished
he'd drawn a more conventional case. Setting down his empty
coffee cup, he walked to the rack of coats and pulled his on. 'I'll
see if I can find this elusive VL. No one you've talked to has any
leads at all?'

'Not a one,' Sellitto said.

The Englishman left. Rhyme told Sachs about the fare card
and recounted their conclusion that Forty-Seven had been at the
jobsite across from the subway two days ago – either taking a
shortcut to avoid the cameras in the government buildings at
Cadman Plaza or, more likely, meeting somebody there, possibly
a worker with an organized crime connection to buy a new gun,
the .38.

'I'll get down there and check it out. Sunday, but they'll have
at least some security there.' Sachs collected her jacket and headed
out the door.

After she'd left, Sellitto received a call and had a conversation.
He disconnected. 'CCTVs from just before our boy took the
subway. He was tagged on Hicks Street, near Pierrepont, a couple

blocks away. Wearing the hard hat and reflective vest. Just walking. Alone. That's all they've got. But he's in the system now, tagged to the location. If he shows up again, we're on the alert.'

Rhyme nodded and wheeled back to the charts. The entries provided some direction, some help. But the prickly dissatisfaction he felt, like a nagging fever, told him that the problem wasn't that the answers were so elusive; it was that he was beginning to think they weren't asking the right questions.

It was then that his phone dinged with a text. He looked at the screen.

'Thom?' he shouted.

'I'm right—'

'Bring the van around.'

'Here. The van?'

'Yes. Bring. The. Van. Around.'

Sellitto regarded him. 'Got a lead?'

'No. This's something else.'

CHAPTER 19

Well, a problem.

Vimal Lahori was sitting across from Mr Nouri at the diamantaire's desk, in his upstairs office at N&B Jewelry. His heart was beating hard, his breath coming fast.

He needed the money. But there was a glitch.

He was staring at the diamond that he'd shaken from the stiff folded envelope, the diamond Mr Nouri was hiring him to cut.

'Something, isn't it?' the man whispered.

Vimal could only nod. He tipped down the loupe and examined the stone under the sharp light from a gooseneck lamp. Turned it over, and over, and over.

Rough diamonds occur in nature in various forms. The most common shape is octahedron – essentially two four-sided pyramids joined at the base. These are cut into separate pyramids and each one is then bruted – smoothed against another diamond or a laser. These become round brilliants: the most common cut, making up tens of millions of stones in rings, earrings, pins and necklaces around the world. This cut features fifty-seven or occasionally fifty-eight facets; it was created a century ago by Marcel Tolkowsky, one of the most renowned diamantaires who ever lived. He applied geometry to establish the ideal proportions for shaping diamonds.

But occasionally shapes other than octahedrons are found: triangular macles, cubics, tetrahedrons and complex or irregular shapes. These are used for 'fancy' cuts – anything that isn't a round brilliant. Marquis, heart-shaped, cushion, pear, oval, emerald and the latest in-vogue cut: the princess.

The stone Vimal was to cut was an elongated complex – a round-edged rectangle. It was, like all rough, not transparent but somewhat milky; only through cutting and polishing does a diamond become clear. But it was still possible to grade a diamond at this stage with some accuracy and Vimal knew that when finished it would be colorless G grade clear, rated VS1 – very slight inclusions, which meant that its few imperfections would be invisible to the naked eye. A superb stone.

Vimal glanced at Mr Nouri and then the plot – a computerized image of the diamond on the monitor next to them, which showed how to most efficiently cut the stone.

Generally a piece of rough is cut into two or three pieces, and algorithms, developed over the years, will produce highly accurate plans for finishing the stones.

Because this diamond was large – seven carats – and of an unusual shape, the plotting software had come up with instructions for cutting it in four places, creating five individual diamonds, each destined for a round brilliant cut. Nouri had drawn the cuts with red marking pen on the stone itself.

'But you can redraw them,' Mr Nouri said, offering the marker. 'See? This is why I need you, Vimal. There is no room for error. One mistake will cut the value of the finished stones by a quarter. Maybe more. I can't do it. Mr Nobody who works for me can do it.'

Vimal lifted the stone to his face once more, flipped down the loupe. 'A pad. A damp pad.'

Mr Nouri handed him a gauze square – similar to what Adeela had used to treat his wounds. Using the pad, Vimal cleaned the red lines off and again studied the stone closely.

Every block of stone, Michelangelo wrote, *has a statue inside it and it is the task of the sculptor to discover it*. Vimal believed this, and it applied to diamonds just as it did to marble or granite.

He took up the marker. Though his heart pounded, his hands were as steady as the stone he was drawing upon. Eight fast lines.

'There.'

Mr Nouri stared. 'What is this?'

'That's the cut.'

'I don't understand what you mean.'

'This.' He indicated the lines.

'What cut is that? I don't recognize it.'

'I'm not separating it.'

Mr Nouri laughed. 'Vimal.'

'I'm not.'

The diamantaire grew somber. 'But I paid so much for it. I need five stones to recoup the cost.'

'Five brilliants like any other five brilliants. They'll add nothing to the world.'

'Add to the world,' the man mused sardonically.

'It has to be a parallelogram.'

'A parallelogram?'

'Think of it as a trapezoid, with parallel sides.'

'I know what the shape is. I studied mathematics at university. It simply has no place as a diamond cut. There's no market for it.'

'You will never see a stone like this again,' Vimal said.

Mr Nouri's shrug said, So?

'No, I won't separate it. I'll only cut the parallelogram.'

'I'll find somebody else.'

'Yes, I'm sure you will.'

Vimal set the stone down and rose.

A rueful smile spread across Mr Nouri's face. 'I will pay you *two* thousand to separate it like I'd planned.'

'No.'

'Two thousand five hundred.'

Vimal started to turn. Then he stopped and leaned down, his face close to the older man's. He whispered, 'Take a chance.'

And thought: So timid with my father, so bold here.

'What?' Mr Nouri asked.

'I know your work. I know the work of your son and the other cutters here. You're all good. You create diamonds that your customers love – the newlyweds and the wives and the husbands and parents and grandparents. You make them happy. And you'll be able to make them happy again and again – with thousands of other round brilliants. But this once, with this stone, do something different.'

'Business is business, Vimal.'

Yes, it certainly is, the young man thought. 'I should go.'

When Vimal was five feet from the door, Mr Nouri said, 'Wait.'

He looked back.

'You think this is best, this cut?'

'It's the cut this stone deserves, I can't say anything more than that.'

Mr Nouri shook his head, as if trying to process this comment. Then he stuck his hand out.

Vimal said, 'Still, twenty-five hundred?'

A nod.

The men shook hands.

Vimal asked, 'Where can I work?'

CHAPTER 20

'Got your text,' Lincoln Rhyme said.

The man lying in the bed glanced up with a brief but glowing smile. Surprise too.

'Lincoln. You came. I mean in person. I just . . . Just wanted to chat. Phone call I was thinking.'

'Barry.' Rhyme directed his chair closer.

The complicated bed was in a room deep in the bowels of a complicated hospital complex on the East Side in Midtown. It had taken some minutes to find the place. Much color coding. It didn't help a lot.

'Thom.'

'Hi.' Barry Sales shifted a bit, tucked under excessively washed sheets and blankets. He found a wired remote control, pressed a button and rose into a sitting position, thanks to the hydraulic mattress. The man was in his late thirties. His skin was pale, his brown hair thinning.

His eyes game but hollow.

Rhyme wheeled closer yet. Both men nodded a greeting and Rhyme at least couldn't help but grin at the irony, which Sales acknowledged with a smile of his own. The criminalist wasn't able to shake Sales's hand because his only working limb was his right. He couldn't use his left.

And Sales's left limb was the only one that remained after a firefight that had nearly killed him.

Rhyme looked around the room. He absolutely did not want to be here. There was not a single memory of medical venues that didn't trouble, or torment, Lincoln Rhyme, since the accident years ago. There'd been accommodation, there'd been a fierce punching down of recollections, there'd been stoic acceptance. But he would have avoided hospitals forever, given the option.

But this wasn't one.

Sales had been a colleague of his years ago when Rhyme was running the crime scene operation for the NYPD.

Sales had been a star. He'd stay on a scene, walking the grid, for hours after any other forensic cop would've released it.

Rhyme hadn't been happy when Sales had decided to move to general investigative work . . . but he'd followed the man's career and learned that, despite his young age, he'd soared to a senior spot in Major Cases and then, after leaving the NYPD, led a suburban police department to distinction.

Rhyme said, 'Do they have a bar here?'

'Jesus, Lincoln,' Sales said. 'Never change.'

'Theorize after a drink. Analyze sober.'

'Sadly,' Sales said, 'the hospital sommelier has the day off.'

'Fire the son of a bitch.' Rhyme nodded to Thom, who produced two bottles of iced tea. That is, they were *labeled* tea. The contents looked suspiciously more golden, like, say, single-malt whisky. The aide set one bottle on the sideboard and opened the other.

'Hell,' Sales said. 'I'm not driving.' Then his voice choked and he struggled to control the tears. 'Fuck me. This's ridiculous.'

'Been there,' Rhyme said.

Thom poured two glasses from the open bottle and handed them out. He retreated to the corner, sat and checked messages.

The men slugged down some of the whisky and judiciously slipped the glasses out of sight when a cheerful Filipina nurse came in to take some vitals. She left, saying, 'Oh-oh, bad boys. Keep those hid.' A grin.

Sales sipped more liquor. Looked at the bottle.

'How'd you do it?'

'A funnel,' Rhyme said.

A moment, a blink. Then Sales laughed.

'You mean, the whole disabled thing,' Rhyme said.

'Yeah, the whole thing.'

'You remember I hated clichés.'

'Yeah, that's right.'

'But sometimes they fit. This one does: One step at a time.'

Rhyme, a quadriplegic, with a break at the fourth cervical vertebra, had suffered a trauma in a league very different from Sales's. He'd been paralyzed from the neck down, with a few glitchy, renegade nerves that provided a bit of movement in a finger. Sales had lost his right arm just above the elbow; all else functioned fine.

But funny how subjective tragedy is, of course. Barry Sales's barometer was measuring his life going forward with what his life had been before the bullets tore through his flesh. Not comparing himself to Rhyme's trauma.

'And there'll be people.' Rhyme nodded toward Thom. Who cocked his head, meaning sentimentality wasn't an option.

'As frustrating and *difficult* as they can be.'

'Aw, you two, you're an old married couple.' Sales had been to the town house a few times.

'There's Joan.'

Sales's face remained completely still. 'I can't stand to be in the room with her. She tries so hard not to look.' He nodded at where his limb had been. 'I tried to make a joke. Could she lend me a hand? She practically had a breakdown.'

'One day at a time. There'll be people. And it's a long road. Jesus, Lord, three clichés in a row. I'm not feeling well.'

Sales had tamed the tears. 'There's a good counselor here. Would you recommend somebody after I'm discharged?'

Rhyme said, 'I tried that. Didn't work. They . . . ' He looked at Thom. 'What's the word?'

'Fled.'

Rhyme shrugged.

'But *most* people benefit. I can get you some names.'

'Thanks.'

But Rhyme sensed the questions about coping with the tragedy were perfunctory, ice breakers. After all, Sales, Rhyme knew, was destined to become just like him, like the vast majority of severely injured patients, spinal cord or otherwise: he'd end up saying to himself, 'Fuck it. I've got a life to lead.' Rhyme, for instance, had finally chosen to ignore his condition to the extent he could. He was on earth to be a criminalist, end of story. No whining, no fund-raising, no public service ads. No political correctness. If he referred to his condition at all, he would use words like 'gimp' or 'crip,' and had once delivered a searing glare to someone who had commented condescendingly that Rhyme was a shining example to the 'disabled-able' community, a term that, Rhyme hoped, never made it into Meriam-Webster.

No, Sales had texted Rhyme, not inquiring about approaches to therapy, but because of a very different agenda.

He brought it up now.

'What do you hear about him?'

There was no doubt who Sales meant.

The shooter.

The man had been collared and was presently on trial.

Sales said, 'I get bullshit from my team, and the chief. They say, "Oh, the asshole's going away." But they say it like they aren't sure.'

Rhyme's rep – now and then – was that he was gruff and impatient, with no tolerance for laziness, and pissy on occasion. But he shot with facts.

'Sorry, Barry. From what I hear it's not so clear-cut.'

The firefight had been, like most, a paroxysm of confusion. The prosecution was fighting to overcome a vigorous defense. And one that was well funded.

He nodded. 'You know, it'd be one thing, facing down some-body. But never seeing the asshole shoot. Never seeing his eyes. Like that time where the perp hung around the scene. The Simpson shooting, years ago. That crazy guy?'

Occasionally suspect would remain at or near the scene. Sometimes out of curiosity, sometimes out of a desire to get intelligence. Sometimes because they were simply homicidal shits. The perp in the Simpson case hid in a meat freezer after gutting the owner. He stepped out and emptied his gun at a shocked crime scene officer working for Rhyme. All the shots missed, thanks to the fact that the perp's core temperature probably hovered about seventy degrees – the meat freezer – and his hand was shaking so badly he hit everything but the officer.

The memory brought a smile to both men. Thom too, when Rhyme explained it.

'God, I want this guy to go away.' Sales licked his lips. 'Bonnie was here. My sister? I asked her to bring Trudi and George. She said sure. But she didn't mean sure. She meant she didn't want the kids to see Uncle Barry like this. Hell, I wasn't thinking. I don't want them to see me like this either. They'll freak out. I can't go to their games. I can't go to their recitals.' He clamped his teeth together.

He inhaled deeply. 'I'm pretty tired. Think I better take a nap.'

'I'll bring the van around front,' Thom said. He took Sales's email address and told him again that he'd send the name of physical therapists and doctors who specialized in prosthetics.

Rhyme moved forward and tucked the second bottle of Glenmorangie "tea" into the bed, beside Sales's left arm. He was about to say something else, but the man had closed his eyes and slipped his head back against the pillow. Rhyme glanced at the tear that Sales simply could not keep from escaping, eased the chair in a circle and wheeled from the room.

CHAPTER 21

Vimal and Dev Nouri walked through a thick door into the factory proper.

Sunday is not the day of rest for most diamond cutters, given the ethnicity and religion of those in the profession, and this was just another workday for N&B. Here, sitting around grinding scaife turntables, were four Indian cutters and one Chinese, all wearing dark slacks and light-colored short-sleeve shirts. They ranged in age from late twenties to fifties and were all men. Vimal knew of only two women diamond cutters in New York. The unfortunate line, which he'd heard far too often, was: Making diamonds is for men; wearing them is for women.

One of the workers was Mr Nouri's son, Bassam, about Vimal's age. The chubby young man's face registered surprise when he looked up. He set aside his dop stick and rose.

'Vimal! I heard about Mr Patel! What happened?'

'It was all on the news. That's pretty much it. A robbery.'

'What're you doing here?'

Vimal hesitated. 'Some work for your father.'

Bassam was clearly confused but Mr Nouri nodded his son sternly back to his workstation and the man picked up his dop once more, lowered his loupe and starting polishing a stone.

Vimal nodded and followed Mr Nouri to an unoccupied station.

Unlike the office, Nouri's workshop was clean and ordered. It was well equipped too. The huge factories in Surat, India, where more than half of the world's diamonds are cut, have largely moved from manual to computerized systems. The 4P machines automatically performed all four stages of processing: plotting, cutting/cleaving, bruting and faceting, or brillianteering. Mr Nouri had two of these machines, which looked like any other piece of industrial equipment, blue metal boxes each six feet long, five feet high and wide.

There was, of course, no software to create a parallelogram, nor would Vimal let a computer handle the cut in any event. This would be handwork exclusively.

'I'll leave you to it,' Mr Nouri said, but he said it uneasily and with a look at the diamond as if he were saying goodbye to an old friend about to sail alone across the Atlantic.

Vimal nodded, only vaguely aware of the words. He was lost in the contours of the diamond, noting the red lines marking his planned cut.

Shaping this stone would mean both cleaving, cutting with the grain, and sawing, against it. The tool for these tasks was a green laser, guided by a joystick and mouse. While proficient at the old-time techniques of mallet, chisel and saw, Vimal Lahori had no problem with lasers, his theory being that diamantaires had always used state-of-the-art technology – ever since the dawn of diamond cutting.

He now spatulaed a wad of cement onto the end of a dop pipe, which was like a large straw. He pressed the diamond into the adhesive, waited until it dried, then mounted the pipe in the laser unit. He closed the access door, powered up the unit and sat in front of the video screen on which he could see a close up of the stone. He rested his hand on the mouse-ball controller.

Vimal moved the crosshairs on the video screen to align with the marked lines, and, working with the keyboard and the mouse, he began the process of forming the basic parallelogram shape. Amid a hissing sound and a pulsing thud, like a medical MRI scanner, the beam started the cut. He paused frequently. After about an hour, he removed the partially cut stone, cleaned it and remounted it at a different angle on a new dop pipe. Then cutting once more. Another pause – to wipe his face and dry his hands of sweat – and back to the task. One more remount. And, after a half hour, the initial cleaving and cutting were done. The diamond was in the shape of a parallelogram.

Vimal removed it and cleaned the cement off and examined it through the loupe. Yes, it was good.

Now the brillianteering, cutting the facets into the stone. Vimal's task, like that of every diamantaire, was to maximize the three essential qualities of diamonds: brilliance (the white flash of light as you look straight down at the stone), fire (the rainbow shades refracted from the sides) and scintillation (the sparkle that flares from the stone when it is moved).

Vimal sat on a stool in front of a polishing station, which was a sturdy table about four feet square and dominated by a scaife – the horizontal cast-iron platter that would spin at three thousand RPMs and against which cutters pressed the diamonds to create the facets. On the wall was a rack containing a number of different dop sticks – armatures on which diamonds were cemented for this grinding process.

Vimal selected a dop and mounted the stone to it. He then started the scaife, about the size of the old LP record turntable his father still had. Oil, impregnated with diamond dust, dripped onto the platter and, resting the dop stick's two padded legs on the workstation, he pressed the diamond against the scaife for a second or two, lifting it to study the progress through the loupe, and grinding away once more. Slowly the facets emerged, first on the girdle – the side – and then the crown and pavilion, the top and bottom of the stone.

The smell of the warm oil – it was olive oil – wafted around his face. And at the moment, there was not a thing in the universe but this stone. Not Adeela, not his brother Sunny, his mother or father, not poor Mr Jatin Patel. Not his sculptures at home, *The Wave* or *Hidden*.

He was not thinking about killers searching for him.

Only this diamond and its emerging soul occupied him.

Touching the stone to the spinning scaife for a fraction of a second, lifting, examining . . .

Again, again, again.

The oil dripped, the turntable hissed, minuscule amounts of the stone vanished into oily residue.

The art of diamond cutting is about resisting that addictive urge to overwork a stone. And so – an hour later or twenty hours or ten minutes; he couldn't say – Vimal Lahori knew the job was done. He shut the scaife off and it spun to silence. He sat back. He gasped, starting with surprise. Four of the other cutters had silently left their stations and had come up behind Vimal to watch him cut the parallelogram. They were huddled close. He had been completely unaware of them.

One, who identified himself as Andy, asked, 'Can I?' Holding out his palm.

Vimal gave it to him. Andy flipped the loupe down and examined it. 'You added an extra facet on the crown. I would not have thought about that. What is the angle?'

'Seven degrees.'

Andy passed it around. The others laughed and examined it through their loupes. The image of their identical astonished, almost reverent, faces was comical.

'Boil it,' another said.

Vimal carried the stone to the wash station, where he boiled it in acid to remove the cement, oil, dust and other materials adhering to the stone.

This could often be a very tense moment. You might think your gem was cut perfectly – only to find that a bit of cement or oil was concealing a mistake. Vimal never worried about this, though. Oh, in his eight or so years of diamond cutting, he had made mistakes. Had ruined stones (and been screamed at by Mr Patel or his father). But he knew instantly when a cleaving or sawing or faceting went wrong. There'd been no errors on this stone. It was as perfect as it could be. The worst inclusions had been in the portions removed (and the remaining ones were in the heart of the diamond and invisible to even the best eyes). The facets were sharp and symmetrical. The balance of brilliance and fire and scintillation, faultless.

He picked up the finished stone with tweezers and looked it over once more – this time not to assess, but simply to admire.

Vimal Lahori had discovered, and released, the stone's soul.

As he studied the finished diamond, noting the flashing of color and white light, he was stabbed by a sudden sorrow that Mr Patel was not alive to see his work.

Then Mr Nouri stepped into the workshop – two cutters had

gone to get him. The bulbous man, with his graying complexion, smiled at Vimal and took the tweezers from him. He dropped the loupe and examined it. He muttered something in Hindi, it seemed, a language Vimal knew little of. His face registered astonishment.

'You didn't flatten the culet.' The very bottom of the pavilion. These were often ground flat, which made a sturdier stone, less prone to chipping. A flat culet, though, tended to darken the diamond. (Vimal believed that the famed Koh-i-Noor had been ruined when it was recut in the nineteenth century on orders from Prince Albert, Queen Victoria's husband; the resulting broad, flat culet imparted a muddiness to the otherwise magnificent stone.)

'No.'

Expecting resistance at his impractical decision.

But Mr Nouri said, breathlessly, 'A brilliant choice. Look at the light. Look at it! The damn customer – whoever they'll be – will just have to be careful. They'll live with it.' Squinting. 'And an extra facet on the crown.'

'It was necessary.'

'Of course it was. Yes, yes. My goodness, Vimal. What a job you've done!'

But Vimal didn't have interest in, or time for, praise. He had to leave and now.

'I should go. Now, you said, twenty-five hundred.'

'No.'

Vimal stiffened.

'Three thousand.'

They both smiled.

That much money would get him out of the city. If he lived cheaply he could make it stretch until he got a job, something modest, menial – perhaps at a university that had a fine arts program. Even janitorial or in the cafeteria. He felt the first blush of what approached joy that he'd experienced in ages.

The man put the diamond onto its sheet and folded the paper, slipped it into his breast pocket. 'I'll get your money.' He stepped out of the workshop and into his office.

Vimal stepped to the basin in the corner to wash up; scaifing is dirty work. As he walked past the others they were regarding him with variations of admiration or awe. He didn't like it. Anything that cemented his ties to the diamond-cutting world left a bad taste. He washed his hands and, as the others returned to their workstations, Vimal walked to the doorway and stepped into the office.

Mr Nouri was putting cash into an envelope. He was offering it to Vimal when the door to the stairwell opened and two figures entered.

Vimal gasped, stabbed by dismay. He was looking at Deepro Lahori. His father. With him was Bassam Nouri; the young, stocky man looked down.

No, no . . .

'Papa. I . . . '

Squat, gray-skinned, his father strode forward angrily.

'Deepro,' Mr Nouri said, frowning, confused.

Papa looked at the envelope. 'That's my son's money?'

'Yes, but—'

His father snatched it from the man's hand. 'I'll take care of it for him. He's not responsible at the moment.' To Vimal he snapped, 'You will come home. Now.'

Mr Nouri was understanding that Vimal had not been completely honest earlier. He said to Vimal, 'He didn't know? You lied?'

'I'm sorry.'

Then Papa walked to the rack of jackets. He reached into the inner pocket of his son's and lifted out his wallet. That and the envelope holding the cash vanished into his own.

Now the answer to the betrayal became clear. Papa nodded to Bassam, a look of thanks. So his father had offered a reward to anyone in the community who saw or heard of Vimal.

Vimal was furious, torn between screaming and sobbing.

He turned his cold eyes toward Bassam, who looked away and muttered, 'He's your father. Respect.'

Vimal wondered how much had been the price on his head. In the mood for blood, Vimal turned suddenly to his father. The man was only an inch taller than his son and was not as broad in the shoulders, nor was he anywhere near as strong. An image of himself pushing his father down, rifling his pocket for his wallet and the cash and sprinting out the door came to him.

But it was a fantasy as insubstantial as diamond dust.

'You'll come home.'

As if there were any other options.

Vimal walked slowly to the door, his father behind him, saying firmly, 'Son, I'm doing this because it's best for you. You do understand that, I hope.'

CHAPTER 22

Amelia Sachs was in Cadman Pláza, at the subway station where their unsub had caught the train to Manhattan after ditching his hard hat and safety vest. She had been canvassing shops and restaurants nearby, those with a view of the subway entrance. The hour-long effort had been useless. No one remembered seeing anybody who'd pitched out the gear. This had not been unexpected.

It seemed that the construction site to which Unsub 47 had some connection wasn't devoted to birthing yet another apartment or office building; it was a high-tech energy project.

She now surveyed the huge jobsite, surrounded by an eight-foot-high plywood wall. Before her was a large sign mounted on two wooden pillars.

Northeast Geo Industries
Harnessing the Earth's Clean Warmth . . .
for You and Your Family

Below this was a small billboard, the background off-white with lettering in green script, as if fashioned out of vines. Paintings of leaves and tufts of grass were prominent. It all reeked of eco. The text explained that the earth was itself a huge solar collector, which absorbed energy from the sun and maintained a constant temperature, however cold or hot the surface. That energy could be tapped for use in heating and cooling buildings. The geothermal facility being constructed now would do just that, servicing hundreds of buildings in the area. Pipes would be sunk deep into the earth and a solution would be pumped through them. When it returned to the surface, the liquid would then pass through regulators to generate air-conditioning or heating.

It was basically a massive heat pump, the notice reported, of the sort that environmentally minded residents used in their houses.

Reducing fossil fuel use for heating and cooling . . . Seemed like a good idea to Sachs.

But not everybody thought so, apparently. Thirty or so protesters stood on the sidewalk holding posters against the drilling. A tall, lean man with frizzy gray hair – and matching beard – seemed to be in charge. From the posters and some lapel pins people wore, she noted that the movement was called One Earth. She wondered what their objections were. Geothermal seemed just another environmentally friendly process. Some of the posters, though, referred to fracking and poisoning the groundwater.

The lean man stepped in front of a flatbed, loaded with girders. He crossed his arms and stood his ground. The rest of the crowd cheered. Every time the truck driver blasted the man with his horn, the protesters exploded with catcalls and applause.

A job for a patrolman, but no patrolman was around.

Sachs walked into the street. 'Sir.' She showed her badge. 'Could you step out of the street?'

'And if I don't? Are you going to arrest me?'

This was, of course, the last thing she wanted to do. It would involve a trip to the local precinct, as she no longer carried her citation book. But there was only one answer. 'Yes.'

'You're in their pocket. The city's kissing their ass.' He nodded at the site.

'Sir, you don't want to go to jail for this. Step out of the way.'

Without protest he did, and her impression was that he'd planned the tactic as a mosquito bite, a small irritation.

'Could I see some ID?'

He complied. He was Ezekiel Shapiro and lived in upper Manhattan.

She handed it back. 'No disrupting traffic. And I hope that can you've got in your pocket is for home repair.'

It seemed to be spray paint. She'd noticed where graffiti had been scrubbed off the sign and the walls of the barrier.

'They're fucking up everything, you know.' He looked at the

site with wild eyes. 'Everything.' He returned to the crowd and many of the people hugged him as if he'd just faced down an entire army.

Then Mother Earth left her thoughts and she got to work. She pulled a small evidence collection bag, red canvas, from the trunk of the Torino, parked nearby, and walked to the subway entrance where the CCTV had captured the unsub's image. She turned, recalled the direction of his route and found the trash bin where he'd disposed of the hard hat and vest. Not empty – that word would never apply to any trash receptacle in New York City – but it was empty enough to see those items weren't inside.

She then spotted the likely gate he would have taken to leave the construction site. The large mesh panels were open and, as she'd hoped, some workers were here, despite its being Sunday. She showed her shield to a trim, vigilant man in a private security uniform, richly toned with a suntan that testified to the fine vacation he'd just taken. She asked if she could speak to the supervisor. He lifted a walkie-talkie and said a detective with the NYPD wanted to speak to him.

The clattering answer: 'Uh, yeah. Hold on. Tell him I'll be there in a minute.'

'Her.'

'What?'

'It's a her. She's a her,' the guard said, casting an awkward look her way.

'Oh. Her. A minute.'

Sachs looked over the site. The project – about three acres square, she guessed – wasn't like most you see in the city, with the dark-red ironwork of skyscrapers latticing upward. This was more like what she guessed an oil rig operation would be. There were a number of drilling locations that measured about twenty feet wide, fifty long, surrounded by green six-foot-high fences; signs labeled them as Areas 1 through 12. Some of these were crowned with derricks rising about four stories high. Other green-fenced sites seemed closed. Maybe the drilling at those locations was completed.

Though the site wasn't that populated, it was noisy. The drills were powered by raucous diesel engines and bulldozers rolled about, picking up debris and dropping it into dump trucks, with huge bangs.

The supervisor had said a minute and he was true to his word. A stocky man, in tan Carhartt overalls and orange safety vest, approached. He wore tinted, stylish glasses whose earpieces were attached to a bright-red retainer, and his yellow hard hat jutted forward, high on his head.

Introductions were made and hands shaken and the supervisor – his name was Albert Schoal – glanced out of the gate toward the protesters. 'So, what's it this time?' he yelled over the sound of the machinery.

'I'm sorry?'

'The complaint.'

She lifted a querying eyebrow.

Schoal asked, 'Didn't somebody file a complaint?' His voice was weary. So were his eyes, behind the gray lenses.

'That's not why I'm here. Why would somebody file a complaint?'

'Oh. Sorry. It's one of *their* tactics. Somebody calls nine one one – from a pay phone or throwaway mobile, natch – and says one of my guys was selling dope to somebody. Or exposed himself. Somebody complained that our guys were killing pigeons but nobody gave a you-know-what.'

'Who's "their"? As in "their tactics."'

'Protesters. The group's called One Earth. They do it to harass us.'

She said, 'Shapiro. Yeah, I met him.'

The supervisor sighed. 'Ezekiel. What'd he do to earn your attention?'

'Stopped a delivery truck.'

'Oh, that's one of their favorites. Graffiti too. And false alarms. Even set fire to some trash cans. No damage but it brought the fire department and clogged the street.'

Though Shapiro was some distance away now, Sachs could see that the scrawny man was worked up. He radiated intensity and passion. Arms waving, head raised high, he led his followers in an indecipherable chant.

'What's their issue?' she asked. 'Fracking? I saw a poster.'

A look of disgust crossed Schoal's face. 'Ridiculous. We build near-surface, closed-loop geothermal. We don't pump anything into the ground. We don't suck anything *out* of the ground. The solution's contained in pipes. It never leaves the system. And the odds of a rupture are as small as a roach's ass. I sometimes think they don't have a damn clue what we're doing. They just need something to protest. Like, oh, it's Sunday, I'm bored, let's hug a tree and go make hardworking people's lives miserable.'

Roach's ass?

'Anyway, so, if none of 'em made any bullshit reports, what can I do for you, Detective?'

She first asked if Schoal had been working on Friday. She wasn't going to share any information if there was a chance that *he* was the person Forty-Seven had met with. But Schoal wasn't on that day. Thursday and Friday were his 'weekend.'

'I'm not so senior.' He said this with a wry grimace. 'That's why I'm working Sundays. Day of rest. Ha!'

She explained that a suspect in a homicide had, they believed, walked out of the jobsite Friday afternoon, though telling him nothing about the nature of the killings.

'One of our people? Jesus.'

'I doubt it. It looks like he exited, was walking to the subway and remembered he was carrying a hard hat and safety vest. He turned around, threw them out and then got on the train.'

'Yeah, nobody in the business'd throw out a hat. A vest maybe but not a hat. What was he doing here?'

She told him the two theories. Using the site as a shortcut, to avoid the CCTV cameras along Cadman Plaza – all the government buildings. Or meeting somebody in the site, possibly to buy a weapon.

Schoal thought the shortcut idea wouldn't make sense. The entrance she'd come through and another, a half block away, for trucks, were the only ways to get inside. 'You basically come out of the site the same place you walked in.'

As for the second theory, he said, 'We screen our people good. For drugs, drinking. I mean, it's New York City construction. Some of my boys might be connected and might have a gun or two to sell. Can't use metal detectors when your crew brings twenty pounds of tools with 'em every day.'

She glanced around the site. 'You have cameras here?'

'Only the supply storage area and the tool rooms. Where thieves'd be more likely to hit. But they're on the other side of the yard. He came out here, this gate, they wouldn'ta caught him. So, whatta you want to do, Detective?'

'Canvass your folks, find out if anybody saw him on Friday. I've got a rough description.'

'Sure, I'll help you. Play cop. My brother's on the force in Boston. South Bay.'

'That'd be great.'

'We'll suit you up. Reggie?' he called to a worker just passing nearby. 'Hard hat and vest for the lady.' He paused. 'For the detective. Ain't the best fashion choice, the vest, but rules is rules.'

She pulled on the orange garment and donned the hat – after banding her hair up in a ponytail. Thought about taking a selfie to send to Rhyme and her mother.

Then decided: Naw.

'How could he've gotten past the guard without a pass or credentials?'

Schoal shrugged. 'Not that hard. Somebody in a vest and hat, they walk in with a bunch of guys, security wouldn't notice. That's not a risk we worry about: It's the trucks that show up off hours to drive away with your 'dozer or ten thousand bucks' worth of copper pipe. Sorry I said "lady."'

'I've been called worse.' She dug into the evidence bag and handed him a picture from the MTA security camera, which, of course, didn't show much at all. The dark coat, the dark slacks, dark stocking cap. The text described a white male, average build and about six feet.

'Detective, what'd this guy do exactly?'

Sometimes you were tight-lipped, sometimes you sensed an

ally. 'He killed a jewelry store owner and two people – a couple – in Midtown yesterday.'

'Fuck me. The Promisor. God. That was terrible. Those kids. Going to get married . . . and he killed 'em.'

'That's him.'

'And you think he bought his gun from one of my guys?'

'That's what we want to find out.'

They began circulating, talking to the workers who'd drawn Sunday duty. The men – and a few women – were more than willing to talk and no one evaded eye contact, any more than normal, or otherwise suggested that he or she was the person Unsub 47 had met with.

After a half hour of no luck they'd been through nearly all the workers on duty and Sachs was thinking she – or Ron Pulaski – would have to return and canvass the rest tomorrow. She didn't like that they'd have to wait. She was sure that Forty-Seven was still on the trail of VL and continuing his hunt for those who'd committed the terrible sin of adorning their fingers with diamond rings.

But a moment later, a break. A tall African American worker listened to her words and then began nodding almost immediately.

'You know, I did see somebody here about when you were saying, Friday. I thought he was corporate. He wasn't in a Carhartt or anything, just a black jacket, with hat and vest.'

The worker's name was Antoine Gibbs.

Schoal said, 'The execs from the head office, they come to the site, they don't wear suits a lot of times.'

Gibbs said, 'So this guy, he was talking to somebody else. I guess one of ours – he *did* have on boots and was wearing Carhartt. They talked, and looked around, and then they walked away, toward Seven. It was kind of odd, suspicious, I guess, but I didn't think much of it at the time.'

'Seven?' Sachs asked.

Gibbs indicated one of the drilling pens surrounded by the six-foot-high green fence. This one did not have a derrick rising from it. Beside a gate was a sign.

Area 7
Drilling: 3/8–3/10
HDPE: 4/3
Grouting: 4/4

As they walked to the site Sachs asked the tall worker, 'Did you see his face?'

'Not clear, no. Sorry. Pretty much the build of the guy was in that picture you showed me. But no face.'

Her eyes were on the battered fence.

'Could they get inside? Maybe they wanted to conduct some business out of sight.'

Gibbs told her, 'If he had a key. A lot of guys do.'

'What's in there?' Nodding at the fence.

Schoal answered. 'Shafts and a mud pit.' He could see she didn't understand and added, 'See, geothermal works by pumping fluid from the surface down hundreds, or thousands, of feet, and back up again.'

'I read your billboard.'

'PR guy wrote it but it gives you an okay idea. The first step is we drill shafts – in this case about five to six hundred feet – into bedrock. Then we feed pipe into it. That loop I mentioned, basically two thick hoses joined at the end – called HDPE, high-density polyethylene – so the fluid can circulate. Since geothermal only works when the piping's in contact with the ground we pour conductive grout down the shaft after the piping's in place. This one, Area Seven, there're twenty shafts. We've drilled them all but they're not scheduled for the piping to go in for a couple of weeks – April third. It's shut down till then.'

She said to the supervisor, 'So there'd be nobody working and they could talk in private. Can you open it up for me?'

Schoal asked Gibbs, 'Mud pit?'

'Haven't dredged it out yet.'

He said to Sachs, 'Just watch your step. The way drilling works is we pump water down with the drill face, and mud and rock're pumped back up into what we call a mud pit. Eventually it's

149

emptied out and the sludge and stone're taken to dump sites but the one in Seven hasn't been emptied yet. Nasty stuff.'

Schoal fished a key from his belt and opened the gate. Sachs walked inside, adding, 'Can you wait out here?'

He nodded, though he didn't get why, his expression said.

She told him, 'Don't want to disturb any evidence from where they might've been standing.'

'Oh, yeah, yeah, sure. Crime scene stuff. We see all those shows, the wife and me. I love 'em. You guys can catch a butterfly that was at the murder scene and there'll be an image of the killer in the damn thing's wings. That's just amazing. You ever do that?'

'Never have.' Sachs reminded herself to share that one with Rhyme.

She donned gloves and put rubber bands on her shoes – to differentiate her footprints from the unsub's – leaving it to the supervisor to draw his own conclusions about *that* high-tech forensic tool.

Butterfly wings . . .

But once inside she noted that this site was useless – *more* than useless, then smiled at the grammatical contradiction that Rhyme would have loved. Like 'extremely unique.'

Or would it be *less* than useless?

The problem, forensically, was that the ground inside was gravel and rock, which wouldn't reveal any footprints, so she had no idea where the unsub and the worker might've stood – if they'd been here at all.

Still, with gloved hands she scooped up about a half pound of stones from the place where they logically *might* have been – near the gate – and placed them in a plastic evidence bag.

The center of Area 7 was the mud pit: a trough, running lengthwise from one end of the fence to the other. It was about fifteen feet wide, surrounded by the narrow rocky walkway. It was filled with what Schoal had described: a mucky pool, deep brown and gray, its surface iridescent with oil or other chemicals. A yellow measuring stick, rising from the middle, showed the pit was just over six feet deep. The smell was a powerful mix of damp earth and diesel fuel.

Nasty stuff.

A dozen of the geothermal shafts, twelve inches in diameter, rose from the pool too. They were covered with plastic bags. To one side was a machine that looked like a small, stationary cement mixer, presumably for pouring the grout into the shafts once the piping was fed down them.

The only way to get across the pit was to walk on planks laid over it, between the shafts . . . and to walk very carefully. They were only about ten inches wide and, because they were eighteen feet long or so, appeared quite springy.

Sachs was wondering if the unsub would have walked over one of them to get to the other side. There was a window cut into the far fence, about head height. It would make sense for the unsub to have walked to it and looked out to see if it was safe to exit. It wouldn't hurt to get a few samples from the ground beneath the window.

She eyed the precarious wooden plank.

Shaking her head. Sometimes it's easy. Sometimes it isn't.

Then smiling to herself and thinking: And when, exactly, has it been easy?

She began across the plank, walking carefully, one foot after the other, as the narrow bridge bounded up and down. On the other side she scooped up stones and dirt from beneath the window and started back.

She was halfway back when the world changed.

The ground around her shook fiercely and she heard a deep rumbling. What the hell was going on? A derrick had fallen, one of the buildings under construction collapsed, a plane had crashed nearby.

A voice from behind her, Schoal's, in a much higher register than earlier, called out, 'Christ Almighty.'

As car alarms began bleating and people screamed, Sachs struggled to stay upright. The plank was bouncing hard and, desperate to keep from falling, she dropped fast and hard on one knee, her bad – well, her worse – one. Fiery pain rose from the limb to her jaw. The plank dipped under her weight, but then rebounded and pitched her off like a swimming pool diving board.

Arms flailing, Amelia Sachs fell toward the mud. In the second before she hit she tried frantically to twist upright, to keep her face to the sky so she could breathe after she landed.

But the maneuver didn't work and she dropped face-first into the brown-and-gray glue, which slowly began to suck her beneath the surface.

CHAPTER 23

'You feel that? That shudder?' Ruth Phillips, putting away groceries in the cupboard, shouted to her husband.

He didn't answer.

This happened a lot. Not that he was hard of hearing. It was more of an architectural issue.

They were in their bungalow in Brooklyn, on the edge of the Heights. The home was a railroad-style structure, which, she'd learned when they moved in decades ago, you saw much more in the South. Railroad, it was called, because there was a long hallway running from the front door past the living room, the three bedrooms and the dining room to the kitchen, in the back. Like the trains you saw from the old-time movies, with a corridor beside the passenger compartments. Ruth didn't think any trains still had this feature but there might have been some somewhere. Her only experience with that mode of transport was the LIRR, which they took out to Oyster Bay to see daughter number one.

Arnie was in the living room, which faced the small street, sixty feet away from her.

The far end of the train.

She set the Green Giant canned beans down and repeated the question. Louder.

'What?' he called.

And once more: 'You feel that? That shudder or something?'

'Supper? Yeah, what's for supper?'

She pulled her yellow sweater tighter about her stocky form and stepped outside, onto the back porch. Car accident? Plane crash? She and Arnie had been on the promenade on September 11 and had seen the second plane hit.

She returned to the house and walked halfway up the hall and noted her husband, still parked in front of the TV.

They were both in their early sixties, just edging close to the time when they could start compiling dreams for retirement. Arnie was inclined to a motor home and Ruth wanted a place by a lake, preferably in Wisconsin, to be near daughter number two and her husband. This set of youngsters was the sort who smiled, with cheerful groans, whenever Arnie made a cheese joke. Which was a lot. The shudder a moment ago had brought back the idea of terrorism and Ruth thought once more: Time to start making firm plans for that move.

'Not "supper." "Shudder," I said. Like something was shaking. Was there an accident? Didn't you feel it?'

'Yeah, I did, something. Construction maybe.'

'Sunday?'

Glasses had shivered, windows rattled. She'd felt the rumbling in her feet; she'd pulled on her slippers as soon as they got back from the grocery store and finished carting the bags inside.

'Dunno.' He had the game on. He loved his games.

Arnie said, 'So anyway. What *is* for supper. Since the subject's come up.'

'I don't know yet.'

'Oh. Thought you were cooking.'

'Already? No.'

She returned to the kitchen. Ruth's procedure for stowage was logical. First, freezer items went to roost. Then perishables that could germify — Arnie's wonderful word — like meat, fish and milk. Then fresh fruits and veggies. Then boxes and finally the long-term stuff. The cheerful Green Giants, in cans, would be the last to get tucked away.

'Then you're baking?' Arnie was in the corridor now. He'd come her way so they could speak in normal voices. 'One of those pies? I was dreamin' about rhubarb.'

'I'm not baking either.'

'Hm.' Arnie now stepped into the dining room, adjacent to the kitchen. His eyes were not on his bride of forty-three years but on the stove. She noted his expression of curiosity and she frowned. 'What is it, hon?'

'The oven's not on?'

She waved to it. Meaning no.

'I could smell gas. I thought you'd turned it on. And it took a minute for the burner to catch.'

'No, but . . . ' Her voice faded. Ruth too could smell that rotten egg scent.

'Maybe the city's doing some work and they hit a gas main. That was the shudder. You know, it's stronger now.'

'Yeah. It is.'

His brows, set high in his well-worn face, knitted close. He brushed at his thinning, curly hair, walked to the front door and looked outside. He called back to her, 'No trucks, no accidents.' He added that a few people were outside of their houses, looking around.

Maybe, Ruth thought, there *had* been a crash and a collision had ruptured a propane truck. But wait, propane didn't smell like natural gas. Ruth knew this because barbecuing was one of their most enjoyable pastimes in the summer.

She walked to the cellar door and opened it. She was hit with the same stink but ten times stronger. 'Honey! Come here!'

Arnie appeared in an instant. He noticed the open door. Sniffed. 'My God.'

He peered downstairs and started to reach for the light, then stopped, as she was about to say, No! Arnie glanced at the fire extinguisher sitting next to the stove. It was seven years old.

She said, 'We should get out. We should get out now.'

'I'll call. We have to call. Isn't there a special number you call for gas leaks? How do we find it?' He reached for the wall phone.

'Gas company?' she asked, incredulous. 'Forget it, hon! We'll call nine one one from outside.' She stepped toward her purse. 'Come on! We have to get out.'

'I'll just—'

From the basement door a tide of flame and smoke exploded outward, enveloping Arnie. As he flung his arms up and covered his face, he was blown against the far wall and landed on the floor, crying out in pain.

No, no, no! Ruth ducked beneath the raging tornado of fire that swirled from the doorway, screaming her husband's name. She crouched and started toward him.

Suddenly a jolt sent her to her knees and the half of the kitchen floor where she was standing dropped three or four feet – the explosion had taken out the joists. As the smoke and flames and dust swirled about them, she could see Arnie – lying on his side, swiping frantically at his burning clothing. He was above her, on the part of the floor that hadn't dropped. From the gap between the sections of flooring flowed dense black smoke, tongues of flame and red sparks like stinging bees.

Ruth struggled to her feet on the slanting floor, looking around frantically. They couldn't use the back door now to escape – with the sunken floor, the exit was too high to reach, and was bathed in flames spiraling up from the basement.

The front. They had to get out the front. But first, Ruth needed to climb up to the level that Arnie lay on.

'Honey, honey!' she called. 'The front! Get out the front!' But the words vanished in the roar. She hadn't known that fire could be so loud.

Dodging the whips of flame, she started to climb up to Arnie, who was choking and writhing in pain. At least, she saw, he'd managed to strip off the burning clothing.

She put her hands on the end of the floorboards at his level and started to boost herself up. 'The front door. Let's—'

But at that moment the portion of the floor she was standing on dropped away completely and Ruth plunged into the basement, landing in a ragdoll pile on the concrete, pelted on head, arms and shoulders by boards, the kitchen table, cookbooks and cans of beans.

Fire was all around her now: storage boxes, Arnie's magazines, Christmas decorations, the girls' old clothing, furniture. And flames licked the cans and jars of flammables on Arnie's workbench – cleaners, paint thinner, turpentine, alcohol. They could be exploding any moment.

Ruth Phillips understood she was about to die.

Thinking of Claire and Sammi. The grandchildren, too. Arnie, of course. The love of her life. Then, now, forever.

She ducked as another joist collapsed and slammed to the floor. It narrowly missed her head.

Choking on the smoke, twisting away from the needle-sharp embers and the fists of heat.

But then, Ruth thought: No.

She wasn't going to die this way. In pain. Not by fire.

She looked around, as best she could through the fog of boiling smoke. The stairs were gone but in the corner, right under the ledge of the floor that remained, where Arnie lay, was her mother's old dresser. She crawled to it and climbed on the top. She wasn't strong enough to do a pull-up and roll onto the floor above her. But she kicked off the slippers, for better grip, stretched her leg high and planted a foot on the mirror on top of the dresser, feeling a thigh muscle drawn to the snapping point.

She ignored the pain.

Flames swelled. A can of turpentine exploded and a swirl of pine-scented fire and smoke ballooned beside her. Ruth turned away, felt the sting of fire on her ankles and arms. But her clothing didn't ignite.

The fire, she saw, was licking a gallon can of paint thinner.

Now. This is it. Last chance.

Gripping the broken hardwood planks above her, she kicked hard and, in clumsy desperation, clawed her way up, rolling onto the kitchen floor beside Arnie.

'Ruth!' Arnie crawled to her. He was down to his boxer shorts. Half his hair was gone, eyebrows too. And there were burns on his face, neck, chest and right arm but they hadn't incapacitated him.

'Out! We have to get out! The front!'

Keeping low, for what little air remained in the house, they started down the hall but got only halfway to the front door. Because of the smoke they hadn't been able to see that the living room and front alcove were a mass of flame too. The bedroom windows weren't an option either. Those rooms were burning as well.

'Garage,' she cried. It was their last hope.

Gripping each other hard, they pushed forward. Just before the heat and flames drove them back – to a claustrophobic, searing death in the narrow corridor – they reached the garage door. Ruth touched the metal knob and let go immediately.

'It's hot,' she said.

A pause. They both laughed, a bit hysterical. Because of *course* it was hot. Everything in the damn house was hot.

She gripped the knob again, twisted it and shoved open the door. They crouched. But there were no flames here, just smoke and fumes roiling into the garage from the vents and up from under the baseboards. They plunged inside. It was hard to see through the eye-stinging clouds but the garage was small and – since it was used for storage only, not parking – they could follow the path to the front between rows of boxes and kitchen appliances and sports equipment from days long ago.

Choking and wiping their streaming eyes, they moved steadily to the front of the structure. Ruth felt light-headed and fell once. She then got a breath of better air, low to the floor, then another and, with Arnie's help, she rose again.

Arms around each other, husband and wife finally made it to the front of the garage. With another laugh, this one of pure relief, Ruth pressed the button of the door opener.

CHAPTER 24

'Just breathe, Detective.'

She nodded to the city medical tech. And tried to follow his orders. Slowly. Okay . . . Inhale, exhale. The coughing began in earnest once more.

Not okay.

Hacking, spitting.

Try again. Control it . . . Concentrating on her lungs, the muscles in her chest. Yes, she controlled it. Breathe in, out. Slowly.

Okay. Controlling it.

No more coughing. Good.

'It's clearing, Detective,' the tech said. He was a cheerful man with curly back hair and skin a mocha shade.

'All good,' she rasped.

Then she puked.

Again, again, again.

Sitting on the back lip of the ambulance, she bent double at the waist and evacuated a mass of the filthy mud soup.

Most had gone into her gut, not her lungs, apparently.

After a moment or two of retching, the feeling subsided.

She took the bottle of water that the EMT offered. Rinsed her mouth and poured it over her face. She couldn't imagine what she looked like from the neck up. She'd shed her clothes and dressed in a set of Tyvek overalls – she kept a carton in the trunk of her car. It felt like her hair weighed thirty pounds. Her fingernails, always short, ended in goth black crescents.

Beside her sat her Glock, which, before she did anything else, she'd cleaned in a mini field strip, including running a patch soaked with Hoppe's solvent through the barrel. It had been dangerously clogged.

'What was that shit?' she asked. 'That I swallowed?'

She posed this question to Arthur Schoal, the Northeast Geo supervisor, who was beside the ambulance. He was still looking mortified at what had befallen her.

'The mud? Just water, soil, clay, maybe a bit of diesel fuel from the drills. Nothing more toxic than that.'

Yeah, she tasted petroleum. And she thought back to her younger bad-girl days: when you needed gas for your Camaro and you had no money but you did have a length of siphoning hose and the inside knowledge of where some local numbers runner or Mafioso wannabe parked his Caddie.

Another bout of coughing, another slug of water. The regurgitation – one of her absolute least favorite activities – seemed at bay.

The important thing, she told herself, was that her knee was fine, after the slam onto the wobbly plank. She was still mobile and free – largely free – from the arthritic pain that had dogged her for so many years.

She squinted away tears from the puking, and noticed ribbons of mud on Schoal's clothes.

'You pulled me out?'

'Me and Gibbs. The guy we were talking to.'

'He here?'

'No, he went to call his wife. See if she was okay.'

Okay? she wondered.

'I'll have to pay you,' she said to Schoal.

The man blinked and nodded, though he'd have no idea what she was talking about.

'For the mud treatment. In a spa they can cost a hundred bucks.'

He laughed.

Sachs did too. And summoned up every ounce of willpower to keep from sobbing.

She'd told the joke not for him but to shove aside the utter horror of being held immobile in the muck, unable to breathe.

It had affected her. Badly. Being held helpless, being sucked down, down, down. She'd almost been buried alive – wet earth or dry, that made no difference. Confinement was her personal hell.

She shivered once more. Recalling a banished memory from years ago. As a girl she'd read a book that she believed was called *Stranger than Fiction*, about real-life occurrences that were, well, strange. One was about exhuming a coffin, for some reason, only to find fingernail scratches on the inside of the lid. She hadn't slept for two days after that and when she did she refused to cover up with sheets or blankets.

'Hey, Detective. You okay?'

She controlled the creeping panic attack, like she'd controlled the coughing. But just.

'Yeah, sure.'

Deep breaths, she told herself.

Okay, okay.

She wanted to call Rhyme. No, she didn't want to. She wanted to drive two hundred miles an hour even if it meant burning out the Torino's engine. No, she wanted to go home and curl up in bed.

Frozen – hands, feet, arms, belly and neck, all held motionless in the wet, slimy grave.

She shivered. Put. It. Away.

The medical technician said, 'Detective, your heart rate . . . '

Her finger was clipped to one of the heavy-duty machines the EMTs came armed with.

Breathe, breathe, breathe . . .

'Better.'

'Thanks.' She pulled the clip off, handed it to the tech. 'I'm good now.'

He was examining her carefully. He understood. And he nodded.

It was then that she noticed that the Northeast Geo workers were talking among themselves, standing in clusters. Their expressions were troubled. And it wasn't Sachs's near-death experience that took their attention.

She recalled wondering about the supervisor's comment that Gibbs, the worker she'd been speaking to, had called his wife to see if she was all right.

Something was going on.

She realized too that there were a dozen sirens in the distance. Ambulance sirens and police sirens.

She remembered the shaking of the ground. And she thought immediately of a terrorist attack. The Twin Towers once again.

'What happened?' Sachs whispered, the tame volume partly from concern, partly because her vocal cords weren't up to a louder task.

A male voice, not Schoal's or the EMT's, said, 'Believe it or not: earthquake.'

A slim man approached, pale, about forty. He was in gray slacks and white shirt and blue windbreaker, beneath the requisite orange vest. His paisley tie disappeared against his chest between the second and third buttons from the top of his shirt, probably so it didn't get caught in machinery gears. His glasses were round.

He looked, Sachs thought, sciencey.

Which made sense because, as it turned out, he *was* a scientist.

Schoal introduced her to Don McEllis, an inspector with the New York State Division of Mineral Resources within the Department of Environmental Conservation. He was an engineer and a geologist and it was his job, he explained, to supervise the drilling that his organization had approved. Since the Northeast geothermal project dug shafts that were five hundred feet or deeper, the DMR regulated the work; above that depth the Division of Water oversaw the construction.

'Earthquake?'

'Yep.'

Sachs recalled some TV show, or maybe an article, about quakes in the New York area. There'd been several.

'Did it cause any damage?'

McEllis said, 'At least one fire. That's the main danger with earthquakes in first-world nations. Even if a building isn't designed to be earthquake-proof, most of 'em'll remain standing. But gas lines can shear. So, fires. San Francisco, nineteen oh six, the city burned, it didn't collapse.'

'I'm standing up,' she said to the med tech.

He looked at her quizzically. 'Okay.'

She'd expected him to say no.

'I am.'

'You can stand up.'

She stood. She was a little woozy but managed to rise without difficulty, though she swayed a bit – mostly from the weight of the mud embedded in her hair.

'How powerful was it?

'Minor. Three point nine – that's the Richter scale.' With a scientist's combination of knowledge and naïveté, he methodically explained that the famous scale everyone knew about was in fact outmoded for measuring most earthquakes; it was used nowadays only for classifying minor tremors. 'Anything larger than five is rated according to the MM, or moment magnitude, scale.'

She didn't want to ask for more information because she knew he would oblige.

But continue he did anyway. 'This magnitude is typical of what we see in the Northeast. The faults in the New York area aren't as active or as well defined as in California, say. Or Mexico or Italy or Afghanistan. That's the good news: Quakes are very infrequent. But the bad news is the nature of the geology here is that if there were to be a bad earthquake the damage would be much more serious and would travel much farther. Also, our buildings aren't made to withstand it. San Francisco's pretty earthquake-proof nowadays. But here? A quake that registered six on the MM scale in New York City – which isn't all that powerful – could leave ten thousand people dead, twice that buried in the rubble. Whole neighborhoods would have to be shut down because the buildings would be too unstable.'

Buried in the rubble . . .

Sachs again forced away the arms of panic. Barely.

'Where was the epicenter?' she asked.

'Nearby,' McEllis said. 'Very nearby.'

Schoal was staring over Area 7, whose gate was still open. They could see the plastic-bag-covered shafts. The supervisor was somber. Sachs recalled that the protesters were complaining about fracking. Maybe Schoal was thinking, despite his comments earlier, that possibly their drilling had caused the quake.

Or maybe it was just that he'd be concerned the tremor would give the protesters ammunition in attacking the project.

Sachs took another bottle of water from the medic and, with a smile of thanks, tilted her head back so she was staring at the sky. She emptied the bottle into her hair. He fed her four more and by the last one, she felt that most of the mud was gone.

Better. Mud-wise and panic-wise.

She was ready. She called Lincoln Rhyme.

'You hear?'

'About what?'

'The earthquake.'

'What earthquake?'

That answered the question.

'Shook up the city, half hour ago.'

'Really? Hm.' His tone said his mind was elsewhere. 'You find anything at the jobsite?'

'I think so. I'll be back soon. Going to stop by my place.'

'Why?'

'Want to clean up first.'

'Don't bother with that. Who cares? Just come on in.'

She said nothing for a moment. He must have wondered about the pause. 'I won't be long.'

Sachs disconnected before he could protest further.

CHAPTER **25**

Vimal's childhood bedroom – also his present bedroom – was small, on the second floor of the modest home in this modest Queens neighborhood, Jackson Heights. This particular area was a largely Indian community.

It was a two-story, single-family brick structure, with small front and backyards, neither of which was any good for football, except to practice footwork.

He'd lived here, within these four very claustrophobic walls, for all of his life. At least he had it to himself now. He'd had to share the space with his brother for a few years until Dada, his grandfather, passed, and Sunny moved into the old man's room.

Upon returning home from Dev Nouri's, Vimal had taken a spot bath – washcloths only – not wanting to disturb the wound that Adeela had so carefully dressed. An examination of his torso revealed that she'd done a good job. There was no more bleeding and still no infection. Now, back in his bedroom, he toweled his legs and chest with one hand and, with the other, manned the remote. He was searching the news on the Samsung.

The murder was a prominent story but it was not the lead; that would be the earthquake that had shaken up Brooklyn and much of the rest of the city.

When the anchor got to the deaths of Mr Patel and the engaged couple, he said there were some new details about the 'daring' robbery, though Vimal wasn't sure how much balls it took to walk into a largely deserted office building, kill three unarmed individuals and run out.

He wrapped the towel around his thin waist and watched the screen. The next bit of news stunned him.

Saul Weintraub, the assayer and evaluator Mr Patel used from time to time, had been killed, as well. The police believed there was some connection between the four murders.

Vimal closed his eyes briefly in dismay and sat, heavily, on the edge of his bed.

So the killer – the Promisor – believed Mr Weintraub had seen something Saturday morning, that he was a witness. Vimal recalled that Mr Patel said he was meeting with the man sometime that weekend.

How had the killer found where Mr Weintraub lived?

Vimal recalled the newscast of the press conference on Saturday afternoon, the police spokesman's urging anyone with knowledge of the killing to come forward immediately.

And Vimal's reading between the lines.

For their own safety . . .

How safe was *he*?

Vimal felt pretty secure, thinking again of his minimal connection with Mr Patel: being paid in cash and keeping nothing personal in the shop to identify him. And trying to track Vimal down by scouring the Diamond District wouldn't be very productive. Unlike in years past, there were few diamond merchants left in the old, musty office building at 58 West 47th. Only one or two cutters, two jewelry stores. And Vimal was sure that no one in the building or on the street would know who he was. He kept to himself, preferring to get home to his studio at the end of the day. And most of the diamantaires and others in the business who might know him were here in Jackson Heights, miles – and a river – away from the Manhattan Diamond District. Vimal had acquaintances who worked in the galleries of SoHo or NoHo, or were studying art where he so wanted to be: Parsons, or Pratt in Brooklyn. But he wasn't close to any of them.

His closest friend in the diamond world was another cutter, about his age: Kirtan Boshi – they'd have lunch or drinks together frequently, sometimes double-dating, with Adeela and Kirtan's girlfriend, an aspiring model Kirtan worked for a diamantaire but some distance from 47th Street, in a building in the Fashion District; the shop had a name that gave no clue as to the Indian ethnicity of the owner – or that it was a jewelry store.

No, it seemed very unlikely that a killer, however determined, could find him.

Vimal tossed aside the towel, pulled on underwear, blue jeans, T-shirt and sweatshirt, his Nikes.

On TV: back to the earthquake. He couldn't hear what the commentators were talking about. Two men seemed to be arguing. A crawl said that an environmental group thought that drilling work deep beneath the city might be to blame.

He shut the set off. Vimal Lahori had his own problems.

Filled with resignation, he trooped downstairs. In the living room, Sunny – younger, though taller, than Vimal – looked up from the TV screen and paused the video game. 'Yo. Dude.'

The eighteen-year-old's eyes revealed his concern, even if his low-key greeting and the deflecting grin hadn't. Sunny was a freshman at Hunter, destined, the boy hoped, for medical school. Vimal believed he would – and should – end up in tech, an opinion he kept to himself.

'You, like, cool?'

'Yeah, fine.'

Awkwardly, the younger brother stood, as if debating whether he should embrace Vimal, who decided the question himself and dropped into the couch before the uneasy moment arrived. Vimal snatched up the controller and resumed the game his brother had been playing.

'Screw you,' Sunny said, laughing hard – too hard.

'You're only at level seven?'

'I've been playing for ten minutes is all. You couldn't get to seven in a day.'

'I got to eight on Thursday. Four hours.'

'Gimme.'

Vimal held the controller away as his brother grabbed for it. After some tame horse wrestling he handed the device over. Vimal took a second controller and they played jointly. A few more aliens died, another spaceship blew up. Vimal found Sunny looking him over closely.

'What, man? It's freaking me out.'

'What?'

'That eyeball shit. Stop it.'

Sunny's character on the screen got vaporized. Not seeming to notice, he asked, 'What was it like?'

'Like?'

'Getting shot at?'

Vimal corrected, 'It wasn't getting shot *at*. It was getting shot.'

'No, shit!'

'Yeah. I walked in. There he was. Bang. Loud, like totally loud. Not like on TV. I mean, *loud*.'

An abrupt voice from behind them. 'You're hurt?' His father had been standing in the hallway, it seemed. He walked into the living room.

Vimal wondered if he'd been hiding, to listen in on his conversation with Sunny. No other reason to be in the hall, except to eavesdrop. Son looked away from Father. 'Nothing. I was just, you know. We were just saying stuff.'

'The news never said anybody was shot.'

'Because I wasn't shot. I was just messing with him.' A nod toward Sunny.

'But something happened,' Papa said sternly.

'The bullet hit some rocks I was carrying. They stung me. That's all.'

Papa was calling, 'Divya! Come here. Come here now!'

Vimal's slim, soft-spoken forty-three-year-old mother appeared in the doorway, looking affectionately toward her sons and then frowning as she saw her husband's expression.

'What is it?'

'Vimal was hurt in the robbery. The man shot at him. He didn't tell me.'

'No! That wasn't on the news,' Mother said, her brow furrowed. She walked directly to her son.

'The bullet didn't hit me. I was saying that. Some bits of rock. It was nothing.'

'My. Let me see.'

'It didn't break the skin. Just some bruises.'

'You will show your mother. You will show her now.' Papa's voice was a slow simmer.

'Where?' Mother asked, gripping her son's shoulder gently.

'My side. It's nothing.' Why had he said anything to his brother?

'Did you go to the hospital?'

'No, Mother. It's all cool. Really.'

'Enough!' Papa snapped. 'Let her look at it!'

Tight-lipped, Vimal turned to her, keeping his back to his father and brother. The woman – a pediatric oncological nurse at Mount Sinai Queens – knelt and lifted his two shirts. Only Vimal could see her blink when she saw the eggplant-purple bruises, the butterfly bandage and the Betadine stains. She carefully examined the wound that the kimberlite splinter had made and probably realized that an ER doctor would have stitched the site. His mother didn't know about Adeela but she would guess that Vimal's reluctance to say anything about the treatment meant that he'd sought help from a non-Hindu friend (that he'd gone to a Muslim he was sleeping with wouldn't enter into any dimension of her thoughts).

Mother looked up. Their eyes met. She lowered his shirt.

'Vimal is fine. Some minor bruises. That's all. Dinner's ready. Let's eat.'

CHAPTER 26

The Lahori family ate traditionally perhaps three nights a week, and Western the rest. There was no set schedule as to which cuisine would be served by Mother on which days, though when Papa was at bowling – he was in a league and very good – she made her sons dishes like meat loaf or spaghetti or pizza or sometimes soup, salads and sandwiches. Tonight she had made roasted chicken, corn on the cob, creamed spinach dusted with nutmeg. The concession to Indian cuisine was naan bread but that was less sub-Asian than a staple at Food Bazaar and Whole Foods and any Korean deli within walking distance.

Who didn't like naan?

Mother was a good cook, with an instinct for seasoning. Vimal loved her food.

Tonight, though, it was no surprise to him that he had no appetite.

The last thing he wanted to do was eat – no, the *second*-to-last thing he wanted to do was eat. Number one on the list was not talk about the robbery. Fortunately, it seemed that Papa sanctioned this protocol. When Mother began to ask about Mr Patel's sister and children and funeral and memorial service, her husband waved a hand to silence her. It seemed to Vimal that the trembling in the man's fingers was worse.

How patient Mother is, Vimal thought, as he had hundreds of times. He wondered if she'd developed this quality from her work. He imagined she would have to be resilient and strong and steady, yet kind, with those under her care, as well as with their parents. And she would have to practice these qualities all day long; doctors came by sporadically, of course; nurses were constants in hospitals.

The conversation skipped about absurdly. Papa asked Sunny

about a test in his biology class. He asked Vimal several times how he had cut the parallelogram. Why had he picked that shape? What adjustments had he made to the dop sticks?

Vimal demurred. He said he couldn't recall. And this was not far from the truth. He was exhausted. And the horror of the past two days had made his heart and mind weary. Every few minutes the image of Mr Patel's feet, angling outward and pointed toward the dim ceiling of the shop, flared. Papa segued to Premier League and the UEFA Champions League as if he were out with his friends after a bowling tournament, sitting at Raga's, over a Kingfisher. The Real Madrid game had been a nail-biter, he told his sons. And in another game, the striker from Man U had twisted and probably broken his ankle. Papa delivered this news, for some reason, with a wink.

Papa reminded Mother to collect a shirt of his from the tailor tomorrow. And complimented her, with sincerity, about the food this evening. He added that it was all right that it needed salt. Better to have to add it later than recook a meal that was over-salted. He smiled approvingly at her resourcefulness.

Vimal sighed. Papa didn't notice.

When the meal was over and Mother cleared dishes, Papa gave a rare smile and asked an astonishing question: 'Scrabble? Do we all want to play Scrabble?'

Vimal stared.

'What?' his father asked.

'I . . . don't feel like playing a game.'

'No?'

'Vim?' his brother asked. Because Sunny would have felt Papa wanted him to. Sunny was often like the second wave of invading soldiers.

'Naw, not tonight.'

Papa nodded slowly. 'Then what would you like to do?'

Looking into the man's eyes, Vimal realized that the time had come. He was tired, he hurt, his plans had been blown apart like the stones he'd carried to Mr Patel's office.

'I'll be downstairs in the workshop.' The inflection of this sentence made it a timid question.

Papa slowly nodded. 'I'll meet you.'

'I'll be a minute. I want a thicker sweater.' Vimal rose and went upstairs. He found what he needed and then walked into the kitchen, to the basement door. He descended the steep stairs and went into the studio.

Here, nervous – actually nauseous – as he waited for his father, he sat on a bench. He was looking over one of his sculptures in progress. He was presently working on pieces in granite, nephrite jade, tiger's eye and celestial-blue lapis lazuli. In the corner of the room was a scaife turntable, similar to what he had polished the parallelogram on, and, on the wall, assorted dop sticks. Papa had been a talented, if uninspired, diamantaire himself and after he'd had to retire from the factory where he worked in the Diamond District, he'd continued to handle some jobs from home, here in the basement, for as long as he could. When he finally had gotten out of the cutting business altogether, Vimal had taken over the workshop to use as a sculptor studio.

This was where he could have spent every waking moment.

These rooms had begun life as an in-law quarters. There was a bathroom and a small kitchen with stove and half refrigerator. On the workbench, in what had been the sitting room, were carefully arranged tools and cartons containing rocks. There was a three-quarter-inch D pneumatic tool, hammers, cup chisels, bushing chisels, wedges and shims for cracking stone, ripper points, hand points. A set of diamond-encrusted blades for the rotary saw – similar to what he might have used for the parallelogram had he not opted for the laser. For the comfort of it he picked up his favorite hammer, four pounds, caressed the dented and scarred head.

Against one wall were cartons filled with a thousand Lahori artifacts, many from his father's family's harrowing flight from Kashmir to Surat in India and their less dramatic journey to the United States.

When taking a break from working on a piece, Vimal had spent time browsing through these cartons filled with the Lahori clan history, which he suspected his father had stowed there purposefully, to ignite within the boy a love of family tradition.

Vimal hadn't needed any prodding. He was fascinated to see pictures of his grandfather in a diamond factory in Surat. Sweaty, gritty, dark, the cutting room in which Dada sat was filled with maybe sixty or seventy employees, four to a scaife, bending forward with their dop sticks. The man had been in his twenties when the picture was taken and he alone, among the twenty or so looking at the photographer, was grinning. Most of the cutters seemed bewildered that someone wanted to record their monotonous chores.

Dada had eventually become one of the top cutters in Surat and thought he could do even better in New York. He used all the rupees he'd saved to bring his wife, young Deepro, and his three brothers and two sisters, to America. The experience had not been a good one. Indians might have ruled the diamond business in Surat but it was the Jews in New York.

Little by little, though, they, and other Hindu cutters, had made inroads.

At his father's insistence, Vimal had gone to his grandfather's cutting shop on the top floor of a dimly lit, moldy building on 45th Street and sat beside him for hours watching the old man's hands, curled around the dop, touching a diamond to the hypnotically spinning wheel.

It was there that the boy decided he was made to change stone into something else.

Though not exactly as his father had in mind.

What would Dada have thought about Vimal's desire to abandon the world of cutting diamonds and become a sculptor? He had a sense that Grandfather wouldn't have minded very much. After all, the man had taken a chance – the extraordinary leap of bringing his whole family to a new and possibly hostile country.

Vimal's mother's ancestry was less well documented, not because Papa wasn't inclined to retain a woman's history (well, not entirely) but because she was sixth-generation American, and the ancestors had come from New Delhi – the forty-million-plus National Capital Region, a very, very different place from Kashmir. Mother was thoroughly Westernized. Her ancestry was potluck, a bit of this, a bit of that. Her family's roots included mixed marriages, divorces, a gay union or two. All this added up, within her, to an *appreciation* of – rather than devotion to – Hindu culture, and the assumption of a quiet, though not fundamentally subservient, role in her marriage.

Vimal now turned on his work lamp over the bench. He closely studied the piece he'd been working on. It was simple, carved from a rich piece of off-white marble from Venezuela: a wave of water at its apogee about to crest and fall down upon itself. He'd grown fascinated recently with the idea of representing the texture and motion of non-stone in stone: wood, steam, hair, and – as with this piece – water. He wanted to do water because Michelangelo had skimped on the waves when he'd carved his reclining Poseidon. Vimal hoped to one-up the master.

Wasn't that an example of a mortal's hubris, which brought the wrath of the gods down upon him?

Come on, he thought, looking up at the ceiling. Let's get this over with. His heart was pounding and his knee bobbed from nerves. He found himself playing with his bracelet and then felt stunned he was still wearing it. Had Father seen? He pulled it off and put it in his pocket.

Now he was hearing the footsteps on the stairs and knew it was time to 'have words,' as Dada used to say. A delicate euphemism for an argument. The look that passed between his father and himself upstairs had made clear that, while a man-to-man talk wasn't possible, a man-to-son talk was . . . and it was long overdue.

His father appeared in the studio. He sat on a stool. Vimal set the hammer down.

Papa wasted no time. 'You wanted to say something.'

'We dance around the subject.'

Because you lose your temper and can't stand anyone disagreeing with you. Which, of course, he did not verbalize.

'Subject?'

'Yes, Papa. But we need to address it.'

'What does this mean, "address"?'

His father had come to America when he was two. He read

two American newspapers a day, cover to cover, and got his news from Publc Broadcasting, in addition to Indian sources. He knew what the word meant.

Waving a tremoring hand, Papa said, 'Tell me. It's late. I will be helping your brother with his homework. Tell me what you mean.'

The man's intentional obliqueness angered Vimal. So he said quickly, 'All right. Here: I don't want to spend my life cutting pieces of carbon that bounce around between women's boobs.'

He regretted the blunt word immediately and feared a fierce reprisal.

But his father just smiled, surprising him. 'No? Why not?'

'It doesn't thrill me, move me.'

Papa jutted out his lower lip. 'Your parallelogram cut. It wasn't like anything Nouri had ever seen. Or me. He sent me a picture of the stone.'

Why did I agree to the cut?

The worst betrayal today had not been Bassam's selling him out; it was Vimal's own lapse. By agreeing to the cut for the money – his thirty pieces of silver – he had bolstered his father's argument that he was a unique and brilliant diamantaire.

I'm my own Judas. His jaw was clenched. See, diamonds ruin everything.

Papa persisted, 'Didn't *that* move you?'

'It was technically challenging. I enjoyed the cut, yes. For that reason. I wasn't, I don't know, passionate about the cutting.'

'Ah but I think you were, son.'

'Whatever *you* want, Papa, I don't want to devote my life to jewelry. It's as simple as that.' This was the most defiant Vimal had ever been.

His father's eyes went to yet another sculpture. The work was a series of geometric shapes, one morphing into another. He called it *Telephone*, after the game in which players whisper a phrase to the person beside them and so on, during the course of which the words become something entirely different. The marble piece had won first prize in a competition at the Field Gallery in SoHo. Vimal couldn't help but reflect that while everyone complimented him on it, no one was interested in buying. It was priced at a thousand dollars, a third of what he'd been paid for the diamond today.

Papa continued, 'I don't understand, son.' A nod at *The Wave*. 'You're an artist. Obviously, you're talented. You understand stone. Not many people do. That's so very rare. But why not be an artist who makes—'

'Money?' Vimal surprised himself by actually interrupting.

'—a difference in the world of jewelry.'

Vimal said, 'There is no difference to make in that world. It's the world of cosmetics. Nothing more.'

He'd just insulted his father and grandfather and many blood relations in the Lahori family. But Papa didn't give any reaction.

'This . . . plan of yours. Running off. What were you going to do?'

Vimal's steam was up. He didn't evade, as he usually did. 'Go to California. Get an MFA.' He'd started college at seventeen and graduated early. Learning, like sculpting, came easily to him.

'California? Where?'

'UCLA. San Francisco State.'

'Why there?'

They both knew the answer to that. Twenty-five hundred miles' distance. But Vimal said, 'Fine arts. Good sculpting programs.'

'You'd have to work. It's expensive there.'

'I intend to work. I'll find something. Pay for my tuition.'

His father examined the work-in-progress again.

'It's good.'

Did he mean this? Vimal couldn't tell from his eyes. He might. But then it might be the way a customer would look over a ring or pendant. The husband or boyfriend's face would shine in admiration. But the lady with him, the recipient? Her mouth would smile and she would whisper, 'Oh, my, lovely.' But her eyes said something different. She'd been expecting more. Flashier. More spectacular.

Or usually what she meant was: bigger.

'Listen to me, son. I can see you've thought about this for a long time.' He sighed. 'And I see too that I haven't really listened to you. This terrible crime with Mr Patel, it's made me look at things differently. I want to understand it. Will you stay here for a few days – let the police catch that man. Then, well, we can talk. I want to hear more about what you want to do. We can work something out. Really. I promise we can.'

Vimal had never heard his father sound so reasonable; so he too had been shaken, fundamentally, by the crime. Vimal felt that tears might swell. He fought the urge. He embraced his father. 'Sure, Papa.'

The older man nodded again at *The Wave*. 'It really does look like water. I don't know how you've done that.' He left, closing the door behind him.

Vimal looked over his sculpture. He pulled on gloves and goggles, powered up the grinder and continued the heavenly task of turning stone to water.

CHAPTER 27

The Henri Avelon was perfect.

Beautiful. No, breathtaking.

Judith Morgan, soon to be Judith Whelan, had been uncertain about the choice. The bridal boutique, on upper Madison Avenue, offered easily fifty different wedding dresses and so the decision had taken some time. Sean couldn't help her with this one, of course. No groom was going to see his bride's wedding dress before the aisle walk. And her mother, a woman who was convinced that price was the best measure of quality, would have bankrupted the family with the dress that she wanted her daughter to wear. Not what Morgan wanted.

The blonde looked at the satin confection in the mirror once more and, while she didn't smile, was pleased beyond words. She turned slowly, viewed as much of the back as she could and returned to pole position. She'd stayed true to her goal of dropping the thirteen pounds and the dress curved the way it should curve, clung the way it should cling, but had plenty of drape and spare room in reserve.

Eyeing the scallops, the reasonable train (half the length of her sister's monstrosity), the shimmery cloth and the tulle at the shoulder, she knew she'd made the right decision.

'It's a winner, my dear,' Frank said and though, sure, he had an interest in selling her the three-thousand-dollar dress, she knew he meant it.

She hugged him. This was the final fitting. Two weeks till launch, but she had a business trip to one of her ad agency's clients starting in a few days and wouldn't have much time after she got back to handle all the plans that a wedding with 257 guests entailed. The get-the-dress box had to be ticked now.

And it had been.

'When is the crew coming in?' Frank asked.

The bridesmaids. For the matching teal dresses, the matching shoes, the matching panty hose, the matching corsages. Frank was a godsend.

'A few days. Rita'll call, make an appointment.'

'I'll get champagne in.'

'I love you, you know,' Morgan said and blew him a kiss.

It was 7 p.m., closing time. When she'd arrived, an hour ago, the shop had been hopping – all the young professional fiancées, busy during the week, had only Saturday and Sunday to select and tailor the dress of a lifetime. Now it was empty except for the two of them, and the tailor in the back.

Frank helped her off the platform where she'd been standing for the final pinning.

As she climbed down, she took one last look in the mirror. And happened to glance at the reflection not of herself but of the front window, opening onto busy Madison Avenue. There was, as always, street traffic on Madison: at the moment, folks headed to dinner, or returning home from a Sunday of shopping, plays, movies and early suppers.

What took Morgan's attention, though, was a man looking into the window.

She couldn't see his face clearly; there wasn't much light on the street any longer and he was backlit from headlights and a streetlamp.

Odd, a man in a dark jacket and stocking cap staring at a window full of wedding dresses.

He moved on. Probably the father of a newly engaged girl, pausing to gaze somberly at yet another expense confronting him after John or Keith or Robert had decided to do the honorable thing.

A few minutes later she was out of the changing room, back in the fatty jeans, which were so delightfully loose around her hips. T-shirt. A reindeer sweater because she was in one of those moods. Judith soon-to-be-Whelan was nothing if not playful. She rolled a scarf around her neck, then pulled on her black cotton jacket and donned supple leather gloves.

She said goodbye to Frank, who was shutting out the lights.

Stepping outside, she turned north toward her apartment.

Thinking about the dress, about the honeymoon. Atlantis in the Bahamas.

Making love while listening to the ocean. Something they'd never done. Ditto, eating conch fritters. Which Morgan knew they served in the Bahamas. She always did her homework.

She stopped at the corner deli, got a bottle of Pinot Grigio and hit the salad bar, throwing into a plastic container lettuce, tomatoes and 'fixens' (she'd once heard a customer gripe about the misspelling but, she'd thought: I'm sorry, is there any confusion? And besides, how much Korean do you speak?).

Then back onto the street and to her building. Yes, it was the Upper East Side, but that included a lot of territory that was not Trump-worthy. Her brownstone was a fourth-floor walk-up, in sore need of a power washing and paint job.

She walked to the lobby door and was just unlocking it and stepping in when she heard a rush of footsteps behind her. The man in dark clothing, the same man outside of Frank's – now with his head encased in a ski mask – pushed her inside.

Her barked scream was silenced by the hand over her mouth. He walked her fast down the corridor to an alcove underneath the stairs, where she and the tenant from the third floor kept their bikes. He swept the bikes aside and shoved her to the floor, a sitting position. He ripped her purse from her shoulder, the deli bag from her hand.

She stared at the pistol.

'Please . . . ' Her voice was quaking.

'Shhh.'

He was, it seemed, listening for voices or footsteps. All was silent – except for the frantic pounding of Morgan's heart, the raw gasp of her labored breathing.

He put the gun back in his pocket and then righted the bikes and leaned them upright against the wall so that anyone looking through the door wouldn't see them on their sides and think something was wrong. Her leg protruded into the hall and he kicked it – gently – back under the stairs, so the limb wasn't visible either. Then he crouched in front of her.

'What do you want? Please . . . just take whatever you want.'

'Gloves,' he snapped.

'You want my gloves.'

He laughed, sarcastically. Then grew angry. 'Why I would want fucking gloves? I want you to take fucking gloves *off*.'

She did. And as he looked at her left hand she curled her right into a fist and slammed it into his jaw. 'You fucker!' She hit him again, aiming low and missing the crotch by a few inches.

He blinked in surprise, not pain. His blue eyes were amused.

Morgan drew her arm back once more but his blow landed first – also to the jaw – and snapped her head into the wall. Her vision grew black and fuzzy for a moment. Then the focus returned.

'No good, lovebird hen.' Crouching over her, he gripped her hair, pulled her close. She smelled cigarette smoke and onions. Doused aftershave. Liquor. It took all her will not to vomit. Then thought maybe that would turn him off and tried to retch.

He shook her by the hair again, fiercely. A whisper: 'No, no, no. No doing that. Okay?'

Morgan nodded. She was aware his eyes weren't scanning her torso as she'd thought they would. His only interest was her fingers. Actually, just the ring finger.

That's what he wanted. And it was clear to her now. Of course. A girl in a fancy Upper East Side bridal boutique. She'd be engaged . . . and she'd be wearing one hell of a rock.

Which she was.

Sean worked for Harper Stanley, on the foreign desk. His dad was a founder of Marsh and Royal, a big hedge fund. His mom was a partner at Logan, Sharp and Towne, a Wall Street law firm.

The ring on her finger had cost forty-two thousand dollars. It was anchored by a five-carat brilliant-cut diamond, with a one-carat marquis on either side.

'Take it,' she whispered.

His eyes flicked to hers. 'Take what? Your virginity? Ha, that is joke. You smell to me like campus slut. How many men before your fiancé?'

She blinked. 'I—'

'Does he know?' He then frowned. 'Or you mean take purse, your credit cards? Hm, hm.' Feigning surprise, he said, 'Oh, oh, my, you meaning your ring. That piece of stone on sad stub of finger. Does your fiancé like your hands? What's his name?'

Crying now, Morgan said, 'I am not telling you.'

The knife – one of those with the sliding blade – appeared. She screamed, until he brandished it and she fell silent.

The assailant looked at the front door. Listened again. No response. In fact, the building was two-thirds empty at the moment. One couple was on vacation. The gay guy was spending the weekend with his friends in the Hamptons. Two units were unrented.

Morgan was sure that Mr and Mrs Kieslowski were in for the night, chewing down Chinese and bingeing on *Game of Thrones*. They'd be of no help.

She stared at the blade.

He's not getting Sean's name, she told herself, though also thinking that if he paid Sean a visit her fiancé would wipe up the pavement with this guy. Sean worked out five times a week.

But the man seemed to lose interest in her love life, so intensely was he drawn to the ring. With a grip she had no strength to resist he pulled her hand close to his face.

'How many carats, they tell you? Four and a half?'

She was shivering in terror. The fuck was this all about?

'How many fucking carats?' he raged softly.

'Five.'

Shaking his head. 'And how much of it they kill?'

She frowned.

'How much they cut off of stone to make *thing* on finger of yours?'

'I . . . I don't know what you mean. I can get you money. A lot of money. A hundred thousand. Do you want a hundred thousand dollars? No questions asked.'

He wasn't even listening. 'You are happy, slicing diamond up?'

'Please?'

'Shhhh, little hen. Look at you. Cryee little thing.' Then he pushed her away and said, 'You were crying when boyfriend bought raped diamond? No crying then. Huh?'

He was fucking insane . . . Oh, God, now she understood. With a sinking heart, she realized this was him, the Promisor. The man who hated engaged couples. He'd killed the couple in the Diamond District on Saturday. And he'd attacked two more. And now she knew why. For some psychotic reason he was protecting diamonds.

For a moment, anger gripped her. She muttered, 'You sick fuck.'

The grip on her hair tightened, pain swelling from her scalp. He pressed the knife against her neck. Judith Morgan went limp, surrendering to tears. She closed her eyes and began reciting a silent prayer, looping and looping through her thoughts. He leaned close, his forehead against hers. 'Lovebird, lovebird . . . I am loving that part of vow, you know. Till death do you part.'

He pressed the knife against her throat.

Oh, Mommy . . .

Then he paused and a faint laugh slipped from his foul-smelling mouth. The blade drooped 'Have fun idea. Better than cutting . . . Yes, I am liking this. You treat diamond like shit. Okay, swallow it. That where it end up.'

'What?' she whispered.

He grimaced. 'Put fucking ring in mouth and swallow it.'

'But I can't.'

'Then, die.' He shrugged again and the knife rose to her throat.

'No, no, no! I will. I'll swallow it. I'll do it!'

She worked the ring off her finger and gazed down at it. What would happen? Lodge in her windpipe and she'd choke to death? Or if it got down her esophagus would the sharp edges cut the delicate tissue? Could she bleed to death internally?

'Or knife on throat,' he offered cheerfully. 'I am not much caring. Choose. But now.'

With a trembling hand, she lifted the ring to her face. The piece seemed huge.

She felt the knife against her neck.

'Okay, okay.'

Quickly she dropped the jewelry into her mouth. She gagged once and the ring nearly fell out but she pushed it to the back of her throat and swallowed hard.

Waves of pain stabbed her chest, neck and head as she worked the muscles over and over and over to get the damn thing down. Tears streamed. The ring made it past her windpipe – she could breathe all right – but then lodged in her esophagus, the sharp sides of the small diamonds slitting the skin. Blood cascaded. She tasted it, and, as some flowed into her windpipe and lungs, her violent coughing fired red droplets from her mouth.

Rasping screams now.

He remained amused. 'Ah, little one. You see how it goes. You fuck stone, stone fucks you.'

Judith Morgan was thrashing against the pain and the sensation of drowning – in her own blood. She gripped her throat with both hands, trying to manipulate the ring up and out. It wasn't going anywhere and the pain only increased. Without a plan, on autopilot, she struggled to her feet then lunged for her purse. He lifted it away and opened it, then removed her cell phone and smashed it on the tile floor. He gave a laugh and strode nonchalantly down the corridor and left by the front door.

Coughing fiercely, consumed by pain from chest to temple, Judith Morgan struggled down the corridor and then up the stairs, heading for the Kieslowski apartment on the second floor.

Praying they had not gone out but were, as she'd speculated, sitting on their lumpy sofa in front of the TV, with takeout, catching up on current events with *60 Minutes* or engrossed in the twisted plottings of the House Lannister and the House Stark.

CHAPTER 28

Another attack.

At eight p.m. Rhyme was listening to a detective from the 19, on the Upper East Side.

'Yessir, Captain,' the man told him. 'That same perp's been in the news. Vic's okay, she'll live. But – can you believe this one? – he made her swallow her engagement ring. She's in surgery now.'

'Scene's secure?'

'Yessir. We've called the CS bus from Queens but since you're the task force on this one, thought you might want to send one of your people.'

'We will. Have the techs wait outside the scene.'

Rhyme memorized it. 'Canvass?' he then asked.

'Five blocks all around. And counting. Nothing. And best the vic could say was white male, blue eyes, ski mask, knife and handgun. Or she nodded in response to my questions. Weird accent she couldn't figure out. All I could get. We only had a few minutes 'fore they got her to the hospital.'

Rhyme thanked him. Then he disconnected and called Ron Pulaski.

'Lincoln.'

'We've got another scene. Upper East Side.'

'I heard some squawk on the radio. Was it our boy?'

'Yep.'

'The vic's okay, I heard.'

'Alive. I don't know about okay.' What did swallowing a sharp piece of jewelry do to you? Rhyme gave the younger officer the address. 'The bus is on its way. I need you to walk the grid and get back here with whatever you can find ASAP. There'll be uniforms and a detective from the One-Nine there. Find out what hospital the vic's in and interview her. And take a pad and pen for the vic to write with. She can't talk.'

'She . . . what?'

'Move, Rookie.'

They disconnected.

The doorbell to the town house sounded and Thom answered it, returning a moment later with the insurance investigator Edward Ackroyd, who nodded, almost formally, to Rhyme and Cooper.

The aide took the man's greatcoat – no, Rhyme thought, changing his opinion of the garment once more. It should be called a mackintosh.

'Another cappuccino?' Thom asked.

'Don't mind if I do, actually.'

'No, no, no,' Rhyme said fast. 'A single-malt.'

'Well . . . now that you mention it, I will do. Save the coffee for another time.'

Thom poured the drinks, pitifully small. Both Rhyme and Ackroyd added just a hint of water to the glass.

'Glenmorangie,' Ackroyd said, after sipping. He pronounced it correctly, emphasis on the second syllable. He held up the glass and eyed the amber liquid as if in a commercial. 'Highlands. You know there *is* a difference in taste between lowland whisky and highland, subtle and I'm not sure I could detect it. However, there are many more highland distilleries than low. Do you know why?'

'No idea.'

'It's not because of the peat or the process but because the Scottish distilleries kept moving north to escape the English excise tax. Or that's what I've heard.'

Rhyme tucked the trivia away, tilted the glass toward the Englishman and sipped the smoky liquor.

Ackroyd took a seat, with that perfect posture of his, in one of the wicker chairs not far from Rhyme.

He told the Brit about the new attack.

'No! Swallowed her engagement ring? Good heavens. How is she?'

'We don't know yet.'

'And payback for buying a cut stone. My, this man's barking mad.' His face seemed bewildered. Then he added, 'Now, let me tell you a few things I've found. I did hear back from my friend in Amsterdam. You recall?'

The dealer who'd received a call from an anonymous number about selling some rough. A nod.

'The seller in New York, with the fifteen carats? He called Willem back. He's legitimate. A diamond broker from Jerusalem. He was in New York and bought a phone at the airport. Didn't want to use the minutes on his personal phone. So, dead end there. Now, I've talked to scores of diamantaires and nobody has heard any inkling of selling the Grace-Cabot rough or rumors of a major underground cut going on. It's absurd but I suppose he really must believe he's saving the stone from the dire fate of being cut into jewelry.

'But, more to the point: About an hour ago I was making calls to dealers and some other people I know, asking about Patel's assistant? Well, one of them, in Brooklyn, told me that it was curious: Someone *else* had called him earlier today, asking about an associate or assistant who worked for Patel. Initials VL. The dealer couldn't help him and they hung up.'

Rhyme lowered his scotch and looked Ackroyd's way. 'He didn't identify himself, of course.'

'No. And, naturally, it was from a blocked number. But here's the important news: The dealer is Russian, and he recognized the caller's accent. He's Russian too. And almost certainly born there and learned English at school in Russia. He worked that out from some of the constructions and choices of words. Probably a Muscovite, or nearby. And he's come here recently. He didn't know the word "borough" or that Brooklyn and Queens were part of New York City. He thought the city was only Manhattan.'

'Helpful,' Rhyme said. And he had a thought of how to best use the information. An idea occurred. He typed out a text and sent it on its way.

The reply arrived almost immediately, proposing a time for a phone call.

Rhyme texted, *K*, and then said to Cooper, 'Mel, write up what Edward found, on the boards, could you?'

Cooper walked to the evidence board and added the new information about Unsub 47 to the list.

A phone hummed and Rhyme watched Ackroyd as he looked at the screen of his iPhone and frowned. Then he typed something in response. There was apparently another exchange. His frown deepened. He looked off, thoughtfully.

The Englishman was aware of Rhyme's gaze and smiled. 'Not about the case. Bit silly, this. Back in London, I'm on a competitive crossword puzzle team. Have you ever done them?'

Seemed like an utter waste of time but Rhyme said only, 'No.'

Ackroyd walked close and held the mobile for Rhyme to see. A look at the screen revealed the familiar grid. Some of the blanks were filled in.

'My husband and I . . . ' A moment's hesitation, then continuing: 'He's on the faculty at Oxford. He and I and two other professors, from Cambridge, are on the team. We're the Oxbridge Four. Silly, I was saying. But Terrance – that's my husband – thinks a puzzle helps you stay on your game. His father was a die-hard fan. He did one a day – often the diagramless ones: without the black square telling where the words start and stop. Terrance's convinced that they kept his dad sharp till the day he died.'

'You competing now?' Rhyme nodded to the phone.

'Oh, no, we'll have to wait on the tournaments until I'm back home. They're held in proper venues. Like chess matches. Supervised. So there'll be no cheating: dictionaries, the Internet. There've been scandals, I will tell you. Quite the controversies.' He regarded the screen. 'This's just a way for us to stay in touch. We compete mostly with cryptic crosswords. You familiar?'

'Not really.'

That is, not at all.

'They're largely a British creation and have appeared in our newspapers for hundreds of years. The creators – we call them "setters" in cryptic crosswords – have a nearly mythical status. They go by one-word pseudonyms like Scorpion or Nestor –

two quite famous ones, by the way. The *most* famous and the one who wrote the rules on cryptics is Derrick Somerset Macnutt, who went by Ximenes.

'Let me explain how they work – you might enjoy this, Lincoln. Cryptics have a grid, similar to regular crosswords, but the clues are word puzzles you have to solve to get the answer, as opposed to just a straightforward clue like "Wife of George the Third." The best setters create clues that are both bloody complicated and absurdly simple.'

Ackroyd's enthusiasm radiated from his otherwise staid face.

'Now, the clue's a puzzle, remember. It contains a definition of the answer and other words or phrases to guide you, including letting you know what kind of puzzle it is: Maybe you have to solve an anagram, find a hidden or reversed word, work out what sound-alike words – homophones – mean.' He laughed. 'I'm sure this makes no sense. Let me give you an example. Here's a classic from the *Guardian* a few years ago, created by a setter named Shed. I'll write it down because it's much easier to find the answer by seeing, rather than hearing.'

Ackroyd jotted:

Very sad unfinished story about rising smoke (8)

'Now, the answer will appear on the crossword grid at fifteen down. All right? Good. Let's get to work. What are we trying to find? See the number eight? That means the answer is an eight-letter word. And the first two words in the clue are the definition of that answer. So, what we need to write on the crossword grid at fifteen down is an eight-letter word meaning "very sad."'

Rhyme had slipped his impatience away and was paying attention. Mel Cooper too had turned and was listening.

Ackroyd continued, 'The next word, "unfinished," modifies the word after it. "Unfinished story." With cryptics you're always mistrusting the literal. If the setter says "story," he means something else, possibly a *synonym* for "story."' Ackroyd smiled again. 'Obviously, I know the answer so I'm short-circuiting the process a bit. I'll pick the synonym "tale." And "unfinished" means the last letter is missing. That gives us the letters "T-A-L." So part of the answer for the clue "very sad" are those letters. You with me?'

'Yes,' Rhyme said, his mind already trying to process the remaining clues.

Cooper said uncertainly, 'Uhm, keep going.'

'Let's go to the last words in the clue, "rising smoke." That could be any number of things but – trial and error again, and given my foreknowledge – let's settle on "cigar." And since this clue is fifteen down, that means "rising" would find the word written backwards: "ragic." So another part of our answer is the letters "R-A-G-I-C." Finally—'

Rhyme blurted, 'The word "about" means that the letters in one of the clues would be split and put on either side of another clue.'

Cooper said, 'If you say so.'

Ackroyd said, with a grin, 'No, no, he's onto it. Brilliant, Lincoln. What're your thoughts?'

'It's obvious: split T-A-L. Put the T before R-A-G-I-C and the A-L after. The answer's "tragical."'

'Congratulations!' Ackroyd said, beaming. 'You've never done this before?'

'No.'

The Englishman offered, 'Some people think it's a waste of time.'

Rhyme tried not to smile.

'But I hardly agree. You know the Enigma machine?'

Cooper answered, 'Yes, the code device that the mathematicians at Bletchley Park cracked. Alan Turing and crew.'

This sounded somewhat familiar but unless information helped with a present, or future, investigation Rhyme tended not to keep it in storage.

Apparently his blank expression showed. The tech said, 'Nazi encryption device during World War Two. The Allies couldn't crack German messages and tens of thousands of soldiers and civilians died.'

Ackroyd said, 'In January nineteen forty-two, the *Daily*

Telegraph had a speed cryptic competition – you had to complete a very complicated puzzle in twelve minutes or under. They published the results, and the War Office took notice. It recruited some of the best competitors to come to Bletchley Park and they helped crack Enigma.' He added, 'One thing I love about cryptic puzzles: They can lie and be completely honest at the same time. It's all about misdirection. Up for one more?'

'Yes,' Rhyme said.

Ackroyd wrote:

Location in Romania rich in oil (4)

Cooper turned back to his equipment. 'Think I'll stick to Sudoku.'

Rhyme stared for a moment. 'A four-letter word that's a location.'

Romania was a nation of which he knew nothing. 'There're thousands of towns and regions and parks in Romania. And someplace rich in oil. Maybe not oil wells. Maybe ports for shipping oil. Maybe banks that specialize in oil industry lending.' He shook his head.

'Remember,' Ackroyd said, 'in cryptic puzzles, you're often looking right at the answer. The problem is that you're not *seeing* it.'

But then he did. Rhyme laughed. 'Yes, the answer is a location in Romania – but not the country. It's in "Romania," the word. The answer's "Oman": r-O-M-A-N-i-a. The Middle Eastern country with oil reserves.'

'Well done, Lincoln.'

Pleased with himself, he had to admit.

Rhyme noticed motion on the front-door monitor and observed Sachs climbing stairs and pulling her keys from her bag. She'd returned from the jobsite where Unsub 47 had, possibly, met with a worker for reasons as yet undetermined.

The time for diversion was over.

CHAPTER **29**

Rhyme regarded Amelia Sachs carefully as she entered.

Hair damp – she'd taken a shower; the skies were gray but there'd been no rain.

I want to clean up first . . .

Her eyes were distant. Her thumb worried a finger, then the digits swapped roles. He could see a bloody cuticle.

She nodded a greeting to Ackroyd, who smiled his modest smile in return.

Rhyme told her, 'Another one. You hear?'

Sachs asked quickly, 'Earthquake?'

'What? No, attack.'

'The Promisor?'

He nodded. And observed that she seemed oddly distracted. Even troubled. He wondered too why it had taken her so damn long to get here.

But he said nothing about it. 'Vic'll live. Made her swallow her ring.'

'Jesus. How is she?'

'I don't know. Ron's walking the grid and getting details. He'll do an interview when she's out of surgery. The shield I talked to at the One-Nine asked a few questions. Didn't add anything – same story you heard: protecting diamonds. And the canvass in the neighborhood didn't turn up anyone. They're still at it.'

Rhyme glanced to Edward Ackroyd, who told her what he'd found – the Amsterdam dealer lead had not paid off but it was likely that the unsub was Russian and probably had come only recently to the city.

Sachs looked thoughtful. 'So, with the kids in Gravesend, he was trying to obscure the accent. Russian. Is that helpful?'

'I'm following it up,' Rhyme said, thinking of the text he'd sent.

Sachs grimaced. 'I've never known a perp to be so damn persistent about taking out witnesses. Hell. Have we had *any* luck finding the boy?'

'Ron hasn't. Like with Edward, nobody's talking to him. Computer Crimes is pulling Patel's phone records. Let's hope Patel and VL talked regularly.' Rhyme's eyes swayed to Sachs. 'So, what happened at the jobsite?'

Sachs blinked. 'Happened?'

'Yeah. What was Forty-Seven doing there?'

'Oh.' She told them he probably hadn't used the site as a shortcut. Yes, there were lots of CCTV cameras on the government building side of the construction area but the limited entrances to the site suggests the shortcut theory was unlikely.

Then she explained about her conversation with the foreman of the geothermal operation. She said that, yes, the unsub had been in the construction site and had met with somebody, identity unknown, for reasons unknown. She could get no better description than what they already had. 'The scene wasn't good – gravel and lots of contamination. Found this.' She handed over two small bags of earth and stones to Mel Cooper. 'It's probably from where he was standing but I don't know for sure.'

The tech took the bags and got to work examining what had been uncovered.

Rhyme noticed that her eyes remained distant, her posture tense. She tugged at her hair, then dug the index finger of her right hand into the thumb of that hand once more. An old habit. She tried to control the self-harm. Sometimes she didn't care. Amelia Sachs lived on the edge, in many senses.

He noticed her hand drop to her knee. She winced.

'Sachs?' Rhyme asked.

'I fell. That's all. Nothing.'

No, it wasn't nothing. Whatever had happened had shaken her. And now she had a brief coughing fit. Cleared her throat. He felt an urge to ask if she was okay but she didn't like that question any more than he did.

Rhyme said, 'Any indication Forty-Seven was picking up that new weapon of his?'

'No, but I didn't get very far. We'll have to keep canvassing.' She turned to Cooper. 'Speaking of the weapon: ballistics?'

He explained that the gun used at Gravesend was a .38 special. Probably the Smittie 36 or the Colt Detective. Both, classic snub-nose. Five rounds. Not very accurate and punishing on the shooting hand. But at close range as wicked as any other firearm.

Cooper added, 'And I heard from the evidence collection techs out of Queens. No sign of the Glock – or anything else – in the storm drains or Dumpsters near Saul Weintraub's.'

Sachs shrugged. 'I was going back to the construction site tomorrow to keep up the canvassing but there's a problem. I met a state inspector down there. Works for the Division of Mineral Resources. He said the city's shutting down construction at the geothermal site until they can see if the drilling's caused the earthquake.'

Ackroyd said, 'Oh, it's a geothermal plant they're building?'

'Right.'

'How deep?'

'I think five, six hundred feet.'

'Yes, I'd guess that could do it. My company used to insure against damage from fracking and high-pressure water mining. Those've definitely caused earthquakes and undermined buildings and homes. But we gave up issuing policies. It was costing us too much. And I have heard of geothermal drilling leading to earthquakes too. In one case a school was destroyed in a fire from a broken gas line. Another one, two workers were buried alive.'

Sachs once more dug an index nail into the thumb cuticle. Deep. The flesh went pink. Rhyme believed he now understood what had happened at the geothermal site.

She continued, 'Northeast is appealing the shutdown but until that's resolved, there won't be any workers on-site. We'll have to interview them at home.'

'How many?'

'About ninety. I told Lon. He'll recruit uniforms. Pain in the ass. But there's no other way.'

Cooper looked up from a computer monitor. 'Got the results from the construction site, Amelia. Same mineral trace as at Patel's and Weintraub's, so he was definitely there. But nothing new, other than diesel fuel. And mud. Was there a lot of mud down there?'

A pause. 'Some. Yeah.'

'Nothing else.'

The door buzzer sounded and Thom let Ron Pulaski into the parlor.

The young officer nodded to those present and introduced himself to Edward Ackroyd; the two had never met. The young officer then handed off to Mel Cooper the evidence bags he'd collected on the Judith Morgan assault on the Upper East Side. The tech got to work, as Pulaski explained to the others what had happened in the latest Promisor assault. Morgan, twenty-six, had been in a bridal boutique, getting some final adjustments to her wedding dress. A man who'd been outside the shop followed her to her apartment and forced her into an alcove on the ground floor.

'He was rambling on and on about how she'd ruined a beautiful diamond by cutting it into a ring. He was going to kill her, she thought. Or cut her ring finger off. But then he changed his mind. He told her that since she'd treated the ring like shit, that's where it was going to end up.'

Sachs asked, 'Did he say anything that'd give us a clue where he lives? Works?'

'No. But she said she could smell aftershave, alcohol, cigarette smoke residue, very foul. And onions. He has blue eyes.'

Sachs said, 'Same as earlier.'

'And that he was foreign but she couldn't tell his accent.'

Rhyme told Pulaski they were pretty sure he was Russian and new to the city.

'She thinks the gun was a revolver – I showed her pictures. And the utility knife was gray metal. That's about it.'

Sachs wrote these finds up on the chart.

Cooper returned to give them the results of the Judith Morgan crime scene search. 'Not much. Too many footprints to find anything more about his shoes. Some black cotton fibers – ski mask, I'd guess. General trace but all typical of that neighborhood. No kimberlite this time.'

Sachs sat down in a wicker chair. She tapped her knee with an index finger, as if she were testing a melon. She was staring at the TV screen. The news was on. Though the set was muted, the closed captioning was telling the story in its own form of clumsy English.

That story was about the earthquake.

Sachs was frowning, Rhyme noted, and she whispered, 'Oh, no.'

He turned his full attention to the story. The anchor was announcing that one of the two fires believed to have started when the tremor snapped gas lines had taken two lives.

A couple in their sixties, Arnold and Ruth Phillips, residents of Brooklyn, had died of smoke inhalation. They had escaped the flames and made it to the garage but there was no electricity in the house to power the opener. Weakened by the smoke and injuries, they couldn't lift the door themselves.

Soon two talking heads were on the split screen, along with a dark-haired male anchor. One of the guests was a middle-aged man in a dark-blue suit, white shirt and red tie. He was a bit pudgy and his head was crowned with trim black hair. He was Dennis Dwyer, the CEO of Northeast Geo Industries, the company building the plant.

The other interviewee was a twitchy disheveled man in his midfifties. He wore a blue work shirt with sleeves rolled up. His gray hair and beard were wild. He was Ezekiel Shapiro. The type on the screen identified him as *Director of the One Earth movement.*

'I saw him down there today,' Sachs said. 'They've been harassing the workers. He's a bit of a – ' She turned to Ackroyd. 'What did you say? Crazy guy?'

'Nutter.'

'Good word.'

The two men on-screen were engaged in a fierce verbal duel. The wide-eyed and broadly gesticulating Shapiro was positive that the earthquake had resulted from the geothermal drilling. And apart from gas line breakage and the risk of buildings collapsing from quakes during construction, the finished plant could lead to groundwater pollution and other environmental risks. He praised the city for stopping the drilling but criticized the mayor and city council for allowing the project in the first place.

Dwyer, much calmer, said the ban was a huge mistake, asserting that drilling could not cause earthquakes. The New York area was far more seismologically stable than most parts of the country, certainly nothing like California. And Shapiro was misinformed about the geothermal process if he thought there was a risk of contaminating groundwater; the system was self-contained, and even a crack in a pipe would result only in a release of inert solution. Shapiro countered that the technology was still unknown.

The anchor added gasoline to the discussion by inviting a third interviewee. He was an even more perfectly assembled businessman than Dwyer. His name was C. Hanson Collier and he was the CEO of Algonquin Consolidated Power – the big electricity provider in the New York area. You would think he'd be against the geothermal project – it seemed to make Northeast Geo a competitor to Algonquin. But Collier was pro. He was saying that near-surface drilling, like Northeast's Brooklyn project, was far safer than deep drilling in volcanic regions to tap steam and high-temperature reserves for the generation of electricity. 'We have to embrace all forms of energy the earth provides,' he said.

As the debate grew increasingly testy and, to Rhyme, uninteresting, the image on the screen switched to the Northeast Geo construction site in Brooklyn, depicting a number of green-fenced rectangular pens. Apparently these were where the shafts were located.

Sachs took one look and rose. 'I'd better go. I need to check on Mom.'

Rose Sachs, who'd had heart surgery recently, was doing fine. Rhyme knew this for a fact since he and the funny, and feisty, woman had had a conversation just a few hours ago. Her reluctance at her daughter's dating a disabled man had faded years ago and she and Rhyme had become good friends. He couldn't ask for a better mother-in-law.

But there was more. Rhyme knew that while Sachs might end up at her mother's house – it was in Brooklyn – she would first take to the road. She was going to jump into her Torino and find an appropriate roadway, out in the burbs, to muscle the car up to eighty or ninety.

This would be in an effort to shed whatever still clung to her from the crime scene. What the shower had not been able to remove: the gut-clenching horror she'd undoubtedly experienced.

If anything could distract her, it was the act of downshifting out of a hairpin, fourth to second, then skidding onto a straight-away and urging the screaming engine to push the needle of the speedometer into three digits.

Rhyme knew and accepted without qualification that she was a risk taker. But speed was a diversion, not a remedy.

'Sachs?' he asked. And he said this in a certain tone, rare for him. She would understand: It was an invitation to talk to him about what had happened at the site. He wasn't going to offer advice, probably not even solace. Just give her a chance to talk.

But the invitation was declined.

Amelia Sachs said only, 'Night. See you in the morning.' She said this to everybody.

Pulaski and Cooper left. Ackroyd pulled his raincoat on. He was hesitating to leave, Rhyme noted.

In a soft voice, the Brit said, 'It's hardly my business. But . . . is she all right?'

'Not really,' Rhyme said. 'She has some issues.' His face wrinkled. 'If that isn't the most useless of assessments. Amelia needs to move, to be free, all the time. I think she was in a cave-in, or got trapped. Wouldn't be a firefight, wouldn't be a pursuit, sniper. Anything like that. She lives for moments like those. But being trapped, caught, not moving: that's hell.'

'I could see her eyes. It must've been bad.'

'I think it was.'

'She'll tell you about it, sooner or later.'

'Probably not. And I know because we're similar that way.'

He gave a smile as he realized he was sharing more of himself than usual. 'A magnet. Opposites attract? Well, in most ways, we're opposite. This, keeping things inside? We're the same pole.'

Ackroyd laughed. 'Just like a scientist to couch matters of the heart in terms of electrical polarity . . . Well, if there's anything I can do, please, let me know.'

'Thank you, Edward.'

The man nodded and left the town house. Soon Thom appeared and said, 'And time for bed for you, Lincoln. Late.'

Exertion and fatigue could adversely affect someone with quadriplegia, a condition where stress can sometimes play havoc with blood pressure.

Still, he had one more task tonight.

'Five minutes,' he told Thom, who began to protest. Then Rhyme said, 'Barry Sales.'

The aide dipped his head. 'Sure. I'll get things ready upstairs.'

Rhyme instructed the phone to dial Sales. He'd been discharged from the hospital and was now at home. Rhyme had a brief conversation with his wife, Joan, who then put Sales on the line. They started chatting immediately and Rhyme supposed that an observer would have been surprised, to put it mildly, to see the criminalist this loquacious. He wasn't taciturn but he typically had no time for idle conversation.

Tonight, though, idle conversation was the game. His and Sales's words ranged far and wide. He'd called the rehab specialist Thom had recommended. They hadn't met yet, but Sales would update Rhyme about the appointment afterward.

Rhyme had to report to Sales that his intelligence revealed that the trial of the man who'd allegedly shot him was moving slowly. Clever lawyering, technicalities, bullying witnesses.

After they disconnected, Rhyme turned briefly to the evidence charts and memorized some of the more enigmatic entries. When this was done he swung around and followed Thom to the elevator. In bed he would use the netherworld, between deciding to sleep and succumbing, to wrestle a little longer with the knottier issues presented by the investigation.

Smiling to himself, he thought suddenly of a line that seemed to define the clues in the Unsub 47 case, words that Edward Ackroyd had spoken earlier, about cryptic crossword puzzles.

They can lie and be completely honest at the same time . . .

CHAPTER **30**

Listening to the raucous sound from his son's workroom – the grinding tools shaping the sculpted stone – Deepro Lahori slipped downstairs.

He stood in the hallway outside the studio, in the basement.

It was late – bedtime – but the boy continued to grind away. They had ended their conversation on a somewhat positive note earlier in the evening. But Vimal was, of course, now being passive aggressive – the grinder shouting a message of defiance to his father.

How foolish, this sculpture nonsense. What a waste of time. And of his talent. If it were only a hobby, fine. In fact, sculpting might enhance his son's skill as a cutter. Better than video games, better than dating girls. But he knew Vimal wanted a career as an artist. Stupid boy. Lahori guessed the percentage of professional artists who made enough money to live on probably hovered around 1 percent. How could he get an Indian woman for a wife, someone who wanted to be taken care of, someone who would show respect only to a man who provided for her?

Apart from the impracticality of devoting his life to sculpture, the truly troubling, truly painful, aspect of his son's behavior was the insulting rejection of his father's – and the Lahori family's – history in the diamond-cutting business. This was a sin, for Vimal was the only one in the family to carry on that tradition. Sunny would have gone into the business – but he had no talent on the scaife; he was embarrassing to watch. Yes, he would be following his mother into health care (though he would be a doctor, of course, not a mere nurse, like Divya). But that was a *maternal* tradition. Lahori needed a son to follow in *his* footsteps.

Downstairs, he approached the door of the studio, pausing as the grinder went silent.

Was he finished for the night?

No, the clatter started up again. Which meant Vimal couldn't hear what was coming next. Lahori took a key from his pocket in a trembling hand and, after some effort, locked the door to the studio. He then placed a security bar, which ran at a forty-five-degree angle; from an indentation above the doorknob to a similar hole in the floor. He affixed this too with a key lock. The bar was three-quarter-inch tempered steel, and the manufacturer assured the world, in its advertising, that only a cutting flame of two thousand degrees Celsius would slice through it. (Though, of course, a flexible disk saw embedded with diamonds would do the trick too, he thought. Just for the record.)

Vimal was now in prison. The door was sealed – and, because this had been a diamond workshop years ago, the low window was barred with thick iron rods.

Lahori congratulated himself silently for the ruse of putting his son at ease, agreeing to some 'compromise.' Had Vimal been the least suspicious that he'd be locked up here, he never would have gone into the room. The insubordinate boy would have sprinted out the door in an instant and been gone, no matter that he had no money and no ID.

Going to California? A state whose only claim to fame, in Lahori's opinion, was the billions of dollars in diamond sales from stores like the ones on Rodeo Drive?

He slipped the keys into his pocket.

What a child Vimal was! He could have been one of the greatest diamantaires of the twenty-first century . . . why, look at the parallelogram cut! Genius, pure genius.

Deepro Lahori had no particular plan, other than to keep Vimal here, locked downstairs, for the next month or so. He was sure the police would catch the killer and the boy would come to his senses. It would be the horror of the robbery, getting shot at, and seeing his mentor die that had upset him so, had unbalanced him. He was, Lahori decided, temporarily insane. A month in captivity would also get his mind off any non-Hindu girls he was vulnerable to.

A touch of guilt. But Lahori reminded himself he was hardly

inhumane, certainly not with his son, whom he loved deeply, of course. The boy would find a comfortable sleeping bag in the closet, along with plenty of food and snacks and water and soft drinks. He suspected his son drank so he'd included some lite beer. There was a TV. No Internet or phone of course. The boy might grow even more unstable and call a friend to come break him out. Or the police, claiming he'd been kidnapped.

There would be some tension between them, because of what Lahori had done. But sooner or later the boy would come to understand that his father knew what was right for him. He would thank him, though Lahori honestly did not want thanks, or even an acknowledgment that he was right. He simply wanted the boy to come to the realization that this was the life he was destined for . . . and to embrace it.

He gripped the bar against the door and tried to shake it. The rod didn't move a millimeter.

He was satisfied. And at last more or less happy . . . after these past few days, when events had tried him so sorely. And unfairly.

He climbed the stairs.

Deepro Lahori was in the mood for that game of Scrabble, and he knew his wife and his other son – his *good* son – would indulge him.

III
SAWING

MONDAY, MARCH 15

CHAPTER 31

Now, where is my *kuritsa*?

Where are you, my little hen?

Aren't you tired of working, aren't you hungry for some curry, some vindaloo shrimp, some basmati rice? And who doesn't love that wonderful raita?

The young man Vladimir Rostov was waiting for was working in a jewelry store that specialized in wedding bands and engagement rings. It was lunchtime and the fucking kid better take a break soon. Rostov had enjoyed his time with the lovebirds – especially the ring swallowing. But now to work. Finding VL and slicing his throat.

That's why he was here in this greasy Irish bar, where he sat on a stool, having a bourbon and studying the building across the street.

Come on, my little *kuritsa* . . . Your Vladimir is getting impatient and you won't like him that way. His knife is sitting heavy in his pocket. The razor blade is lonely.

His Persian, no, Iranian, *kuritsa*, Nashim, had come through for him, and delivered the name of a young man who had worked for Patel a year ago and stayed in touch with the diamond cutter and those who worked for and with him. His first name was Kirtan, and Nashim didn't know his home address but he did know where he worked: the store that Rostov was staring at right now. He had a passing regret that because of the Persian's success, Rostov had no excuse to visit Nashim's plump daughters, Scheherazade and Kitten.

Ah, families, families, families . . .

After his parents had gone their separate ways and fled the suburbs of Moscow, twelve-year-old Vladimir had found himself in Mirny, a town of about twenty thousand, smack in the middle of Siberia. If Hell had been ice, rather than fire, Mirny could be the Underworld.

The village had sprung from the frozen steppes seventy or so years ago when a vast diamond pipe was discovered. *Mir* means 'peace' in Russian. The geologist who found the lode sent a coded message to Moscow that he was about to 'smoke the pipe of peace,' which meant he'd made an amazing find. The town was called Mirny, the mine Mir, and in its heyday it produced two thousand kilos of diamonds a year, 20 percent of them high-quality. Upon its discovery, Mir sent shivers of panic through the staid halls of De Beers, which knew that its output could cause the price of diamonds to plummet. (Still, ever conscious of controlling the market, the Russians manipulated output and bought up reserves – De Beers's included – to keep prices sky-high.) The mine began as an open pit, ultimately seventeen hundred feet deep, and when that was played out the state company began digging tunnels.

It was in these unforgiving shafts that Gregor Rostov insisted his nephew work, when he wasn't studying in high school and, later, the polytechnic college. Gregor claimed he used his 'pull' to get the boy a job, when in reality the mine was begging for workers mad enough to descend into the shafts.

Digging the open pit had been an engineering challenge – jet engines to heat the ground and softened it enough to dig – but tunneling was a nightmare. Workers were often drowned or crushed, stone dust burned out lungs faster than three-pack-a-day smoking habits, chemical fumes destroyed eyes, tongues and noses. Unstable explosives neatly removed other parts of the body.

It was far warmer down there than at the gray, skin-cracking surface, of course. But more important to Vladimir, it was popu-lated only with rock and dust and diamonds – not the crew-cut youths who leered and bullied the outsider from Moscow, the girls who ignored him, the glum aunt and uncle who resented having to share the tiny apartment with the boy.

Because he was younger, he wasn't expected to heft the loads of the adult laborers and was treated as something of a mascot.

He was safe here. With his stone. Working double shifts. Sometimes staying for days at a time. Wandering the shafts.

Once, he was discovered without his pants, which lay in a pile near him in a deserted shaft. A supervisor had made an unexpected visit to the location. As Rostov dressed hastily the man noted what the boy had been up to. He chose not to reprimand him but firmly told him to confine such activities to his bedroom at home; more deviance would not be tolerated.

Vladimir frequently ignored the warning. He just made sure that he would find long-abandoned nooks and rock faces where there was no chance of discovery.

But staying in the mine forever was not an option. He had to surface and return home to the fourth-floor walk-up apartment.

Uncle Gregor . . .

Gone to the stone . . .

He was, by appearances, the meekest of men. A skinny man, as thin as his fiercely strong Belomorkanal cigarettes – the brand named after the infamous White Sea canal dug by gulag prisoners in the 1930s, with more than a hundred thousand perishing during the work. Gregor's angular face was like Vladimir's, protruding brows, broad lips tending toward purple, shoulders bony. His work in the mine involved instruments and clipboards. He had probably never lifted a shovel in his life. Vladimir thought his fingernails were remarkable. They were long and pale and perhaps sharpened. At least, so they seemed; in the games that were played almost nightly in the dim, cluttered apartment, the nails left red, painful trails along Vladimir's spine.

Aunt Ro was the opposite, physically, of her husband. She was as sturdy as the cinder-block building they lived in. When the boy first met her, his impression was of a globe. At five two, she was formidable and, when she wanted something, that desire was all that existed in the universe.

Impatient too. And if Vladimir didn't please her, she too left angry marks – though not with her nails. She would turn her engagement ring around as she laid into him. The diamond, which had come from the Mir mine, occasionally drew blood.

The years passed and at twenty he found himself a supervisor (you found few old men in the mines). After his uncle, and then aunt, died, he lived in the apartment attending school part-time, halfheartedly. He finally attained a degree in geology, barely passing.

His passion for the mine, the sensuous shafts, the warmth, the water, remained as strong as ever, but Rostov the young man had hungers that he doubted could be satisfied in Mirny.

In any event, the decision was made for him. The mine closed, the lodes largely depleted.

Russia was one of the biggest producers of diamonds in the world and he might have found work elsewhere. But, he decided, no. He wanted more.

Hungers . . .

It was around then that Vladimir Rostov came to accept that he wasn't right. The time in the mine, the time on the living room floor – the bed of rocks his uncle and aunt had strewn out for him to lie on . . . All those times had turned him into something as hard as a diamond. And just plain off.

Where to go?

The Chechnyans were misbehaving then. So why not the army?

Being gone to the stone was perfect training.

For the army and for what came later.

The life that had brought him, now, to glorious, fucking America.

Another sip of bourbon in the Irish bar . . .

Come along, Rostov thought angrily.

Then he brightened. Inside the store, Kirtan shook a customer's hand, a farewell gesture, and pulled on his jacket.

Rostov finished his drink – an off brand but not bad, and cheap. He wiped the glass with a napkin to remove his prints. This was a bit paranoid but Vladimir Rostov was still alive and not in prison when, by rights, he should have been jailed or more likely killed long ago.

One fond glance back at the waitress's fine ass, then he was out the door into the cold, damp air. A diesel truck went past, spewing exhaust, reminding of home. No city on earth did exhaust better than Moscow. Beijing maybe, but he'd never been there.

He stayed on this side of the street – too many cameras in the windows of the ancient, ten-story structure, part of whose ground floor was occupied by Kirtan's employer, Midtown Gifts. This, like many jewelry stores and diamond factories, avoided any mention in the name that gems were involved. A practice that, while it made sense for security, made tracking down Mr VL fucking hell.

The building would have had a nice basement – nice and *silent*, that is – but he couldn't have his chat with the *kuritsa* down there because of the cameras, as well as the armed guard in the arcade; there were two other jewelry stores on the first floor and a furrier that sold, wholesale only, mink, chinchilla and fox. The African American guard was fat and looked bored and seemed to be the sort who didn't like wearing – much less using – his pistol, which was an old-style revolver.

His plan was to follow the boy and approach him somewhere deserted. An alley would be good but Manhattan seemed to have no alleys, at least none that he could find. Queens, yes, Brooklyn, yes. But not here. Manhattan had sexy women, cheap liquor, wonderful diamonds and plenty of magnificent shopping districts . . . but no fucking alleys.

He wondered how far he would have to follow the boy before he got him alone. He hoped it was near and he hoped it was soon. If not, he'd have to trail him home, after work. And Rostov was impatient. He needed VL and needed him now. There weren't a lot of other options. None of his other sources had yielded up what he needed. And Nashim had been able to come up with only Kirtan's name.

But it turned out that the round, dark-haired kid didn't go very far. Despite his sub-Asian ethnicity Kirtan didn't opt for curry or tandoori chicken. He walked into a tried-and-true New York City coffee shop. A waitress pointed him to a booth and he sat.

Would this work for him? Rostov was doubtful. Too many people. But he'd check it out. It wasn't the best opportunity. But it was *an* opportunity.

Rostov, who wore the ski mask rolled up into a normal-looking stocking cap, stepped inside the restaurant. He sat at the counter and ordered coffee. Before it came, he rose and went into a back corridor, where the restrooms were located. He went inside, coughed hard for thirty seconds, regarded the paper towel, then pitched it out and returned to the corridor.

He found something else too. An unlocked door, leading to the cellar. He supposed restaurant supplies were stored down there and employees might come down at any minute. Everyone, though, seemed busy in the kitchen.

The only question was: Would the kid pee after lunch?

Nothing to do but wait and see.

He returned to the counter and sipped his coffee while the boy ate his sandwich, examining his phone's screen – maybe texting, or wasting time with Facebook or some kind of nonsense like that. Kirtan signaled for the waitress. Oh, please, don't have dessert.

But, no, he wanted the check. He paid.

Rostov drained his coffee and again used his napkin to inconspicuously wipe the cup. He pushed it aside and the waitress swept the chipped ceramic away. He left her a five.

Well, Kirtan? Bodily functions calling?

Yes, they were! The *kuritsa* pulled on his jacket and walked down the corridor to the restrooms.

This was, yes, a risk. But sometimes your mind clicks and it snaps and you do things a sane man – even a killer – wouldn't do.

Gone to the stone . . .

More often than not his madness worked to his advantage. That should be a lesson for everyone, Rostov sometimes thought.

As the boy walked inside the bathroom Rostov waited in the corridor near the cellar door.

His back was to the men's room. After three or four minutes, he heard the door open and glanced at Kirtan, exiting. The boy said, 'Excuse me, sir,' and Rostov turned, smiling, glanced around to make sure there was no one to see and with a short but fierce blow punched the boy directly in the throat. As he started to drop, Rostov caught him, pulled open the cellar door and shoved him down the rubber-treaded stairs headfirst.

It was a noisy tumble and Rostov turned to see if anyone had heard.

No. People eating, people talking, people examining cell phones.

The Russian slipped inside, onto the top step of the stairs, closed the door behind him and, pulling out the razor knife, started down into the cool, dim cellar.

Sachs was leaving her mother's house, where she'd spent the night – in her childhood bedroom – when her phone trilled.

She dropped into the driver's seat of her Torino and hit Answer. 'Rodney.'

A senior detective in the NYPD's Computer Crimes Unit, Rodney Szarnek was a curious creature. The man, of ambiguous age but probably thirties, loved code, hacks, algorithms, boxes (*the* term for computers) and all things digital. He also mainlined rock music at illegal decibels. She heard Led Zeppelin pounding away in his office.

'Amelia. I called Lincoln and told him we had a break. He said to call you directly. You're closer to where you have to be.'

'And where do I have to be?'

'Queens.'

'And why?'

'Remember we got a warrant and the provider coughed up Patel's cell phone records?'

'Right.'

'I finally pieced together his calling patterns: his sister, other diamond merchants, overseas numbers – South Africa and Botswana – presumably for diamond orders. No calls to anybody with initials of VL. But there were a dozen calls in the past month to and from a Deepro Lahori.'

'Okay.'

'I did some homework. Actually a lot of homework. The last name – the L – intrigued me. Was that half of VL? I think so. Deepro's son – apparently a diamond cutter – is named Vimal. Hold on, Amelia. I love this riff.'

She heard an electric guitar shred. She yawned.

'Could you hear it? You want me to replay it?'

'Rodney.'

'Okay. Just asking. I got a DMV picture. Just sending it now. Check your texts.'

Her phone dinged and she was looking at Vimal Lahori's driver's license photo. The image could easily have been that of the young man exiting the site of the killing through the loading dock on Saturday.

The address on the license was 4388 Monroe Street in Jackson Heights. A half hour away.

'Thanks, Rodney.'

'Disclaimer alert: Can't say he's your boy, not for certain.'

Only one way to find out . . .

CHAPTER 32

Monroe Street in Jackson Heights, Queens, was one of those spots that could not decide if it wanted gentrification or just to be left alone.

To be comfortable, to be quiet, to exist the way it had existed for fifty or maybe a hundred years. Who knew? Workers in small factories and warehouses and on jobsites lived here. Some white-collar entry-level kids in advertising, brokerage houses, publishing, fashion. And then the artists.

At the moment, on the street, near where Vimal Lahori lived, only a few people were outside on the sidewalk. One woman, in a black quilted coat and beret, was trailing behind a small dog on one of those retractable leashes, which was getting quite the workout because a series of suicidal squirrels waited until the last minute to zip away from the energetic canine.

A boy on a bicycle, maybe playing hooky. It was a school day, it was early afternoon.

A businesswoman in raincoat and silly rain hat – clear plastic, like a bonnet, printed with yellow daisies.

Everyone moved quickly, presumably because of the damp, pasty chill.

But these fuckers didn't have it so bad.

Moscow this time of year was a hundred times worse.

Thinking of his home city, Vladimir Rostov decided that this neighborhood of New York was much like the Barrikadnaya area northwest of Moscow; it differed only in that here the homes were single-family row houses. In Moscow – ach, in *every* Russian city – people lived in apartment buildings, towering, stolid and forever gloomy, the color of Stalin's uniform.

Rostov had parked his Toyota up the street and was standing by a tree – the dark trunk obscuring, he hoped, his dark jacket

– and studying the modest home of Vimal Lahori and his family.

Rostov was proud of his detective work. Kirtan had come through – the boy with the crushed larynx and, it turned out, a broken wrist from the stairway tumble, so sorry, *kuritsa*. After the fall, Rostov had dragged the choking boy into the corner of the basement, behind an oil tank, pungent with the eye-stinging fumes from spilled fuel for the furnace. The ancient heater muttered softly, as flames roiled inside, and the two men – one on the floor, one crouching over him – were bathed in heat.

The boy couldn't talk, of course, which made the process of extracting information a bit more complicated. But the silver lining was that he also wouldn't be able to scream in pain and that had been the more important factor at the time.

Rostov had pushed the blade from the utility knife, and tears began streaming in earnest from Kirtan's eyes, leaving glossy tracks on his matte-olive skin. He'd shaken his head no, no, no. He'd mouthed something else as well, perhaps explaining – *trying* to explain – to Rostov that he had little to give him. Rostov had then noticed the boy wore a pinkie ring, gold with a diamond in it. It was one of those showy, pointless pieces. Diamonds only come alive when light bombards them from all sides and enters the facets on the girdle, the pavilion and crown. In a pinkie ring, made for uncultured businessmen, the diamond is cut very shallow and surrounded by metal, with no opportunity to breathe. Pinkie rings invariably contain inferior stones.

A waste of a noble diamond.

Rostov had smiled and turned his attention to the boy's finger once more, caressing it. Kirtan tried to pull away. Useless. More caressing with the razor.

'No, no, baby *kuritsa*, don't bother, no.'

It had taken only two brief cuts on the left-hand finger pads for the kid to jot down Vimal Lahori's name and address with his right. A bit more information and Kirtan's lunch hour – and his life – had come to a quick end.

Now it was time to get to work.

Still pressed against the tree, Rostov waited until the pedestrians, the dog and the bicyclist were gone and he made certain no one else was around. He started toward the Lahori house.

This neighborhood differed from Barrikadnaya in another regard: there was more landscaping here. Rostov took advantage of the cover offered by hedges and trees to get close to the house and not be seen by neighbors.

He noted lights on in the house and, through the lace curtains covering most of the windows, it was clear that there were inhabitants inside. Kirtan had told him that Vimal lived with his parents and a brother. The father was on disability, the mother was a nurse who worked irregular hours and the brother was a college freshman. Any or all of them could be at home.

Rostov would kill them all, of course, but to do so he would have to plan carefully. Those inside could be in different rooms and that meant a risk that somebody would hear the intrusion, dial 911 and drop the phone behind a couch. In a city like New York, the cops would arrive in minutes. He'd have to do some surveillance, wait till they were together, move in fast, brandishing the gun. Tie or tape them. Then the knife. It would have to be the knife. The houses were so close a gunshot could be heard by dozens of people.

In a crouch, taking cover behind evergreen bushes, he skirted the house, which was pale green, in need of paint. At a window toward the back, where he could see shadows in motion, he rose to full height. This allowed him to peek inside the kitchen. A woman of about forty-five stood at the stove. She was obviously Indian. Pretty enough but not appealing to Rostov, with her gray-brown skin and short, wavy black hair, shiny like the plastic do on a doll. He could see her face was troubled. As she absently stirred a pan, she cocked her head and Rostov believed that she was listening to something that upset her: voices. He listened carefully and he could hear them too. Male voices engaged in an argument, it sounded like, though Rostov could not hear the words. They were quite muted. He heard pounding like soft hammer blows at a distance.

A moment later she turned and a man in his fifties, gray and paunchy, appeared from what seemed to be basement stairs. He was agitated. Rostov ducked but kept his ear cocked toward the window.

The woman avoided his eyes and said, 'You shouldn't be doing this.'

'It's for his own good. He's full of stupid ideas. Stupid! You were too indulgent when he was young.'

This was probably true, Rostov thought.

Women.

Good for one thing. Well, that and cooking.

He now heard the muted sound of a power tool somewhere in the house. It sounded like a grinder, electric sander. Somebody was doing some construction.

Another voice asked something. Younger, male. Rostov couldn't detect the words.

The man who'd come from the basement, surely Vimal's father, barked, 'Sunny, you will go to your room. Don't worry about this. It's not your business.'

A response, indiscernible.

'He's in his studio working on a sculpture. He's fine. Go. Now!'

Sunny. Vimal's brother. This meant it was Vimal whom the father had been arguing with in the basement.

You shouldn't be doing this . . .

What would that mean?

So then: four people inside: mother, father and two brothers.

This was a challenge, indeed. But he decided that simple was better. If Vimal was in the basement, he'd slip into the house and take the first person he came across by surprise, slash their throat, then when someone came to see the disturbance, kill that person. And so on. Vimal wouldn't hear, with all the racket from his sander. He'd then walk downstairs and have his visit with the boy.

All right, you *kur*. Here we go.

He turned toward the front of the house and made his way, crouching, to a bush beside the porch. He dipped his hand into his pocket to grip the knife. He was almost there when he heard the sound of an urgently approaching car. He stepped back fast, and a flash of red appeared in his periphery. An old American car skidded to a stop in front of the *kuritsa*'s house.

Shit. He dropped behind the bushy shrubs, fragrant with dog pee.

A woman climbed out of the car. She was trim and tall, her dark-red hair pulled back into a ponytail.

No, no, no!

This fucking *kuritsa* is a cop. He saw a badge on her hip, just peeking from beneath her dark sport jacket. And he noted how her hand absently slipped farther back to orient herself as to where the grip of her long-barrel Glock was. He knew this was a *kuritsa* who knew how to draw and shoot.

Rostov was furious.

If only he'd been a half hour earlier, this would have been finished.

At least she hadn't called in backup. The boy was no suspect, only a witness. She'd just want to ask him questions. And warn him that he'd be in danger. And probably take him to protective custody.

Then Rostov squinted. He was only about fifteen feet away and noted something else about her. A faint shimmer: She wore, on her left hand, the heart finger, a ring with a stone that glinted blue. Was it a diamond? Her engagement ring, then probably yes.

A blue diamond . . .

He thought of the Winston Blue. This was tinier. Flawed, undoubtedly.

The Winston would never be his, of course.

But this one?

The cop woman was at the door now, ringing the bell. He heard it, muted, chiming inside.

He revised his plan but only slightly. He decided this might be a godsend. The woman would gather together everybody in one room to talk to them and interview Vimal.

The hens would be rounded up together, never expecting the fox to burst in on them with his gun and his razor knife claw.

CHAPTER 33

'So you're telling me that Vimal isn't here?' Amelia Sachs was asking.

'I'm afraid not.'

She was speaking to Deepro Lahori, who, despite his easy smile, exuded discomfort, if she could read his body language right.

'What did he say when you heard from him?'

Priming the pump.

'Oh. Well, it was yesterday. He said all was good. He would be away.'

'I see. What was your son's connection with the victim? Jatin Patel?'

'Oh, no, no, not at all.'

That wasn't a response.

'His connection?' she persisted.

'No, no connection at all, really. He just did a little work for him.' Lahori was a short but broad man, with sunken eyes and dark circles under them. Dark-complexioned, grayish skin. His thick black hair was streaked with gray. His wife, Divya, had a handsome face and sharp eyes. Sachs had seen a laundry hanger in the hall with a set of woman's hospital scrubs under the plastic. She was a doctor or nurse, apparently.

And she was clearly uncomfortable with her husband's words. Crossing her arms and shooting him a dark glance.

'A *little* work?' Sachs asked.

'Some diamond cutting.' Lahori seemed irritated that his wife's body language had tipped off his deception. He glared. She ignored him and said, 'Vimal was Mr Patel's apprentice.'

He snapped, 'Not apprentice. That suggests he worked all the time with Mr Patel. He didn't. He didn't study with him.'

Sachs wondered why Lahori seemed to feel that the nature of

the boy's chores for Patel correlated to what Vimal knew or didn't know about the robbery and murder.

The noise of power tools rose. Somewhere in the house, somebody was doing some construction work. Power sanding, it seemed.

'Someone else is in the house?' Maybe another family member who knew something about where the boy might be.

But Lahori said quickly, 'Only some workers.'

'What did he say about the murder? He was there.'

'No, he wasn't there. He was *going* there but it happened before he arrived and he left.'

'Sir, the evidence shows that someone fitting your son's description was present and was injured when the suspect shot at him.'

'What? Oh, my goodness.'

Lahori was an appallingly bad actor.

A young man appeared in the open, arched doorway to the living room. She thought at first he was Vimal but then noted he was younger by a few years, a teenager.

Sachs was about to play the obstruction of justice card with the father; instead she smiled at the teenager and asked, 'You're Vimal's brother?'

'I am, yes.' Looking down, looking up, looking sideways.

'I'm Detective Sachs.'

'I'm Sunny.'

'Go to your room,' Lahori snapped. 'This doesn't involve you.'

But Sunny asked, 'Have you found that man yet? The one who shot at Vimal?'

Lahori closed his eyes and grimaced. Busted by his own child.

'We're working on that now.'

His father snapped, 'Your room.'

The boy hesitated and then turned and left. Sunny would be a backup – if the father didn't start cooperating soon. She sensed the wife would not directly cross her husband, though Sachs knew that she had information about her son.

The grinding, from downstairs, ceased. Sachs was grateful. The sound had been piercing.

'I need to know where he is. I need to know now.'

'He was so upset about what happened that he went away,' Lahori said. 'With some friends. Maybe skiing. The cold weather lately. The resorts are still open. Have you heard?'

His wife stared at him – with the look of someone whose family had never even seen a ski resort.

'This is serious, Mr Lahori. You've followed the news, the man they're calling the Promisor? Well, that's who's looking for your son.'

'He wouldn't be interested in my boy. He didn't see anything!'

'He's already killed another witness.'

'But Vimal couldn't have seen him. There was a mask. I *heard* there was a mask. On the news. So he'd have no reason—'

'Enough!' This, from Divya Lahori.

'No,' Lahori growled.

'Yes, Deepro. This has gone on too long,' the wife said calmly. Then looked imploringly at Sachs. 'You have to protect him.'

'We will. That's why I'm here.'

So, wrong about Divya. She could stand up to her husband.

There was nothing to be gained by a cold glare at Lahori. But Amelia Sachs glared anyway. Then she asked, 'Where is he?'

'He's downstairs. In the basement. His sculpting studio is there,' the boys' mother said.

She remembered that they believed the boy was a sculptor. The grinding sound would be Vimal working on a piece. She should have picked that up.

No matter. She'd soon have him in protective custody. She'd arranged for a safe house, and she would put a detail here too, to keep the family safe.

'So you lied to me.'

The father said defiantly, 'I'm only trying to protect him.'

There was more to this than the father wanting to protect his son, though, Sachs assessed. Most parents would get the police on board as fast as possible.

But she said only, 'Please, go get him now.'

His wife held out her hand, palm up. Lahori's face tightened. He was fuming. He dug into his pocket and angrily handed over a set of keys with a trembling hand.

His father had *locked* him in the basement?

Divya Lahori was paying for her defiance with an icy gaze from her husband. She looked at his face once, then glanced away and walked toward the back of the house.

CHAPTER 34

With a gloved hand, Vladimir Rostov tested the front door of the Lahori residence.

Ah, ah, the helpful *kur* had left it unlocked.

This saved him from a dramatic – and potentially risky – entrance by kicking in a window. Subduing those inside would probably have required the use of his extremely loud pistol.

Stifling a cough – very bad time for a spell of hacking – he looked through the lace curtain in the door. His form would be visible if anyone looked but not obviously so. The overcast was thick and there was little backlight to cast a shadow in the entryway.

The *kuritsa* cop and the husband were in the living room, to the left. It seemed that the wife had gone to get Vimal, who was somewhere else in the house. The other boy – probably the brother – was not to be seen. It would be logical for the cop to bring Vimal into the living room too. She'd want to question them all.

All my little *kur* in a single hen house.

Rostov could just see the redhead's back from the doorway. She was five strides away. Rostov had an idea. He looked around and lifted a large brick from the garden. He returned to the door and peered in again. Yes, yes, this would work. Rostov would step inside fast, bring the brick down on her head and keep the father at bay with the gun. He'd get the cop's gun and cuff her hands. Then take care of Vimal and the rest of the family.

And her? The cop? Rostov caught one more glimpse of the blue diamond on her pale finger. So alluring.

Gone to the stone . . .

Rostov pulled the ski mask down, took the gun in his left hand and slipped the brick under his arm. He gripped the doorknob.

Here we go, little *kur*. Here we go.

Then there came a cry from the back of the house. 'No!' A woman's voice. Vimal's mother. She burst from a door in the back, in the kitchen. The door that Rostov had seen a few moments ago, the one that seemed to lead down to the basement. She paused in the hallway. Still, on the front porch, Rostov crouched. But he didn't need to see the drama. He could hear clearly enough.

'He's gone! Vimal is gone!'

'How could he be gone?' Lahori raged, as if it were her fault.

'The saw? The one he uses for his sculpture? He used it to cut through the bars on the window.'

So the father had locked his own son in a cell in the basement.

Now the fucking *kuritsa* had escaped?

Rostov risked a look to see if they were coming out the front door. But, no, all three adults hurried to the back of the house and down the stairway to the cellar.

He backed away from the front door and down the steps. He walked into the neighbor's property and jogged to the backyard.

Hiding behind a hedge, he peered into the Lahoris' yard. No sign of the boy. But he did see thick metal bars lying on the grass in front of a low window.

He sighed and turned, striding quickly to the sidewalk. He got into his car. For ten minutes he cruised up and down the streets of the placid neighborhood, with no success. He searched for only a brief time, though, assuming that the redheaded *kuritsa* would call other officers to scour the neighborhood too.

Glancing to the seat beside him, he noticed some cold Roll N Roaster fries. He shoved them in his mouth, chewing absently and swallowing fast. He lit a cigarette and enjoyed the inhale. A setback, yes. But Vladimir Rostov wasn't as upset as he might be.

The Promisor is savvy, the Promisor is devious.

And, even though he's completely gone to the stone, he always has a backup plan.

CHAPTER 35

Three p.m.

This was the time Lincoln Rhyme and the man he'd texted yesterday, after meeting with Edward Ackroyd, had agreed on for a phone call.

And it was with, no less, a spy.

Lincoln Rhyme had a relationship with the American espionage community. It was ambivalent and infrequent but undeniable.

The reason he'd been unable to participate in the El Halcón case – the Mexican drug lord who was on federal trial for murder and assault – was due to a meeting in Washington, DC, to assist a new U.S. security agency.

Rhyme and Sachs had come into contact with the organization on a recent case. They, on the one hand, and the Alternative Intelligence Service, on the other, had butted heads over a clandestine operation the AIS had run in Naples, Italy. In the end, Rhyme and Sachs had saved the organization's reputation – and some lives in the process. The director had been so impressed with their forensic work, he'd tried to recruit them.

But working for the AIS would involve considerable foreign travel. Given Rhyme's physical limitations, he was not inclined to sign on, despite the intriguing jobs the organization promised. Besides, New York City had no lack of challenging cases. Why fish elsewhere? It was also his and Sachs's home. He had, however, been happy to jet down to DC, to help the AIS set up a new division to use forensics and physical evidence as an intelligence resource.

At the first meeting in DC, one of the congressmen involved in the creation and funding of the AIS had said, 'Glad you're here, Captain Rhyme, Detective Sachs. We know you can help us in our task to parameter a new dynamic for evidentiary intelligence analytics and weaponization.'

Rhyme, who otherwise would have engaged in a bit of verbal fencing about verbosity and about turning 'parameter' into a verb, reminded himself he was inside the Beltway, and simply ignored the bullshit. The concept was clever: The new division would employ crime scene and crime lab skills to gather and analyze intelligence . . . and, yes, to 'weaponize' evidence.

Need to identify a mole within the American consulate in Frankfurt, when everybody passes the polygraph? Just find the one employee bearing a molecule of trace evidence that can be matched with a molecule of trace in the Generalkonsulat der Volksrepublik China.

Need a North Korean hit team in Tokyo taken down? Just deliver to the Japanese Keiji-kyoku some trace evidence and shoe prints suggesting they have illegal weapons, and, bang, they're in jail – for a long, long time. So much more humane than snipers. And more important, somebody other than the U.S. government does the dirty work.

The name would be the EVIDINT Division of the AIS, a word coined by Rhyme himself. As in 'evidence intelligence.' Spy-speak. Like HUMINT, human intelligence. Or ELINT, electronic intelligence.

It was the director of the AIS, Daryl Mulbry, whom Rhyme had texted when Ackroyd told him of Unsub 47's Russian roots. Mulbry's text suggested a 3 p.m. call.

Espionage apparently engendered promptness and at 3:00:42, his phone rang.

'Lincoln, hello!' The man, Rhyme recalled, was pale and slight and with thinning hair a light shade of brown. To judge by his patois, his roots were the Carolinas or Tennessee. When Rhyme had first met him he'd thought Mulbry was a minor, regulation-bound low-level diplomat. The man's appearance and self-effacing manner gave no clue that he ran a hundred-million-dollar intelligence operation, including tactical teams, who, if they wanted you to disappear, could fulfill that task with a minimum of fuss.

'So sorry it's taken this long to get back. Had a brouhaha in

Europe. Was a mess. It's largely – though not completely – cleared up now. But more about that later. What can I do for you? You want to know how your baby, the EVIDINT's going? Swimmingly. Though that's not a word I really understand. It's not all that easy to swim. And one *can* drown, course.'

'Something else and it's urgent.'

Mulbry was used to Rhyme's impatience. 'Of course.'

'We've got a perp in town. Recently, looks like. My diagnosis: he's pretty unhinged. Obsessed with diamonds. Got away with a couple million worth of rough, it's called. Uncut stones. He murdered some innocents. Tortured, in a couple of cases.'

'Torture? What was that about?'

'Mostly to track down witnesses. But probably for his own amusement too.'

'Details?'

'Not much. Russian national, Muscovite, fluent-ish in English. White. Blue eyes. Average height and build. Fashion choice leans toward dark casual clothing – off the rack – and ski masks.'

'You're a card, Lincoln. Why the theft? Funding terrorism? Money laundering?'

'This is the odd part. He wants to save diamonds from dese-cration. Our British consultant describes him as a "nutter."'

'He thinking of heading back home for the Motherland's borscht or does he have more mischief in mind?'

'Staying put, at least temporarily, we'll assume.'

'Recently here, you said. How recent?'

'Unknown. But we've checked for similar MO in the databases and nothing shows up. So let's say the past week, ten days. Though that's a big assumption.'

'Means of dispatching people?'

'Glock, short-barrel thirty-eight and razor knife.'

'My. Any indication of military training?'

'That'd be speculation too. But he's smart. Careful with CCTVs and evidence.'

'All right and you want to know if I can find any names of Russkies who've come to the U.S. in that time. Of questionable backgrounds or circumstances.'

'Exactly.'

'Okay, Russian, diamonds, psycho, access to weapons. I'll see what we can find. I'll get the kids and the bots on it.' Rhyme heard typing. Fast as train wheels over old track.

Mulbry came back on. 'Might be a while . . . and you might end up with quite the list. We don't stop them at the border, those Russian folks, you know? The Cold War is over, haven't you heard?'

Rhyme had to laugh at this.

'Now, Lincoln, as long as I have you, let me pose a question.'

Rhyme recalled what the man had said a moment ago.

More about that later . . .

'Hm?'

'That incident I was talking about. We wrapped up a radical cell in the suburbs of Paris. All good. But in the process our team vacuumed up some unrelated digital traffic that caught our attention. It was between Paris, Central America and New York City. That triad rings terrorist profile bells.'

Rhyme said, 'Must be about a million emails a day along those routes.'

'You bet there are. But these were different. They were encrypted with duodecimal algorithms. Virtually unbreakable. Which makes us a tad nervous.'

Rhyme, who had a science background, knew the duodecimal numbering system, also called base 12 or dozenal. The binary system has two digits only, 0 and 1. The decimal has ten: 0 through 9. Duodecimal has twelve, 0 through 9 plus two extra symbols, usually ᘔ and Ɛ.

Mulbry continued, 'The encryption package is so "righteous" – that's what the geeks say – that we're treating the software as a weapon. It's considered munitions under the International Traffic in Arms Regulations, State Department. Since New York is one of the points of origin of the messages, I'm curious if anybody at NYPD has ever run across duodecimal encrypted emails or texts.'

'No. Never heard of it.' He looked up at Cooper. 'Mel, any duodecimal encryption in cases you've run?'

'No.'

'Call Rodney and see if he's heard of anything.' Back to the phone. 'We'll talk to our expert here. We'll see.'

'Thanks. It's got us troubled. We're checking locations he or she or it were at when the messages were sent. Those're hard to find too. Proxies, of course.' Another laugh. '*Righteous* ones.'

'I'll let you know if we find something.'

The men said goodbye and disconnected.

Hm, interesting idea, dozenal as a basis for encryption. Though Rhyme's background was chemistry primarily, he harbored an interest in math and he knew that a number of mathematicians believed that base twelve was far easier to learn and use in making calculations. He'd even read about a dozenal clock, in which a minute equals fifty seconds of current time. A clock reading 7:33.4 Ɀ in dozenal, for instance, was 2:32.50 on a standard timepiece.

Fascinating.

But, of course, irrelevant. And Rhyme pushed the thoughts away. He hoped he could help Mulbry but Unsub 47 was his priority. His phone hummed. The number was unfamiliar.

Hoping for the caller's sake it wasn't a telemarketer, he answered, 'Hello?'

'Mr Rhyme? Captain Rhyme?' The accent was Spanish, and it was light.

'Yes?'

'My name is Antonio Carreras-López. I'm an attorney from Mexico. I'm in New York at the moment, and I wonder if I may have a moment of your time.'

'I'm very busy. What would this be in regard to?'

'One of my clients is presently on trial here.' The man's voice was low and melodic. 'I'd like to discuss a matter that's come up. It involves you.'

'Who is your client?'

'He's a Mexican national. If you follow the news, you might have heard of him. Eduardo Capilla. He is better known as El Halcón.'

Lincoln Rhyme was rarely shocked. But the ping in his insensate body was manifest as a significant throbbing in his head.

This was the very case that he'd so wanted a piece of, but had been unable to participate in because of his commitment to Daryl Mulbry and the AIS down in Washington.

'I'm familiar with him. Go on, please.'

Carreras-López continued, 'I know you understand the protocols of criminal trials. The prosecution is obligated to give the defense its evidentiary files prior to trial. In that material we received from the U.S. attorney, we discovered your name listed as a potential forensic analyst and witness. But a notation said you were not available.'

'I submitted my name to consult for the prosecution but I had to be out of town.'

'I looked you up, Captain, and was, I must say, impressed at your background and expertise. Extremely impressed.' He paused. 'I gather that the consulting work you do is exclusively for the prosecution.'

'Some civil work – for plaintiffs and defendants – but in criminal, yes, I work for law enforcement.'

With the occasional spy thrown into the client mix.

'Yes, well, if I may take just a few moments of your time to explain. The trial is under way and the prosecution is presenting its case now. In looking over the evidence, our experts believe they have found something troubling. That the evidence, *some* of the evidence, has been manipulated by the police or FBI. My client is unpopular, and – frankly – he's not such a very nice person. He has done some bad things in his life. But that does not mean he is guilty of the crimes he's on trial for.'

'And you want to hire me to see if I can find proof the evidence was manipulated?'

'I think you are not a man who cares much about money, though we would pay a substantial fee. I think you are, however, a man who cares about right and wrong. And there is something very wrong about this case. But I can find no one who wishes to help me prove it. Of the four former prosecutors and retired forensic officers, and two professional forensic analysts I approached to help us, all have declined.'

'You've made a motion to exclude the evidence, or for a mistrial?'

'Not yet. We don't want to do so without some substantive proof.'

Rhyme's thoughts tumbled. 'From what I read there were multiple charges.'

He heard a chuckle. 'Oh, yes. Since you and I don't have an attorney–client relationship, I will refrain from saying anything specific. But let me give you a hypothetical. A suspect is charged with five counts. There is no doubt he is guilty of one – let us say entering the country illegally. And there is ample evidence for that. And the jury will certainly convict. But the other, more serious counts, assault with a deadly weapon and attempted murder, he is absolutely *not* guilty of. Someone else committed those crimes and my client, my hypothetical client, was not even present when they happened.'

'Justice,' Rhyme whispered.

'Justice,' the lawyer repeated. 'Yes, the very issue at hand. Mr Rhyme, in reading about you, I saw you once testified at the petition of a man seeking release from prison on the ground that the laboratory technician had intentionally altered DNA results. You told the court that whether it was intentional or innocent, a forensic scientist's errors in processing evidence are inexcusable. Truth is paramount, you said.'

He recalled the case, easily picturing the face of the man who'd served eight years for a rape he did not commit. The convict's eyes, fixed on Rhyme's, had been filled with hope and desperation. The woman technician who'd intentionally written the false report, because she believed him guilty, had not looked up from the floor.

Rhyme said, 'I never make a judgment about the moral nature of the defendants in the trials I work. I'm in the midst of a big case at the moment but if you want to come to my town house, we can talk about it.'

'Ah, really, Mr Rhyme? I am so grateful.'

'I can't promise anything but I'd like to hear the details.'

They chose a time and Rhyme gave his address. They disconnected.

Rhyme wheeled up to the evidence charts. Cooper was writing up some recent information from the crime lab in Queens: The DNA and fingerprinting from the jacket found in the storm drain had come back negative. So had the hairs and swabs from the Gravesend attack.

Rhyme noted the words on the whiteboard. He tucked them away and then returned to thinking about what the Mexican lawyer had told him. He thought too of Sachs, Sellitto, Cooper and the others hard at work on the Unsub 47 case and reflected, *What would they think if they knew I was considering signing on with the drug dealer's team?*

There was no good answer to that question and so he ignored it and returned to the evidence.

CHAPTER 36

The word 'bedridden' didn't really fit for the now. It fit for the then.

The long-time-ago then.

The Jane Austen then. The Brontë Sisters. The novels that Claire Porter used to read and reread – in college and after. Recently, some of them.

Bedridden.

Often, in those books, a character was tucked away under down comforters and thick blankets, with a compress on a feverish forehead, because of some mysterious unnamed disease. Or exhaustion. Exhaustion was a common malady in the then. When reading about life in the eighteenth and nineteenth centuries, Porter always wondered what could be so stressful back then that you had to recuperate by staying in bed for weeks at a time. Or taking a cruise (if you were one of the posh people).

Posh. Another good then word.

Nothing posh about *my* bedridden life, thought the thirty-four-year-old.

Lying on her Sealy Posturepedic in the bedroom of their first-floor apartment in Brooklyn, Porter looked out the window at Cadman Park, monotone and wet and chill today, which fit her mood pretty well.

The slim brunette barista had been sidelined not by exhaustion or a novelist's anonymous disease but because she'd tripped over a dog. Not even hers, but a fuzzy little thing that'd slipped a lead while she and her husband had been out jogging and darted in front of her. She'd twisted away, instinctively, and heard a pop in her ankle. Down she went.

Hell, a sprain, she'd thought.

Wrong. It was one fucking nightmare of a break.

Two surgeries to start, then a battle with infection, then under the knife again – to place steel pins. Bionic woman, her husband had joked gamely, though he was clearly shaken by her pain – and, understandably, dismayed by his new responsibilities; the couple had an eighteen-month-old daughter. Dad – a graphic designer in Midtown – was now living a double-shift life. And she couldn't even think about his cheerfully forced nod when the doctor said it was best to avoid 'intimate relations' that would put the ankle at risk for at least six months. (Something Victorian about the MD's phrase too, come to think of it.)

With a crutch, Porter could just about handle the basics: the bathroom. A trip to the mini fridge that Sam had set up in this, the guest, bedroom. She could get a bottle and the solid food to feed Erin, whose small bed was beside hers. That was about the extent of her activity until the wound healed. How she loved to cook, how she loved to run, how she loved the barista job – the banter, the quirky and bizarre people she met.

But it was another month of being bedridden.

Claire Porter resolved to be good and follow orders. Another fall, the doctor warned, could make the injury far worse. Infection, necrosis of the skin. Ick. And though he hadn't mentioned amputation, Google had. And once seated in her mind, that thought stuck like a leech and wouldn't let go.

At least she could continue her online studies. Barista now, owner of a small restaurant consulting business in two years. She lifted the Mac onto her tummy, glanced at the crib. Thank you for snoozing, honey doll! Hell, she wanted to kiss the girl's toffee-blond hair. But that would be a big project.

Bedridden.

She booted up and worked for a few minutes, then, goddamn it. The urge. She needed to use the bathroom.

It's funny how we can anticipate exactly where and how pain will get us. Porter went through the instinctive choreography of shifting one leg, the other, her torso and arms in a complicated pattern to let her sit up without bringing tears to her eyes.

Or puking.

She negotiated the sitting-up with relatively little discomfort. And she managed to snag the crutches pretty well.

Now the standing-up part.

A deep breath, everything coming into alignment. Okay, scoot forward.

Then . . . okay slow . . . then up.

Porter, who weighed in at about 110 pounds, felt the force of gravity tugging her down, down, down. The crutches did this, turned her into a load of bricks. But she managed. A few steps. She paused as her vision crinkled a bit. She was light-headed. Lowering her head, breathing deeply, she reminded herself to get up slowly next time. Fainting? She couldn't even imagine what a fall would do to her fragile bones.

Then her head cleared and she moved toward the hall. She paused to look down at Erin, who slept the sleep of youthful oblivion, with dreams, if at all, simple and kind.

Claire Porter hobbled onward to the bathroom. Sam had modified it – he'd put a shower seat in the tub and replaced the wall-mounted head with a handheld unit. He'd added a high seat on the toilet so she didn't need to put much weight on her foot.

One good thing about the accident. No fashion choices. It was sweats, sweats, sweats . . . Just tug the turquoise bottoms down with the panties and sit. Job done.

Getting up was a bit harder but she knew how to manage it.

Anticipation . . .

Up and pain-free. Damn, my right leg's going to be solid wood by the time this is over.

As Claire Porter was washing her hands she felt a shudder throughout the apartment. Windows rattled and a glass sitting on the shelf leapt off the edge and died in a dozen shards on the tile floor.

Porter gasped.

My God. What was that? Another one of those earthquakes? She'd followed the news. Something about that drilling – the construction site they said was responsible was a half mile from here. There was a lot of protesting. Environmental folks versus big business. She couldn't remember exactly.

Wow, a quake in New York! This was something. She'd have to tell her mother about it when they talked next. It had been a fairly minor tremor – no damage to the walls or windows.

But that *was* a problem.

And a serious one.

Bare feet. Broken glass.

Stupid, she thought. She had slippers (well, *slipper*; nothing was going on the bad foot) but hadn't bothered to put it on. And now five feet of obstacle course to get to the hallway.

She looked down. When the glass hit, it hit hard.

Shit. It would be impossible for her to clean up the mess. Bending over was no option. She could use the crutch to push the bigger pieces out of the way but she couldn't see the smaller ones on the white tile.

Towels. She would cover the floor with bath towels and place her good foot only where there were no lumps. The smaller ones wouldn't penetrate – she hoped.

She pulled the thickest towels from the racks and strewed them on a path to the door.

One step. Good.

She paused to find a spot for the next one and froze.

What was that? She smelled natural gas.

'Jesus, Jesus . . . '

Porter recalled the terrible news story about what had happened after the first earthquake. The damage from the shaking hadn't been bad at all. A few broken windows. But some gas lines had broken. The resulting explosions and fires had killed several people: a couple, trapped in their burning house.

Well, she and her daughter weren't going to be victims.

They were on the first floor. She'd get Erin and clutch her tight and hobble outside, shouting her head off for the other tenants to get out too.

Move, move, move!

Another step.

One more. And then the glass splinter leveraged through the towel like a scorpion's stinger and pierced her heel.

Porter screamed and fell backward. She released the crutch

and got her hand behind her head just in time to keep her skull from cracking on the side of the porcelain bathtub. Pain careened through her body. Her vision crinkled again – from the agony. It then returned, though blurred by more tears.

The smell of gas was stronger here: Her face was beside the access panel to the bathroom pipes, which led down to the basement, where the cracked gas line would be.

Go! Somehow, she had to get to the room and save her baby.

Crawl over the fucking glass if you have to!

An image came to her: the news footage of the buildings burning following the most recent quakes – that horrifying tornado of orange flames and oily black smoke.

Save your daughter.

'Erin!' she cried involuntarily.

The girl must have heard – or perhaps she'd been woken by the foul smell of the gas – and she started screaming.

'No, honey, no! Mommy's coming!' She struggled to roll onto her belly, so she could start her frantic crawl to her daughter.

But she hadn't realized that her broken ankle had become wedged beneath the bathroom's heavy wooden vanity. As she rolled over, she felt, and heard, the gritty snap of the delicate bone work giving way. Breathtaking pain exploded within her entire body.

Screaming in unison with her infant daughter, Claire Porter looked at her foot. The metal rods that the surgeon had implanted just the other day had ripped through the skin and, bloody, were poking out of the top of her foot. She gagged and felt her head thud hard against the tile floor as blackness embraced her like oily smoke.

CHAPTER 37

Vimal Lahori was back in his beloved bus station, the Port Authority.

Better this time. Less pain. The horror of the killing had diminished. And he had money.

At home last night, before he'd gone down to the studio to 'have words' with his father, he'd walked upstairs on the pretext of getting a sweater. He'd done that . . . but he'd also taken the three thousand dollars – *his* three thousand – that Nouri had paid him, as well as his wallet. He had lifted another two hundred of his father's because he was owed that, and much, much more, for the cutting jobs his father had rented him out for. He got his phone too. A razor, toothpaste and brush, the antiseptic Adeela had given him. Some bandages. And of course his Book, his most precious possession.

Vimal had been planning all along to escape last night as soon as his parents were busy with their game or had gone to sleep. He'd agreed to some ambiguous peace treaty with his father, which Vimal hadn't meant a word of. But then it turned out that his father hadn't meant a word of it either. He should have guessed that Papa was lying – and going to entrap him in the basement prison; the bottled water stacked up, the food in the fridge, the sleeping bag. Lite fucking beer?

Goddamn it.

He shivered with rage.

Vimal was now walking away from the Greyhound window. The one-way ticket cost him $317.50. The journey from New York to the station at 1716 7th Street, in Los Angeles, would take sixty-five hours.

Thinking about what was coming next, Vimal Lahori was sorrowful, he was terrified.

But these emotions were outweighed by the exhilaration he felt, and he knew he was doing the right thing. He turned his phone on and texted his mother that he loved her. And texted his brother that he loved him too and he'd be in touch from someplace out of town.

He then bought a soda – a large Cherry Coke, a secret delight (his father never let him have any beverage with caffeine because he was, for some reason, convinced it would make his son's hands shake, resulting in a flawed diamond facet). Vimal bought a slice of pizza too. He stood, eating and sipping, at a dirty high-top table. There were no chairs for customers. To encourage turnover in the 'dining room,' he guessed.

He looked into what amounted to his luggage – a canvas bag he'd bought for a dollar at a grocery store. And he took out what gave him as much comfort as the Port Authority itself.

The Book. A holy book in a way. It was something he turned to a lot, something that comforted him, that never failed to astonish.

The Collected Sketches of Michelangelo had been printed years ago, in the early part of the prior century. Vimal considered the master to be the greatest sculptor who'd ever lived and, given his own passion, it was logical that he'd be drawn to the man and his art. The artist was Vimal's god. Oh, he liked pop music, manga and would have liked binge-worthy TV, had his father allowed him to watch much of it. But he *loved* Michelangelo and, in those moments when his ancestral country's religious legacy – reincarnation – seemed plausible to him (this was rare, usually after wine), he fantasized that the ancient sculptor's soul – part of it, at least – resided within Vimal himself.

Of course, Michelangelo was a prodigy. He was under thirty when he sculpted *David* and *Pietà*. Vimal didn't rise to that level yet, though his own works, crafted in marble and granite and lapis, usually placed first or second in competitions around the New York City area.

But it had occurred to Vimal, with a shock, recently, that there was possibly a subtler, a subconscious, reason for his obsession with the man. Once, flipping through the pages, on break at Mr

Patel's, he realized that the majority of Michelangelo's sketches depicted in the volume, while superbly executed, were incomplete.

The man seemed incapable of finishing his drawings.

His 1508 study for *Adam* was merely a head and chest and floating, detached arms. His sketch for a *Risen Christ* featured a nearly faceless Jesus.

Incomplete . . .

Those sketches are just like me, Vimal had concluded, while acknowledging that this "disembodied" theory of his sounded like bad pop psychology on a bad TV show.

There was another parallel too between the two men. Vimal had shared this with Adeela and she'd given him one of her wry smiles. Meaning, Really? Aren't you carrying this a bit far?

Well, no, he wasn't.

The analogy was this: Michelangelo considered himself a sculptor before all else and only reluctantly would take on commissions for paintings. He wasn't exactly a hack at this, of course, having produced the Sistine Chapel ceiling in merely four years, as well as *The Last Judgment* and dozens of other master-pieces. But Michelangelo's passions lay elsewhere, with marble, not canvas. And for Vimal, it was marble, not jewelry.

Painting and diamond cutting, in their respective cases, simply didn't ignite that undeniable, searing fire that flares when you're doing the one thing that God, or the gods, or whatever, put you on earth for.

As he finished the greasy slice and slurped the last of the soda, anger at his father once more swelled. Then he tamped it down and, with a last look at the *Poseidon* statue, closed the book and replaced it in his bag.

Walking with his head mostly down – he wore a black baseball cap – he left the pizzeria and avoided the clusters of police, making his way to the waiting area. The bus would be leaving soon.

He sat down on a plastic chair, next to a pleasant-looking girl in her late twenties. He noticed from her ticket that, for the first leg of the journey at least, she would be on the same bus that his ticket was for. The address sticker on her guitar case was

Springfield, Illinois. She wasn't very Midwest in appearance, at least from Vimal's limited knowledge of the region. Her hair was green and blue and she had three nose studs and a ring in her eyebrow. Vimal supposed that her dreams of stages and cabarets and theater in New York had come to an end. Her stoic face suggested this too. Wistful, as if she'd lost something important and given up looking. Which seemed sadder than sad.

Then Vimal reflected that this might be his imagination and she was going to spend a few days with some former roommates from college, drink plenty of wine from a box, sleep with a local bar boy and have the time of her life.

What was the truth?

The older he got, Vimal Lahori had decided, the less he knew.

A staticky voice – of indeterminate gender – announced that the bus was ready to depart. He leaned down, gathered his bag and rose.

'Any idea where he's run off to?'

'None,' Sachs replied to Rhyme, who'd asked about Vimal Lahori, after the young man's prison break from his own house. Clever, pretending to grind away on sculpture when all the while you're cutting steel bars.

Sick, of course, that his father had decided to play jailer.

Sachs continued, 'He took about three thousand from his father – though his mother tells me that it's really his. Lahori takes everything the boy makes as a diamond cutter and banks it. He gives the kid an allowance.'

'At his age? Hm.'

The doorbell rang and Thom went to answer it. He returned a few moments later with Edward Ackroyd, dressed in a two-piece suit, pinstripe light gray, perfectly pressed. White shirt and red-and-blue-striped tie. Rhyme pictured him wearing this getup for a meeting at 10 Downing Street.

'Lincoln. Amelia.'

He'd given up, at last, on the 'sir' and 'ma'am.' Rhyme imagined that Scotland Yard protocols were largely baked in.

The insurance man said hello as well to Cooper.

242

'Any new leads?' he asked.

Rhyme offered the latest developments.

'Vimal Lahori.' Ackroyd nodded. 'A bit more to go on. But locked in his basement?' A brief frown at this news. 'And now he's vanished. Doesn't he know he's in danger? Well, pointless question. Of course he does. But why doesn't he want help?'

Sachs said, 'The basement's a clue. My guess is he's avoiding his father as much as he's avoiding Forty-Seven. We bring him in, he can't escape dad.'

Thom offered to take his coat but Ackroyd said he couldn't stay; he had a meeting with another client.

The Brit said to Sachs, 'So you met his family. Surely they must have some idea where he's gone. Friends, other relatives.'

'They gave me a few names but nothing panned out. Vimal didn't share much with anybody in the family. Dad offered five hundred dollars as a reward and the son of a diamond cutter Vimal was working for turned him in.' A shrug. 'I suppose the father's doing the same thing again. Maybe that'll give us a lead. And they'll contact me, if they hear.'

'You're sure?' Rhyme asked. 'They won't try to lock him up again?'

'I waved the obstruction-of-justice flag. I think they'll toe the line.'

Ackroyd told them that he himself was making little headway. 'The diamond rough your unsub, the Promisor, stole at Patel's has just vanished, which bears out that he's a madman and hoarding the stones. No one else has reported any calls from him, asking about the apprentice. And people are even more reluctant to talk than ever. He's scaring everyone. I've heard anecdotes that sales of engagement rings are down twenty percent.'

Well, Unsub 47 may have been psychotic but, if his goal was to make a statement about the sanctity of diamonds, he was pretty damn effective.

'Now, I could have called that in, of course. But I wanted to stop by. Brought you a present.' He was speaking to Rhyme. He reached into the plastic bag he held and extracted a box about six by nine inches, glossy, pictures of some electronic product on the top. He stripped off the plastic wrapping and extracted what seemed to be a tablet device. He set it next to Rhyme's chair and pushed a button on the side. It came to life and a menu appeared. 'Electronic crosswords. These are cryptics. There're over ten thousand, all different levels of difficulty.'

Rhyme explained to Sachs that Ackroyd and his husband competed at crossword tournaments. And he gave her a brief description of how cryptics worked.

She was even less a game person than Rhyme but admitted that she found the idea intriguing.

Ackroyd said, 'And this unit? It's voice-activated. Made for . . .'

'You can say "crip" or "gimp." I do.'

'I was going to say "handicapped." I don't think that's correct, however.'

'My response is what is a four-letter word starting with "s" and completing the sentence, "I don't give a . . . "?'

Ackroyd laughed briskly.

'Well, thank you, Edward.' Rhyme was truly pleased. He played chess some – and had tried Go, an Asian board game that was even more complicated. The cryptics seemed more up his alley. He loved words and how they fit together. The puzzles would be a good way to keep his mind active, a shield against his worst enemy: boredom.

After Ackroyd left, the team received a call from Rodney Szarnek. He said that Vimal's phone had been detected. 'He's out of the area. GPS puts him on an expressway in Pennsylvania. Headed west. Doing sixty miles an hour or so. He's driving or on a bus.'

'Bus probably,' Sachs said. 'The family only has one car and my security team'd spot him if he snuck back to take it.'

'Maybe a friend's driving him,' Cooper suggested.

'He made that call from the Port Authority on Saturday,' Rhyme pointed out. 'Maybe he was checking out bus schedules then. I'd go with bus. You and Lon Sellitto set up a tracking operation. Get in touch with the state police in Pennsylvania.'

When he disconnected, Rhyme called Lon Sellitto to arrange to intercept the vehicle.

The doorbell rang again and Rhyme glanced at the security video screen. A short, round balding man stood there. He didn't recognize him but had a pretty good idea who he was.

Thom slipped a glance toward Rhyme, who said, 'Go ahead, let him in.'

A moment later the man was in the doorway. He glanced around the lab. He seemed impressed – and pleased – more than surprised.

'Captain Rhyme.'

Rhyme didn't introduce him to the others. He said 'Let's go in the den. Across the hall.'

If Sachs or Cooper was curious about the visitor, their interest didn't show and they went back to their work. Just as well.

What would they think if they knew . . . ?

CHAPTER 38

Antonio Carreras-López wasn't as portly as he'd seemed in the security video, though he was a solid man. Rhyme wondered if he'd been a weight lifter or wrestler in his youth. Now apparently in his late fifties, he still seemed quite strong though some of the weight was gone to fat.

His black hair, what remained, that is, was swept back and fixed in place with spray or cream. He wore glasses with thick tortoiseshell frames, perched atop a fleshy nose. His eyes were amused. Quick too.

The men were in the small formal room, across the entry hall from the parlor. Three walls were lined with bookcases and on the other hung four muted prints of pen-and-ink drawings of New York City in the nineteenth century. The guest said, 'As I told you on the phone, I represent Mr Eduardo Capilla – El Halcón – though I'm not admitted to the bar here in the United States. I am, however, supervising his defense.'

'Who are the lawyers representing him here?'

Carreras-López mentioned three names – all lawyers from Manhattan, though the trial was in the Eastern District of New York, which included Long Island, Staten Island, Brooklyn and Queens. Rhyme knew of the lead trial attorney, a high-profile and respected criminal defense lawyer. Rhyme had never testified in a case involving any of his clients.

He wasn't sure this would have been a conflict but the situation was certainly fraught with the smoke of impropriety so he thought it best, if he proceeded, that there be no connection with El Halcón's legal team. The prosecutor on the other side was Henry Bishop, and Rhyme knew he hadn't been involved in a case he'd prosecuted.

'Now, Captain Rhyme, as a first matter . . . '

'I'm retired and, please, "Lincoln" is fine.'

'And I am Tony. Now the first thing. I will give you this.' He pushed an envelope toward Rhyme. 'It's a one-thousand-dollar retainer. Which makes you a contractor with the defense team. The attorney–client privilege extends to you now.'

So they would not have to speak hypothetically any longer.

Carreras-López hesitated as he held out a receipt, his eyes on Rhyme's arm.

'I can sign,' Rhyme said, and he took the pen the lawyer offered and jotted his signature on the document. 'Now. The details?'

'Yes. In essence: My client came into the U.S. illegally. We admit this. He flew to Canada on a commercial flight and entered legally into that country. But then he flew in a helicopter to Long Island, entering *illegally*. Yes, the craft flew under the radar, but that is not illegal in a helicopter. There are no minimum altitude requirements. So there is no FAA violation. El Halcón was met by a bodyguard who worked for the owner of a warehouse that El Halcón was going to buy. While the pilot waited, they drove to this complex so Mr Capilla could look it over and discuss the purchase with the man.'

'Any controlled substances anywhere in this scenario?'

'No, sir. Absolutely not. The warehouse was solely for a transportation company that my client wanted to start up in America.'

'Aside from this, any warrants on your client?'

'None.'

'Then why enter illegally?'

'The answer is that my client's profession in Mexico is well known. It is suspected that he is responsible for the influx of large quantities of drugs into the U.S. He was concerned that he would be detained at Passport Control on technicalities. Perhaps imprisoned on trumped-up charges.'

'Go on.'

'At the warehouse my client met with the owner of the facility—'

'His name?'

'Christopher Cody. They discussed the terms of the deal and my client took a tour. Now, it happened that Cody was under investigation on some weapons charges. Completely independent of my client. El Halcón did not know this. A local police officer was conducting some surveillance. When my client and the bodyguard showed up he grew suspicious. He thought these might be arms dealers. He sent a picture of my client to his office, which alerted the FBI. They identified my client, checked with Border Protection and learned he had entered illegally. A team of FBI and some local police hurried to the warehouse. A gunfight ensued. Mr Cody and his bodyguard were killed, and one FBI agent and the local officer who had taken the photos were badly injured.'

Facts Rhyme was aware of.

'The prosecution claimed what?'

A shrug. 'What they always claim. That officers and agents approached, calling for surrender, and the men inside opened fire.'

'And your client's story?'

'The officers fired first without identifying themselves and the men in the warehouse returned fire. They believed it was a robbery or hijacking. In any event, my client did not participate. He was in the restroom at the time. On the floor, hiding, so he would not be hit by a stray bullet. And, quite frankly, terrified. There he stayed until the firing stopped. He came out, saw what had happened and was arrested.'

'Did the other men with him, inside, give any statements?'

'Mr Cody was killed instantly, a shot in the head. The bodyguard survived for a day but never regained consciousness.'

'Tell me about the tainted evidence.'

'You see, when my client was being arrested he was placed facedown on the floor of the warehouse. At one point, an agent or officer – he couldn't see who – came up to him and searched him. But then my client felt something pressed against his hands and clothing. It was cloth. He is sure the officer was transferring gunshot residue he'd lifted from Cody's hands. When he asked what the man was doing, my client was told, "Shut the fuck up. Two of our guys're shot to hell. You're going away forever."'

Rhyme said, 'So the prosecution claims that after Cody was killed, your client picked up his gun and shot the officer?'

'That's right.'

'Friction ridges – fingerprints – on the weapon?'

'Only Cody's, not my client's. There were no gloves or rags nearby he might've used to hold the gun but the prosecutor's position is that he undid his shirt cuff button and held the pistol in the sleeve. That would explain the gunshot residue and the absence of fingerprints.'

'Clever theory. What are the exact charges?'

'The illegal entry into the U.S. – it's called "entry at improper time or place" under the statute. The charge carries a fine and imprisonment of up to six months. A federal misdemeanor. The other charges are what you'd expect: weapons, assault on a law enforcement officer, attempted murder of a law enforcement officer, Cody's death – felony murder. We admit he was in the country illegally and he is willing to plead to that. So, now, that is our situation.' He eyed Rhyme closely. 'You said you were busy. Working a big case.'

'I am, yes.'

'I am asking you is it possible to take some time and look at the evidence, see if you can find proof that the officers at the scene planted that residue?'

Rhyme's head eased back. He gazed at the ceiling for a moment. Thoughts swirled.

Finally he said, 'I'll need all the forensic files. Yours and the prosecution's.'

Carreras-López said, 'I'll have copies of the files sent over. A half hour. *Gracias*, sir. God bless you.' He pulled on his coat and left.

Rhyme placed a call to Ron Pulaski. He would have liked to pursue the El Halcón tainted-evidence matter on his own but that wasn't possible. There'd be some fieldwork.

'Lincoln.'

'Need you to do something for me.'

'Sure. This about Forty-Seven?'

'No. A different case. There'll be a box of files over here in a half hour. I'll need you to collect it and take it home.'

'Home?' the officer asked. 'As in home-home?'

'Exactly. I need a complete analysis of all the firearm, electro-statics, clothing, and surface trace from the scene.'

'Sure, Lincoln.'

'Then I need you to do something else.'

'What's that?'

'Keep quiet. Don't say a word about this to any other living soul. You got that?'

Silence.

'You *got* that, Rookie?'

'Yes.' Pulaski was whispering, as if speaking any louder would itself be a breach of the rules.

CHAPTER **39**

'Another earthquake.'

Rhyme glanced toward Mel Cooper, who'd just delivered this news. The tech's eyes were on the TV.

He followed the man's gaze. On the screen, news cameras were filming an apartment in Brooklyn, engulfed in swirling flames and smoke. The cause was, as the others, a gas line rupture, which had followed on the heels of the second quake.

Now the scene shifted to a press conference at City Hall. Rhyme read the closed-captioned account of the mayor's words: In light of the second quake, the city had decided to reject Northeast Geo's request to resume its geothermal drilling even on a limited basis. The talking heads appeared again: Ezekiel Shapiro – the bearded activist leader of the One Earth movement; Dwyer, head of Northeast Geo; and C. Hanson Collier, CEO of Algonquin Power.

As they spoke, the scene shifted to the blazing apartment building, surrounded by the clutter of fire trucks and emergency vehicles.

The text at the bottom reported three fatalities. The victims had been engulfed by flames.

The door buzzer sounded. Thom was out, at the store; Rhyme looked at the security camera screen. It was Lon Sellitto. Didn't he have a goddamn key? After all these years? They should have one cut for him. Rhyme buzzed him in.

'Okay. Are you ready for this?'

Rhyme sighed and lifted an eyebrow.

Sellitto nodded at the screen, on which were stark images of brawny, spiraling flames, a black torrent of smoke.

The crawl at the bottom of the screen: *Multiple fatalities.*

The detective said, 'Linc, that wasn't from the quakes. All the fires were arson – just staged to make it look like the earthquakes caused 'em.'

'What?' Mel Cooper asked.

'That latest quake, the second one? Right after, this woman at home by Cadman Plaza – it's near where the epicenter is – smells gas really strong. She thinks the quake broke the line and it's gonna blow. She's home with her kid, a baby. But the good news is she's got a broken ankle. I mean, a totally fucked-up ankle. She falls and breaks it again and passes out.'

Good news . . . ?

'But then she wakes up a few seconds later and she's trapped. So what's she do?'

'Move it along, Lon.'

'She has a brainstorm. She can't get out, can't walk, but maybe she can keep the gas from blowing up. She opens the access door in the bathroom, the door to the pipes, you know? And she turns a handheld shower sprayer on full and douses the basement, hoping to hit the pilot light of the water heater and put it out. While she's spraying, she's screaming her head off and somebody hears and gets the fire department and police there. They shut the gas off outside and get the woman and her baby out, and the other tenants.'

Rhyme glanced at the TV screen, the cyclone of fire. 'So that fire was a second one.'

'Yeah.' Sellitto added with a grimace, 'Three fatalities. It was a couple blocks from Claire's.'

'Who?'

'Claire Porter. That shower thing. She was really thinking on her feet.' Sellitto winced. 'Bad choice of words. She's in emergency surgery right now for her ankle. Anyway. A marshal goes down to the basement to check out the leak. Guess what he finds?'

Rhyme lifted an eyebrow.

'If looks could talk,' Sellitto said.

'They can. Mine did. Let's keep going.'

'IED on the gas line.'

Now Rhyme's full attention settled. An improvised explosive

device. He said, 'Set up to cut through the line and let the gas flow for, what, five minutes then ignite it?'

'Ten minutes.'

'And the water she sprayed disabled it.'

'Bingo, Linc. Sometimes you do catch a break. The device was plastic and housed in a thermostat casing. If it works right and ignites the gas, there's virtually nothing left and even if the fire marshal finds something, it'll look like a melted, burnt-up thermostat, sitting in the rubble. Perfect arson. No evidence. No accelerant.'

The door buzzer again. It was a solid man in a black suit, holding a large carton. Rhyme hit the intercom. 'Is that from Tony?'

Carreras-López: El Halcón's lawyer.

The man leaned close to the speaker. 'That's right, sir.'

The case files he'd asked for, regarding the evidence-tampering claim. He glanced at Sellitto to see if he was paying any attention. But, no. The detective and Cooper were staring at the scene of the fire on the TV.

'Just leave it inside the front door. On the table.'

'Yessir.'

Rhyme hit the door lock, and the man set down the box of the El Halcón case files and left.

He turned to Sellitto. 'Fire marshal's gone back and checked out the prior fires?'

'Yep, every fire that started after the first and second earthquakes? There're the shells of fake thermostats. Just like at Claire's.'

Serial fires with sophisticated IEDs. What's that about?

'As if that wasn't interesting enough, here's the juicy part. As soon as it was labeled arson the fire marshal called RTCC to pull the nearby video cams from the past few weeks.'

The computer surveillance center down at One Police Plaza.

He held up his phone. 'And look who got videoed slipping into and out of Claire Porter's building last week. The basement.'

It was a screenshot of a man in dark clothing and a stocking cap, carrying an orange vest and yellow hard hat. A bag was slung over his shoulder. It appeared heavy.

Identical to the image of Unsub 47 as he'd left the geothermal site later that same day, heading for the subway – minus the bag.

Sellitto said, 'I had RTCC pull all the videos from her apartment to the drilling site. He walks right to the construction site, puts on his hat and vest and vanishes inside. It was an hour before he left and walked to the subway. And then I ordered videos near the sites of all the other gas fires. Within the space of two hours, Unsub Forty-Seven broke into every single one of them.'

Jesus. The unsub planted gas line bombs meant to mimic fires after the quakes? What was this about? Rhyme said, 'I want to see the device. Get it here fast.'

'Already ordered. I thought you would. It'll be here any minute.'

'And have an ECT crew walk the grid around where it was found in Ms Porter's building. Probably contaminated as hell but we'll give it a shot.'

'K. Will do. Thanks. I gotta go. Mayor wants a briefing. You'll copy me on all your brilliant insights, right?'

Rhyme grunted.

Sellitto pulled his jacket off the hook and left. Just as he stepped through the door, Ron Pulaski arrived, nodded to the lieutenant and continued into the hallway. Rhyme wheeled into the hallway to greet him.

The young officer sniffed the air and said, 'I smell gas.'

Rhyme realized he did too, very faint. 'It was Lon.' He explained about the IED that ate through the line at Claire Porter's apartment. 'Disarmed before it ignited. But anybody nearby would've picked up some odorant.' Since explosive – and suffocating – natural gas was odorless, sulfur-based chemicals, reeking of rotten eggs, were added to warn of leaks.

He explained they'd learned that the fires after the earthquakes were actually arson.

The young officer frowned at this. 'Who set them?'

'It appears . . . and note that word. It *appears* to be Unsub Forty-Seven.'

'No way,' Pulaski muttered.

'We'll see.' Rhyme nodded toward the box of files that Carreras-López's driver had delivered. 'Those're the files in the El Halcón. Can you run the analysis tonight?'

Not really a question.

'Sure.'

'And I'm going to need you to walk the grid at the scene.'

'What scene?'

'Long Island. The warehouse where the El Halcón shoot-out took place. It'll all be in the file. And remember—'

The Rookie whispered, 'Not a word to anyone.'

Rhyme winked. Pulaski blinked at the alien expression.

The young officer collected the box for his furtive assignment and left.

Back to the parlor – where nobody seemed to have noticed Pulaski's arrival, *sans* box, or his departure with it.

The buzzer rang yet again and Rhyme recognized the caller. He instructed the security system to open the door.

Into the parlor walked an officer from the Bomb Squad, based out of the 6th Precinct in Greenwich Village.

'Brad.'

'Lincoln.' Lieutenant Bradley Geffen, a compact, gray-haired man, strode forward and had no hesitation shaking Rhyme's somewhat functioning right hand. Often people were intimidated by the disability but this was a man who would lie on his belly with tweezers and screwdriver and dismantle IEDs that could turn him into red vapor. Not much fazed him. If he resembled anyone, it would be a drill sergeant, with his sinewy, etched face, crew cut, piercing eyes.

He nodded a greeting to the others and stepped to an examination table in the parlor.

'What do we have?' Rhyme asked.

'Our boys and gals went over it.' He extracted an evidence bag from the attaché case he carried. 'Never seen anything like it. But it's pretty damn smart.'

He held it out for Rhyme to look at. Inside the bag was what appeared to be a typical white plastic thermostat housing along with some other metallic and plastic parts, none of which he recognized.

Turning it over, Geffen said. 'There. See that hole? A timer opened a little spigot. Acid dripped out and melted the gas line. About ten minutes later, this part . . . ' He touched a small gray box with two electrodes on it. 'It would strike a spark. That would ignite both the gas and the solvent – it's very flammable. Now, the delay was smart. It let the room build up with gas but not force all the air out.'

A room filled with gas only will sometimes not blow up. As with all fires, both air and fuel are required.

'We'll take over, Bradley. Thanks.'

Geffen nodded and stepped out of the room. He moved stiffly, the result of an IED that detonated at a woman's health clinic during the render-safe operation. (There was grim irony in the fanatics' tactic: They'd planted the bomb between two buildings – the clinic and what they hadn't realized was a church's daycare center. If the structures hadn't been evacuated, the daycare center would have sustained far more damage and injuries than the clinic.)

Cooper filled out the chain-of-custody card and began his analysis. He found no prints, and sent swabs out for DNA testing. He took a sample of the acid and ran it through the gas chromatograph. It would take some minutes for the results.

'Detonates by digital timer,' Cooper said as he examined the components with tweezers and a probe. 'Battery life about two months.'

'It doesn't look handmade,' Rhyme observed.

'No. Professionally assembled. Sold on the arms market, I'd imagine.'

'Any idea where it would've come from?'

'Nope. Nothing I've ever come across.' Cooper looked over the chromatograph/spectrometer. 'Got the acid used to melt the line. Well, it's not acid. It's trichlorobenzene. Gas pipes are usually polyethylene and impervious to most acids. But benzene derivatives will melt them. And—'

'No. Can't be.' Rhyme was staring at the evidence charts.

'What, Lincoln?'

What he was thinking seemed impossible. Or would have, if he hadn't just learned about Unsub 47's likely planting of the gas line IEDs.

'Get Lon back here. And do you have Edward Ackroyd's number?'

'Somewhere.'

'Find it. I want him here. Now.'

'Sure.'

'Dial Sachs,' he commanded his phone.

She answered a minute later. 'Rhyme.'

'I need you to run another scene, Sachs. Well, to be accurate, to run a scene you've run before but to look for something else.'

'Where?'

'It's the geothermal site. The drilling shafts again.'

Where, he deduced, though she hadn't mentioned it, she'd nearly been buried alive.

Sachs was silent.

There were plenty of competent evidence collection techs who could walk the grid and could probably find what he needed. But no one was better than Amelia Sachs. He wanted her, and only her.

'Sachs?'

'I'll run it,' she said in a flat voice. 'Tell me what I'm looking for.'

CHAPTER 40

Forty minutes later Sellitto and Ackroyd were in the parlor, along with Mel Cooper. Amelia Sachs was joining them, walking through the elegant archway that separated the hallway from the parlor.

Rhyme noted that she didn't seem troubled to have revisited her near-burial ground. The hollow look on her face was gone completely and she wore the keen expression of a hunter. He noticed mud speckling her jeans.

Sellitto asked, 'What's this all about, Linc?'

'Let me try this out on you. Theory only. But let's see. Whatever our unsub's interest in diamonds is, he's got another mission. He's behind the earthquakes.'

Edward Ackroyd gave a brief laugh. 'Behind the earthquakes? You mean . . . somehow he's *caused* them?'

'Exactly.'

Sellitto said, 'Better keep going on this one, Linc. Fill in the gaps. I see a lot of 'em.'

Rhyme was staring at the ceiling. His face knotted. 'We . . . *I* should've thought better. Why would Forty-Seven go to the trouble to get a hard hat and go into the jobsite to buy a weapon from somebody? They'd meet in a bar or on the street somewhere. No, he needed *access* to the site itself.'

'Why?' the detective asked.

Rhyme looked at Sachs, who said, 'I was just down to the site again. I found traces of RDX near several of the shafts.'

The main ingredient in C4 plastic explosive.

'At a construction site?' Sellitto asked. 'C4's never used commercially.'

It was a military explosive.

'And the site manager told me that one of his workers has

258

gone missing. It was right after Unsub Forty-Seven was in the site. And there was a half ton of grout missing from the pallets in Area Seven.'

'Grout?' Cooper asked.

Rhyme explained, 'It's Forty-Seven's plan. It's why he's here: planting gas line bombs and C4 charges to mimic earthquakes. Last week he placed the gas line IEDs in buildings near the geothermal site. Then he goes to the site, in his hard hat and vest, and meets the now-missing worker, who takes him to Area Seven. He drops C4 charges down some or all of the shafts, and the worker pours grout down them so that when the charges blow, you won't hear the explosion. Then Forty-Seven ditches the empty shoulder bag and leaves – where we see him on the subway. Later that night, I'm guessing, he kills the worker and disposes of the body.'

'Pretty fucking bizarre, Linc. But can that even happen, explosions causing earthquakes?'

'That's why I asked our expert here.' He looked at Edward Ackroyd. 'You know if there've ever been any insurance claims because explosions in mines caused earthquakes?'

The Englishman reminded them of his earlier thoughts, about fracking and geothermal drilling potentially leading to quakes. 'But as for explosions? I've never heard of that. But I'll ask my research associate again. Somebody here or in London could have a look, I'm sure.'

'Do that, if you would.'

Ackroyd stepped to the corner and pulled out his phone. After a brief conversation he returned. 'Sorry to report, our head researcher's never heard of an earthquake induced through explosions. She'll ask at headquarters in London and our other offices when they're open. My initial thought is that it's rather unlikely.'

Rhyme noticed Sachs open her purse. She withdrew a business card, read a number and placed a call.

Waiting for the connection, she said to the room, 'Don McEllis, the state mining inspector.'

A voice answered, 'Hello, Amelia. How are you feeling?'

'Fine,' she said shortly. 'Listen, you're on speaker here with Lincoln Rhyme, an NYPD consultant, and a few other people.'

'Oh. Sure.'

'Dan, this is Lincoln.'

'Don,' Sachs corrected.

'We need to know if somebody can induce an earthquake by explosion.'

There was a pause. 'You think these quakes in the past few days aren't naturally occurring?'

'We aren't sure. Can explosives cause an earthquake?'

'Well, in theory, yes, but you'd need a nuclear device, in just the right place, just the right megatons. But short of that, no.'

'C4 couldn't do it? Do you know C4?'

'Plastic explosives, sure. But, no, it'd be impossible. Even a ton or two placed right on a fault line. That's not how quakes work. But . . . '

Silence.

'Hello?' Rhyme asked.

They heard fast keyboarding. 'Okay, okay. Give me an email address. I want you to see this.'

Cooper did so and a moment later a tone announced the arrival of a message.

McEllis said, 'I've sent two seismograms.'

Cooper's astute fingers typed on the keyboard, and the charts – with the familiar waves anyone with a TV and a love of natural disaster blockbusters would recognize – appeared on the screen. 'Got them.'

The inspector continued, 'The top one is from the most recent tremor here.'

At the far left, the stylus's black line rose and fell only a little as it moved to the right over the course of several minutes. Then halfway along the chart the line jumped up and down in a series of broad, sharp waves. As time passed, they tapered and grew smaller and smaller until the line returned to what it had been before the tremor.

'Now look at the second chart. It's a record of a real earthquake, one in California. It seems similar but there's one subtle difference. In the real quake, we can see just a bit of pre-quake ground motion a few seconds before the main disturbance. There's none of that in the tremors here.'

Rhyme said, 'So the explosions weren't inducing an earthquake; they were mimicking one.'

'Exactly.' A moment later McEllis said, 'But then how do you explain the fires . . . Ah, wait: Unless they were caused by charges too – separate ones, to make it more credible that it was a quake.'

When no one answered, he asked in an uncertain voice, 'What exactly is this all about, Amelia?'

'We're not sure yet, Don. But if you could – please keep it to yourself.'

'Of course. Sure.'

She looked at Rhyme, meaning: Anything else?

He shook his head. She thanked McEllis and they disconnected the call.

Rhyme echoed, 'And what *is* this all about? What's our unsub up to?'

'Terrorism,' Sachs suggested, then shook her head. 'But nobody's come forward. And why make an attack look like a natural disaster? That's not the terrorist profile.'

Sellitto said, 'One idea: He staged the quakes to cover up the arson. Maybe he's working for a landlord wants to torch his buildings for insurance.'

Ackroyd said, 'With respect, Lieutenant, it'd be the most elaborate insurance scam in history. And, besides, professional arsonists never risk murder or assault charges. They only torch buildings when they're empty.'

'Granted.'

Rhyme said, 'Well, there's another way to look at it. What McEllis suggested: The fires were cosmetic. Just to give more credibility to the quakes – so that nobody would look too closely at suspicious seismograms. He wants them to seem real . . . How's this: He wants to stop the geothermal operation.'

Sellitto offered, 'Who's on that list? Energy industry companies would see geothermal as a threat. Somebody wants the drilling site land. It's prime real estate.'

'Environmentalists,' Cooper suggested. 'That One Earth crowd? Though I don't think tree huggers use C4 very much . . . or burn down buildings with people inside.'

Sachs said, 'Whatever he's up to, Forty-Seven seems like a triggerman or mercenary to me. Access to the arms market for the C4 and gas devices. Knows weapons. Doesn't hesitate to kill. Somebody hired him, I'll bet.'

Rhyme was inclined to agree. He then said, 'One thing: We've got a decision to make.'

Sachs was nodding. 'To tell or not to tell.'

'Announce the fact they're fake?' Cooper asked.

'Right. He could have a dozen more IEDs planted in the shafts.'

Sellitto said, 'There'll be some panic. Everybody'll think terrorism.'

'So, they think terrorism,' Rhyme countered. 'I think we have to. And tell people in the general area of the drilling site that there might be a bomb on their gas lines. They should look for them. And announce that if there's another tremor, they should evacuate or check for gas immediately.'

'It'll be the commissioner's and City Hall's call, but if we do announce, we tip our hand,' Sellitto said. 'The perp might book on out of town. Evidence'll disappear.'

As for the last concern, Rhyme was amused: It was very difficult to make evidence disappear from him.

'If I may make an observation?' Ackroyd said.

'Yeah, sure,' Sellitto offered.

'I don't doubt this fellow is deranged and has some perverse obsession with diamonds. But if he's basically a mercenary, hired to sabotage the drilling, well, as soon as he finds out we're onto him, he could sell my client's rough as soon as he can and leave town. I think I should contact dealers again and explore that possibility.'

Sellitto and Rhyme agreed. Ackroyd pulled on his overcoat and, looking even more like a stolid British detective inspector, left to pursue that lead.

Sellitto too slipped on his jacket. 'I'll go talk to the commissioner and the mayor, recommend we announce the whole thing is probably fake. And I'll have ESU and Bomb Squad set up a staging area down there. They'll send a robot down the shafts, see if they can find any more IEDs and render safe.'

For his part, Rhyme had a task too. He placed another call to his spy down in the nation's capital.

CHAPTER 41

Trooper J. T. Boyle had had, over the course of his fourteen-year career with the Pennsylvania State Police, some bizarre assignments. Chasing an Amish horse and buggy hijacked by a very non-Amish drunk college kid. The typical cats up trees ('Not our job, ma'am, but I'll do the best I can'). Birthing babies.

But he'd never pulled over a whole bus before.

This job came as a courtesy to the NYPD, whom Boyle had worked with before and generally liked, though the language of some officers he didn't approve of. On board the Greyhound he was now trailing was a witness on the run – and, no less, a witness from a case that'd made the news. WKPK, at least. The Promisor – the serial perp murdering young couples who'd just bought their engagement rings. That'd be one sick pup.

A New York detective was sure this witness was on the bus. Their computer department had found his phone and done some kind of high-tech thing so that its GPS kept working, and beaming the location, while incoming and outgoing calls were disabled, so no one could warn him that the police were after him if someone was inclined to do so. The screen showed *No Service*. He'd get suspicious after a while but after a while didn't matter; Boyle had him now.

He lit up the Greyhound, which was on its way to Indianapolis. There, according to the ticket the witness, one Vimal Lahori, had bought, he would transfer to a bus for St. Louis. And onward and onward to Los Angeles. They knew his itinerary because they had tracked the phone to the Port Authority bus station in New York and run a scan of the CCTVs in the ticket seller's cubicles, noting that a young man who fit the description of Vimal had bought such a ticket.

Except he wasn't going to get any farther than the county

lockup ten miles from here. Solely for his own protection. This Promisor knew about him and had already killed one witness. Though Trooper Boyle had to admit that the odds of the suspect getting all the way out here were pretty slim.

The bus eased to the side of the road and Boyle climbed out of his car. He wore the standard PSP trooper outfit: dark slacks, gray shirt, black tie. He pulled on his gray Smokey-Bear hat, with chin strap, and strode to the bus.

The door sha-hushed open.

Eyes scanning the passengers. No obvious threats. Not that he expected any. 'Looking for somebody you got on board,' he said softly to the driver, a slim African American whose face registered concern. The decision had been made by the NYPD to not radio or call him earlier; they didn't know what kind of actor he was and were concerned that the boy would catch any wary behavior, jump off the bus and flee. 'He's not armed. There'll be no issue there.'

''Kay. Feel free.'

At least the New York detective, a gruff-sounding guy, *said* he wasn't armed. Witnesses generally weren't but sometimes they were. This kid seemed like he fell into the unarmed category. Besides, he was Indian, as in overseas Indian, and in Boyle's admittedly limited experience there didn't seem to be a lot of firepower packed by people of that extraction.

Boyle had memorized the picture of Vimal, and he now made his way through the bus, looking, with a neutral expression, at the faces of the passengers he passed. Terrorism would be on everyone's mind, of course. A bomb on the bus. Someone with a gun ready to blast away in the name of Allah or for no reason at all.

He nodded when smiled at, and answered questions like 'What's wrong?' and 'Is there a problem?' with a noncommittal 'Won't keep you long, folks.'

But darn. He didn't spot the boy. There were a couple of darker-skinned men but they were all much older and seemed Latino, not Indian.

He returned to the front of the bus and called that detective in New York.

''Lo?' Lon Sellitto asked.

Unprofessional. But then again these were New Yorkers he was dealing with, whole different kettle of fish.

But by way of object lesson, he said, 'Sir, this is Trooper J. T. Boyle again. I'm on board the bus and've taken a look at all passengers. I don't see him.'

'Did you—'

'Checked the john too, yessir.'

'—ask the driver if anybody got off at any stop?'

Boyle hesitated. He turned to the driver asked if anybody'd gotten off at any stop.'

'No, sir.'

'No, Detective, nobody got off,' Boyle said, then added, 'Detective. Can you call it?'

'What?'

'Can you call the boy's phone?'

'Oh. Hm. Good plan. Hold on.'

There were some clicks and then Sellitto said, 'I've got that detective at Computer Crimes who's been tracking it. Trooper? You're on with Detective Szarnek.'

'Hey,' came the voice. Boyle heard rock-and-roll music.

These New York folks simply were not to be believed.

'Detective . . . ' He didn't try the name. 'This is Trooper J. T. Boyle, state police.'

'Hi, Trooper.'

'Uhm, hi. Could you call the phone?'

'Sure. I'll activate it.'

A moment later, the default ringtone of an iPhone bleated. The sound was coming from a row three back from the front. Boyle walked forward to find a passenger reaching into the side compartment of her bag, a frown on her face, and pulling the phone out, staring at it.

'Miss, am I right in figuring that's not your phone?'

She looked up at him. Her face, surrounded by blue and green hair, was pretty, though in the trooper's opinion spoiled by the nose studs and the ring in her eyebrow. She said, 'No, sir. And I have no idea how it got here.'

*

Ron Pulaski entered the lab and Rhyme knew immediately two things: He'd had some success and he was as uneasy as hell about it.

'Rookie?'

He nodded broadly and furtively, if doing both simultaneously were possible. He would have made an absolutely terrible spy.

'The den,' Rhyme said. He glanced back.

What would they say if they knew . . . ?

The men crossed the hall and stepped, and wheeled, inside.

'What do you have?'

'I'm not feeling great about this, Lincoln.'

'Ah, it's all good.'

'"All good." You know, that sort of rates with that other phrase, "No worries." You notice people say them when all is *not* good and when there *is* something to worry about. I mean, *you* didn't just break the law.'

Pulaski had been out to the warehouse where the shoot-out had occurred involving Eduardo Capilla – El Halcón.

'I doubt you did either.'

'Doubt? The place was sealed. You know it was sealed.'

'It's a crime scene. I would assume it was sealed. Nobody was there, though?'

'No. Just the tape. And the notice that said not to enter. Oh, it also shared that entering was a federal offense.'

'Oh, you don't take those things seriously, do you, Rookie?'

'Those *things*? Federal offenses. Of all the things I take seriously, federal offenses hover near the top.'

Rhyme was amused. *He's sounding more and more like me.*

'Let's get going. Where are we?'

From his bag Pulaski extracted a sheaf of eight-and-a-half-by-eleven-inch pages. 'The ballistic and trace analysis from the prosecution and defense reports. Scene photos, diagrams.'

'Good. Spread them out.'

He did, filling the old, walnut coffee table, whose legs ended in carved claws. Rhyme studied them. He then said, 'And samples from Long Island?'

In the interest of keeping the El Halcón mission on the

down-low, Rhyme had retained a private forensic lab to analyze the new trace Pulaski had collected from the warehouse and had dropped off there earlier. Pulaski opened an envelope from the service and displayed the results.

'Turn the pages, if you would be so kind, Rookie.'

'Oh, sorry.'

Rhyme read the dense type.

'Now the files from PERT.'

'Not enough that I break into a crime scene. You've got me stealing from the FBI headquarters.'

'You didn't steal a thing, Pulaski. Don't exaggerate. You took pictures. That's all.'

'Sounds like a fellow saying he only *borrowed* that watch from the jewelry counter at Macy's. I'm just saying.'

The box delivered to his door by the lawyer's driver wouldn't have all of the crime scene and agents' reports, merely what was going to be presented at trial. Rhyme needed to see everything.

From another envelope Pulaski pulled out a dozen more sheets of paper. He'd printed out the images taken at the FBI's evidence room on his phone's camera. He set these too in front of Rhyme and, like flipping pages of the score for a pianist, he lifted a page away once Rhyme had finished reading it, exposing the one below.

All right. Good. Taken together, all the paperwork detailed many things that he was interested in: the gunshot residue and other trace found on El Halcón's hands and clothing, the trace on the floor of the warehouse, the location of the many bullets that had been fired – in the walls and ceiling and floor and into the victims' bodies. The data confirmed that El Halcón's prints were not on the weapon in question, as Carreras-López had said, though his cuff contained gunshot residue – just where the drug lord had said the arresting officer had smeared a rag or piece of cloth containing the GSR.

Rhyme read everything again.

'What is it, Lincoln?'

Was he being *that* transparent? He was dismayed by what he'd found.

A failing like this? At least he could be grateful for El Halcón's attorney – for coming to him and raising the falsified-evidence question. If not for the round, mild-spoken Mexican, the damage would never have come to light.

Pulaski persisted, 'Is there a problem?'

'No, no. You're a godsend, Rookie.'

'You're being sarcastic.'

'No, I mean it. My delivery doesn't always match my intent. That's a quality for us all to guard against.'

'All right. Acknowledged. But come on, tell me. Am I going to get into trouble for this?'

'How much trouble can you get into when your mission is a higher cause?'

Pulaski pulled a tight grimace. 'You know, Lincoln, my father always said you can never trust anybody when they answer a question with a question.'

CHAPTER 42

'Hank, there's a problem.'

The man uttering these words, a slim, baby-cheeked young assistant prosecutor, had not sounded too alarmed when he'd uttered the 'P' word. Henry Bishop, the senior federal prosecutor for the Eastern District of New York, remained in high spirits. The case against El Halcón was proceeding well. The groundwork had been laid, and they were just getting to the rock-solid forensics that the experts would present.

Bishop himself was slim, though at six feet, five inches, he appeared far more willowy than he really was. The blond, clean-shaven man worked out daily, and beneath his Brooks Brothers suits lurked muscle. He ticked off a notation on a list – on which many more notations required death by ticking – and looked up. 'Yes?'

Larry Dobbs – whom Bishop thought of as First Assistant – continued, 'I just got a call from somebody at PERT.'

The FBI's physical evidence response team.

To Dobbs, Bishop said in a cool voice, 'Let's be clearer. Can you do that?'

'Sure.'

'Good. Now. Specifics.' Bishop was sitting in his office, overlooking the borough of Brooklyn. He noted a haze of smoke on the horizon. From the fire after that earthquake, which had not been far away. He'd felt the tremor in his office.

The young, buttoned-up assistant prosecutor said, 'NYPD officer, a uniform, had some questions about the case.'

'Our case?'

'Right,' Dobbs confirmed.

'Well, say, the El Halcón case.'

'Sorry, Hank. The El Halcón case.'

'Not "the case." There're a lot of "the cases."'

Dobbs, standing across the bulky desk, said, 'El Halcón.'

Bishop mused, 'So New York City cop. Questions. Hm.'

The El Halcón investigation involved federal crimes and state crimes but New York had deferred to the feds. Yes, after Bishop got his convictions of El Halcón, the man would also be charged under the state penal code. But that prosecution would be icing on the cake and largely irrelevant, since the Mexican would never get out of federal prison to serve time in the state pen. So why would NYPD get involved? El Halcón had no city nexus.

Dobbs said, 'The uniform comes into PERT. He knows all the codes, knows the case numbers, knows the people, knows the filing system. He asks to see the evidence logs. The gatekeeper lets him see everything. 'Cause he was in uniform and he knew everything about the case.'

'You said "gatekeeper". The way you phrased it, using that word. Assigning blame, are we?'

Dobbs swayed back and forth slowly. Skinny, a live wire of energy. 'Occurred to me. Evidence room supervisor lets in a patrol officer whose name isn't on the official roster and turns over records.' Dobbs added, 'Tsk-tsk.'

The man actually said that? Bishop then asked, 'Who was running the room? A special agent?'

'No. A civilian with Justice.'

'Oh, good. Heads can roll. And they will. But please. Keep up the narrative.'

'Anyway, the uniform said it was an allied case.'

'Allied case, NYPD? Makes no sense. Nassau County maybe. But not New York City. No NYPD jurisdiction on this one, period. What did he say?'

Dobbs offered, 'He didn't. Just asked for the files. Asked to take copies but the gatekeeper wouldn't let him. It's pretty likely, though, the uniform took cell phone shots.'

'The shit, you're saying,' Bishop barked.

'Once he was finished he made a call. And the gate—'

'Got it, just say "civie." Fewer syllables.'

Dobbs seemed pleased to deliever the next bit of information. 'The civie, she heard him say, "Lincoln, I got everything you wanted. Anything else?"'

Oh. The civie gatekeeper was a she. Harder to roll a female head, though it could be done.

Then he focused.

The assistant continued, '"Lincoln." As in Lincoln Rhyme, I'd think. Rhyme works with NYPD a lot and knows PERT. He helped set it up. The guy wrote the book on forensics and crime scene. He's in a wheelchair, you know.'

'Wheelchair,' Bishop mused. 'What the hell did he want our evidence for? And unauthorized copying?' He tried to figure this out. He couldn't make any headway. He waved Dobbs into a chair – he'd been hovering – and called a friend, a dep inspector at NYPD, and asked if he knew anything about it. But he learned that, no, the NYPD wasn't pursuing a case against El Halcón. They thought the Mexican was a turd, who didn't? But the only deaths he'd caused in New York City were from overdosing on his product; the shootout was outside the city limits.

He hung up, staring out the window. Dark-gray smoke still rose. The fire had been bad.

Mentally he kicked around several theories about Rhyme's involvement. If, in fact, he *had* been involved.

'Rhyme's off the force, right? The wheelchair thing, you mentioned.'

'Oh, yeah, Hank. For years. He consults.' Dobbs was really quite a bundle of eager.

'For NYPD. Us too, right?'

'Yeah.'

'Has he ever done any consulting for a defense team?'

'We've got a team on El Halcón's attorney and the rest of his entourage, right?'

Dobbs said, 'To the extent we can, Hank. There're a lot of them. A dozen came up from Mexico City.'

'Find out if any of 'em ever went to Rhyme's home or office.'

'Sure.'

'Now.'

'Sure.' The assistant made a phone call, had a conversation and a few moments later disconnected. 'Well. Try this on, Hank.'

Oh, please. But he just lifted a querying eyebrow.

More eager than ever now. 'Tony Carreras-López, El Halcón's main lawyer from Mexico – we're on him twenty-four/seven. He was at Rhyme's place, Central Park West, today. Before that, just before that, he stopped at a bank. Chase. He was inside for fifteen minutes. Then to Rhyme's, then back to his hotel.'

'Money? Withdrawal? Wire transfer?'

'Don't know. No probable cause for a warrant, of course, so we couldn't get any details.'

Was Carreras-López hiring Rhyme as a consultant, for the defense, to look for holes in the case?

Our case.

My case.

Bishop paused and closed his eyes momentarily. He couldn't imagine what problems there might be. Of course, no crime scene officer was perfect, no lab analyst was perfect. And someone like Rhyme could very well find something that might derail the entire investigation.

And help that horrific piece of murdering shit, El Halcón, escape justice.

After a moment or two of thought, Bishop decided he had a way to make sure that wasn't going to happen.

He picked up the phone and dialed a number.

'Yessir?'

'Come into my office.'

'Right away.'

A moment later a clean-cut, gray-suited man of thirty-five stepped into Bishop's office. He nodded to Bishop and Dobbs.

'Have a seat.'

The man did and Bishop continued, 'I need you to start a criminal investigation. Immediately. Tonight.'

'Yessir, of course,' said FBI Special Agent Eric Fallow, withdrawing a notebook from his pocket and uncapping his pen.

CHAPTER **43**

Daryl Mulbry from Alternative Intelligence Service was calling back.

'Hello. Lincoln, this just keeps getting better and better! First, your unsub – what were you calling him?'

'Unsub Forty-Seven.'

'First, Mr Forty-Seven is a brilliant diamond thief, then it seems he's a psychotic serial killer who dubs himself he Promisor, and now we see he's actually a mercenary hired to do some nasty deeds in Brooklyn. Though still a psycho, by the looks of it. Never a dull moment.'

'Daryl?'

A chuckle. 'I know, you want to get down to business, First, here's what I've got about your Russian. Or *a* Russian. Or *some* Russian. Probably yours. First, some background. There are known routes that operatives and assets take when they leave certain countries, Russia, for instance, and want to come into the U.S. We call it "purging," as in they purge their background by flying to three or four different cutout locations. One pattern is pretty common: Moscow to Tbilisi to Dubai to Barcelona to Newark. Four separate tickets, four separate identities. And that's what we think this Russian did. There was no one individual on all of those flights – the separate tickets, separate names. But we took a peek at flight manifests – shhh, it'll be our secret – and found there was one constant with all of them.'

'The luggage,' Rhyme interrupted.

Sachs was nodding. 'He checked the bags separately on each flight but they weighed the same.'

Mulbry laughed with delight. 'See, Lincoln, Amelia, I *told* you you're *just* the material we need at AIS! Exactly. What're the odds that four different men on four different flights would check two bags weighing exactly twelve point three kilos? Nonexistent. Pictures would prove it, and I'm sure you'd love one of his mug but we can't get those from Passport Control. That would involve the NSA and, well, getting you data for a domestic case would be so . . . "illegal" is the word that trips into my mind. But we're convinced it's your boy.

'The passport for the final leg, when he landed at Newark, was Georgian. Josef Dobyns. Not a watchlist baby. And his address here was a fake one in Patterson, New Jersey. I'll send you all the names he used on the flights. You can check hotel registries. Though my bet is he's got another ID that he hasn't used before.'

'*Five* passports?' Sachs asked.

Mulbry only chuckled.

Rhyme gave the man Mel Cooper's email and asked him to send the names on the passports.

'Now,' Mulbry continued, 'you were asking about explosives. About a week ago we had an alert about a weapons package that was reportedly smuggled into the East Coast: three one-kilo packets of C4 and a crate of a dozen *lehabah*s.'

'Of *what*?'

'Gas line bombs. *Lehabah*s. The word's Hebrew. It has two meanings: "flame," and "the tip of a spear or weapon."'

Which, Rhyme reflected, described the mean little things pretty well. He asked, 'A Mossad invention?'

Now that he dabbled in the world of espionage, he'd done some homework on the various intelligence agencies around the world. None was more clever at weaponry, or more talented at its deployment, than the Mossad.

'Yep. For just what you're talking about: making it seem that there was a gas leak and explosion. Who knows how many Hamas or Hezbollah terrorist homes have gone up in flames quote "accidentally"?'

Three loads of C4. They didn't know how much the unsub had used for the IEDs in the Northeast Geo shafts. They'd have to assume he had some left for at least one more 'earthquake.' He had other *lehabah*s too. How much more carnage did he have in mind?

Mulbry now asked, 'So, please, Lincoln, give. What's this all about?'

'You followed the earthquakes in New York? And the fires?'

'Yes, sure. It's big news everywhere.'

Sachs explained that Unsub 47 was creating the phony quakes and accompanying fires.

'So that's what he was using the devices for. Hm. Clever.' His job, as head of the AIS, was to come up with ways to, well, alternatively engage the enemy. Faking earthquakes as a mask for arson fell squarely within the AIS toolbox. Mulbry was clearly impressed. 'Why?'

Rhyme said, 'That we don't know. Our best guess is to stop the drilling. Somebody doesn't want that geothermal operation up and running. We don't see it as political terrorism.'

Mulbry said, 'I agree. The C4 shipment and gas bombs raised eyebrows – anything like that always does, of course – but our algorithms scoured the intel and they couldn't pin the explosive to known terrorist actors. We'll keep an eye on that side of it, though.'

'Please do,' Sachs said.

'While I've got you on the line?'

'Yes, Daryl?'

'I got your email about the dozenal coding – that nobody at NYPD or FBI New York knew anyone who'd ever used it. Thank you again for checking, by the way. Now, actually there's more to the matter. We were never able to decrypt the messages but we did trace the traffic pattern of a couple of them. To a hotel – a long-stay residence hotel – near the Seine in Paris. The Left Bank. Have you been?'

'No. Go on.'

'It's remarkable – a whole different smell and feel. And the cultural history. Hemingway, Simone de Beauvoir, Jean-Paul Sartre, existentialists. I digress.'

True.

'A couple of EVIDINT folks got inside and, my, had the place been scrubbed. And I mean literally: *Beaucoup de* bleach and *le* Windex for DNA and fingerprints. Traces of sandpaper to remove something from the floor and Gorilla Glue in places where trace had lodged, then pulling it out. I mean, really, whoever this person or cell is, they're very, very good. But they missed one thing, a small piece of metal. Didn't show up in any metal parts database. Homemade. We scanned it. Positive for radium. Not nuclear-device-quality but it might be part of a dirty bomb. Makes us all a bit nervous. Could you take a peek?'

'I will, sure, Daryl. Tell me: What does it look like?'

'Flexible, springy, silver-colored. Typical of mechanical detonators. There's a trend away from electronic. You know, EMPs – electromagnetic pulses – can take out the digital detonators.'

'Send it overnight.' He gave the man his address.

As soon as they'd disconnected. Rhyme's phone trilled. It was Crime Scene headquarters in Queens. He picked up and, via speakerphone, had a conversation with an analyst there. The man reported that searching the basement in Claire Porter's apartment, near Cadman Plaza, had revealed that the fingerprints on and around the gas line were the superintendent's or were very old and, in any case, came back negative from the IAFIS database. The lock was easily jimmied with basic tools, and whoever did it had apparently taken these with him when he left. The local precinct told him that a canvass of tenants and residents of nearby buildings found no one else who had seen the man in the hard hat and vest.

While he'd been talking to the detective in Brooklyn, Lon Sellitto had called.

Rhyme now called him back at One Police Plaza and hit Speakerphone.

'Got some news. Vimal sent his phone on a bus ride. Trooper tracked it down in Pennsylvania. Slipped it into the bag of some girl. So he's back to being MIA. Damn smart kid.'

'Well.' Rhyme sighed. Smart indeed.

Sachs said, 'He's got a two-hour head start, wherever he's going to. He'll take Amtrak or public transit to Jersey, get to a smaller Greyhound station there. Or Westchester.'

Rhyme told him about the conversation with Mulbry. He had

Cooper email the names of the four passports they suspected the unsub had used to travel here.

'K, Linc. I'll order a canvass of hotels.'

Rhyme reminded him that their spy believed the unsub would have yet another identification, though.

Sellitto said, 'Yeah, I'd guess. But we gotta do it.'

'Now, you'll find this interesting, Lon.' Rhyme reported on the explosives that Mulbry had learned of.

'Israeli intelligence gas bombs? Fuck me.'

'Daryl's still doing some looking.'

Sellitto said, 'Well, one thing you should know, Linc: ESU and Bomb Squad talked to the mayor's office. They decided not to send robots down the shafts at the geothermal site to try to render it safe; they'd just put a bomb curtain over the openings. They think another explosion'll at least give people in the vicinity ten minutes' warning to evacuate. And the fire department's sent extra trucks and crews to stage around the geothermal site – since it's the hub of the attacks. If there's another detonation, they'll be ready to go at the first report of a fire. And . . . '

Silence.

'Lon?'

'Fucking hell,' the lieutenant muttered.

'What is it?'

'Just saw on the wire: Forty-Seven got another vic.'

Sachs asked, 'Engaged couple?'

'No.' A pause, while Sellitto presumably read. 'But it's related. Somehow. Got to be. The vic was Kirtan Boshi. About Vimal's age, Indian. Worked in the diamond business. An apprentice cutter. Just like Vimal. Can't be a coincidence.'

'Circumstances?' Sachs asked.

'Basement of a coffee shop in the Fashion District. About a block from where he worked.' Sellitto paused. 'Some employees just found the body but looks like he was killed around lunchtime today. Son of a bitch broke his windpipe. Killed him with the box cutter.'

'Kirtan was probably a friend of Vimal's and knew where he lived. He probably gave the address up.'

'Yeah. He'd been tortured. A mess. And the unsub cut Kirtan's ring finger off and put it in his mouth. Postmortem, but still.'

'Goddamn it,' Sachs muttered.

Rhyme looked her way.

'We canvassed for anybody who knew Vimal in every store in the Diamond District, Jackson Heights, other parts of Queens and Brooklyn. Never occurred to me to look for diamond cutters in the Fashion District. But Forty-Seven did. He outthought me.'

Us, Rhyme corrected silently. He outthought us. But he knew the words would mean little to her. Any failing to which she contributed, however small her part, she owned.

Sellitto said, 'He's got the Lahoris' address now and he doesn't know the boy's on the run. Amelia, tell your security team at their house to stay out of sight and expect Forty-Seven might show up.'

'I will,' Sachs said. 'Though I think he's too smart to fall into a trap like that.' She sighed. 'I'll walk the grid at the coffee shop.'

Sellitto gave her the address and she hurried from the parlor, tugging her jacket on absently. A moment later Rhyme heard the engine of her big car fire up and a squeal as the tires slung her into traffic.

His eyes drifted toward the sounds out the window, gazing over the dun dusk.

So Unsub 47 had spent all day, last week, planting gas bombs meant to mimic the fires after earthquakes. Presumably more existed, and announcing that the authorities knew the quakes were being faked wouldn't change the fact that they were timed to explode.

And even if his plans were now exposed, Unsub 47 would have no incentive whatsoever to remove the devices or let the police know where they were.

CHAPTER 44

The Promisor's backup plan.

Vladimir Rostov steered the stolen Toyota carefully along the streets of Queens. East Elmhurst to be specific.

Somewhat carefully. He was used to driving in Moscow, where one didn't need to be very careful; the congestion left little risk of high-speed collisions.

Here, though, the weaving was due to the fact he was digging beneath the passenger seat, as best he could. Making a sharp turn had catapulted his Roll N Roaster beef sandwich to the space between front passenger seat and door.

Where, where the hell, where?

Ah, he got a corner of the bag and pulled it out, ripped the paper apart with his teeth and began chewing the cold, but still tasty, sandwich.

Why the fuck don't we have these in Moscow?

In three minutes the sandwich and fries were consumed. He belched and lit a cigarette. He noted that in America very few people smoked in cars any longer, unlike Russia. Of course, when he was through finding Vimal, the little *kuritsa*, and he was done with the car, he'd make sure it did plenty of smoking. This was a joke: The only way to get rid of the evidence in a vehicle was to burn it to the rims – which was, in fact, the source of an expression used in certain criminal circles in Russian. 'Rim it,' a mob boss might say. Usually the automobile *flambée* contained merely evidence. Sometimes, a corpse. Sometimes, depending on your playful mood, the person might not yet be a corpse when you tied them up inside and set the gas tank ablazing.

Rostov now thought of the red-haired *kuritsa* cop once more. A fantasy blossomed in his mind: the woman as cowgirl. Vladimir Rostov happened to love the Louis L'Amour novels of the American West. He thought they were finely crafted jewels, adventure tales that gave you a peek at life back then. Russia had the Cossacks and, from Mongolia, the Tartars. But there was nothing romantic about marauding drunks and rapists. The American West . . . ah, those were the days of heroes! He owned all the Sergio Leone films. John Ford's movies, too, starring John Wayne. And there was no better Western than Sam Peckinpah's *The Wild Bunch*.

He sometimes thought about living back then. The Germans were in Mexico. The Spanish and Portuguese in South and Central America. The French in Canada and the Caribbean.

There must have been *some* Russians in the nineteenth-century New World.

Oh, how he would have loved to be among them.

With his six-shooter and horse. And bourbon, of course.

And the whores.

His thoughts returned to the cowgirl *kuritsa*, the one with the red hair and the blue diamond on her white finger.

His blue diamond, *his* white finger.

He turned the corner and slowed. Vladimir Rostov was feeling proud of himself, for being smarter than the cowgirl cop.

Because I know where Vimal Lahori is going.

His backup plan.

When Rostov had his chat with Kirtan in the basement of the diner in the Fashion District, he'd learned more about Vimal than just his name and address and family. A cut here, a cut there. He'd found out Vimal had a girlfriend.

I'll tell you but don't hurt her!! Kirtan had written (the crushed throat matter).

'No, no, *kuritsa*. I won't hurt a hair on her head. I just need to have a talk with Vimal. I won't hurt him either. That's a peeing promise.'

Rostov had had to read the response twice, to make it out – the kid's hand was shaking so. The message was: *Will die before I tell you if you hurt her.*

Which made no sense.

'Hair on head. Really.'

Peeing promise. Rostov had just made that phrase up but he liked it. He'd use it again.

He'd bent down and slid the knife along the kid's fingernail.

In three minutes, poof. Vimal's girlfriend was Adeela Badour. And she lived in East Elmhurst, Queens, a mile or so from Vimal's family.

A check of Google revealed that a Mohammad Badour lived at the address. And, yes, he had two daughters, Adeela and Taalia, twenty-two and ten. Though, sadly, no online pictures of the little creatures. Some parents were *so* protective.

'Anyone else?' Rostov had asked. 'That Vimal is close to?'

Kirtan had shaken his head vigorously. His last gesture. Rostov had slit his throat then. It was a favor, he reasoned. The kid would have lived with guilt his whole life, for having given up Vimal and his friend.

After he died – which took some messy time – Rostov had cut his pinkie finger off and placed it, still holding the travesty of a ring, into Kirtan's slack-jawed mouth. The Promisor didn't have to limit himself to making statements only about diamonds on the fingers of slutty fiancées.

Adeela Badour . . .

He'd be at her house soon.

At a traffic light, he took a napkin from his pocket and coughed into it for a moment. Fucker, he thought angrily. A problem all his life. Cigarettes, of course. He'd stop smoking someday. The condition would go away.

He wondered if this Adeela was sexy. He generally preferred pale-complexioned women. But since he'd been thinking of the little Persian *kur*, Kitten and Scheherazade, he was of a mind to spend some time with a darker girl, an Arab girl. Hell, didn't matter if she was sexy. He was hungry. He needed a woman. Now.

Oh, and the Promisor would keep his peeing promise to Kirtan. What was going to happen to her wouldn't damage a single hair on her head.

CHAPTER 45

'It'd be an adventure.'

'Adventure,' Adeela Badour replied to Vimal, clearly troubled by his choice of words. 'What is this? A quest? *The Hobbit.*'

They were in her backyard. The Badours had a nice house, brick with red wooden trim, in East Elmhurst, Queens, about a mile from Vimal's family. This neighborhood embraced LaGuardia airport and on days when the wind wasn't kind, residents would have to endure the scream of jets skimming over houses to land on Runway 4. Today the air was, more or less, quiet.

The Badours' home was bigger than the Lahoris'; Adeela's father had a good job with a big tech company, her mother – like his – was a nurse. The place featured a yard with a well-tended garden, both rare here.

As far as Vimal was concerned, though, one of the better features was a detached garage, behind the house, which opened onto an alley, shared by all the homes here.

Better, because it was in the musty structure that Vimal and Adeela had first kissed – daringly in the backseat of her mother's Subaru – after the adults had gone to sleep, of course – and where they had explored, touching and tasting, growing warm, teasing open buttons and finally a zipper or two.

At the moment, though, the mood was different. The only agenda item was escape.

He directed her into the garage, just to be out of sight, though he wasn't concerned the ski-masked man had found his way here – that would be impossible. But he didn't want neighbors to see him and call his father.

She leaned against her car, an old dark-green Mazda (fond memories there too, though the backseats were comically small). There was no room inside the structure for a second vehicle.

Much of the rest of the space was occupied with a shabby work-bench and limp storage cartons, inscribed with faded labels describing contents. *Mothers dishes. Clothes for goodwill. Textbooks/diapers.*

He said, 'I'm not making, you know, light of it or anything. I mean, it'd be a change for you.'

'California?' she asked. 'Why California?'

'Have you ever been?'

Adeela fired a thoughtful look, tilting her head. 'In a land long ago, far away, there was a magical place out to the west, beyond the far reaches of humankind.'

Vimal sighed. Now she was being sardonic. 'I'm just—'

'Disney, Legoland, San Francisco, Yosemite. I skied in July at Mammoth.'

'I didn't mean it to sound like you were . . . what's that word?'

'Young, provincial, naïve?'

He sighed, but only slightly. Then recovered. 'So? Did you like it?'

'Vim! Of course. That has nothing to do with anything. How can you just pick up and go – and expect me—'

'Not expect.'

'—to go with you?'

'UCLA has a fine arts program with a sculpting track. And a great medical school. I checked.' Then he took her hand.

'This isn't the time to be thinking about that.' Her brown eyes narrowed. 'You're a witness to a murder. Do you get it, that this is not a normal time? Is that registering with you? You're joking about adventures. This is serious!'

'I'm not saying we jump on the train today. I'll go and then I'll find a place and—'

'Train to California?' Her beautiful sculpted brows furrowed. 'Oh, because you *can't* fly because you're on a watchlist. People don't take trains across the country, Vim. Does that tell you anything?'

He fell silent. 'Would you consider it?'

'Vim, just tell him you don't want to cut anymore.'

He released her hand, stepped away and walked to the small

window in the side wall of the garage, grimy and half obscured by a persistent weed. He laughed softly at her comment, which appeared to be a non sequitur, but was in fact the whole point of his fight.

His father, the person the police couldn't protect him from.

The person he was fleeing as ardently as he was the killer.

Vimal loved Adeela Badour. He'd fallen for her the first time he'd seen her. It was in a coffee shop in Greenwich Village – one of the old-time ones, way-way-way pre-Starbucks. She'd been poring over a detailed diagram of the heart in an anatomy book and whispering the names of veins and arteries and muscles – or whatever medical students need to know about the pump, which was presumably everything.

He'd sat down and opened his Michelangelo book.

The ice-breaking conversation was, of course, anatomy. Flesh and blood, in one case. Marble, in the other.

They'd begun dating not long after that and had been in a monogamous relationship since then. From early on the subject of marriage surfaced regularly in his thoughts. On some days, he viewed marrying her as a goal that could be achieved by practical planning, like with most couples. Other days, more frequent, their saying 'I do' was about as feasible as using their arms to fly.

The problem was that *Romeo and Juliet* thing.

The Lahoris were Kashmiri Hindu. Kashmir is a beautiful region in the north of the Asian subcontinent, but one that has for ages been the center of conflict. It's claimed by India as well as by Pakistan and, halfheartedly, by China. For more than a thousand years, rule of the region as a whole, or portions of it, has traded hands among Hindu, Muslim and Sikh leaders – and the British too, of course, who came up with one of the more curious names ever for a country: the Princely State. In recent years the Hindu population of Kashmir, largely Saraswat Brahmin, lived in Kashmir Valley. Representing about 20 percent of the region's inhabitants, they were a people moderate in their religious practice and they comfortably blended spiritual and secular lives, avoiding as much as they could the simmering turbulence of the area.

Inevitably, the peace and isolation didn't last. In the 1980s a militant Kashmiri independence movement arose, composed largely of radicalized Muslims. Its mission was ethnic cleansing, which resulted in the infamous Exodus of 1990, in which more than 150,000 Kashmiri Hindus fled. Those who didn't, risked death. In the end, only several thousand Hindus remained in the valley.

Vimal was born in the United States and had no personal knowledge of these events – which were, of course, hardly topics touched upon by world history classes in American schools. But he was an expert on the independence movement, the rapes and murder, and the Exodus because Papa lectured him and Sunny on the topic frequently. Papa had been in the United States when the Exodus occurred but a number of his relatives had to abandon their homes, leaving all behind, to be relocated to India proper – the congested, polluted urban sprawl of the National Capital Region – Delhi. Several older aunties and uncles died prematurely, Papa was sure, because of the resettlement.

Papa harbored deep, unrelenting resentment toward all people Muslim.

Adeela Badour, for instance – had he known about her.

It didn't matter that the Badour family had lived here for more generations than Papa and that their forebears had no connection with the radicals in the valley, or that they were moderate in religion and secular in worldview. Nor did it matter to Vimal's father that Muslims in India suffered their own abuse at the hands of the Hindu majority.

No, no matter.

What irony here: His father had finally and reluctantly abandoned his insistence on an arranged marriage for his sons; Vimal could have married any Hindu woman of his choosing (though Papa occasionally reminded him that Akbar the Great, the most famous ruler of the Mughal Empire, and his courtesans vastly preferred Kashmiri women for wives and – yes, his father actually said – concubines, because of their beauty).

Possibly, eventually, with a great deal of lobbying by his mother, Vimal's father might have accepted someone non-Hindu.

But Muslim?

Never.

But it was a Muslim who, sipping tea in Greenwich Village and looking over a drawing of a human heart, had stolen Vimal's.

He now turned back to her, as she leaned against the car, arms folded.

Adeela repeated, 'Tell him. You have to.'

I tried, Vimal Lahori thought. And I ended up a prisoner in my own basement.

He told her, 'You don't know him.'

'I'm Muslim, Vim. I know about parents.'

Silence filled the garage, then was suddenly broken by the sound of rain, loud, since the roof wasn't insulated. Vimal glanced up and saw an abandoned bird's nest.

With a faint gaze of resignation she said, 'Do what you think you have to. I have three years in New York. After that, residency, which'll be flexible. Maybe California. I could probably make that work. But I need those three years here.'

Her message wasn't a threat, not by any means. Adeela was never threatening. She was simply and clinically pointing out the undeniable truth: A lot can happen in three years.

'You're going to go, aren't you?'

He nodded.

Her eyes closed. And she hugged him hard. 'Do you have money?'

'Some.'

'I've got—'

'No.'

'You can borrow it. And I know somebody in Glendale.'

'Where's that?'

She laughed. 'Los Angeles. Do your homework. She taught at NYU for a year. She and her husband, they're good people. Wait here. Taalia's in the house.'

Adeela's parents did not know she was dating Vimal but she was close to her younger sister, and the two girls and Vimal had seen a few movies together and had some fast, furtive meals. Better to have no witnesses.

Vimal noted on the workbench her phone, car keys and purse. This gave him an idea. He'd borrow her car and drive it to a suburban town that had a train station, Westchester or somewhere. He'd leave it there. She could take the train to pick it up. And he could get a ticket to another train, Amtrak, and head up to Albany, then find a train going west.

He pocketed the keys. She'd understand.

Then he paused. He heard a car roll into the side street and the brakes squeal as the vehicle stopped. The engine went silent. He looked out and didn't see the vehicle.

Nothing, he was sure. A neighbor. And reflected again that the odds of the killer finding Adeela's house were just about zero.

He leaned against the workbench and waited for his Juliet to return.

CHAPTER 46

What a time this was.

As she walked up the stairs from the backyard into her house, she reflected that she could understand Vimal's wanting to escape his father. Her own – as she'd said – could be overbearing. Oddly, in a culture often male-dominated, it was Adeela's mother who was the formidable partner in the marriage. (This was the opposite of Vimal's Hindu family.) After graduating, Adeela would get an internship and residency out of arm's reach of her mother.

But not too far away. Probably Connecticut (Adeela Badour loved autumn foliage, just *loved* it). Maybe Long Island.

That was as far as she was willing to go.

California? Of course not.

And it wasn't right for Vimal either. But she supposed it was not a bad idea for him to leave now, get to the West Coast for a time. Until they caught that madman.

She glanced into the living room and saw Taalia, on the couch. The ten-year-old was in a *Phineas and Ferb* T-shirt, and jeans. Adeela had to smile. What a child of our times! The girl was texting on the same phone that was pumping music through the massive pink headset embracing her ears and watching, distractedly, a muted Disney Channel cartoon.

Climbing the stairs to the second floor, Adeela stepped into her room, glancing at a poster on the wall: A periodic table of the elements, each represented by Japanese anime characters – from Sailor Moon as hydrogen to Vegeta as Ununoctium. She'd made it herself, inspired by a similar one she'd found online. Adeela was amused, recalling the fight she'd had with her mother about taping up other posters on her walls when she was in middle school: boy bands. Which depicted boys she had no interest in, bands that played music she never listened to. She'd done it simply out of defiance.

So *totally* mature of me, she now thought.

She pulled her checkbook from a folder and sat for a moment. Adeela had a decent-sized bank account. She'd worked a number of jobs since high school, and, though medical school was excruciatingly expensive, she had a student loan for most of it (the day of reckoning was some years away). She looked at her balance. A sigh. She wrote Vimal a check for two thousand dollars.

She tore the check out; the noise seemed particularly odd and troubling, something surgical. She thought of Vimal's wound and his refusal to go to the ER.

Another sigh.

She walked down the stairs and into the kitchen, heading for the back door, when she heard a familiar click.

The front door opening.

Oh, no! Her mother must've returned early. But why the front door? The woman would have parked in the alley beside the garage.

Adeela walked to the doorway and peeked around the corner to the living room. She froze and gave a quiet gasp.

A man in a black coat and ski mask, holding one of those box-cutting knives in his right hand, was looking around. He spotted Taalia and moved quietly up behind her.

No, no, no!

Adeela stepped back, looked around the kitchen and ran to the island. A moment later, holding a ten-inch carving knife, she strode into the front hall. Her gaze toward him was pure steel.

The man blinked, glanced at the knife and smiled. 'Ah, little bird. Look at what you have there. You are the big one, Adeela.'

This would be the killer.

'And cute little Taalia, little birds.'

How the hell did he know their names?

'What do you want?' Her voice was firm. In fact, she didn't feel an ounce of fear. She had told herself that this man was an infection, a weak blood vessel, a shattered bone. This was a clinical problem to be addressed.

He stepped closer. She lifted the knife to waist level. The sharpened side of the blade was up. She'd learned this in some spy movie.

He blinked and paused.

A gun appeared in his other hand, fished from his pocket.

Her resolve faltered for a fraction of a second. But then returned. Somehow, Adeela smiled. 'A gunshot. The neighbors are home. They'd hear. You'd get arrested.'

He nodded at her sister, still lost in the oblivion of pixels and digital sound. He asked in an oddly accented voice, 'What she listens to? Music kids listening to now. Lots and lots of crap, aren't you thinking? I like strings, I like smooth horns, you know what it is.'

'You want money? You want the TV?'

He glanced. 'Sixty-inch Sony? Ah, yes, yes. You help me carry to car? Thank you, birdie. No, no. You know what I want. And you tell me.'

He pointed the gun at the back of Taalia's head.

'No,' Adeela growled and stepped closer. Still holding the knife. 'Don't point that at her. Turn it away.'

'Ah, but you sure I not fire gun. Scaredy of the noise. So why you worry?'

'Now.'

He hesitated, not sure what to make of her, and pointed the gun at the floor.

'If I tell you what you want to know, you'll leave?'

'When parents are coming home?'

'Soon,' she said.

'And father, he is cop or soldier with big gun he carry all the time. Right? And knows karate like Bruce Lee.'

'No. But the more people, the more fucked your are.'

'Ha! No, no, am thinking nobody home for long time. You have nice knife, I have knife. Maybe we roll around and see who is the stabbed one first.' A sick grin.

Still Taalia had no idea of the drama behind her. Her small, perfect head nodded in time to a song.

He lifted the gun to Adeela now. 'Not having time for shit like this.' The smirk vanished. 'Vimal. Where he is?'

'I don't know.'

'Yes.'

He replaced the gun in his pocket and, with his thumb, pushed the blade farther out. He stepped closer to Taalia.

Adeela stepped closer to him yet, chest heaving from the deep breaths, heart pounding, blood pressure through the ceiling, she thought with manic clarity, adrenaline levels soaring.

The man's blue eyes were cold as marbles. He'd kill a child as easily as talk to her.

But then the frown. He cocked his head.

The sirens were just audible.

At last!

He looked past Adeela, into the kitchen – on the wall, where the central station alarm panel door was open, revealing the panic button for the police that Adeela had pressed when she'd picked up the knife.

The man's shoulder's rose and his eyes filled with madness. He lunged toward Taalia, maybe thinking he'd kidnap her and, somehow, trade her for Vimal.

This was not going to happen. Adeela jumped toward him, slashing with the knife. No design, no strategy, just swinging the blade toward his face, so fast the metal was invisible.

He was far larger than she, surely far stronger – and undoubtedly had experience with his knife. But he hadn't expected her assault and he stumbled back. Adeela put herself between Taalia and him.

He stood still for a moment, and she fully expected that he'd pull the gun out and kill them both. Not for any particular reason – he had the mask on; she couldn't identify him. But he would murder simply because he was insane.

Now the sirens were louder.

He grimaced. 'You fucking bird. I am remembering you. I come back and visit.' He fled out the front door. Adeela followed and ran onto the porch. She saw him leap into a red Toyota and speed away. She didn't get the license.

Adeela ran to her sister and pulled her to her feet. The headset fell off the girl, who gave a shriek of surprise and fear.

'What?'

'Come with me.'

'Why? I—'

'Now!' the older sister commanded.

Taalia's round face – darker than Adeela's – nodded slowly, eyes filled with fear. She was looking at the knife.

Holding the girl's hand, Adeela sped out the back door and into the garage.

There, Vimal was looking out the window. He said, 'I hear sirens. What's that—' He stopped speaking as he turned and saw the blade and Taalia in tears.

Adeela raged in a whisper, 'He was here. That man was here.'

'That man?'

She spat out, 'You know who I mean!'

'No! Where is he?'

'He drove off. I called the police.'

'Are you all right?'

In an even softer, even angier voice, she said, 'After a knife fight, yeah. I'm great.'

'What?' He stared.

She glanced out the window – to make sure the intruder hadn't circled back.

'We have to go. Get away. Now. We'll drive to Westchester. You come with me for now, drop me at a train station.'

'No,' she said.

'Yes, get in the car. Please. Hey, Taal, want to go for a drive?' He had forced a smile on his face.

Taalia stepped behind her sister, wiping the tears. 'What's going on?'

'It's okay,' Vimal said kindly.

'No, it's not okay,' Adeela whispered.

Vimal opened the garage door, looked out.

'It's clear,' he said, dropping into the driver's seat of the car. 'Get in. Get your phone and purse.' Nodding toward the workbench. 'We'll call the police and your parents on the way.'

'No,' she whispered.

'I have to go! I don't want to leave you here.'

She gave him a soft smile. She walked to the window. And bent down.

He said, 'You're not coming?'

'No.'

She leaned forward and kissed him.

'I love you,' he whispered.

'I love you too,' she said.

And plunged the knife into the car's front tire, which gave a slight shudder and hiss and then settled down to the rim.

CHAPTER 47

Vimal Lahori was in protective custody. Finally.

Their unsub – the Promisor – had learned the address of his girlfriend and had gone there to, apparently, torture her into giving up the boy's whereabouts. But the young woman had had the presence of mind – and grit – to summon police and fight him off.

In his parlor, Rhyme was learning these details from Amelia Sachs, who was relaying her conversation she'd had with the young man in an NYPD safe house on Staten Island.

Sachs added that the officers arriving on the scene moments later had radioed for assistance in locating the man's car – a red Toyota, model unknown – and then detained Vimal.

The young man was sullen but cooperative, Sachs reported. She'd interviewed him in the Staten Island safe house where she'd stashed him. He couldn't, however, provide any helpful additional insights. He explained that his failure to come forward had been out of fear, though Rhyme suspected it had also to do with the soap opera drama of his family life, as Sachs had suggested. He'd too had in his pocket, Sachs had reported, some chunks of stone – the kimberlite, it appeared. They had bits of crystals, possibly diamonds, in them, and Rhyme wondered if it was some of Patel's inventory that he'd kept for himself. The fact he'd taken the stones that weren't his would also have made him reluctant to go to the police.

As for the day of the killing on 47th Street, he'd returned from running an errand for Mr Patel when he walked in on the horrible scene. He'd called 911 and told them what he'd seen.

She added that Vimal knew nothing of the rough that was stolen, nor had there been any discussions with his mentor, Patel, about recent security issues. The man never mentioned to his protégé concerns about anyone casing the place or unusual calls. There'd been no drop-in customers who might be inquiring about diamonds but who seemed more interested in cameras or guards. Patel had never, as far as Vimal knew, had any rivalries in the business that might give rise to such violence. While Vimal didn't know for certain, it was ludicrous that Patel had had any connection to organized crime or had borrowed money from a loan shark.

In answer to Sachs's question, Vimal confirmed what they'd deduced: He was an amateur sculptor, hoping to make it big in the art world. This explained the other trace found at the scene: the jade and lapis.

A search of Adeela's house for evidence shed by Unsub 47 during his home invasion revealed nothing. Nor had there been any sightings of the red Toyota.

Other inquiries, to use Edward Ackroyd's charming Scotland Yard inspector's word, were not proving successful either. A check of hotel registrations revealed no guests under the name of Dobyns, nor any of the other aliases the AIS had discovered that Unsub 47 had used.

Homeland Security and the bureau had continued to check out terrorist threats – of which there were plenty but none involving C4 or *lehabah* devices smuggled into the country, fake earthquakes in downtown Brooklyn or fires nearby.

A systematic search for future targets – wood-based apartments and buildings within a half mile of the drilling site – revealed no *lehabah*s on the gas lines.

Edward Ackroyd had found no one trying to move the rough on the underground market.

Rhyme wheeled to the window and gazed out upon the gray, still day. Even the evergreens seemed muted, their color bleached away. Across the street, a man walked by, minding the icy patches. His dog – a small fluffy thing – pranced over them without a care in the world.

Rhyme closed his eyes in frustration.

Then, as sometimes – not often but sometimes – happens, a break in the case came unexpectedly.

It arrived in the form of Ron Pulaski, who stepped into the parlor, nodded greetings to Rhyme and Sachs and said, 'May have something here, Lincoln. On Forty-Seven.'

To differentiate this intelligence from their other – clandestine – assignment, working for the defense attorney representing El Halcón.

'Well, *I* don't have a fucking lead at all. So, what?'

'I was wondering who'd have a motive to stop the drilling. We talked about environmentalists. But that seemed too obvious. So I started looking into energy industry competitors.'

Rhyme said, more reasonably, 'Good. Initiative. What'd you find?'

'Unfair trade practice complaint with the FTC against Algonquin Power.'

Well, this was interesting.

'Apparently the company hired an oppo lobbying firm—'

'A what?'

'Oppo firm. They dig up – or *make* up – information that trashes business competitors or political candidates you're running against.'

'Oppo. Makes sense. Though for some reason, I dislike the term. Go on.'

'The firm was hired to discredit alternative energy sources – any technology that would siphon off income from traditional oil and gas electrical production. For instance, they planted rumors that wind farms kill seagulls. And that solar panels make roofs heavier and more prone to collapsing in fires – and injuring firemen. Employees actually left seagull corpses near wind farms – killed elsewhere – and published pictures of fires in buildings equipped with solar panels, even though the panels had nothing to do with the roofs' collapsing.' He smiled. 'And they looked into research as to whether—'

'Geothermal drilling created earthquakes.'

'Exactly.'

'Algonquin,' Sachs mused. 'Who'd we see from the company on TV?'

It was Thom who recalled. 'C. Hanson Collier. President or

CEO.' The aide frowned. 'But didn't he say he supported geothermal?'

Sachs said, 'He'd have to do that, wouldn't he? Play innocent. And now that I think about it, didn't he say something like it wasn't *likely* there'd be earthquakes? It was *generally* safe. Damning with faint praise.'

Rhyme then tossed a glance toward her.

She nodded and said to Pulaski, 'Let's go for a drive.'

Amelia Sachs had been here before.

Not long ago some individuals at Algonquin Consolidated Power and Light in Astoria, Queens, had been suspects in a series of crimes involving the New York City power grid.

Sachs and Rhyme had drawn the case.

The company, which supplied electric power and steam throughout much of the New York area, had its main facility and headquarters on the East River – across from Midtown Manhattan. The operation covered a number of blocks, with the main building – its façade was huge red and gray panels – rising two hundred feet above the streets. This, where the turbines were located, was the working heart of the complex, and massive pipes and electric wires – thick, inflexible cables – ran everywhere.

High above the street level, where Sachs, driving, and Pulaski were now pulling up to the plant, were four towering smoke-stacks, also red and gray, topped with blinking red lights as a warning to low-flying aircraft. In the summer the stacks seemed to exhale no vapor at all but today, with the March chill that just wouldn't quit, wisps of steam trickled upward to dissolve in the dull white sky.

She braked the Torino Cobra to a stop and flashed her badge to the security guard at the main gate and told him she had an appointment with the CEO. The massive man, skin as pale as the overcast, glanced at her and Pulaski, who was in uniform. He made a call and, nodding to no one, told her where to park.

A second guard met them in a lobby and took them to the same place Sachs had been a few years before, on that prior case:

the executive offices. The floor was right out of the 1950s, 'modern' furniture upholstered in brown and white and tan, the designs geometric.

The art was black-and-white photos of the power plant over the years.

The employees here – mostly men – were dressed as if they too had been locked in time for seventy years. White shirts, dark ties, dark suits with jackets often buttoned. Hair was trim. Sachs imagined she could smell the Brylcreem her father wore, though surely this was a psychological, not an olfactory, sensation.

The guard deposited them in a waiting room outside the office of the CEO, C. Hanson Collier. He had not been head of the company when she and Rhyme had worked the prior case but she wondered if she'd passed him in the halls back then.

She glanced down at the kidney-shaped coffee table, on which sat copies of trade magazines. *Electricity Transmission Monthly. Power Age. The Grid.*

A limp *Time*, dated circa six months ago.

'How're we going to handle it?' Pulaski asked.

'Rattle his cage,' Sachs said. 'Let him know you found the memo. Watch his reaction.'

Sometimes you closed a case through DNA and trace evidence. Sometimes, through a blink and a bead of sweat. A friend and colleague of Sachs and Rhyme was a state police investigator in California. Kathryn Dance. Her expertise was body language. Though not as savvy in the art of kinesics as Dance, Sachs, as a former street cop, had some talent at this esoteric skill.

They didn't have many options, in any case. No forensics linked the CEO to the earthquakes or to Unsub 47. In fact, she knew that, if he was the mastermind, he would not personally be involved – other than making payment arrangements to the perp. And even that wasn't certain. The oppo firm might have hired him themselves and sent Collier the bill for 'media analysis and story placement.'

A precise young woman, in a brown suit, stepped into the doorway and asked Sachs and Pulaski to follow her. They navigated another long corridor, arriving finally at the CEO's office. The assistant gestured them inside.

Collier looked like a former coal miner – a career guess that would not have been unreasonable, given that he now headed up a power company. But Sachs had done some homework and learned that prior to this gig he'd been CEO of a major clothing manufacturer. She supposed the principles of business apply equally whether you're selling bras or voltage.

'Come on in, Detective. Officer.'

Hands were shaken and Collier gestured for them to sit. Same chairs, couches and coffee table as a few years ago.

'Now, what can I do for you?'

Sachs took the lead. 'Mr Collier, are you familiar with the stories about the earthquakes in Brooklyn?'

'Of course. Very odd.' He unbuttoned his dark-gray suit. The American flag pin in the buttonhole of his lapel was upside down. 'Speculation that somebody's using explosives to mimic quakes. Nobody's sure why. Maybe to get the geothermal plant shut down. That's what the journalists are saying. Industrial sabotage.' More wrinkles folded into his creased, pale face; it was naturally patterned, not from the sun. It was as if he still worked – and even lived – deep underground. 'And why are you here exactly, Detective? Is it why I think?'

'The memo. The FTC complaint against Algonquin.'

Collier was nodding. 'You know, those dead birds? Nobody killed them. Our firm hired somebody to drive around and find dead seagulls. Can you imagine some intern, first day on the job? "Need dead birds, kid." Though the fact is the windmill blades *do* kill them. The firm just added a few extras – for effect. And the fires with solar panels? That's a known fact. The pictures weren't exactly of ceilings that collapsed *because* of the panels. But what's a little license among capitalists? You're thinking we're setting the explosions to make it look like the drilling was causing earthquakes.'

'Are you? Your oppo firm researched it. That was in the memo.'

'It was in the memo. But if you heard me on TV, which I guess you did, you'll recall I was *defending* Northeast and geothermal drilling.'

'That's not answering my question. Are you sabotaging the site?'

'No. Is that enough of an answer for you?'

'What about the oppo firm?'

'Fired them a year ago. The bad publicity wasn't worth it. A couple of dead seagulls. Died of natural causes. You should have seen the hate mail we got.'

'Which,' Pulaski said, 'might have taught you to be more careful.'

'No, Officer, it taught us to be smarter – in how we deal with alternative energy. We don't try to run them out of business.'

He dug up a corporate brochure from his desk drawer and dropped it in front of them. Opening to the first page, he tapped a passage. Algonquin's wholly owned subsidiaries included three wind farms in Maine and a solar panel manufacturing operation.

'We *buy* them.' He opened another drawer, extracted a thick legal document and dropped it with a loud smack in front of her. 'We'll keep this one secret, you don't mind. It's not public yet.'

Sachs looked at the front page of the document.

Purchase Agreement

WHEREAS, Algonquin Consolidated Power and Light, Inc. ('Algonquin'), desires to purchase twenty percent (20%) of the outstanding common stock (the 'Shares') of Northeast Geo Industries, Inc. ('Northeast'), and Northeast desires to sell the Shares to Algonquin,

NOW THEREFORE, in consideration of the mutual obligations herein recited, the parties hereto do agree as follows:

She didn't bother to flip through it. 'You're buying stock in the company?'

'Eventually, if it's profitable, we'll buy the rest. It has to prove itself. Deep-drilling geothermal – tapping into volcanic reserves

– for electrical generation is profitable. Near-surface drilling on a large scale? The jury's still out on that. Do you have a furnace at home or a heat pump?'

'Furnace.'

'Exactly. Heat pumps're for wimps. Geothermal's a heat pump. But there're a lot of ecological wimps out there. So I'm hoping our investment will pay off. We'll see.'

Sachs's phone hummed with a text. She looked down at it.

She stood up. Pulaski glanced her way and rose too.

'Thanks for your time, Mr Collier.'

'Ms Evans will show you out.' He said nothing more, didn't rise. He opened a folder and began reading.

The assistant appeared and escorted them down the hall.

As they walked into the parking lot, out of earshot of the employees, the young officer whispered, 'We just going to let it go, like that? He showed us a contract. He might've had it printed out in case somebody called him on the earthquake plot. How do we know he's not behind it?'

'Because of this.'

Sachs showed him her phone, the text she'd just gotten from Lon Sellitto.

'Oh. Well. We're going to New Jersey?'

'We're going to New Jersey.'

CHAPTER 48

This is a place where earth meets water in stark and stunning beauty.

This is a place where the rocks take on the texture and sheen and contradiction of art.

This is a place where brush, bush and trees rise along sheer cliffs with the effortless ease of smoke.

This is a place where someone whose life was devoted to the earth might, fittingly, die.

The body of Ezekiel Shapiro, in a fire department rescue basket, was now being winched to the top of the hundred-foot cliff of Palisades Park.

In the chill early evening, their breath easing in visible wisps from their mouths, Sachs, Pulaski and a number of New Jersey state troopers stood watching the fire department and rescue team. They were beside Shapiro's dusty and dinged car, which was surrounded by protective yellow tape.

Suicide is, after all, a crime.

It had not been the police but insurance man Edward Ackroyd who'd made the discovery that Shapiro had hired Unsub 47.

When Ackroyd told Sellitto what he'd found, the lieutenant had sent patrol cars to Shapiro's office and home but apparently the environmentalist had seen them and realized that the authorities had learned about the plot.

He'd posted a suicide note online, driven here and killed himself.

Shapiro had hired Unsub 47 for two missions. The first was to close down the geothermal drilling as environmentally unsound. The second was to single out Jatin Patel for attack and robbery. The diamond cutter was apparently known for working on stones from mines that displaced indigenous people and polluted villages and rivers. The stolen rough, Ackroyd had learned, would be sold by the unsub and the proceeds given to Shapiro, who would distribute it to environmental organizations to help the unfortunates.

I don't think tree huggers use C4 very much . . . or burn down buildings with people inside . . .

Mel Cooper had been wrong.

Shapiro's suicide note made clear, though, that he'd miscalculated. He'd wanted to scare the city, sure. The deaths by fire were not his idea, but had been the brainchild of the madman he'd hired – somebody who shared his fury at the destruction of the earth, but who had decided, on his own, to plant a series of incendiary devices to kill and injure.

Perhaps the deaths, though unintended, had been what pushed him to take his own life.

'Hey, Amelia.'

She turned to see a tall, blond officer, about her age. He was in uniform – dark slacks with an orange stripe down the outseam and a powder-blue shirt and tie. Latex gloves and booties too. Ed Bolton was a sergeant with the Crime Scene Investigation Unit of the New Jersey State Police's Major Crime Bureau. He now pulled off the cornflower-blue accessories and stuffed them into his pants pocket.

Knowing that Bolton had run the scene was a relief. He'd have done as thorough a job as she would have.

She introduced him to Pulaski, who asked, 'How'd you get onto it?'

'Trooper saw the car here and ran the plate. There was an area-wide out after you guys found he was behind those earthquakes and murders on Saturday and Sunday.'

'Positive ID? It's Shapiro?'

'Uh-huh. One of our tac people rappelled down. Did a field FR. It's him. Prints were on file after an arrest at a protest rally a few years ago. Pretty crazy, faking earthquakes.'

She asked, 'So how does the scene look?'

'Nothing says anything other than suicide. No wits. And he drove here from the city, so no tollbooths.'

All the bridges and tunnels were toll-free entering New Jersey. There was no toll-taker video of someone else driving Shapiro's car, with the activist in the trunk, for instance. That was improbable, of course. No one would have a motive to kill him – except, she supposed, Unsub 47, if he'd decided to keep the diamonds for himself. But even then, why kill Shapiro, why not just take the diamonds and go back to Russia?

And if he'd truly wanted to murder Shapiro, he wouldn't've staged it. He would simply have shot the man, at a time and place of his convenience. The Russian was clever but apparently cared little for nuance.

Sachs asked, 'The evidence's gone to Hamilton?'

The state police's crime scene headquarters.

'That's right. We'll get you copies as soon as we can, autopsy too.'

Sachs and Pulaski watched the basket in which the body was strapped breach the top of the cliff. Two muscular fire fighters, one a man, one a woman, pulled it closer, unhooked the cable and carried the body to a waiting ambulance.

The view of Manhattan from here was spectacular in clear weather. Now the haze made the place look dystopian. Not many lights shone through the gray fog, though you could see the outlines of buildings large and buildings small. It seemed like a ghost town.

'Let's run his house,' Sachs said, 'see what we can find.'

CHAPTER 49

The U.S. attorney's office was quiet.

This was one of those moments – early evening, of a weeknight – that Henry Bishop liked. Much of the rest of the building was empty, most of the support staff gone.

But those who remained were loyal and diligent and blindingly focused.

The sort of person that the lean, admittedly tense prosecutor preferred.

This place was comforting to him in the way that the Upper West Side apartment where he'd been living by himself for the past thirteen and a half months was not.

Bishop looked out over the dark night, and in his thoughts were a dozen – no, two dozen – matters about the El Halcón case. Every case was important but this one was more important than others of late. The crimes the Mexican had committed – the assaults on federal officers and the local policemen – were all terrible. But the crimes the man *would* commit – if he went free to continue to expand his operation to the United States – required that he be stopped now.

It was an adage in this business that you can't try someone for future crimes. But Hank Bishop felt that in one way you could: Try somebody for his present crime, put him away for as long as you can, and you've 'solved' any future crimes that person might have committed.

Bishop was going to make sure that El Halcón was out of commission for a long, long time. He would delay the Mexican cartel's move into the United States for a significant period, severely limiting the river of drugs cascading into this country. And crimping too the enforcement murders, bystander killings, underage prostitution, arms dealing and money laundering that were subsidiary enterprises in the El Halcón empire.

Considering this goal, Bishop happened to think of the one sore spot for him in the whole prosecution: that he hadn't been able to learn the identity of El Halcón's American partner, the man who was going to be running his operation after the Mexican returned home. The man who was the ultimate owner of the warehouse (Chris Cody, the man killed in the shoot-out, was merely a front, Bishop knew).

How Henry Bishop wanted this co-conspirator too.

But at least putting El Halcón away would slow up the expansion of the Mexican OC operation into America.

A knock on his doorjamb.

Special Agent Fallow stood there.

'Come on in.'

The man strode into the room and sat stiffly in the chair across from Bishop's large desk, which was covered with a hundred file folders.

'And?'

Fallow opened his own folder and looked at some notes. 'I think we're good. There's a CI we've got in Mexico City. He knows one of the guys up here in the Carreras-López entourage.'

Bishop loved confidential informants – snitches. They were either cowards or without consciences. Either one made them extremely valuable.

The agent continued, 'Apparently, it's true, Lincoln Rhyme's been hired to analyze our evidence and look for improprieties. The withdrawal from Chase? Was a down payment that's in Rhyme's possession now. And the bulk – a half million, if he gets results? It'll be wire-transferred. He's got Rhyme's bank's routing and account number. Oh, and he gets two hundred fifty K, even if he doesn't find problems with our case.' The agent shrugged. 'But there's nothing he did illegal. I tried to find conflict of interest but he's never had any connection with anybody on the prosecution or the agents involved. Nothing.'

Bishop sneered. 'And what does he think he'll find? We're buttoned up, aren't we? Completely buttoned up.'

Fallow said nothing, but nodded.

'Why would Rhyme undermine us? Doesn't he know what kind of evil El Halcón represents?'

Okay, a little melodramatic. But Bishop often addressed people – and himself – as if he were making closing statements to a jury.

'Next steps, sir?'

'Did you find the uniform who raided the PERT office?'

'I did. He's Ronald Pulaski. Technically Patrol Division but generally works Major Cases. No discipline issues. Citations for bravery.'

Under other circumstances, Henry Bishop would have had some qualms about putting a decorated officer in jail. But Pulaski's collaboration with Rhyme was a clear crime – and a stupid one, to boot. He should've known better. Also, Pulaski was a male and – presumably – white. Safer to destroy the career of somebody like that.

'Charges for Pulaski?' Fallow said. 'We need to hit them hard, I'd say. Shut them down.'

Shut them down? Odd choice of words. But in principle, Bishop agreed.

The agent continued, 'Obstruction. Conspiracy.'

'Theft of government documents too.'

'Good.'

'There're probably some NYPD confidentiality and protocol rules he's tripped over. But that's not our issue. We'll let their Internal Affairs handle that. I'll put him in federal prison. The state can do what they want after he's out. In ten years. Warrant him – Pulaski. Pick him up ASAP.'

Before he and Rhyme found one of those *improprieties* they'd been hired to hunt down.

Fallow asked, 'You're just going to let Rhyme . . . ' Apparently Fallow was going to say 'walk,' but he changed his mind. 'Let him go?'

'No. We'll get him for receiving stolen government files. Is there any facility that can handle him?'

'Lockdown medical unit in detention.'

'Good.'

'He's got a caregiver.'

'A what?'

'An aide. Somebody who takes care of him.'

Bishop scoffed. 'Well, he's not going in with him. There'll be some orderly or nurses who can do what they have to.'

Fallow said, 'I'll let the medical unit know.'

Bishop looked out the window. 'And another thing. I'm going to make sure absolutely every law enforcement agency in the country knows what Rhyme's done. He'll never work as a consultant again. I hope he has a good retirement plan. After he gets out of jail, he'll spend the rest of his life sitting home and watching soap operas.'

IV
BRUTING

TUESDAY, MARCH 16

CHAPTER 50

'Think we've got everything,' Sachs said. Rhyme wheeled closer to her in his parlor.

She explained to him, Pulaski, Ackroyd and Sellitto what evidence they had uncovered, and then added her and Cooper's analysis.

'The environmental outfit – One Earth? Didn't find anything there, other than some trace linking Shapiro to it, but he was director, so of course he'd be there every day. The New Jersey State Police crime scene analysis from the suicide site at the Palisades didn't turn up anything about the Russian or gas bombs. Shapiro's car, though – we've got trace of the kimberlite.'

Rhyme said, 'Linking Shapiro to the drilling site or to Unsub Forty-Seven, or both.'

'Right,' Sellitto said, adding that the find supported what they had surmised but it offered no new information.

Sachs continued, telling those present that the search of Shapiro's small apartment in upper Manhattan, where he'd lived alone, gave up no leads either. But it did offer explanations.

Hidden under a mattress she'd discovered a map of the geothermal site, with the shafts of Area Seven circled, five hundred thousand Russian rubles – about eighty-five hundred dollars, presumably a bonus for Unsub 47 when the job was finished – and two burner phones, presently inoperative. Their call history was cleared.

'I printed the phones – negative on that – and I sent 'em down to Rodney. We'll see if the computer geniuses can extract any info. The guy he hired? The Russian? Sure, he's a mercenary. But he's also cut from the same cloth, I'm betting. Saving the earth, getting even for the damage we've inflicted. He just did Shapiro one better: the torture, the gas line bombs.'

Sachs added that she'd recovered a great deal of trace evidence in Shapiro's apartment, some situating the activist at various places around the metropolitan area: samples of minerals and soil and sand and diesel fuel and plant material. Some might have been carried into Shapiro's home on Unsub 47's shoes but without more evidence to narrow down the locales they did the investigators no good in finding him.

Rhyme noticed Sachs looking at the chart on which she'd written the findings. Her face seemed wistful. She looked back and noticed his gaze. She said, 'It was sad, you know.'

'Sad?' Sellitto muttered. 'The asshole killed a half-dozen people.'

'Oh, I know. He got carried away, lost in the cause. But you should've seen his apartment.' She explained that it was filled with easily a thousand books, mostly about the environment. There were dozens of protest posters and photos he'd taped up on the scabby walls: of Shapiro and colleagues in jail or being arrested – once being teargassed – as a result of various protests. She imagined he'd mounted them with pride and fond memories.

'It was like a shrine to his cause. He did a lot of good. Up until now, that is.'

Murder was, of course, murder.

Rhyme noticed another picture Sachs had taken in Shapiro's apartment: a black-and-gold ceramic urn on which was a bronze plaque. It contained his wife's ashes. He commented on it. Sachs added, 'I looked her up. She died of cancer, probably due to a toxic waste spill when she was a teenager.'

Rhyme now turned and wheeled closer to their insurance expert, Edward Ackroyd, who was the man of the moment – since it was he who'd been instrumental in cracking the case. He was trying to get in touch once more with the diamond dealer in Manhattan who had put him onto Ezekiel Shapiro. The activist had called the dealer asking about Jatin Patel's source for diamonds. Was it true that he bought them from mines that exploited indigenous people?

Ackroyd hoped that the dealer might have additional information – maybe even a lead about the Russian who Shapiro had hired.

Rhyme focused out the window. A lethargic ice storm during the night had encased the vegetation in front of his town house. He wondered if the sharp crystals had killed the plants, or if the ice had had no effect whatsoever other than to temporarily enwrap leaves and buds in a clear cocoon, which would flash with rainbow fire, like a diamond, under the sun.

Now Ackroyd was disconnecting his phone. 'Okay. I got through to him: the dealer. He's still jittery but I think the guilt got to him – that Patel was killed after he told Shapiro about him. I'll go have a chat with the gentleman.'

Rhyme watched the man pull on his coat with precise movements.

Ackroyd added, 'Let's keep our fingers crossed.'

His voice hesitated as he glanced Rhyme's way, suddenly recalling, it seemed, that Lincoln Rhyme was not a person who had the ability to cross any fingers.

Their eyes met and they shared a smile.

From a very sour-smelling vantage point in a stand of bushes in Central Park – apparently popular with urban dogs – Vladimir Rostov watched the medium-built, sandy-haired man in the beige overcoat step outside the town house he'd learned belonged to one Lincoln Rhyme. The man drew the garment tighter about him, against the chill.

Cold, cold? Ha. This is nothing, *kuritsa*. Come to Moscow in January.

The man walked down the disabled-accessible ramp and onto the sidewalk, avoiding a few patches of ice. He turned north and walked to the cross street, then west, away from the park.

Rostov pushed through the bushes and strode quickly after him, passing between two cabs. Closing the distance, Rostov kept his head down. You assumed CCTVs were everywhere and fitted with high-definition lenses. He also supposed some had facial recognition software, though he wasn't, as far as he knew, in any FR databases. At least not here, in the United States.

Ah, *kuritsa*, slow down, slow down. You're walking too fast for a whore of a hen.

Rostov's mood had improved and he'd overcome his anger at the latest setback – at the house of Adeela, the raven-haired Arab girl. Making it worse, as he'd fled, the police approaching, he'd caught a glimpse of Vimal himself in the garage! He was *at* the house. And he'd be in protective custody now.

Angry then, better now.

Concentrating on the task ahead of him.

Yes, the Promisor has yet another backup plan, *kuritsa*! Don't you know?

Rostov saw the man he was following approach a gray Ford and push the fob button. The lights flashed briefly. Rostov was only twenty feet behind him and he sped up, head still down. When the man pulled open the driver's door and dropped into the seat, Rostov did the same on the passenger side.

'*Kuritsa!*'

The driver reared back in shock, blinking. Then he and Rostov locked eyes.

The Russian smiled. And stuck his hand out. The driver shook his head, with a wry laugh, gripped Rostov's meaty palm and, with his left hand, pressed the man's biceps, a gesture conveying a cautious warmth. It was the sort of greeting that might transpire between two soldiers who'd been enemies in the past – and might yet be in the future – but who, for the moment at least, were allies with a common cause.

CHAPTER **51**

'So, *kuritsa*, what I am calling you? What is name? Surely not Mr Andrew Krueger?'

'Using my real name? Now, what do you think, Vladimir? No, I'm Edward Ackroyd.'

'Yes, yes, I like that. Distinguished fucker. Is real somebody?'

Krueger didn't explain that the identity he'd stolen, Edward Ackroyd, was, yes, a real employee of Milbank Assurance – a company that insured hundreds of diamond and precious metal mines and wholesalers. Ackroyd, as he'd told Rhyme, was a former Scotland Yard detective and presently was a senior claims investigator with Milbank. Beyond that, Krueger knew nothing of the real Ackroyd; he'd made everything else up, like riffing on his sexuality: He played his fictional version as gay – a casting choice intended to work his way, subtly, through Rhyme's defenses; the consultant seemed like a man who valued tolerance. (Krueger had told his business partner in his company, Terrance DeVoer, the most hetero man you'd ever meet, that Terry and Krueger were now married – to the South African's great amusement.)

The cryptic crossword puzzles – which were a hobby of Krueger's – were also intended to ingratiate himself with the criminalist. A number of Krueger's clients were British, so he could easily feign being English.

In the driver's seat of the rental car Krueger eased back a bit from the Russian. Rostov stank of pungent cigarettes and onion and excessive drugstore aftershave. 'And you? You're not Vlad Rostov, I assume.'

'No, no.' The Russian laughed. 'So many fucking names in the past week . . . Now I am Alexander Petrovitch. I was Josef Dobyns when I landed. Now Petrovitch. I like better. Dobyns could be Jew. You are liking Alexander? I do. It was only passport this asshole in Brighton Beach had. Charge me fortune. I like Brighton Beach. You ever go?'

Rostov was known, in the diamond security industry, to be a loose cannon and also more than a little crazy. The rambling was typical.

'You know, Vlad—'

'Alexander.'

'—I'm not here to sightsee.'

'Ha, no, we are not tourists, you and me.'

Krueger was feeling more at ease now. He was over the shock of Rostov's sneaking up on him, though he'd known the man would appear sooner or later. He found it refreshing too not to have to use the British accent. It was getting tedious. In fact, he was South African, and his natural intonation was of an Afrikaner speaking English. He'd been on his guard every time he'd spoken with Lincoln Rhyme and Amelia Sachs and the others, struggling to get the Brit upper-crust tongue correct.

Façade upon façade . . . what a time this past week had been.

It was Andrew Krueger, not Vladimir Rostov, who was the real perpetrator, whom the police were calling Unsub 47: the man who had killed Jatin Patel and Saul Weintraub. And who, under the guise of Edward Ackroyd, had talked his way into the police investigation of the case.

Krueger had been stunned when the 'Promisor' appeared, mimicking Krueger's role, right down to the ski mask, gloves and box-cutting knife. It didn't take him long to realize that it was probably Rostov. He, or his employer in Moscow, would have hacked Krueger's computers and phones and would be sucking up real-time details of the South African's progress here as he communicated with his own company and his employer for this mission. Rostov knew everything about Krueger's crimes even before the police did.

Krueger had swapped phones and installed new proxies, but finally sent a message on a phone he knew had been hacked. 'Rostov. Contact me.' Though he'd expected a phone call, not the man's sudden appearance in his front seat.

'How'd you find me here?'

'Ah, you put all kinds of shit in your emails to your client, my friend. Careless, careless!'

Krueger started the car. 'Let's go talk someplace. Out of the way. We have a problem, Vlad, and we need to address it.'

'Yes, yes. Can we go to restaurant somewhere? And remember. *Nyet* "Vladimir." I am Alexander. I am Alexander the Great!'

A half hour later the two men were in a restaurant in Harlem.

Andrew Krueger didn't know New York well. He had come to the city only a week ago, to put the plan into operation. But he had believed Harlem to be mostly black and working-class, so he would be unlikely to run into somebody involved in the police investigation in a place like this. Krueger was mildly surprised to see that this modest establishment was filled with as many white people – a lot of them hipsters – as black.

Pleasant enough.

But heaven to Vladimir Rostov. He was loving Martha's Authentic BBQ. Krueger sipped a Sprite. He'd feigned a love of single-malt scotch to ingratiate himself further into the world of Rhyme and Amelia. The fact was he drank very little alcohol, mostly only red Pinotage, a wine unique to his home country.

The Russian was on his second bourbon. He had a coughing fit. 'Fucking cigarettes.' He held up his glass. 'This helps. Good for you.'

Krueger knew Rostov had worked in the diamond mines of Siberia from a young age. No, his tattered lungs weren't failing from cigarettes, not entirely.

Krueger and the Russian had crossed paths, and swords, for years and Krueger well knew that the Russian was larger than life, a big drinker (though he hated the national beverage of vodka). Also, a food lover. He was presently working away vigorously at his order: the full baby back rib meal, what looked like a kilo of meat, along with mounds of soul food accoutrements.

Krueger picked at the salad he'd ordered. He was in crisis and not the least hungry.

He noted Rostov's eyes following the ass of the server. She was a tall, solid woman whose skin was the color of perfectly done toast. The Russian, he knew, was largely insatiable in all appetites.

'What did you call me?'

'Call you?'

'When you got in the car?'

Rostov laughed – loud. 'I say, "*kuritsa.*" My little *kuritsa*. It is hen. A bird. Everybody is *kuritsa* to me! I might even be *kuritsa* to someone. I love you, you know, Andrew. You are my brother, you are my father!'

Eyes slipping to and fro around the restaurant, Krueger sighed. 'As they say here, take it down a notch.'

'Ha! Yes, yes.' Rostov ripped the meat from a rib with his yellow teeth and chomped it down. An eerie smile filled his face. 'First!' He tapped his glass to Krueger's. 'To you, my friend. To you. You are genius. This fucking great plan you have came up with! Genius.'

Krueger's lips tightened. 'Except it didn't work quite the way I'd hoped.'

We have a problem . . .

'So,' Rostov asked, lowering his voice, 'you working for Nuevo Mundo – New World Mining – Guatemala City.'

He'd know this from the hacking . . . Goddamn Russians.

Krueger said, 'Right. New client. Never worked for them before. You know them?'

'I hear of them, yes, yes.'

'And you're here for Dobprom, of course?'

This was the Russian quasi-state-owned diamond-mining monopoly based in Moscow. *Dobychy*: mining. *Promyshlennost*: industry. It was the biggest diamond-mining and -distribution operation in the world. Rostov was a regular troubleshooter for them.

'Who the fuck else I working for? Look at my shitty clothes, look at my belly fat from eating cheap food. Tell me, *kuritsa*. New World pay you up front?'

'Of course. Half.'

'Ach. Never for me. Fuck Marx, Lenin and Stalin!' He winked and washed down a mouthful of ribs with bourbon.

Krueger sighed.

The 'fucking great plan' – and the circumstances of these two men's paths crossing here in New York – had begun some weeks ago, thanks to a curious occurrence.

A contractor – that is, a hired-gun 'troubleshooter' – working for New World Mining had contacted Krueger and explained that the famed Manhattan diamantaire Jatin Patel had come into possession of some kimberlite, drilled up by Northeast Geo Industries at its geothermal site in Brooklyn. The analysis showed the rocks were diamond-rich, with very high-quality rough. Now, it was likely that the kimberlite find was a freak occurrence – serpentinite, a related stone, was common in New York, but its diamond-embedded cousin was not.

But if the lode was large and the quality as good as it seemed, and the owner of the land learned of the find, he would license mineral rights to a mining operation, surely an American company. The output could depress the price of diamonds world-wide. And worse, a U.S. diamond mine would have a vast marketing advantage over foreign mines. Why would consumers buy possibly suspect third-world diamonds when U.S. mines were unquestionably ethical? This would be an utter disaster for over-seas mines; the United States accounted for more than half the retail diamond purchases in the world, around forty billion dollars' worth a year.

The contractor had then proposed that New World would pay Andrew Krueger's company a million dollars for one of its specialties: 'downwardly modulating production output.'

In other words: sabotage, threats and bribery, and occasionally worse, to make sure that finds of precious metals, uranium and other valuable ores and gems never saw the light of day. The diamond industry had a long – and violent – history of suppressing production and competition.

The specific plan that the contractor came up with was bril-liant: Krueger was to kill Jatin Patel, after getting the names of anyone who knew about the kimberlite find. And kill those individuals too. He'd bribe a Northeast Geo employee to give him access to the site, where he would collect and dispose of as much kimberlite as he could. Then he'd drop explosive charges down some of the shafts and seal them with grout, and plant gas line bombs in buildings nearby. Each C4 charge was timed to detonate just before a gas line blew. This would mimic an earthquake and the resulting conflagration.

The city would close down the site, citing the risk of more quakes. That would be the end of drilling up more kimberlite.

He'd gotten the devices planted fine and then had turned to eliminating anyone who knew about the kimberlite.

Under Krueger's knife, Jatin Patel gave up Saul Weintraub's name. But Patel swore no one else knew about the kimberlite. After the man was dead, though, into the shop comes the young man – Vimal Lahori, it turned out – obviously an employee, since he knew the door code. Krueger shot him but he got away. And it was clear he knew about the kimberlite, too, because the bullet had struck a bag of the stuff.

Knowing that the young man would call 911 at any moment, Krueger had tried to figure out what to do. He didn't have time to go through all of Patel's papers and learn his identity – a fast search revealed nothing. Then, looking at the white squares of envelopes of diamonds he'd scattered on the floor, to make the police believe the crime was a simple robbery, he had an idea.

He would trick the police themselves into helping him find the boy and anyone else who might know about the kimberlite find.

In his job as a hired-gun for the diamond and precious metal industry, Krueger often used identity theft as a tool (just as Rostov had done). He would do the same now.

In Patel's shop, he'd found an empty diamond envelope and had written on it the names and specifications of four multi-million-dollar diamonds, along with the name of Grace-Cabot, a real South African mining operation. The phone number he wrote down, however, was a burner phone of Terry DeVoer, his business partner in South Africa.

Krueger left the envelope at a work station and, taking the hard drive and its telltale security video with him, fled.

He then called DeVoer in Cape Town to have him change the voicemail announcement on the number to Grace-Cabot and be ready for a call from the police about the stolen rough. He was to play the role of Llewellyn Croft—a real executive with the company. "Croft" would sound shocked about the loss and then send the police to the company's insurance investigator, a man with experience in tracking down diamonds, a man who could assist them.

Krueger assumed *that* identity himself: Edward Ackroyd, with the real insurance company of Milbank Assurance, whose identity he'd "borrowed" in the past. Ackroyd, who was about Krueger's age, was British, former Scotland Yard. And there was no picture of him on the Milbank website. Krueger had had Milbank cards printed up with Ackroyd's name and that of the insurance company but with one of his own burner phone numbers on it.

Absurd, indeed. The plan could fall apart at any moment. There was a knife-edge chance it might work. Krueger had to take the risk.

His luck had held . . . for a time. The police believed his fake identity, the C4 charges went off as planned, the fires roasted a few people, the city halted the drilling, he found and killed Saul Weintraub and he was making some headway in finding Patel's protégé.

But then he'd run smack into a brick wall: Lincoln Rhyme and Amelia Sachs, who managed to link the two parts of the plan that absolutely should not have been linked: That the man who'd killed Patel had also been present at the geothermal site. And, even worse, that he was behind faking the earthquakes. He could still recall with dismay how Rhyme had called him into the parlor to describe in perfect detail, thanks to the CCTV videos, what their suspect was really up to, faking the earthquakes and fires.

It's Forty-Seven's plan. It's why he's here: planting gas line bombs and C4 charges to mimic earthquakes . . .

It had taken all Krueger's willpower to stay calm. He was sure Rhyme would turn to him and say, 'I know you're the one! Arrest him, Amelia!'

But, no. The Ackroyd fiction held. And, thank God, Rhyme and Sachs hadn't made the leap that the reason for the scheme was sabotaging the diamond lode at the geothermal site. They identified the kimberlite too, but fortunately it had no particular significance to them.

Of course, then, on top of it all, the unstable, meddling Russian, Vladimir Rostov, blusters his way into the action.

'All right. So you decide to become my doppelganger and—'

'The fuck is that?'

'A double, you know. You imitated me. You hear me on the phone, talking about the witnesses I have to find, and you decide to help me out.'

'Yeah, yeah. I find this Iranian asshole – Nashim – and he gets me to Vimal's friend, Kirtan. And *he* gives up Vimal's name and girlfriend, Adeela. I am fucking good detective, huh? Columbo!' A shrug. 'I got close. But didn't work.' He grimaced broadly. 'Fuck me.'

Krueger now asked, point-blank, why he'd done it. Dobprom's goal was the same as New World's: to keep the diamond lode secret. Why not just let Krueger handle the matter?

Rostov tossed back his bourbon and poked a toothpick Krueger's way. 'Look, my friend. You are not offended by my saying it, I hope: But this is big fucking deal. What happen, if you fucked up? That kimberlite, oh, is sweet. I am reading assay report. You see carats per ton?' He nodded his head out the window, presumably indicating the geothermal site in Brooklyn. He whispered reverently, 'That is Botswana yield.'

Although it varied considerably, the rule in the industry was that on average a mine had to process one hundred to two hundred tons of rock to produce one carat of quality diamond. In the African nation of Botswana, the diamond concentration in ore was ten times higher. The best in the world.

The New York lode was the same.

'I am so very *prosti*, so very sorry, *kuritsa*, if you are sad. But we could not take chance. So, cheer up! Here I am come to help you. You are the Batman and I am the Robin! Pat me on back!'

CHAPTER **52**

'I'm not making this call. You never heard it. And you're not reactin' to it. Anyway, anyhow. Got that?'

Amelia Sachs, standing in the corner of Rhyme's lab, was listening to the caller. Fred Dellray, special agent with the FBI's New York office.

'Okay.'

'Is Lincoln nearby?'

The hell was this all about? she wondered.

'Yes.'

Rhyme was across the parlor, speaking with Ron Pulaski.

'Can he hear you?'

'No. Explain.'

'Okay, here's the deal, and it ain't so nice, Amelia. I heard through the vine, Lincoln's under investigation. Ron too. Us. FBI, Eastern District.'

She didn't move, felt the warmth of shock wash over her. 'I see. And why would that be?'

Dellray was the bureau's expert in undercover ops. The lanky African American was the epitome of subdued, as one would have to be when playing the role of an arms dealer offering to sell munitions to a twitchy neo-Nazi, pointing a Glock his way to aid in the negotiation process. But now, she heard dismay in his voice – a tone she'd never heard before.

'They've been helping the defense in the El Halcón case.'

She struggled not to utter any words of shock or disappointment. 'And that's confirmed?'

'Oh, yeah. Pretty boy Hank Bishop, prosecutor going after El Halcón, he's got all the evidence he needs for an arrest. Both of 'em. Ron and Lincoln.'

She was stunned. 'I see.'

Sachs recalled that Ron had been acting secretive lately. He'd gone off on several missions that seemed unrelated to the Unsub 47 case. And there was that visitor the other day, a man who was Hispanic in appearance. Maybe he was one of El Halcón's aides or lawyers.

'I'm thinking he signed on because there was some funny business with the evidence. Maybe an agent or evidence tech played fast and loose, just to make sure El Halcón got put away good and long. I mean, he *is* a triple-A-rated shit. I can see Lincoln getting in a knot about that. But . . . ' His voice dipped. 'He didn't go to Bishop or anyone else. He just took on the defense's case on his own and . . . fuck, he's getting paid for it. Bunch o' money. In the K's. Makes it look bad.'

Jesus, Rhyme. What the hell have you done?

'It's going down soon, Amelia. They'll be in federal detention for a time. Bail's gonna be a problem because El Halcón's trial's goin' on hot and heavy now, and Bishop doesn't want anything to fuck up the case until after closing arguments.'

'Even . . . ' She paused, thinking of a word. 'Even given his condition?'

'Yep. Medical wing in the detention center. Thom won't be allowed. Nurses'll take care of him.'

She glanced toward Rhyme. She could imagine how they'd treat him.

No, this couldn't be happening . . . A nightmare.

'So,' Dellray continued, 'I'm telling you this but I'm not telling you this. Get a lawyer fast. It might help some. And you and Lon'll have to take over on Unsub Forty-Seven. I gotta hang up. Good luck, Amelia.'

The line went dead.

Sachs intentionally looked away from Rhyme. Her eyes would clearly reveal how troubled she was.

'Lon?' she called.

Sellitto looked her way. She nodded to the front hall, and he followed her out there.

'What's up?'

She sighed, took a breath and in a low voice told him about Dellray's call – that is, the non-call.

The rumpled detective rarely displayed emotion. Now his eyes grew wide and he was momentarily speechless.

'He couldn't. It's a mistake.'

'With Bishop?' Sachs asked cynically. 'He doesn't make mistakes.'

'No,' Sellitto muttered. 'And taking money? Jesus. I know he charges a fee for his work, but from an asshole like El Halcón? This's gonna be bad. Even if he beats the case, that's it for consulting for us. Probably everybody.'

Then Sellitto said, 'Okay. Well. Innocent until proven guilty.'

Though one crime he was guilty of, no debate on that: Rhyme hadn't told her about taking on the assignment for El Halcón's defense team. This cut her deeply.

Welcome to married life, she thought – even more cynical now.

But Sellitto was right in one sense: Rhyme – and Ron Pulaski too – would need to find an attorney. And, from the urgent tone of Dellray's call, they needed one immediately.

He said, 'I've got some names. Ballbusters who've represented some high-profile perps I've collared. I don't like 'em, but they're top-notch. I'll start calling now.'

Sachs heard some noise in the back of the town house. Pots and pans. Water running.

She sighed. 'And I'll tell Thom.'

Andrew Krueger sipped his soft drink.

He scowled at Rostov. 'All right. Granted Dobprom wanted to make sure nobody learned about the lode. But what the hell was that "Promisor" crap? What, you heard that I used a razor knife and wore a ski mask at Patel's, and you went out and bought the same things?'

Rostov said proudly, 'Of course! I am clever fucker! No?'

'Then going on and on, nobody treats diamonds right? They're the soul of the earth? You made that girl swallow her ring? Cutting fingers off? What kind of bullshit was that?'

Rostov's eyes turned savvy. 'What kind bullshit? Hm. Bullshit whole *world* believe! After Promisor arrive, *nobody* thinking Patel got killed because kimberlite or diamonds is in Brooklyn.

CNN says crazy man attacking pretty little fiancées, so has to be true.'

Krueger could hardly argue.

Then the Russian leaned forward, and he spoke in a low, steady voice. 'But, *kuritsa*, tell me the true word. You know what most diamond companies do: cut up beautiful stone into pieces of shit for shopping malls. Ruin lovely rough to make little bastard diamonds for girls' fat fingers.' His eyes grew dark and angry. 'A fucking crime.' He waved for another drink and was silent until it arrived. A fast sip. 'Yes, yes, Dobprom, my *wonderful* employer, they sell to dealers like that. They pay my fucking salary. But I bitch about it anyways. And you, my friend? I know you thinking, in that heart of yours, yes, yes, Promisor is *right*. Make those *kur* who don't know diamond from a piece of glass hurt, make them cry.'

Another shot of liquor. 'Okay, okay. I am fucked up. Gone to stone. But maybe little part of you crazy like me?'

Andrew Krueger wanted to argue. But he had to admit that Rostov was right on this point too. Diamonds were the most perfect thing on earth. How could you not feel some contempt for those who treated them shabbily?

But he too was on a salary. There was work to be done. He pushed his soda aside and said in a low voice, 'Now our problem.'

A scowl from Rostov now. 'Yes, yes, they are knowing your earthquakes was fake. But you made it that Greenpeace asshole did everything.'

Krueger said, 'Not Greenpeace. One Earth.'

'Ach. They all assholes.'

Once Rhyme and Amelia learned that the earthquakes were sabotage, Krueger needed a fall guy. He had seen the ranting Shapiro at the site and decided to pick him. He'd broken into the man's house, planted some incriminating material there and, when Shapiro returned, cracked his skull. He'd then called Lincoln Rhyme and said he'd learned that Shapiro was targeting Jatin Patel for cutting compromised diamonds.

Then he'd driven to Palisades Park in Shapiro's car. After flinging him over the edge, Krueger had taken a bus to the George

Washington Bridge transit hub, for a subway trip back to his place.

'So, genius plan guy? What we are going to do?'

Krueger said, 'It's not as bad as it seems. The man at the site who helped me rig the explosions?'

'Yes, I saw in your emails.'

Krueger gave him a sour look.

'So this guy, where he is?'

'Dead. He told me most of the shafts are drilled. There won't be that much kimberlite dug up anymore. I can find it and get rid of it. The big problem is the boy, Vimal. On Saturday, those samples he was carrying with him? He didn't get them at the drilling site – I'd cleared it by then. Either somebody else gave them to him – maybe another assayer, like Weintraub – or he got them at another location. We have to find him. Get him to tell us where the samples came from and if anybody else knows.'

The last of Krueger's appetite vanished at the sight of Rostov's enthusiastically digging between his teeth with a fingernail to excavate bits of food. 'So?'

Krueger leaned forward. 'Here's my thought. This Amelia? She knows where Vimal is. We'll get her to tell us. We can't kill her – she's police. That's too much.'

Rostov asked, 'But hurt, okay?'

'Hurting is fine.'

Rostov's face brightened. 'Yes, yes, I will say. I am not so happy with her. I had little *kuritsa* Vimal very close. And she fucked me up. How we get to her?'

'I told her and the other cops there's a dealer in Manhattan who's got good information. I'll tell Amelia he'll agree to meet her, only her, in private. We'll find a quiet shop somewhere – not one in the Diamond District. We go there first, you and me, kill the dealer. You take his place, and when she comes in, you do what you want to find out where Vimal is and how we can get to him. We take care of the problem and you and I go home, get our bonuses.'

Rostov gave an exaggerated frown. 'Bonus? You fucker, Guatemalan bastards pay bonus?'

'Doesn't Dobprom?'

Rostov laughed sourly. Then he leaned forward and rested a creepy hand on Krueger's forearm. 'This Amelia, this *kuritsa* . . . You have seen ring she wears? Is diamond, no?' His eyes were narrow and his voice suggested this was a very important question. 'Not fucking sapphire?'

He said, 'Yes. Diamond.'

Rostov asked, 'What is grade?'

The Gemological Institute of America graded diamonds according to the four C's: carat weight, color, cut and clarity. Krueger told Rostov, 'I haven't seen it up close but I'd say two carats, a blue, brilliant, and I'm guessing a VV1 or -2.'

Which meant it wasn't flawless but only had very slight inclusions, invisible to the naked eye. A respectable stone.

'Why are you asking?' Krueger wondered, though he supposed he had an idea of what the madman had in mind.

'We need to hurt her and I need a souvenir.' He eyed Krueger narrowly. 'You are not minding that?'

'All I care about is you finding Vimal. Whatever you want to do short of killing her, that's up to you.'

CHAPTER **53**

Rhyme was looking around the town house, aware that Sellitto and Sachs were elsewhere. That was curious. They hadn't left – their coats were hung on a nearby rack.

He wanted them here, to keep examining the evidence charts, to see if the notations might reveal any more clues about the whereabouts of their Russian unsub or the next bomb. The whiteboards, decorated with careful jottings, remained silent and far more cryptic, and coy, than usual.

As he was about to summon his wife and the detective back to the parlor, there came a pounding on the door.

Rhyme and Ron Pulaski looked at the security camera monitor: four men, in suits. One was holding something up to the video camera. It seemed to be an ID card.

Rhyme squinted.

FBI.

Ah, got it.

Sachs, Sellitto and Thom all appeared quickly from the back of the town house. Rhyme noted their expressions. And he thought: They knew about El Halcón.

'The hell's going on, Lincoln?' Mel Cooper asked.

'I'm not completely sure but I think the Rookie and I're about to be arrested.'

'What?' Pulaski barked.

'Well, open the door, Thom. We hardly want them to kick it in, now, do we?'

The four people stepped quickly into the lobby and then the parlor. Three were FBI agents and were properly diverse, like the actors in an ad for a consulting company: white woman and a black and Asian man. They were humorless but that was a plus quality in a lot of professions, law enforcement ranking high among those. They would know that there was likely no threat from the occupants but their quick eyes took in everyone, assessing risks.

The fourth of the foursome was Henry Bishop, the lean federal prosecutor from the Eastern District. He towered over everyone in the room.

'Lincoln Rhyme.' The special agent speaking to him was an athletic-looking young man named Eric Fallow.

To him, Rhyme said, 'Can't raise my hands. Sorry.'

Neither the agent, nor anyone else in the room, gave a reaction to the joke.

Bishop said to Fallow, 'I'll speak to Mr Rhyme. You secure Officer Pulaski.'

Fallow stepped to the younger man. 'Officer, just keep your hands where we can see them. I'm going to take control of your weapon.'

Pulaski faced him. 'Hell you are. What's this about?'

Though his perplexed expression rang false. He knew exactly what it was about.

'Linc,' Sellitto said, then fell silent. He and Sachs had probably been briefed by Dellray – if he was indeed the one who'd delivered the news about Rhyme's assignment for El Halcón – to play dumb. Rhyme looked to Sachs, but she was avoiding his eyes.

Understandably.

The other two agents stepped forward. One took Pulaski's Glock.

Fallow said, 'Hands behind your back please.'

'That's really not necessary,' Rhyme said in a voice that was perhaps a bit too singsongy. The patina was mockery. Which was a tad unfair.

Fallow cuffed Pulaski anyway.

'Answer me, Bishop. What's going on?' Sellitto had recovered and was offering a credible performance of surprise.

'Really,' Rhyme said. 'Unnecessary.'

Bishop said, 'Mr Rhyme, you and Officer Pulaski are in a great deal of trouble. We're placing you both under arrest for felony obstruction of justice and conspiracy, unauthorized use of evidentiary information.'

The Rookie's eyes turned slowly to Rhyme.

How much trouble can you get into when your mission is a higher cause . . . ?

The prosecutor continued, 'You've been helpful in the past, Lincoln. I admit it.'

Only helpful? Rhyme reflected sourly.

'And that will be taken into account in the future, when we come to plea discussions. But now, Agent Fallow, read Officer Pulaski and Mr Rhyme their rights.'

Sellitto gave up. 'Is it true, Linc?' A sheen of dismay on his face.

Rhyme noted too Sachs's tight lips. The look in her eyes.

And he decided it was time.

'All right, everyone. All right. Henry – can I call you Henry?' Rhyme asked this.

Bishop was taken aback. 'Uhm. Hank, generally.'

'Okay, Hank. The fact is, I was just about to send you a memo on our situation. It's nearly finished.'

The prosecutor's eyes wavered not a bit but Rhyme believed some surprise shone through. He nodded at the computer screen, on which there was, in fact, a lengthy email addressed to Bishop's office. Bishop didn't follow the lead but remained fixed on Rhyme, who said, 'The Nassau County supervising detective who was shot at the El Halcón takedown on Long Island?'

Bishop said, 'Sure. Barry Sales. He'll be a witness for us in a few days.'

'Barry was my colleague years ago. One of the best crime scene cops I ever worked with.' Rhyme paused. 'When I heard about the shooting, I wanted to volunteer to consult for the prosecution, handle the evidence. I wanted to make sure that whoever was behind it, we'd marshal an ironclad case against him. And I wanted to handle the evidence in the case.'

'Yes, I remember,' Bishop said. 'You were number one on the list for expert forensic witnesses.'

'But I had to be in DC on other business. A regret, but there was nothing to do about it. Then, a few days ago, El Halcón's lawyer calls me. He wants to hire me to prove that someone on the arrest team planted evidence incriminating El Halcón.'

Bishop blurted, 'Well, that's just bull—'

'Hank. Please?'

With a grimacing expression on his face, the man lifted a go-ahead palm toward Rhyme.

Rhyme continued, 'You're aware of the weaknesses in your case?'

The tall man shifted uneasily. 'It's not clear-cut, no.'

'First, they're claiming that El Halcón was in the bathroom the whole time, hiding. Second, that the gunshot residue was planted. He never fired Cody's gun.' Rhyme nodded at the computer. 'I've just proved that those are both wrong. I refute their theories entirely. The bathroom? There's a distinctive cleanser residue on the floor that El Halcón claims he was lying on. Officer Pulaski walked the grid there and took samples. I know the adhesive property of the chlorine ingredient of that particular cleanser. If El Halcón was in the bathroom, matching molecules would have shown up on his clothing or shoes. There were none.'

Bishop's eyes slipped toward Fallow, who, as lead investigator, should have made this discovery himself. The agent's face remained utterly expressionless.

'As for proving he fired the gun at the officers, true, El Halcón's fingerprints weren't on the weapon. But your contention is that El Halcón unbuttoned his shirt cuff and pulled the sleeve down and held the gun that way? That explains the absence of prints on the gun but the presence of gunshot residue.'

Bishop nodded. 'Theory, yes. But I'm hoping the jury will infer that that's how he held the gun when he was shooting.'

Rhyme stifled a scowl. 'They don't need to infer it. I *proved* he was holding the gun in his sleeve.'

Bishop blinked. 'How?'

'The gun was a Glock twenty-two, firing Luger nine-millimeter rounds. The impulse recoil velocity would be seventeen point five five feet per second and the recoil energy would be six point eight four foot-pounds. That's plenty of power to compress the fibers in the loose-knit cotton shirt El Halcón was wearing. The lab took microscopic pictures to show visual traces of the gunshot residue. I just looked over them and saw what the recoil had done to the fibers. Only shooting a firearm would create that compression pattern. It's all in the memo I wrote. The jury *will* have to infer that it was the bullet El Halon fired that hit Barry, but that's a logical conclusion, since the timing strongly suggests that Cody was dead by the time Barry was shot.'

Bishop was momentarily speechless.

'I, well, good, Lincoln. Thank you.' Then he frowned. 'But why didn't you tell me ahead of time?'

'What if there was a grain of truth to their claim?' Rhyme shot back. 'What if somebody *had* tainted the evidence? If so, I was going to find out who and how bad it was and let you know. Or, frankly, if you'd been the one who'd done the tainting, I would have called the attorney general in Washington.'

Drawing a smile from Sellitto.

'So you pretended to sign on to help El Halcón to shore up our case?'

'Not really. That was just serendipitous. Obviouly there was another reason.'

'Which was?'

'To find Mr X, of course.' Rhyme scowled. 'At which I wasn't very successful.'

'Mr X?' Bishop squinted. His lips tightened for a moment. 'Oh. You mean El Halcón's U.S. partner?'

Obviously . . .

'He might not have been at the shoot-out but he's behind the whole operation.'

Fallow nodded. 'We're sure his company owns the warehouse complex, but we couldn't trace it.'

'And he's as responsible for Barry Sales's injury as El Halcón. But I couldn't find any connection.'

Bishop sighed. The frustration was evident in his face as he said, 'We've done everything. We've looked everywhere. Every document, followed every lead. Nothing.'

Fallow added, 'CIs, surveillance. I even called the CIA and NSA about overseas communications. Whoever this guy is, he's a ghost.'

Rhyme said, 'I hoped there'd be some bit of evidence, some reference in the notes that led me to the U.S. partner.' A shrug. 'But nothing.'

'Well, you nailed down the case against El Halcón, Lincoln. Thank you for that.'

Bishop gave what Rhyme supposed was an uncharacteristic smile. He said, 'So how're you going to handle the money, fee he paid you?'

Rhyme said, 'Oh, I put it in an irrevocable trust for Barry. Anonymous. He won't know who it came from.'

Sellitto laughed. 'Don't you think Carreras-López ain't gonna be too happy about that? Whatta you think he's going to do?'

Rhyme shrugged. 'He's a lawyer. Let him sue me.'

Bishop nodded to Fallow and glanced at Pulaski's wrists. The agent uncuffed him and, without saying anything further, the foursome left.

Rhyme watched them leave. Pulaski or Cooper said something. He didn't hear. He was preoccupied with a single thought. An image, actually. Of Barry Sales, his friend.

He thought once more about the word he'd uttered when Carreras-López had first come to him, a word that the defense lawyer undoubtedly took in a very different context from that which Rhyme had had in mind when he uttered it: justice.

Rhyme glanced toward Sachs, who was still avoiding his eyes. Then he heard her phone hum.

She glanced at it. 'Edward Ackroyd.' She answered and had a brief conversation. He could tell from the way her eyes narrowed – just slightly – that the news was important.

When she disconnected, she said, 'That dealer? The one who put Edward onto Shapiro? He's agreed to talk to us. But only plainclothes, no uniforms. He's worried about customers seeing cops. Edward suggested me and he agreed.'

Then she walked close to Rhyme and bent close. Only he could hear her say, 'Not completely forthcoming, hm?'

She'd be referring to the clandestine operation involving El Halcón's lawyer. Reflecting on it, he wasn't in fact sure why he hadn't said anything. Maybe he wanted to keep her at arm's length in case something went south. Condescending of him, he now understood.

His lips grew taut. He held her eye. 'No. I wasn't. I should've been.'

She smiled. 'I mean both of us. I didn't tell you about what happened at the drilling site. You didn't tell me about your little investigation.'

He said, 'After all these years, we're still kind of new to it, Sachs. I won't make that mistake again.'

'I won't either.' She kissed him hard and then headed for the door. 'I'll call in from downtown.'

CHAPTER 54

Amelia Sachs felt every cobblestone in her back as the old Ford rocked over the worn streets of the Lower East Side. The fall at the construction site – the initial tumble onto the plank, not the cushioning, though horrifying, mud – had twisted her spine in some elaborate way.

Another thud.

Ah, that one hurt bad.

There was some asphalt but a lot of stone, brick and road repair steel plates.

The Torino Cobra is a car made for smooth.

Sachs had always had a soft spot in her heart for the neighborhood – abbreviated by some as the LES, which she could never accept. Far too precious and hipster a moniker, the antithesis of the place. It had a more colorful and varied history than any other part of Manhattan: In the late nineteenth century, the place became the home of Germans, Russians, Poles, Ukrainians and other European immigrants. The teeming neighborhood, filled with dark and claustrophobic tenements and chaotic pushcart-cluttered streets, gave birth to entertainers like James Cagney, Edward G. Robinson and the Gershwins. Film companies like Paramount, Metro-Goldwyn-Meyer and 20th Century Fox could trace their ancestry to the Lower East Side.

The neighborhood became the first truly integrated enclave in New York City after the Second World War, when black and Puerto Rican families joined the white longtimers and everyone lived in relative harmony.

The Lower East Side was also the site of the city's worst tragedy until September 11. The *General Slocum*, a ship chartered to take thirteen hundred German Americans to a church event, caught fire in the East River. More than a thousand passengers perished, and the sorrow that spread like plague through the community spawned a migration. Virtually every resident of Little Germany on the Lower East Side moved several miles north and resettled in Yorkville.

Discovery Channel stuff aside, Amelia Sachs had a special connection with the area. It was here, many years ago, that she had made her first felony bust – stopping an armed robbery in progress while off duty. She'd been on a Sunday brunch date, and she and – what was his name? Fred. No, *Frank*. She and Frank were walking back from a numbingly massive meal at Katz's Deli when her companion had stopped abruptly. He'd pointed with an uneasy finger. 'Hey. Does that guy, see him? Does he have a gun?'

Then Sachs's doggy bag was tumbling to the sidewalk, her Glock was in her hand and Frank was being shoved unceremoniously to safety behind a Dumpster. She charged forward, crying to passersby, 'Get down, get down, police!' Then things turned ugly. She traded a few rounds with the crackhead, who'd had the doubly bad judgment to stick up a wholesale lamp store (a window sign read, *Credit Cards Only*) and to point his weapon her way. NYPD procedure dictated that if an officer shoots, he or she should shoot to kill, but Sachs hadn't been prepared to make an existential decision under those circumstances. She'd sent a slug into his hand, removing the weapon and any future threat. An easy shot for her and, far better, less paperwork than with a fatality. Chatting manically the entire time, Frank had walked her to the subway and never asked her out again.

She now turned off this very same *High Noon* street – the Bowery – and made her way through the labyrinth until she came to a shadowy canyon. Those same tenements that had survived for 150 years still rose five stories toward the rectangle of, today, gray sky. The tall buildings bristled with fire escapes. One featured a real, old-fashioned laundry line, on which ghosts of shirts and jeans and skirts fluttered. Maybe to lessen, in a small, small way, a carbon footprint.

The street was mostly residential, but there were some ground-floor retail stores. A dry cleaner. A 'vintage' (that is, used) clothing shop. A secondhand bookstore, specializing largely in the occult.

And Blaustein's Jewelry.

She parked half on the sidewalk, tossed the NYPD placard on the dash and climbed out. The cool day kept people home and the absence of much to do on this street kept the sightseers elsewhere. The sidewalk was deserted.

She walked to the front of the store. There was a *Closed* sign on the door, but Edward Ackroyd had told her that Abe Blaustein was expecting her. She peered inside. The showroom, filled with display cases, was empty and dark but there was a light in the back and she saw some motion there. A man in a dusty black suit and wearing a yarmulke glanced up and waved her in.

The door wasn't locked and she pushed inside.

Sachs got no more than three feet. She tripped over something she hadn't seen and fell forward, landing hard on the old, oak floor with a grunt of pain.

Just as she was noting with shock the thick wire strung at ankle level, the man in the back charged forward and dropped onto her back, his knee knocking the air from her lungs, filling her with nausea. Pain consumed her and she cried out. The yarmulke was gone; he'd pulled on the familiar ski mask.

As she reached for her weapon, he fished it from her holster and pocketed it, along with her phone. His hands were encased in cloth gloves. Then he snapped her own cuffs around her wrists, behind her. And, unnecessarily, slammed a fist into her lower back. She cried out as a new agony radiated through her body, next door to the pain from the fall against the plank at the jobsite.

The man paused, as he had a coughing fit. She felt his breath and spittle on her neck. The smell was of liquor and garlic and copious, sweet aftershave.

She was aware of the assailant leaning close. She tensed, waiting for his fist again. But, no, this was weird. He was only rubbing the third finger of her left hand, as if he was studying her wedding or engagement ring.

She began, 'People know I'm here. This is a bad idea—'

'Shhh, little *kuritsa*,' came the Russian-accented voice. 'Shhh.'

She then was half carried, half dragged into the back of the shop. He deposited her hard on the carpeted floor of the office, right next to the still, pale body of a man, surely Abraham Blaustein, the owner. From his pocket, the Russian extracted a utility knife and worked the thumb button, to slide out a shiny razor blade.

And she recalled what Lincoln Rhyme had said.

I won't make that mistake again . . .

The last words he would ever speak to her.

CHAPTER 55

'Poor Abe,' the Russian was muttering.

He was looking through her wallet, her shoulder bag, clumsily because of the gloves. None of the contents seemed to interest him. He tossed everything aside.

'Poor *kuritsa*. Abe-ra-ham. Poor Jew. Did stupid things, talking about Ezekiel Shapiro and me.' He clicked his tongue. 'I saw him talking to asshole insurance man. Was stupid, don't you think he was stupid?'

He crouched beside her. 'Now, now. I am needing some things. I need to know where to find boy, Vimal? You know him, yes, you do. And insurance man. Abraham told me – after we play a few games.' A nod at the knife. 'He told me he was talking to this Edward. You tell me where Vimal and this Edward's last name and where to find them . . . and all good. All good for you.'

A trap, of course. The unsub had forced Blaustein to call Ackroyd and arrange a meeting with the police. But not just anyone. The unsub wanted *her*. She knew where Vimal Lahori was.

The pain assaulted from all directions, her ribs, her head – and her wrists. She realized she'd never been cuffed before and the steel was tight against bone and skin. Sachs was helpless. Still stunned and in searing pain from the crippling drop of his knee into her back. It had emptied her lungs. She still was struggling for breath.

Fainting . . .

No, can't faint.

Not acceptable.

He had, it seemed, realized just then that he was still in disguise. He brusquely pulled Blaustein's jacket off and tossed it aside. Then the yarmulke.

'Jew jacket.' He coughed briefly. Wiped his mouth and looked at the napkin. 'Good, good. All good.'

She looked past the disgust and tried to analyze her situation. She could smell liquor but he didn't seem drunk. Not drunk enough to be careless. How much time did she need to buy? Long enough for Rhyme to call her phone to ask what she had found? Without an answer, he'd get uniforms here in three or four minutes. The precinct wasn't that far away.

But that would be a very long three or four minutes.

He leaned close. 'Now, you . . . '

He looked again at her ID.

'You, Policewoman A-melia. You are helpful girl. You can help me. Good for you. You help me and you go free.'

'What's your name?' she ventured.

'Shhh, *kuritsa*.'

'There's another gas bomb, we know. Maybe more. Tell me where they are.'

This gave him pause. His blue eyes kept slipping in and out of focus. Not from drugs, though. His mind was manic. Yes, he was a mercenary and a hired killer. But the Promisor and his crazy mission were not complete fictions. Her initial diagnosis held.

He's just plain crazy . . .

She continued, 'We'll work with the DA. And the State Department. We'll cut you some kind of deal.'

'State Department. Why, look at you! A little trussed-up *kuritsa*, ready for the pot, and still scratching at chickensfeed, looking for helpful *things*. Am I a national? Am I a Russki? What does Homeland Security know about me? Clever. Now, I like you, *kuritsa*. Things won't go painful, you help me.'

With her breath coming more consistently now, she was aware that the pain from the fall and his blows was dissolving.

Thinking: Steady. A plan. Have to buy time.

Time . . .

'We have information about you. You're from Moscow. The Dobyns passport. The others, from Barcelona and Dubai.'

He froze. It was as if he'd been slapped.

She said evenly, 'It's only a question of time till they find you.

Your description, it's gone to a watchlist. You'll never get out of the country.'

He recovered, nodding broadly. 'Yes, yes, but maybe I have own way of getting out. Or maybe I stay in nice country here and drive for Uber! Now my question. There is boy I need to find. And insurance asshole. Edward. You will tell me.'

'We can work with—'

He rose suddenly, his eyes completely mad. He drew his foot back and swung an oxford shoe hard into her side. The kick didn't break a rib but it reignited the pain on all fronts. She cried out once more and tears flowed. He once again crouched near and lowered his lips to her ear. When he spoke his voice was raw with anger. 'No talk but to answer question.'

She fell silent.

'Okay?'

She nodded.

Nothing more to do. Sachs closed her eyes. Her thought was: At least he's leaving a trove of evidence.

Amelia Sachs knew she was going to die.

She thought first of her father, Herman Sachs, a decorated NYPD officer.

Then of Rhyme, naturally. Their lives had coursed parallel for so many years.

I won't make that mistake again . . .

Then of her mother, of Pam – the young woman whose life she'd saved and who had become something of a daughter to her. Presently studying in San Francisco.

The Russian now rolled her completely face down, kicked her feet apart. Her cheek rubbed against the gritty floor. He gripped her cuffed left hand, pulled it up, agonizingly, and again caressed her ring finger. He was apparently examining the blue diamond in the engagement ring Rhyme had bought her.

Could she bargain his interest into some time? She began to speak. 'Listen to—'

'Shh, shh. What I tell you?' He rubbed the blade against her ring finger. 'Okay, *kuritsa*. Now. What I am saying is question. That boy. That Vimal boy. Stupid little *kuritsa*. I need to talk to him. Have little talk. You need tell me where he is. And insurance man.'

'That won't happen.'

'I won't hurt him. No, no! Don't want to hurt him. Just talk. Chat.'

'Surrender now. It'll be a lot better for you.'

He laughed. 'You are some other thing else! Now Vimal. Tell me how I pay visit.'

With one hand he pulled her ring finger taut, moved the razor knife closer yet, she could feel.

She struggled, with all her strength, to keep her fingers curled but he was far too strong. He straddled her, pressed all his weight down on her hips. She was frozen in place.

A sting on her finger.

Jesus, he's cutting it off! He's going to cut it off!

She gritted her teeth, thinking, How's this for irony? He's about to remove my left ring finger – the same one that, after Lincoln's accident, had been the only digit of his that continued to function.

'Vimal?'

'No.'

She felt him tense as he was about to start cutting.

Sachs inhaled. Squeezed her eyes shut. How bad would the pain be?

Then the Russian stiffened. His grip relaxed. He seemed to be looking up. He began to stand, the knife rising from her finger. He gasped.

The air pressure from the gunshot, painfully close, slapped her body. The Russian dropped immediately, falling backward onto her legs.

Then the man was being hauled off her and she was rolling onto her back, looking up into the horrified face of Edward Ackroyd. He stared at his own hand, holding a Glock. Not hers. He dropped the gun on the desk as if it were red-hot and lifted her away from the Russian's body.

His lips were moving. She wondered for a moment why he'd lost his voice. Then realized that she had been temporarily deafened by the shot.

He was, she guessed, asking if she was all right.

So this was the question she answered, with 'Yes, yes, okay.'

Though his hearing too was useless and he responded, manically, with words that seemed to be, 'What, what, what?'

CHAPTER 56

Outside the jewelry store, in the shadows of buildings erected two centuries past, Sachs sat on the ledge of the ambulance. She'd refused a gurney.

The medical tech announced that there was no serious harm; she had suffered no broken ribs – from the Russian's knee or his shoe – but there would be contusions. A slight cut from the knife resided at the base of the fourth metacarpal of her left hand – the ring finger – where the amputation had been about to commence. A bit of Betadine and a bandage were the only fixes needed.

Edward Ackroyd stood beside her, subdued. His faint smile was back but was understandably hollow. Which also described his hazel eyes. He explained that he'd decided to come to the dealer's to meet with her and Abraham Blaustein to see if he could help. He peered in and couldn't see anyone so he'd entered. Then to his shock he'd seen a man straddling her and bending forward with a razor knife. He had noted too a pistol in the pocket of a black jacket on the counter – the Russian's; he'd taken it off to dress in Blaustein's garment.

When the man saw him and rose, lifting the knife, he pulled the trigger.

'I didn't think. I just shot. That's all. I just . . . All those years on the Metropolitan Police. Never fired a gun. Never *carried* a gun.' His shoulders were slumped. Manically, he flicked a forefinger against a thumb.

'It's okay,' she said.

Though she knew it wasn't. The first one stayed with you. Forever. However necessary, however instinctive, that first fatal shot was etched indelibly into your mind and heart and soul.

Several times Ackroyd had asked the medical crew and the responding officers if the Russian was in fact dead, clearly hoping he'd just wounded the man. One look at the result of the hollow-point slug, though, left no doubt.

Sachs said, 'Edward, thank you.' An inadequate expression, of course. But what possibly *would* suffice?

Sachs was, however, of mixed feelings about the incident. Her digits were intact, her life was spared. But not only had Unsub 47 died but so had the easiest – and perhaps only – chance to find out where the last gas bomb devices had been planted. As the medical examiner tour doctor was finishing the preliminary examination, Sachs dressed in CSU overalls and bent to the corpse to see what, in death, it might tell her.

'Know this is a hassle, sir. But, between you and me, I wouldn't worry about it overly.'

Andrew Krueger nodded and tried to bring a bit of uncertain concern to the equation. 'I . . . just don't know what to say.'

The detective was a large African American, driving his unmarked police car to a precinct house that he had assured Krueger was not too far away. Krueger was in the front seat of the Chrysler. He wasn't under arrest. The detective himself had made the determination that the shooting was justified and he would 'go to bat for you, Mr Ackroyd.'

Still, there were formalities. He would have to make a statement, there'd be an investigation, and all the findings would go to an assistant district attorney, who would make the final determination about his fate.

'One chance in a million it'll become a case. I'd bet my pension not. No ADA's going to screw up his reputation by bringing a charge on this one. Besides, you've got a ringer.'

'A what?'

'Oh, means like a get-out-of-jail-free card.'

Krueger still didn't get it. 'Sorry?'

'Don't you have Monopoly in England?'

'Unfair business arrangements?'

The detective seemed amused. 'Never mind. Just that Amelia

– Detective Sachs – you saving her hide? She's a big deal in the department. That'll count for more than beans.'

They drove in silence for a time.

He continued, 'Happened to me. I've done it. Once. Twenty-four years on the force I never fired my weapon. Then, just eighteen months ago . . . ' His voice faded away. 'Domestic call. The guy was nuts, you know, off his meds. He was going to shoot his mother, and my partner and me were talking him down. But then he swung the weapon on Jerry. No choice.' A pause for the length of one block. 'It wasn't loaded. His weapon. But . . . well, you'll get over it. I did.'

Or not.

'Thanks for that,' Krueger said with as much sincerity as he could dredge up. 'I'm not sure that I'll ever be the same.'

This, from a man who had murdered at least thirteen people – though only three with firearms.

He was recalling Rostov's expression when he'd seen the gun pointed at his head. Shock, then an instant of understanding, knowing that he'd been set up. Krueger had fired fast, before the Russian could call out his name and tip Sachs off that they knew each other. Aiming right at the temple.

Vladimir Rostov's death had been inevitable.

And planned out for some time. Krueger had decided to kill him as soon as he'd figured out that the Russian had hacked his phone and was in New York, playing the role of the 'Promisor.' He'd known by then that Rhyme and Amelia were brilliant and he needed to give them both a mastermind – the fanatical Ezekiel Shapiro – and his hired-gun eco-terrorist, Vladimir Rostov.

Krueger's strategy was to walk into Blaustein's and kill Rostov with Krueger's own unregistered Glock – the one that he'd used to shoot at Vimal and to kill Saul Weintraub. In the confusion after the shooting at Blaustein's, he'd planted 9mm rounds in Rostov's jacket to better link the man to the shootings at Patel's and Weintraub's. Krueger had also pocketed Rostov's mobile and the keys to his motel and the Toyota.

The minute Krueger's interview with the police was done, which he didn't think would take very long, he would hurry to

Rostov's room, scrub it of evidence, then ditch the Russian's burner phones, computer and car.

The police car now arrived at the precinct house and Krueger climbed out. The detective directed him toward the front door.

'This way, Mr Ackroyd. Now, just to let you know. You're not being arrested. No fingerprinting or pictures. Any of that. It'll just be an interview is all.'

'Thanks, Officer. I truly appreciate your words of reassurance. What happened, well, it was pretty upsetting.' He thought about wiping faux tears from his eyes but decided that would be out of character.

CHAPTER 57

Amelia Sachs returned to Rhyme's town house with several things.

The first was a collection of evidence from Vladimir Rostov's hotel in Brighton Beach and the dealer's store where she'd nearly lost a finger to the crazy Russian's knife.

The second was a New York state mining inspector.

Rhyme glanced toward the man they'd spoken to before, Don McEllis, without much interest and reseated his gaze on the evidence cartons that Sachs was carting in. She noticed the direction of his eyes and said, 'Not going to be easy, Rhyme.'

Referring to their urgent mission: finding out where the next gas bombs had been set.

'I'm hoping McEllis can help.'

He was a slim, earnest-looking man – okay, 'dowdy' came to mind – who was here, Sachs explained, to look over the maps and the details of the prior fires and see if he could help them narrow down the search for the devices.

Sachs said, 'I'm thinking that he'd plant them close to fault lines in the area, if he wanted the quakes to look authentic. If so, maybe Don can point them out.'

The detective shrugged. He didn't seem enthusiastic. His phone hummed. 'City Hall. Jesus.' He took the call and stepped aside.

McEllis asked to use one of the computers to load some geological maps of the area. Cooper directed him to one. He wanted to see too where the previous gas bombs had been set, and Sachs pushed toward him the whiteboard on which was taped a map of the city. The fires were marked in red and they made a rough ellipse around what was the epicenter: the geothermal drilling site near Cadman Plaza. McEllis called up the geological diagrams of the area and began poring over them.

Cooper and Sachs both dressed in gowns and face masks and

began to look over the evidence that had been collected at Blaustein's jewelry store and Rostov's motel in Brighton Beach.

Rhyme had some information too. After Sachs had sent him the unsub's identity, he had contacted Daryl Mulbry at AIS once more, requesting details on the killer. The man had sent a report summarizing what he could find on short notice. Vladimir Ivanovich Rostov. The forty-four-year old's history was Russian military and then FSB – one of the successors to the KGB – and then for the past ten years a 'consultant,' whose clients included some of the big Russian quasi-governmental organizations, like Gazprom, the oil and gas company, Nizhny Novgorod Shipping, which made oil rigs and tankers and – significantly – Dobprom, the biggest diamond-mining company in Russia.

Mulbry had learned that Rostov had worked in the Mir mine, in Siberia, from ages twelve through twenty. 'Fellow's a bit off, from what we could learn. Rumors that he killed his uncle, who was in a mine shaft with him. Head crushed with a rock, but there wasn't any rockslide. The police tended to look the other way when it came to the biggest employer in the region. His aunt died too, not long after that. Apparently one night, she got trapped on the roof of the building, locked out of the access door. No one could figure what she was doing there. She was wearing a flimsy nightgown and no shoes. It was December. The temperature was minus twenty. The authorities looked the other way on that one too. There were complaints that she'd been *ne podkhodit*, not appropriate, with some youngsters in the building.'

Quite a background, Rhyme reflected.

Mines. Well, that explained the obsession with diamonds . . . and Rostov's interest in the fake earthquakes at the geothermal site.

The spy had added that Rostov was non grata in Germany, France, Sweden, the Czech Republic and Taiwan, suspected of assault, extortion and illegal business practices, as well as a number of financial crimes. Witnesses would not come forward with statements, so he'd never been brought to trial; he was simply told to leave and not come back. In Kraków, Polish authorities detained him after a report that he sexually assaulted a woman and beat her boyfriend. He was quietly released after some intervention by Moscow.

At the jewelry store, she'd found the man's real Russian passport – in the name of Rostov – plus a forged passport in the name of Alexander Petrovitch, the .38 Smith & Wesson, loose .38 and 9mm Finocchi rounds – the latter for the Glock – ski mask, cloth gloves, the bloodstained utility box-cutting knife, cigarettes and lighter, cash (dollars, rubles and euros). No keys to the Toyota, though there was no guarantee that the red car outside Adeela's house had been Rostov's. He didn't have a mobile on him, either.

He had no room keys on him but a fast canvass of motels and hotels in the area revealed that one Alexander Petrovitch was staying at the Beach View Residence Inn in Brighton Beach, Brooklyn, which Sachs had searched carefully. But she didn't find much. More .38 ammunition, junk food, bottles of Jack Daniels, the actual passports of the other identities that Mulbry had learned of. No computers or telephones, car keys or trace of or references to *lehabah*s, the gas line IEDs, or to where they might have been planted.

And no rough diamonds worth five million dollars.

Where were the stones? And Rostov's electronics? She supposed he kept everything, hotel key included, in the Toyota, in case he needed to make a fast getaway. The car key was likely hidden in the wheel well. After *Breaking Bad*, the TV series, a surprising number of perps had been doing this.

The lack of leads, she'd explained to Rhyme, had inspired her to conscript the geologist – a bit of a desperate move, she admitted. Though a reasonable one, in Rhyme's opinion.

Sachs transcribed the sparse evidentiary finds on a whiteboard and stepped back, hands on hips, worrying a thumbnail with an index finger. Staring, staring, staring.

Rhyme was doing the same. 'Anything more?' he called to Cooper.

'Just checking the last of the trace from the hotel room. Should be a minute.'

But what would that show? Possibly some substance from a shoe print unique to where he'd planted a bomb. But what a long shot that would be.

He grimaced in frustration. A glance toward McEllis. 'Anything, Don?'

The engineer was hunched forward, studying both the online geological maps and the hard-copy one that depicted the previous fires. He said, 'I think so. He seems to have set the bombs along the Carnarsee fault. See? It goes through downtown Brooklyn, near Cadman Plaza, then into the harboir. It's two miles long, but most of that's underwater. Abour a half mile is on land.' McEllis indicated a line through the densely populated borough.

Hell, Rhyme thought, too many basements to search. 'We've got to narrow it down more.'

Mel Cooper called, 'Got the last of the trace. Nothing pins Rostov to a particular place. Tobacco ash, ketchup, beef fat, soil associated with Brighton Beach geography. More kimberlite.'

Without looking up from the map, McEllis asked, 'Kimberlite?'

Rhyme said, 'That's right. Our unsub picked some trace up at the first shooting. It's on his clothes and shoes. He's left it at a couple of the scenes.'

'Then you mean serpentinite. Not kimberlite. They're in the same family.'

'No, it's kimberlite. There're diamond crystals embedded,' Cooper said, looking up. 'I thought that made serpentinite into kimberlite.'

'It does,' McEllis whispered. 'But . . . well, can I see a sample?'

Cooper looked toward Rhyme, who nodded.

The tech prepared a sample and set it on the stage of the compound microscope.

McEllis sat on the stool, bent forward and began adjusting the light above the stage. He focused. Sat back, looked away. Then back to the eyepiece. He used a needle probe to poke through the dust and fragments. His eyes remained against the soft rubber eyepieces but his shoulders rose, as did his heels, slightly. His body language suggested he was looking at something significant. He sat back and gave a soft laugh.

'What is it?' Sellitto asked.

'Well, if you found these rocks in New York City, then you've just rewritten geological history.'

'Kimberlite,' Don McEllis was telling those in the parlor. 'You could call it the elevator that carries diamonds to the surface of the earth from the mantle – the part that's just below the crust. Where diamonds are formed.'

The inspector returned to the microscope, as if he couldn't resist, and studied the minerals on the instrument's stage again. He continued sifting through the samples. 'Hm. Well.' McEllis sat back once more and turned the stool to face the others. 'Diamond-rich kimberlite – like this – has never been seen anywhere in New York State. The geology of the area doesn't lend itself to diamond formation. New York is a "passive margin" area. We have stable tectonic plates.'

'Impossible for kimberlite with diamonds to be found here?' Rhyme asked.

The man shrugged. 'Better to say very unlikely. There're about six thousand kimberlite pipes in the world but only about nine hundred contain diamonds . . . and only a couple of dozen have enough rough to make mining profitable. And none in the U.S. Oh, there was a bit of production years ago – in the South. Now they're all tourist mines. You pay twenty bucks, or whatever, and pan for diamonds with the kids. But then again in Canada miners didn't find kimberlite or diamonds until recently and now it's a major producer. So, I suppose it could happen here.'

The inspector peered briefly into the microscope once more. 'Where did you find this again?'

Rhyme responded, 'Several places. At the shop where Patel, the diamond cutter, was killed. Vimal – his apprentice – had a bag with him. We didn't think anything of it. We thought he was going to make it into jewelry. Or sculpt it. That's his hobby.'

'You couldn't carve kimberlite like this. The diamonds would make that impossible. Too hard.'

Rhyme scowled. 'Assumption.'

'And the other sources?' McEllis asked.

Sachs said, 'There was some trace at Saul Weintraub's house – a witness who was murdered. It came from either the killer's shoes or clothing.' She shrugged. 'That's what we thought. I suppose it might have come from Weintraub himself.'

Assumption . . .

Rhyme asked, 'Say there were some larger pieces of this stuff. Would they be worth a lot? Worth killing for?'

'The odds of finding any worthwhile diamonds in small samples of kimberlite are like winning the lottery.' Then he was frowning. 'But . . . '

'What?' Sachs asked.

'Nobody would kill for a rock like this. But they might for what it represented.'

'How do you mean?'

'If this sample came from a large lode? Well, I could see people killing either to get the mining rights or to destroy the source, make sure no one found out about it.'

'Destroy?' Sachs asked.

McEllis said, 'Historically there're two industries where companies will do whatever it takes to sabotage potential finds, to keep prices high. Oil and diamonds. And when I say whatever, I mean that. Murder, sabotage, threats. It doesn't happen with industrial-grade diamonds – the cheap ones for grinding, filing, machinery. But for gem-quality, like these.' Another nod toward the microscope. 'Oh, yes. Definitely.'

Sellitto said, 'Linc, you're thinking some diamond company heard about a lode and sent the unsub here to kill anybody who knew about it.'

Rhyme nodded. 'Northeast Geo— they dug up the stuff. So Rostov faked the earthquakes to have the city shut down the drilling and make sure no more kimberlite got dug up.'

McEllis said, 'It's not as outlandish as you'd think. There're even quote "security" companies that you can hire to make sure potential mines never open or existing ones're closed. Dams get blown up, government officials are bribed to nationalize mines and then destroy them. Russians are particularly active.'

'And Rostov,' Rhyme said, 'had worked for Dobprom in the past, the Russian diamond monopoly.'

'Oh, they're definitely players in sabotage. A lot of other producers too but the Russians are number one in the dirty-tricks department.'

Sachs said, 'Weintraub. He was an assayer. Maybe he wasn't killed because he was a witness. Maybe he was killed because he'd analyzed the kimberlite and found out about the diamonds.'

Sellitto muttered, 'We weren't thinking. At Patel's: Weintraub left before the unsub got there. How much help would he've been as a wit? Not much. Our unsub wanted him dead because he knew about the kimberlite.'

Sachs said, 'The crimes at Patel's weren't about stealing the rough. They were about killing him and anyone who knew about the find. That's why he tortured Patel – and pistol-whipped Weintraub. He wanted to know if they had any more kimberlite or if anyone else knew about it.'

Rhyme eased the back of his skull against the headrest of his chair, eyes now closed. Then they opened. 'Somebody finds a sample at the drilling site. Takes it to Jatin Patel, who has it analyzed by Weintraub. Word gets back to Dobprom. They send Rostov to stop the drilling and kill anyone who's learned about it.'

McEllis said, 'Dobprom wouldn't want a major U.S. diamond operation to get started. Hell, *no* foreign mine would. It would cut their revenues in half.'

Mel Cooper asked, 'But is there really a risk to the companies? I mean, how realistic is it to mine diamonds in Brooklyn?'

McEllis replied, 'Oh, it wouldn't be hard at all. A lot easier, actually, than digging subway and water supply tunnels, which the city does all the time. Some legal hurdles but they're not insurmountable. My department would need to approve the plans and there'd be other licensing red tape. We won't allow open-cut mining, for instance. But you could easily set up a narrow-shaft automated system. From an engineering stand-point, piece of cake.'

But, Rhyme thought, if the goal was to stop the drilling, that means—

Giving voice to what he had been about to say, Sellitto offered, 'So Ezekiel Shapiro, he wasn't a suicide. Rostov murdered him and made it look that way. Kidnapped him, tortured him to get his Facebook passcode, left the suicide note.'

Rhyme was grim as he said, 'He needed a fall guy because we'd found that the earthquakes were fake and the fires were from the gas line devices.'

Then it struck him. Like an electric jolt.

'Rubles,' he whispered.

'Hell.' Sachs apparently was with him. 'Rostov wouldn't plant *rubles* at Shapiro's. They were evidence that pointed to him. It was somebody *else* who broke into Shapiro's apartment, who killed him – somebody who wanted to make it seem like *Rostov* was behind the plot. Sure, the Russian was involved: He attacked the couple in Gravesend and that girl from the wedding dress store. And Kirtan – Vimal's friend. Attacked me, too. But he wasn't the mastermind.'

And the conclusion was inevitable.

In a quiet voice, eyes on Rhyme, she said, 'And that was the person who shot him.'

Rhyme knew this was right. 'Edward Ackroyd.'

'But,' Sellitto said, 'we vetted him. And he knew all about Patel. About the diamond rough that had been stolen.'

'What diamond rough?' Rhyme asked cynically. 'Did we ever find it? Did we ever see any trace of it?'

Of course not.

'Because it never existed,' Sachs said,

Rhyme nodded. 'He faked the diamond envelope at Patel's. It never occurred to me! Why leave it? He could have just taken the stones *in* the envelope. He did that to work his way into the investigation . . . to find out who VL was. And we let him into the chicken coop. Goddamn.'

'How'd that work, Linc?' Sellitto asked. 'Amelia called Grace-Cabot Mining in South Africa.'

Sachs exhaled. Her face was taut and her words angry. 'No, I didn't. I called the number on the envelope for the rough. I didn't look the company up online. Is it even a real company?'

'Well . . . ' Rhyme cut an impatient glance to Pulaski. He nodded and found the Grace-Cabot receipt, then went to Google.

He was nodding. 'It is a real diamond mine. But the office number isn't the one on the receipt.' He tried that one. 'It just says leave a message.'

'Llewellyn Croft?' Rhyme asked.

Pulaski scrolled through the site. 'He *is* the managing director of Grace-Cabot.'

'If you found him, then Ackroyd – I mean our real unsub – could've found him too.'

Sachs continued, in a soft, disgusted tone, 'The man we talked to, pretending to be Croft, was an associate of Ackroyd's. Probably in one of those security companies Don was telling us about. He sent us to Milbank Assurance. Same thing, a real company but he faked his connection to it.'

Rhyme snapped, 'Now. I want to find out now.'

The ensuing series of phone calls to Grace-Cabot and Milbank Assurance confirmed that the scam was just as they believed. Llewellyn Croft was managing director of the former but he assured them now that he'd never sent any rough to Patel for cutting. He himself hadn't been in the United States for several years. Nor was Milbank their insurance carrier.

At Rhyme's request, the FBI special agent Fred Dellray contacted someone in the State Department. They confirmed, from Customs and Border Protection, that Croft had not been in the country recently. Calls to Milbank bore out the fact that the insurance company had no connection to Grace-Cabot. Yes, the company had a senior investigator by the name of Edward Ackroyd and, yes, he was a former Scotland Yard inspector. But he had also been in London for the past week, at the company's home office.

His face a sardonic mask, Lon Sellitto said, 'Okay, for the slow guy: I'm lost. The fuck's going on, Linc?'

'Some diamond-mining company learns about the kimberlite find and is worried a competitor's going to start production. Ackroyd's hired to set up the earthquakes and stop the geothermal drilling. And to find out who knows about the kimberlite and kill them too: Patel and Weintraub and Vimal. He murders the first two but the boy gets away. So Ackroyd claims that his client's rough was stolen, to work his way into our investigation so he can find out where Vimal is.'

Sellitto asked, 'How does Rostov fit in? Were they working together, for the Russians?'

Rhyme said sourly, 'You don't usually shoot your partner in the head.'

Sachs said, 'No. Two different companies both heard about the kimberlite. One sent Ackroyd here and Dobprom sent Rostov. Ackroyd set up Rostov to take the fall, if everything went south.'

Rhyme muttered, 'I should have seen it! Black polyster fibers at the Patel and Weintraub scenes. Only black cotton at the other. That meant maybe two different types of ski masks. Two different weapons. Glock and Smittie. Look.' He pointed to the recent evidence chart. 'Rostov had some nine-millimeter rounds on him at Blaustein's store but Ackroyd could have slipped those into his pocket.'

'Rhyme!' Sachs sounded alarmed.

He suddenly understood. 'Hell. There's another reason to kill Rostov.'

'Why?' Sellitto asked.

Sachs said, 'To make it look like Unsub Forty-Seven's dead – and Vimal is safe. So we'd release him from protective custody.'

'Is he out?' the lieutenant asked.

Sachs grimaced. 'Hell, yes. I called the security detail on Staten Island and they were driving him to the ferry. And Vimal doesn't have a phone anymore. There's no way to get in touch with him. I'll call his family.' She swept out her mobile.

Rhyme said to Sellitto, 'And call the precinct in Brooklyn where they took Ackroyd. Tell them to detain him.'

'I'm on it.' The detective placed the call. He had a brief conversation, then, with a grimace, disconnected. 'Ackroyd, or whoever he is, he's been released without charges. His phone's dead. And the address he gave the shield's fake. Nobody knows where he is.'

CHAPTER **59**

And now?

Vimal Lahori climbed to the street, out of the oppressive, salt-scented atmosphere of the subway. The tunnel had featured a hint – just a hint – of urine too.

He inhaled deeply. The air was chill and damp, the sky was gray. He was walking past single-family homes, modest homes with trim yards. Populated by husbands and wives and young children, he knew – though there was no visible evidence of the kids. In the suburbs, yards like these were repositories of tricycles and toys. Not in the city.

There weren't many people on the street here – a woman in a yellow raincoat and carting a grocery bag. A businessman. Both had heads down and shoulders lifted against the chill breeze. What kind of homes were they returning to? Vimal wondered. Pleasant, comforting, he bet. That this was pure speculation didn't matter; he envied them because he wanted to envy them.

Pausing, he watched a sheet of newspaper float past on the wind. It settled near him on the sidewalk.

Laughing softly, he thought: Paper covers rock.

He crouched and studied the stone at his feet. On this block the walk was bluestone – laid a hundred years ago, maybe more. The name came not from the original color at the quarry – it was gray – but from aging. Over time the rock had transformed to reveal azure shades and sometimes green and red tones. He pressed a hand against one, wondering what it would be like to carve. In this particular piece he saw a bas-relief – a shallow three-dimensional figure of a fish. It would be a good complement to his sculpture *The Wave*. It would be an easy thing to sculpt. He would simply, like Michelangelo, remove the portions of the slab that were not the koi.

Rising to his feet again, he continued toward his house.

The pleasant thoughts of the fish and of his carving tools awaiting him at home were suddenly, and inevitably, dislocated by another image: Mr Patel's feet motionless on the floor of his studio, angling toward the ceiling. This memory kept recurring. Hour after hour. Then that image was in turn displaced by the memories of his own father locking him into the studio, Mr Nouri's son's betrayal, Mr Weintraub's death, the police.

Diamonds. Diamonds were to blame.

He shivered briefly in anger.

Then the question rose once again: What now?

In a few minutes Vimal would see his father. What would the man say? Vimal's desire to leave town was undiminished. But now he didn't have the excuse to escape – the excuse that a killer was after him . . . and the excuse that he would be arrested for 'stealing' Mr Patel's kimberlite, which apparently had no value, after all. The horror was over. And his father would put on the pressure to stay. Would Vimal have the courage to say no?

Safe from the killer. And yet no comfort. How cruel was this?

Well, he would say no. His stomach tightened at the thought. But he'd do it. He would.

He found himself walking more and more slowly. This subconscious braking almost amused him.

About two blocks from his house, he passed a driveway that ran to the back of a brick bungalow. He heard a man's voice calling out. 'Somebody, can you help me? I fell!'

Vimal glanced up the alley. It was the businessman he'd seen a moment ago. He was lying on the ground beside his car.

Yesterday he would've been suspicious. But now, with that Russian man dead, he wasn't worried for his own safety. Not here. In Manhattan, in the Diamond District, he was always on guard. But in this part of Queens, no.

Muggers rarely looked like accountants and wore nice over-coats.

The man had slipped. His leg was bent and he was gripping the limb and moaning. He glanced toward Vimal and said, 'Oh, thank God. Please, can you reach my phone? I dropped it under the car.' He winced.

'Sure. Don't worry. Is it broken? Your leg?'

'I don't know. I don't think so. But it hurts like hell to move it.'

Vimal was nearly to the man when he saw something in the bushes. It was a square of white.

A metal sign. He paused and leaned in. He read:

For Sale
Under Contract

The name of the brokerage firm was underneath it.

He glanced at the windows of the house. They were dark.

In a second, he understood that the man didn't live here at all! It was a trap! He'd pulled the sign out of the front yard and hidden it so he could lure Vimal here.

Shit. Vimal turned fast but by then the man was on his feet and snagging him, spinning him around. He wasn't a large man, and his eyes, the color of yellow agate, were placid. Still, when he slammed Vimal into the side of the car, the blow stunned him. The assailant easily dodged Vimal's sloppy, swinging fist and dropped him to his knees with a fierce blow to the gut. Vimal held up a wait-a-minute hand and vomited.

The man looked around to make sure they were alone. He said, 'You going to be sick again?' An oddly accented voice.

Vimal shook his head.

'You're sure?'

Who was this? A friend of the Russian?

'What do you—'

'Are you sure you're not going to be sick?'

'No.'

The man bound his hands with silver duct tape and pulled him to the trunk. He seemed to be debating taping his mouth too but was probably worried that he might in fact puke once more and choke to death. He chose not to gag him.

Apparently the assailant was determined to keep him alive.

At least for the time being.

CHAPTER 60

Driving through a rugged part of industrial Queens, looking for a suitable place for what was next on the schedule.

Andrew Krueger knew, since he'd been released by the police, that they didn't suspect him. And while he supposed Rhyme and Amelia were quite capable of figuring out the entire scheme given enough time, he knew that didn't enter into their thoughts much at all, since they were frantically trying to find the next gas bomb. He had placed that one in an old wooden residential building – a literal tinderbox. The fake earthquake would rattle windows soon and not long after, the gas line would start to leach its delightful vapor. Then the explosion.

But Krueger no longer cared about scorched flesh; his only concern was to answer the final question: Where had Vimal found the kimberlite he'd been carrying on Saturday?

Krueger pulled his rented Ford into an industrial park area and found a deserted parking lot of cracked asphalt and weeds. He looked about. No one nearby. No cars, no trucks. No CCTV, though he hardly expected any; the warehouse's roof had collapsed years ago.

The boy had stopped pounding on the trunk and Krueger had the troubling thought that he might be dead. Could you suffocate in a trunk in this day and age? It seemed unlikely. Had one of the jostling bumps on the roadway or here broken his neck, some freak accident?

Damn well better not have.

He lifted the lid and looked down at Vimal Patel. He was doing fine – if that word could be used to describe somebody who was utterly terrified.

Unlike the late and unlamented Vladimir Rostov, Krueger wasn't a sadist. He took no pleasure in the boy's dread. Oh, he would kill anybody he needed to – setting the gas line fires in the apartments, for instance, or Patel and Weintraub – not to mention Rostov himself. But he didn't torture, at least not for pleasure. Death and pain were simply tools like a dop stick, a scaife turntable and diamond-infused olive oil for brillianteering.

But if he took no pleasure in the boy's misery, neither did he feel an ounce of sympathy. His mission. That was all that mattered. Keeping the price of diamonds floating high, just shy of heaven.

He pulled the boy from the trunk.

'Please, what do you—?'

'Quiet. Listen to me carefully. Saturday, you walked into Patel's shop with a bag of kimberlite.'

Vimal frowned. 'You were there? *You* killed Mr Patel?' Anger replaced the fear in his eyes.

Krueger brandished the razor knife and the boy grew quiet. 'I asked you a question. Tell me about the kimberlite. How did Patel get it? Look, I can hurt you a lot. Just tell me.'

'All I know is somebody found a piece in Brooklyn where they were doing that drilling. In a scrap pile.'

'Who?'

'I don't know. A scavenger or somebody, I guess. I'm a sculptor. I do the same thing at construction sites. I pick around for rocks. He probably saw the crystals and thought it might be valuable. He just picked Mr Patel at random to sell it to.'

'And how did you end up with that bag?'

'Mr Patel wanted more. I went to look for them but the company? The one doing the drilling? They'd had everything hauled off to a scrapyard.'

Vimal was continuing. 'Mr Patel had me go to the yard to look. I went four times, or five. I finally found a pile of it. That was on Saturday. I was bringing some back to show him.'

Krueger asked, 'How much kimberlite was there?'

'Not much.'

'What do you mean by not much?'

'A dozen bigger pieces – about the size of your fist. Mostly fragments and dust.'

'Where is this yard?'

'Near Cobble Hill. C and D Waste Transfer Station Number Four.'

Construction and demolition, Krueger supposed.

'What's Cobble Hill?'

'A neighborhood. In Brooklyn.'

Krueger said, 'Where?' He called up a map on his phone and the boy glanced down but then gazed off.

Krueger said, 'Look. Don't worry. Killing you wouldn't fit my plans. The one taking the blame for this whole thing, a fellow from Russia, he's already dead. For you to die now, that means the police would start looking for *another* suspect. You're safe.'

A nod. He was miserable and angry but he saw the logic.

Faulty logic though it was: Of course, the boy *would* be dead soon . . . and the killer identified as a partner of Rostov's, another – a fictional – Russian. After killing Vimal, Krueger would rip his clothing, as if he'd fought with his assailant. He'd then plant a bit of evidence here, near the body, things he'd taken from Rostov's motel – tobacco from a Russian cigarette, a few ruble coins – that would appear to have been scattered in the struggle. And he'd leave a prepaid phone somewhere nearby, too. The phone, free of fingerprints, had a dozen or more calls to Dobprom and various random numbers in Russia embedded in memory. Krueger had placed the calls himself after he'd shot Rostov.

Perfectly tidy? No. But a reasonable explanation for the boy's death.

'Well?'

Vimal hesitated and then pointed to a spot on the map. It was not far away.

Krueger helped him back into the trunk, closed the lid and then drove out of the desolate parking lot. In twenty minutes they were at the dump site.

C&D Transfer Station #4

He drove through the wide gate, ignored by the few workers here, and the vehicle rocked slowly along a wide path, marred with deep tire treads. The yard was easily the size of a half-dozen soccer pitches. Hundreds of twenty- and thirty-foot-high piles of refuse rose like miniature mountains, composed of stone, plasterboard, metal, wood, concrete . . . every building material you could imagine. He supposed that salvage companies, for a fee, were allowed to prowl through the refuse and pick what might be valuable. He smiled to himself thinking that these companies would be delighted to find copper pipe and wiring, and ignore the diamond-rich kimberlite, which was the clue that somewhere in the ground not far away lurked material worth a million times more.

He parked behind one of these mounds, out of view of the highway, the entrance and the workers.

He climbed out of the Ford and pulled Vimal from the trunk.

Krueger lifted the knife. Vimal shied. 'Just the tape,' the man told him. He sliced through it, freeing his hands. He put the knife away and displayed the gun in his waistband. 'Run and I'll use it.'

'No. I won't.'

'Go on.' They started through the dun and gray valleys, moving parallel to the water, where the barges were being filled with debris by bulldozers and dump trucks. The sound was over-whelming.

'Where?'

The young man looked around, orienting himself. 'That way.' He nodded his head toward the waterfront. The two of them weaved through the yard, Vimal pausing occasionally and gazing about, then continuing on, turning left and right. He muttered, 'There's been more dumping. A lot of it. It doesn't look the same.'

Krueger's impression was that the kid wasn't stalling. He seemed truly confused.

Then he squinted. 'That way. I'm sure.' Another nod.

They searched for ten minutes. Then Krueger paused. He glanced down and saw a bit of kimberlite in the rut left by a large truck tire. He pocketed it.

They were headed the right way.

What a grim place this was. The March weather had cast a gray pall over the earth, turning it to the shade of a corpse at a postmortem. Humid and cold, crawling up your spine, along your legs and thighs to your groin. It reminded Krueger of a huge open-cut diamond mine he'd been to years ago in Russia. A thought occurred to him: His job, of course, was to make sure that the pipe containing the kimberlite was never discovered, and no diamond-mining operation opened here. But what, he thought, might workers have found if a mine *had* opened? His evaluation was that the lode contained very high-quality gems.

Could it be that beneath the earth at the Northeast Geo Industries site there rested a diamond for all time? Krueger thought of stones from his own country: The Cullinan, which when mined weighed over thirty-one hundred carats, making it the largest gem-quality diamond ever found. The stone was cut into more than one hundred smaller diamonds, including the Great Star of Africa, more than five hundred carats, and the Lesser Star of Africa, more than three hundred. Those two finished gems are part of the British Crown Jewels. Krueger's favorite South African stone was the Centenary Diamond. The weight as rough was 599 carats. It was cut to more than 270. A modified heart-shaped brilliant, it was the largest colorless flawless diamond in the world.

Krueger's role in keeping such a diamond buried would sting. But this was his job, and he would see it through.

'Keep going,' he muttered to Vimal. 'The sooner we finish, the sooner you can get home to your family.'

CHAPTER **61**

Amelia Sachs was just off the Brooklyn Bridge, a few minutes from the Northeast Geo operation, her destination. The Torino's engine sang at a high pitch.

Rhyme's thinking had been that Ackroyd – or whatever his name might be – didn't want simply to kill Vimal Lahori. Not yet. He needed to find out where the boy had picked up the kimberlite on Saturday morning before he'd walked into the carnage at Patel's. Ackroyd's assignment would be to destroy or dump every bit of kimberlite he could find, before fleeing, and the one logical place for that would be the drilling site.

The operation was still closed, and Ackroyd and Vimal could wander it with impunity, as the boy pointed out where the kimberlite samples had been found.

She was about to exit the highway when her phone hummed. She tapped the Answer button, then Speaker, and set the phone on the passenger seat to downshift from fourth to third. The car skidded around a slow-moving van.

'I'm here.'

Lon Sellitto said, 'Amelia. I've got somebody who wants to talk to you. I'm patching her through.'

Her?

'Sure.' She eased off the gas.

A click and another. Then a woman's voice. 'Detective Sachs?'

'Yes, who's this?'

'I'm Adeela Badour.'

'Vimal's friend.'

'Yes, that's right.' The woman's voice was concerned but steady. 'Detective Sellitto called and told me Vimal has disappeared. You're trying to find him.'

'Do you have any idea where he might be?'

'I don't know for certain. But Detective Sellitto told me about the diamonds and the drilling. And that the man who might have kidnapped him was interested in some rocks Vimal had. Well, on Saturday, the morning he was shot, he called me from the subway. He was angry. Mr Patel had given him a job – to go to a junkyard somewhere and prowl around to find something. Some particular kind of rocks.'

The kimberlite, Sachs understood.

'And when I saw him later that night, he had a piece of rock lodged under the skin.'

'Yes, the bullet hit a bag of stones he had. Lon, are you there?'

'Yeah, Amelia.'

Sachs said, 'That's where they're going. He's taken Vimal to the junkyard. To find the kimberlite. Not to the drilling site.'

'Got it. I'll find out where Northeast Geo dumps their waste.'

'Get in touch with the site manager. A guy named Schoal. Or if he can't get through to him, call the CEO. What was his name? He was on the news. Dwyer, I think.'

'I'll get right back to you.'

Sachs asked, 'Adeela, did Vimal say anything more about where he was on Saturday?'

'No.'

'Well, thanks. This's important.'

'I gave Detective Sellitto my number. If you hear anything . . .' Now Adeela's voice cracked. She controlled it instantly. 'If you hear about him, please call.'

'I will. Yes.'

The young woman disconnected.

Sachs veered onto the shoulder to wait, earning two horns and a middle finger. Ignored them all.

'Come on, come on,' she whispered, a plea to Lon Sellitto. Her leg bobbed impatiently and she resolved not to stare at her phone.

She stared at her phone.

Then put it face down on the bucket seat beside her.

Three excruciating minutes later Sellitto called her back. Schoal had told him that all the stone scrap and drilling residue from the Northeast Geo operation in Brooklyn was hauled to C&D Transfer Station #4. On the water, east of Cobble Hill. He explained, 'Hundreds of companies use it, from all over the city.'

'Got it,' she said. She slammed the shifter forward into first and popped the clutch, hitting the flow of traffic in three seconds and exceeding it in five.

She knew the scrapyard and barge dock. They were south of the Brooklyn Bridge Park Piers, about five minutes away – at least in the Torino – if traffic cooperated. Which it decidedly was not doing. She set the blue flasher on her dash, downshifted and returned to the shoulder. She accelerated again, hoping fervently that nobody would have a flat and swerve in front of her.

'Lon, my ETA's five minutes, I hope. Get uniforms and ESU to the scrapyard. Silent roll-up.'

'Will do, Amelia.'

She didn't bother to shut off the phone, letting Sellitto disconnect. Sachs didn't dare remove her hands from the wheel as she sped along the rough shoulder, with side-view mirrors inches from the concrete abutment on the right and traffic on the left.

Thinking: Am I too late?

She traded sixty miles an hour for eighty.

CHAPTER 62

Sachs beat the blue-and-whites and ESU to the debris transfer station.

She skidded into the site – a sprawling yard, which she remembered as a dusty, shimmering sprawl in the summer but was now forbidding and gray. The large gate was open and she saw no security. There was no parking lot, per se, but as she cruised around, the Torino bounding over the rough ground, she came upon a level area, free of scrap, between two large mounds of shattered concrete and rotting wood and plaster. A Ford was parked here, by itself; all the other vehicles were dump trucks and bulldozers. The few personal vehicles were pickup trucks and SUVs.

She skidded to a stop and climbed out. Drawing her weapon, she made her way cautiously to the Ford. Nobody inside.

She reached inside, pulled the trunk release.

A huge relief seeing the empty space.

Vimal Lahori was, possibly, still alive.

A flash of motion caught her eye. Two squad cars from the local precinct sped up and stopped nearby. Four officers, all in uniform, climbed out.

'Detective,' one said, his voice soft. She knew the slim, sandy-haired officer. Jerry Jones, a ten-year, or so, veteran.

'Jones, call in the tag.'

He fitted an earbud – to keep his Motorola quiet – and put in the request. Adding, 'Need it now. We're in a tactical situation. K.'

She nodded to him and the others – two white men and an African American woman. 'You got the description of our perp?'

They all had.

Sachs said, 'We've got one of his weapons but assume he's

armed again. Glock Nines may be his weapon of choice. No evidence of long guns. He'll have a knife too. Box cutter. Remember that the younger man with him is a hostage. Indian, dark hair, twenty-two. I don't know what he's wearing. The suspect was last seen in a tan overcoat but he's worn dark outer clothes, too. We want this perp alive, if there's any way. He's got information we need.'

Jones said, 'He's planted those gas bombs, right?'

'Yeah. It's him.'

'What's he want here?' the woman officer asked.

'A pile of rock.'

The uniforms glanced toward one another.

No time to explain further.

'Jones, you and I go west, to the docks. You three, south. You're going to stand out in your uniforms, against the landscape.' It was beige and light gray. 'So keep your eye out for sniping positions. He'll kill to take out witnesses. No reason to think he won't target us.'

'Sure, Detective,' one of the uniforms called and the trio started off.

She and Jones moved perpendicular to them, toward the water.

Jones's radio gave a quiet clatter. He listened. She couldn't hear the transmission. A moment later he told her, 'ESU, ten minutes away.'

The two of them moved quickly through the valleys between the piles of rock and refuse. Jones cocked his head – he'd be receiving a transmission through his earbud. And whispered, 'K.' He then turned to Sachs. 'Vehicle on monthlong lease from a dealer in Queens. Lessee is Andrew Krueger. South African driver's license. Address in Cape Town. Gave an address in New York but it's a vacant lot.'

The uniform lifted his phone and showed an image of the driver's license photo. 'That him?'

Confirming that Krueger had been acting the role of Ackroyd all along. She nodded.

Like Rostov, Krueger would be one of those security operatives in the diamond business, working for a competitor to Dobprom.

You don't usually shoot your partner in the head . . .

Now Sachs brought all her senses to the game. In a recent case a suspect – a bit psychotic, more than a bit fascinating – had decided that Sachs was an incarnation of Diana, the Roman goddess of the hunt.

One of her finest compliments, even if it had come from a crazy man.

They moved as fast as they dared. Sachs and Jones kept low, scanning constantly, left right, the ridges of the trash mounds, which were indeed perfect sniper nests. Breathing hard, muscles knotted.

Oh, how Amelia Sachs loved this.

She ignored the pain in her left side from the fall at the muddy grave at the construction site, ignored the pain from her run-in with the Russian. There was nothing in her mind except her prey.

She used hand signals to tell Jones where to look, when to hurry, when to slow. He did the same from time to time. She suspected he'd never been in a firefight. Uneasy, tense but willing . . . and able: He held his Glock with confidence and skill.

They proceeded slowly. She didn't want to stumble on Krueger and force a gunfight; she needed to find him, unawares, for a bloodless takedown.

Alive . . .

She also didn't want him circling around on her and Jones. Two hundred feet away a huge backhoe was filling a barge with scrap. The roaring engine and the clatter and boom of the rock tumbling into the vessel obscured all sounds. Krueger could easily get close to them without their hearing.

So she scanned forward, to the sides and behind. Constantly.

Another fifty feet. Where, where, where?

She and Jones were nearly to the water when she spotted them.

Between two large piles of rocks and timber and twisted metal, Krueger was pulling Vimal along behind him. In a gloved left hand he gripped the kid's collar; his right was under his short, dark jacket. He'd be holding his weapon.

Jones pointed to himself, then to the crest of the scrap pile near Krueger and Vimal. It was on the officer's right, about twenty feet high. He then pointed to Sachs and made a semicircular gesture, indicating the pile on the left.

Good tactical plan. Jones would cover Krueger from above and Sachs would flank him. She pointed back to their staging area, held up three fingers – meaning the other officers – and pointed a palm his way. Meaning to have them hold position. Sachs didn't want the others stumbling onto the scene and she had no way of explaining to them exactly where the target was.

Jones stepped aside and made a quiet call to the others. He holstered his weapon and began climbing the debris pile. Sachs trotted to the left, around the base of the mound to the right and began to close on where she'd last seen Krueger and Vimal.

As she eased around the pile, she noted that, yes, it was going to work, if she could just get closer. Jones was atop the debris heap to the right and had his weapon trained on Krueger. Sachs just needed to close the distance a bit more so she could demand his surrender – over the sound of the chugging backhoes and bulldozers.

Jones looked her way and nodded.

She reciprocated and then moved closer yet toward the suspect and Vimal, who had stopped. Krueger's cold face – so different from the man he'd pretended to be – bent close and whispered something into his ear. The kid, who was crying and wiping tears, nodded and looked around. Then he pointed and the two of them turned abruptly and hurried down another valley, away from Sachs and Jones. Apparently Vimal had spotted the piles of kimberlite.

She glanced at Jones, who shook his head and pointed to his eyes. He'd lost sight. Sachs rounded the base of the mound closest to Krueger and began to follow. Then she looked beyond them. Oh, no . . .

Not far away one of the male NYPD officers was crouching, with his back to Krueger, no more than twenty feet away. Without hesitating, Krueger whipped his pistol from beneath his jacket and fired a round into the officer's back. The uniform plunged forward, dropping his own weapon. Sachs had noted that they wore body armor but at that range, even a slug stopped by armor would incapacitate him. He struggled to rise.

Krueger flung his left arm around Vimal's throat, so he wouldn't run, pulling him close. Together they moved toward the injured officer.

Sachs, behind them, stepped closer to the downed cop, drawing a target. 'Krueger!' she shouted. 'Drop the weapon.'

He didn't hear and took one step closer, aiming, about to fire a fatal round.

Any incapacitating shot she might try would possibly hit Vimal too.

So, with the thought in her mind that only Krueger knew where the deadly gas bombs were planted, Amelia Sachs lowered her center of gravity, settled the white dot of the front sight on the back of Krueger's head and gently added pressure to the trigger until her weapon fired.

CHAPTER 63

Now that they knew the name Andrew Krueger, they could assemble an accurate dossier on him.

While Sachs was searching the deceased's residence motel in Brooklyn Heights, Rhyme, Fred Dellray from the FBI, the South African Police and ever-helpful Alternative Intelligence Service began filling in details.

The killer's residence was a flat in Cape Town, not far from the water, in the Victoria & Alfred Waterfront area. According to the South African Police, it was quite the posh neighborhood. The man had no criminal record but following his discharge from the army he'd been associated with some 'dodgy' businessmen in the diamond trade. Though his father had been a vocal advocate of apartheid, Krueger himself rejected those prejudices, either because they were repugnant to him or, more likely, because they were not economically beneficial. He would work for anyone in the trade who would pay him, including some of the more dangerous 'black diamond' businessmen, whose roots had been in the impoverished squatter townships but who were now wealthy. When in the army, Krueger worked demolition. In civilian life, in his younger days, he'd been in mining and had studied engineering, which explained how he could rig the explosives to mimic earthquakes. It was his military connections, of course, that gave him access to both the C4 and gas line bombs.

Krueger's company was AK Associates. He was managing director; his partner was a former mine labor enforcer, Terrance DeVoer. The company specialized in 'security work' for the gem and precious metals and materials industries.

That vague description translated, one SAP detective told them, as 'corporate mercenary.' Attempts to interview DeVoer were unsuccessful; he and his wife had disappeared.

When he'd been among Rhyme, Sachs and the others, Krueger, as Ackroyd, had professed a knowledge of the diamond world and this wasn't fiction. A raid on his Cape Town digs by the SAP revealed a genuine obsession with the stones: Hundreds of books on the subject, photographs, and documents about diamonds, from the scientific to the cultural to the artistic. He himself, one inspector said, had even written poetry about the gems.

'Very bad verse, I will tell you.'

They found actual diamonds too. Rough and finished. Close to two million dollars' worth, another investigator said. An odd display sat on Krueger's bedside table, the officer added. A low-power spotlight was aimed upward from underneath a lens of clear glass, on which Krueger had placed a dozen diamonds. The light beamed the translucent forms of the stones onto the ceiling, like constellations, the edges of each one radiating with the colors of rainbows.

Rhyme recalled that the name for this refraction was 'fire.'

The raid revealed the likely employer. Bank records showed that two wire transfers of $250K each had been deposited at Krueger's company. They originated from a numbered account in Guatemala City. These had been received within the past two weeks. The memos on the wires reported the payments were for 'Installment 1' and Installment 2.'

The police also found printouts about a company called Nuevo Mundo Minería – New World Mining – a diamond producer located in Guatemala City.

But nothing in the raid or an examination of police records, including Interpol and Europol, had revealed what they needed so desperately: information about where the final gas IEDs had been planted.

Maybe the evidence from Krueger's motel would have that answer. He was about to find out. He could tell this from the roar of a sports car engine and the squeal of brakes in the street outside his town house.

Sachs had walked the grid – twice – at Krueger's extended-stay motel in Brooklyn Heights.

Lincoln Rhyme and she were now looking over the results of her efforts. Mel Cooper was processing some of the finds, as well. McEllis was still present, waiting to help them narrow down the possible locations where the bombs might be, based on his knowledge of the half-mile-long fault.

In Krueger's motel were diagrams of the geothermal site, photos of the drilling operation, maps of the area around the site, articles about explosions whose seismic profile had been mistaken for earthquakes, emails from untraceable accounts with attachments on the diamond content of kimberlite samples, echoing what Don McEllis had told them. Krueger had researched Ezekiel Shapiro and the One Earth movement as well. The dead environmentalist's address was on a Post-it note.

Sachs had found an attaché case that matched the one Krueger'd had with him at Patel's. It contained a small but powerful portable microscope, some tools and pieces of kimberlite. He'd taken it with him to Patel's shop to analyze the rock, Rhyme supposed. If the kimbmerlite proved diamond-rich, he'd steal it and torture Patel to find more information. Here too was a carton that contained traces of RDX, the main component of C4, and another with the label on the side: מיטסטומרת. Which was Hebrew for 'thermostats' – which the gas line IEDs were meant to impersonate.

Sachs taped up pictures of the rooms. She said, 'One thing real? His love of crossword puzzles. He had dozens of puzzle books.'

This reminded Rhyme.

He glanced at the present – the electronic cryptic crossword device that the killer had given Rhyme.

Edward Ackroyd – the man he thought he could become friends with.

Five-letter word beginning with *J* meaning 'betrayer.' Then he shot *that* moment of melodrama dead.

He told Mel Cooper, 'See if there's a transmitter inside.'

'A—'

'See if he fucking bugged us.'

'Ah.' Using a set of miniature computer tools, Cooper removed the backing. He looked it over and scanned it with a transmission-detecting wand.

'Nothing. It's safe.'

He started to reassemble it. But Rhyme said softly, 'No, throw it out.'

'You don't want—'

'Throw it out.'

Cooper did, and Rhyme and Sachs returned to the evidence.

Where the hell were the gas line bombs?

No maps or notes suggested an answer. Krueger's computer was locked and had gone to Rodney Szarnek downtown, along with two burner phones, and the one he'd had with him at the waste site in Brooklyn – which was not locked and showed calls to a number in Moscow. The numbers had been dialed after Rostov had died, and Rhyme believed that Krueger himself had done so to make it seem that Vimal's killer was an unknown associate of Rostov. This was exceedingly unlikely – especially since Sachs also found a Russian cigarette and rubles in Krueger's pocket, meant, obviously, to be strewn around Vimal's body. A feint.

Unlikely, yes, but until Rodney confirmed the calls were made at the same place that Krueger's phones had been located, Vimal would stay safely in a local precinct house.

Sachs had also found the keys to the now-infamous Toyota – though its whereabouts weren't known – and Rostov's residence.

Mel Cooper said, 'I've got some things on the mining company in Guatemala. New World. Big outfit with diamond mines throughout Latin America, producing mostly industrial-grade. Not the nicest crew on earth. They've been accused by environmentalists and the government of destroying rain forests with strip mining, clear-cutting, things like that. They pay small miners, *garimpeiros*, to raid indigenous lands. There're battles – real battles. Dozens of miners and Indians have been killed.'

Rhyme called Fred Dellray at the FBI once again, and asked if he could tap some of his State Department contacts to have security and the U.S. embassy or consulate in Guatemala City talk to executives at the mining company.

As if they'd cooperate, he thought sardonically.

'Let's look over the trace,' Rhyme said.

Among the items found by Sachs were raw honey, rotting felt, clay soil, shreds of old electrical wire insulation, bits of insect wings, probably from genus *Apis* (bees – the honey helped in this speculation, though they might be unrelated). Also, on a pair of boots in the motel she'd found traces of unusual agricultural soil – lightweight, absorbent shale and clay and compost containing flecks of straw and hay – and organic fertilizer.

'Ah.'

'What, Lincoln?'

He didn't respond to Cooper but went online and gave the Google microphone a command. 'Composition of Rooflite.' Sometimes you needed esoteric databases, sometimes you didn't.

The answer came back in milliseconds.

'Yes!'

Sachs, Cooper and McEllis turned his way.

Rhyme said, 'It's sketchy but we don't have much else to go with. I think he planted one device, at least, north of the government buildings in Cadman Plaza. In Vinegar Hill.'

This was an old area of Brooklyn, adjacent to the old Navy Yard. Named after the battle in Ireland in 1798 between Irish rebels and British troops, the neighborhood was a curious mix: quaint residences from Victorian times encircled by grim, imposing industrial structures.

'How do you know?' Cooper asked.

He knew because, though he couldn't prowl the streets as he used to when he was mobile, Lincoln Rhyme still studied every borough, every neighborhood, every block of his city. 'A criminalist is only as good as his or her knowledge of the locale where the crime occurs,' he wrote in his forensics textbook.

The specific answer to the question was the combination of bee wings, honey, that Rooflite soil, fertilizer and felt. He believed those materials had come from the Brooklyn Grange at the old Navy Yard. It was the largest rooftop farm in the world, two and a half acres devoted to raising organic fruits and vegetables. Rooflite was a soil substance in which vegetables could grow quite well but that weighed far less than regular soil, which would be too heavy for rooftop gardening. The Grange also was a major producer of honey.

The closest residential area to it was Vinegar Hill, filled with old wooden structures. Perfect targets for Krueger, whose goal had been to rouse the city and state into banning the drilling. The more deadly fires the 'earthquakes' caused, the better.

Don McEllis hunched over the map of the city and with a red marker drew exactly where the fault line ran under Vinegar Hill. It headed northwest then jogged north into the harbor.

'Here. I'd look about three blocks on either side of that.'

It would be a much more concise search than the entire fault, but there were still scores of buildings whose basements might contain the gas line devices.

'Scan the map, Mel, and get a copy to the supervisors – fire and police – in the area. Do it now.'

'Sure.'

'Sachs, you and Pulaski get down there.'

As they hurried out the door, Rhyme said, 'Mel, call Fire . . . and the local precinct. Get as many bodies as they can spare, checking basements. Oh, and call the Detective Bureau, too. Larceny. Have somebody pull recent break-ins where nothing was taken.'

Cooper nodded and picked up his phone.

Rhyme called: 'And not just Patrol. I want anybody with a badge. *Anybody!*'

CHAPTER 64

Almost impossible.

That was Sachs's impression as she sped her Torino, a deep-red blur, along the Manhattan Bridge into Brooklyn. She was glancing to her left – at Vinegar Hill. Ron Pulaski was probably feeling the same.

How could anyone possibly find the devices? Dominated by a single, towering smokestack from Algonquin Power's electrical substation, the neighborhood was bigger than she'd expected. Six square blocks, the precinct commander had told her. But small blocks they were not.

She downshifted and tore off the exit ramp, skidding onto Jay Street, drawing a faint gasp from Ron Pulaski, though after all these years he was pretty immune to her Danica Patrick approach to driving. The blue flasher cut silently but urgently through the shadowy street, lined with industrial buildings, houses, apartments and residential lofts. The brick and stucco and stone walls were scuffed and scraped but largely graffiti-free. The trash cans were battered and cracked but the garbage remained inside.

The muscle car had bad-girl suspension and she felt the road in her back and knee, still sore from the abuse of the past few days. And the streets of Vinegar Hill were not all fully paved. The original Belgian block, sometimes erroneously called cobblestones, had worn through in many stretches. In others the granite rectangles, smoothed by centuries of horse, foot and wheel traffic, had never been asphalted over and were the only roadway.

Sachs swung the car toward John Street, the agreed-upon staging area. It was across from the substation, the sprawling yard like a science-fiction film set. Gray metal boxes, wires, transformers. She skidded to a stop in front of a red brick industrial building. Probably a factory in a former life, it was now home to a half-dozen advertising agencies, design firms and boutique manufacturers. 'Monti's Gourmet Chocolates' occupied the ground floor, and her nose told her the company made their enticing products on-site. She wondered when she'd last eaten. Couldn't remember. Then forgot the question altogether.

In addition to four fire trucks and an FDNY battalion chief's car, a half-dozen blue-and-whites and an unmarked sat clustered on the substation side of John Street. There were eight uniformed officers, two plainclothes detectives and a captain from the precinct, wearing a suit. He was a tall African American, lean, with skin very dark and a perfectly bald head. Archie Williams. She'd worked with him before. Liked his humor. He'd once put a very shaken assault victim at ease by saying, No, no, it would be easy to remember his name: Archi*bald*. And he pointed to his shiny skull.

Williams said, 'Detective.' He then glanced at Pulaski, who identified himself. A nod.

Beside the captain was the FDNY battalion chief, in uniform. The pale, stocky man was in his mid-fifties. Vincent Stanello. When he shook hands, Sachs was aware of an extensive scar, from a burn years ago.

He explained that fire fighters were spreading out throughout the neighborhood with gas keys – long rods used to shut off gas mains underground, whose valves were accessed through small square doors on streets and sidewalks and in yards. 'We've got a half-dozen shutoff teams working. Captain Rhyme said to stick to a swath through the center of Vinegar Hill. His office sent us this.' He held up his phone, which showed Don McEllis's map.

'It's the fault line. We need to search about two blocks on either side.'

Stanello sighed. 'You know, we've got miles of pipes here. And you have to remember, we can only shut off utility-supplied natural gas. A lot of customers use propane from private companies. There's no way to shut that off except at the tank in the home or office.'

Williams said, 'I've told our Central Robbery people to drop everything else and start checking the paperwork. And we've got a bot running the nine-one-one tapes from Vinegar Hill.' He shrugged. 'But unless somebody saw him in the act, I'd bet it wasn't even called in.'

Williams asked, 'When did he plant the device?'

Pulaski said, 'Sometime in the past week, we think. Ten days. We aren't sure.'

'So CCTVs won't do much good,' Sachs said. Looking around at the hundreds of structures – all old and largely built of wood.

Sachs said firmly, 'Evacuate.'

'Evacuate what?' Stanello asked.

'Everything. Every building for two blocks on either side of that fault.'

'That'd be chaos,' Stanello said uncertainly. 'There could be injuries. Elderly residents, children.'

Williams said, 'And the press'll have a field day if there is no bomb.'

'And what'll they say if there is one and we don't get people out?' Amelia Sachs hated to have to state the obvious.

The supervisors, Williams and Stanello, regarded each other.

The battalion chief asked, 'You sure there's a device in Vinegar Hill?'

Sachs thought: Sure? What exactly is sure?

She said, 'Absolutely.' Then added a truthful component: 'And he's set one every day for the past two days. No reason to think he'll change his pattern now. And if the prior devices're any indication, we're late in the day at this point. I'm thinking it'll detonate at any time.'

A moment of silence. Then Williams said, 'All right, we'll do it. Evacuate as many as we can, check the gas lines in the basements, mark them safe and the residents can go back in.'

Stanello nodded. He lifted his radio to his lips and gave the command to his officer to start evacuating residents.

'And there's a school here, right?' Pulaski asked.

'PS Three Oh Seven. A few blocks away.'

'Empty it,' the young officer said.

'It's not along the center line,' Stanello said, nodding at the map on his phone.

Sachs was about to intervene but Pulaski said firmly, 'It's a school day. Evacuate it.'

Stanello paused a moment. 'Okay, I'll do it.'

Williams walked to his officers. 'Everybody, into cars. Loudspeakers. Just say there's a possible gas leak, and everybody should leave the buildings immediately. Don't take any belongings, just leave.'

'Come on,' Sachs said to Pulaski. 'We'll start knocking on doors too.' She called to Williams and Stanello, 'We'll start south, work our way east then north.'

They piled into the Torino and sped down to York. Pulaski was looking around, his face troubled. 'How many people you think live here? Where his target zone is?'

She guessed the population of Vinegar Hill was fifty thousand or so. Much less in the area around the fault but she supposed a good number. 'This time of day, eight thousand.'

'How many you realistically think we can evacuate?'

Sachs's answer was a grim laugh.

CHAPTER 65

Carmella Romero often said, gravely, that she was a spy.

The fifty-eight-year-old had shared that comment with her four children and eleven grandchildren. The basis for her claim was that she worked for the government as an agent.

Though in her case, the employer wasn't the CIA or James Bond's Secret Service. It was the New York City Traffic Enforcement.

The stocky, gray-haired woman, a lifetime resident of Brooklyn, had decided two years ago after her last daughter had flown the nest that she was going to get a job. A fan of TV shows about police, like *Blue Bloods*, she thought a career in law enforcement might be nice (and Tom Selleck could be her commissioner *any* day!).

Being a gun-toting cop wasn't in her future, given her age (the cutoff at NYPD is thirty-five), but there was no age limit for TEAs. Also, she was regularly furious when Mr Prill, a neighbor, parked wherever the hell he wanted to – in front of the hydrant, on the sidewalk, in the crosswalk. And he was rude when you called him on it! Imagine. And she decided she'd had it. He and people like him weren't going to get away with anything anymore. Then too Carmella Romero had a sense of humor and appreciated that quality in others. She'd loved it when Traffic Enforcement put up signs: *Don't Even Think of Parking Here*. How could she not want to go to work for an outfit like that?

No, she wasn't in the *Blue Bloods* world of law enforcement but now she had a chance to do something a little closer to what real cops did. She and all the others TEAs (never 'brownies,' don't *ever* say that), as well as every city worker in this part of Brooklyn, had been enlisted to evacuate buildings and get into basements in Vinegar Hill to see if there was a little white device that looked like a thermostat attached to the gas line.

An IED!

Improvised explosive device. (She knew the phrase thanks to, ta-da, a case that Tom Selleck's son had run; it didn't come up much in Traffic Enforcement briefings.)

Carmella Rosina Romero was Bomb Squad Girl for a day.

The block she had been given contained three-, four- and five-story walk-ups. Like many in Brooklyn, with easy access to Manhattan, they would be packed with tenants. And the construction was old. Oh, there should have been recent renovations to bring them up to code – maybe, if the landlords were honest – but the buildings still would be tinderboxes, compared with new construction.

She was walking to the first one on her 'beat,' on the corner, when she froze.

Beneath her there was a trembling.

Was that it? The fake earthquake she and the other city folks had been briefed about?

Her radio clattered, 'Be advised. All those on evac duty. That was confirmed as a detonation of an IED near Cadman Plaza. Evacuation is now critical. You've got about ten minutes until secondary explosion and fire.'

Romero sped forward on stocky legs, feet pointed outward, to the corner building, intent on hitting the intercom and ordering the evacuation.

Flaw: no intercoms. Not even a doorbell. You apparently had to let somebody know ahead of time you were coming to call. Or maybe you just shouted your arrival.

She shouted.

No response.

Think, woman. Think, Agent! What the hell? Pulling a loose paver from the street, she smashed the glass of the door and leapt back from the falling shards. She opened the door from inside and burst into the building, calling, 'Police. Gas emergency, evacuate the building!' Pounding on doors and repeating the warning.

A door in the back opened and a Latino man in T-shirt and jeans stepped out, frowning. He was, it turned out, the superintendent. She told him about the danger and, wide-eyed, he nodded, promising he'd tell the tenants.

Her radio clattered, 'TEA Romero, come in. K.'

With a thumping heart – she'd never been summoned by dispatch before – she called in. 'Romero here. K.'

'You're on Front Street?'

'Affirmative. K.'

'Further to the evac, Central Robbery in Brooklyn reported a break-in a week ago. Eight Oh Four Front. Somebody in hard hat and safety vest was seen using a bolt cutter to get through the basement window. Nothing was missing. That's the profile of the suspect. We think he might've put the device in there.'

'It's three doors down from me!' Then she reminded herself of protocol and said, 'K.'

She said this coolly. But was thinking, *Dios mío!* Crap!

'We've got Bomb Squad on the way, Romero. Try to get out as many as you can. You've got about nine minutes left, till it blows. Keep that in mind.'

In the distance, sirens began to wail.

'Roger. K.'

She sprinted to the building, an old one, four stories high. It wasn't the biggest on the street but it was the most vulnerable, given its all-wood frame. It would go up like a gasoline-soaked rag. The windows were closed against the March chill but she could see lights inside some of the front-facing ones.

No intercom again.

And this building didn't have a door containing a window; it was solid wood.

Hell.

Eight minutes left, she reckoned.

She looked at the basement windows, protected by metal grates, which were secured by heavy-duty padlocks.

'Get out!' Romero began shouting. 'Gas leak. Get out!'

Nobody responded. She picked up a stone and flung it at a second-floor window – the first-story windows were, like the basement, protected by gratings. The projectile shattered a pane. If anybody was inside, they didn't notice or chose not to respond.

Yes, this was the target. She could smell the gas now.

'Evacuate!'

No response.

Looking around, she noted a line of cars parallel-parked across from the building. She noted a Lexus and other nice vehicles too, in addition to some more modest wheels. If Agent Carmella Romero knew anything, it was cars. She walked up to the Lexus and kneed it hard in the front fender, denting the metal. The alarm began braying.

She passed by the Taurus and a Subaru. But slugged a Mercedes and an Infiniti. Horns sounding fiercely.

Windows began opening. On the top floor of the building, Romero noted a woman and two small children looking out.

'Get out! There's a gas leak!'

Her uniform apparently added authority to the command. The woman disappeared fast. Several others appeared in windows too and she repeated the command in English and Spanish.

Romero looked up and down the street. No Bomb Squad yet. No other police.

Six minutes now.

The front door was opening and people were running out. The smell of gas was very strong. She held the door and encouraged them to run, as she shouted loudly into the dim hall, 'Gas leak, gas leak! Evacuation. The building's going to blow!'

If even just three-quarters of the apartments were occupied, there had to be at least twenty or thirty people remaining inside. Some asleep maybe, some disabled.

No way to get them all out.

A deep breath. Carmella Romero, flashing on Commissioner Selleck, ran to the basement door. She descended the rickety stairs on her thick, sure legs. Her nose tightened at the rotten-egg smell of the gas odorant. A wave of nausea hit her.

The basement was damp and dim, the only light from the gated windows in the front, small ones, above eye level. It was hard to see anything at all, let alone a tiny device on a gas line, which was probably intentionally hidden from sight. But there was no way she was going to click a light on.

Thinking: We're looking for bombs in basements; they damn well could've issued us flashlights.

Four or five minutes left, she guessed.

There seemed to be three rooms down here, large rooms. The one in the front, where she stood, was mostly for storage. A fast examination revealed wires overhead and sewage pipes but nothing that seemed to carry gas. The second room contained the furnace and water heater, dozens of pipes and tubing and wires. The smell of gas was stronger here. Romero was growing light-headed and felt about to faint. She jogged to a window, shattered a pane with her elbow, took a deep breath and returned to the second room, searching among the labyrinth of pipes and tubing for the device.

She glanced toward the water heater but noted that it was electric. She found the furnace. The unit was hot but wasn't running at the moment. Of course there'd be a pilot light or some kind of ignition device. Apart from the bomb that man had planted, the heating unit itself might turn on at any moment, igniting the gas. She found and pressed the emergency cutoff switch.

Dizzy once more, she dropped to her knees. Apparently natural gas was lighter than air and was rising to the ceiling; there was more breathable air down here. She filled her lungs again, fought the urge to gag, and then rose. She located the furnace gas feeder hose and followed it to the incoming pipe. It was about one inch in diameter. In one direction it disappeared into the concrete wall. In the other, it continued into the third room. She hurried there and, after debating, flicked on the flashlight of her phone.

No explosion.

She played the beam along the pipe, to where it disappeared behind a dozen boxes and other items stored by tenants: rolled carpets, battered chairs and a desk.

One minute remaining, she guessed.

She heard voices calling from the open window, behind her. Ignored them.

No backing out now.

Blue Bloods . . .

She swung the light from right to left and, yes! There it was! A small white plastic box taped to the gas line. Beneath it a half-inch hole gaped and gas hissed out.

She lunged forward, scrabbling over the mountain of furniture and boxes. She had no real plan, other than to rip the box from the line. Maybe then spit on the leads. Pull the battery out, if there was a battery. She'd sprint for the window, throw it out.

Now with the images of different faces in her head – her late husband and the most recent addition: twin grandsons – Carmella Romero ripped the device from the line and sprinted toward the stairway.

Only seconds later, as she was looking down at the device, noting it had no switch, it uttered a snap, almost silent, and a flash of blue flame filled her vision.

CHAPTER 66

Amelia Sachs sped the Torino Cobra around the corner to Front Street.

She braked to a stop quickly, as the entire avenue was packed with fire and other emergency vehicles.

Climbing out, she hurried to the ambulance where a solid woman, Latina, in a uniform, sat on a gurney.

'Agent Romero?' Sachs asked.

The woman, being tended by a male NYC medical technician, squinted.

'Yes?'

Sachs identified herself and asked, 'How are you?'

Traffic Enforcement Agent Carmella Romero, in turn, asked the medical tech, 'How am I?'

The wiry man, name of Spiros, said, 'Oh, fundamentally fine. The eyebrows? Well, you're gonna need makeup. And a bit of heat rash, you could call it. Bactine. But that's all you need. Hands? Well, that's another matter. Nothing serious and you won't feel it yet – I've got it numbed. You were a man, you'd lose some or all of the hair and the smell'd be with you for a bit. Look at me. Ape hair. What my wife says.'

Romero turned to Sachs. 'I guess that's how I am.'

Spiros said, 'But consider yourself lucky.'

'I do, sir.'

Though, Sachs had learned, there hadn't been much luck involved. When the *lehabah* detonated, the building, along with the dozen people still inside, had been saved by Romero. She'd gotten the device away from the basement, which was filled with gas, and into the stairway before it blew. The fiery blast that injured her was from the initiator, a mechanical sparking device, igniting the remaining chemical that was meant to melt the gas line. It was highly flammable. She was far enough away so that the gas in the basement had not blown.

'I've told your supervisor, Agent Romero. There'll be a citation.'

She blinked, apparently dismayed.

A double-take. Then Sachs smiled. 'Oh, no, not *your* kind of citation. Parking. I mean, you'll be decorated. It'll come from the commissioner himself.'

Her eyes lit up at this and it seemed that here was some kind of an inside joke about the NYPD commissioner of police that Sachs wasn't getting.

The crime scene bus pulled up and Sachs rose – a bit stiffly.

She waved to the van and the driver, an Asian American evidence collection tech Sachs had worked with before, nodded to her and drove close.

'Oh, Detective?'

She turned to Romero.

'Had a little problem,' the traffic enforcement agent said.

'What's that?'

'Only way to get the people's attention? I had to knee a few cars. Get the alarms going.'

'That was smart.'

'I suppose. But I kicked this Lexus. And the owner, he's not too happy about it. He's going to sue me. He said personally. Should I get myself a lawyer? Can he do that?'

'Where is he?'

Romero pointed to a man in his thirties, in a business suit, cropped Wall Street hair and round glasses. His long face had a smirky, put-upon smile and he seemed to be delivering a condescending lecture to a patrol officer, stabbing a finger toward the uniform's chest.

Amelia Sachs smiled. 'Don't worry. I'll go have a talk with him.'

'Are you sure, Detective?'

'Oh, it'll be my pleasure.'

* * *

Vimal Lahori was thinking that the old-time car he was riding in gave off a much more powerful scent of gasoline and exhaust and oil than modern vehicles. Of course, these aromas might have been due to the fact that it was being driven flat-out by a wild woman.

'You all right?' Detective Sachs asked him.

'I'm. Well. Yes.' He gripped the seat belt of the old-time car in one hand and the armrest in the other.

She smiled and slowed a bit.

'Force of habit,' she muttered.

After she had saved his life and shot that terrible man, the one who had killed Mr Patel, Detective Sachs had told him that they'd found a phone on the body. It was suspicious. It had been used to call Russia *after* the Russian killer had died. Was there another person involved? She and Mr Rhyme had not thought so, but better to be smart, so Vimal had stayed at the precinct house in Brooklyn until some computer expert at the NYPD found that the phone was a trick, to divert suspicion away from Andrew Krueger. Vimal was free to go and he had asked if Detective Sachs could drive him home.

She'd said she'd be delighted to.

She now made the turn and pulled up in front of the young man's house in Queens. Even before he climbed out, the front door of the house flew open and his mother and Sunny were hurrying through the misty day toward him.

He said to the detective, 'Can you wait here for a minute?'

'Sure.'

He met the family halfway up the walk and they embraced. The brothers awkwardly at first, then Vimal ruffled Sunny's hair and they starting pushing and wrestling, laughing hard.

'You aren't hurt?' his mother asked, looking him over with the eye of a diagnostician.

'No, I'm fine.'

'Dude, another gunfight? You're like dangerous to be around. It was on the news.'

No more than ten minutes after Detective Sachs had shot the

killer, a dozen news vans had appeared, magically, at the dumping site.

Sunny said, 'Kakima called – all the way from the NCR! You were on the news over there!'

The National Capital Region – New Delhi. Which meant tens of millions of people might've seen him.

Auntie was seventy-eight years old and spent more time online than any teenager Vimal knew.

His mother hugged him once more and walked to the maroon Ford. She bent down and spoke with Detective Sachs, undoubtedly thanking her for saving her son's life.

Sunny was asking if he'd seen the man get shot. Then 'Was it right in front of you?'

'Later, man. I've got to get something in the house.'

Vimal noticed the family car was gone. His father would be elsewhere. Thank goodness. He had no interest in seeing the man. Now. Or ever.

He walked inside and down to the studio. He noted that the bars had been replaced, which made sense, since this was New York City, and one could never have too much security. But the locks and hasps had been removed from the door, as had the fixture for the iron bar. The food and cartons of beverages were gone.

The studio was no longer Alcatraz.

Vimal walked to the closet and found what he sought, wrapped it in a sheet of newspaper. And returned to the front yard.

He told his mother and brother that he'd be inside in a moment and walked to the passenger side of the detective's car and sat back in the passenger seat. 'I've got something for you. And that man you work with, Mr Rhyme.'

'Vimal. You don't need to do that.'

'No. I want to. One of my sculptures.'

He unwrapped the object and set it on the dashboard. It was the four-sided pyramid he'd carved last year and been thinking of in the moments before he'd believed he was going to die. The piece was seven inches high and the base seven inches as well. Sachs leaned forward and looked at it, then stroked the dark-green granite sides. 'Smooth.'

'Yes. Smooth. And straight.'

'They are.'

Michelangelo believed you needed to master the basic inanimate shapes before you could render a living form in stone.

Vimal said, 'It's inspired by diamonds. Most diamonds are found in nature as octahedrons. Two pyramids joined at the base.'

She said, 'Then they're cleaved into two pieces for cutting. Usually for round brilliants.'

He laughed. 'Ah, you've had quite the education about our business.' He too leaned forward and touched it with a finger. 'It won first prize at a juried arts competition in Brooklyn last year, first at a competition in Manhattan and second in the New England Sculpting Show.'

Which, he reflected, his father had not allowed him to enter. A friend had entered it for him.

'First prize,' she said, clearly trying to sound impressed – while studying the mundane geometric shape.

Vimal said playfully, 'Not bad for a paperweight, hm?'

Looking at him with a wry smile, Sachs said, 'There's more to it, I've got a feeling. Do I push a secret button and it opens up?'

'Not quite but you're close. Look at the underside.'

She lifted the sculpture and turned it over. She gasped. Inside was a carved-out impression of a human heart – not a Hallmark card version but an anatomically correct heart, with exact reproductions of veins and arteries and chambers.

It had taken eighteen months to craft the piece, working with the smallest of tools. It was, you might say, a negative sculpture: the empty space, not the stone, was the organ.

How did I do, Signore Michelangelo di Lodovico Buonarroti Simoni?

'It's called *Hidden*.'

'Vimal, I don't know what to say. It's astonishing. Your talent . . . ' She set it back on the dash, then leaned forward and hugged him. His face burned with a blush and he awkwardly pressed his palms into her back.

Then he climbed out of the car and walked back to the house, where some, though not all, of his family waited.

CHAPTER **67**

At 9 p.m. Lincoln Rhyme decided: Time for a drink.

With an unsteady but determined hand, he poured several fingers of Glenmorangie scotch, the bourbon cask variety, into a Waterford glass, which contained a few drops of water. This, he believed, opened up the whisky.

The Waterford represented a victory for him. Though he'd never in his life been inclined to luxurious items like this, he'd been determined to graduate from unbreakable plastic tumblers – which he, as a quad, had used for years – to something elegant. Had his grip failed, $137 would have shattered on the floor.

But he'd mastered the vessel. And was convinced, without objective proof, that the whisky tasted better from crystal.

Sachs was upstairs, showering. Thom was in the kitchen, whipping up something for dinner. Rhyme deduced it involved garlic and some licorice-oriented herb or spice. Perhaps fennel. No gourmand, nor even much of a diner, Rhyme nonetheless found it helpful to know foods. A few years ago he'd run up against a hired killer whose hobby was cooking, and ingredients for various dishes provided important clues in his capture. (The killer's avocation was not only a source of great pleasure for him but also gave him the chance to put his extremely expensive – and sharp – knives to work on the job. Witnesses tended to tell everything he wanted to know in the face of a razor-sharp Japanese filleting knife.)

Heavy glass in one hand, Rhyme used a finger of his other to maneuver to the front of the Unsub 47 evidence charts. He was certainly grateful that both Rostov and Krueger were out of the picture and that none of the officers running the case had been injured seriously. The mayor had called to express his thanks. Dwyer, the head of the geothermal operation, had too. But the case wasn't completely over, from his perspective. There were some loose ends. For instance: the disappearance of the Northeast Geo worker who'd helped Krueger plant the C4 charges in the drilling shafts. He was surely dead but Rhyme would devote whatever time and effort were necessary to locating the body, for the sake of his family.

Justice . . .

The South African Police were apparently more than eager to pursue the employees in Krueger's 'security' company. They rounded up some lower-level administrative people and located Terrance DeVoer and his wife, in Lesotho, the landlocked country surrounded by South Africa. Not a wise choice of escape route for a fugitive, considering he'd be on airline watchlists and, if he wished to drive, he would have to return to the very country that had warrants out for his arrest.

DeVoer would be handed over to the SAP in a day or so.

As to the diamond mines behind the plot, the NYPD foreign liaison division and the FBI, working with State, had contacted them both. Dobprom hadn't replied and Rhyme had been told not to expect a response. The Guatemalan mine that had hired Krueger, New World Mining, had at least returned phone calls but vehemently denied any involvement in the incident.

This portion – the Russian and Central American legs – of the investigation had stalled.

Rhyme was, however, determined to unstall it.

Another, more pressing, issue was whether there was in fact another device. Just because three kilos of C4 had been delivered didn't mean there were only three bombs in the Northeast Geo shafts. Maybe Krueger had divided the plastic into four or five lumps and planted other gas line bombs. The police were still canvassing possible targets along the fault line in the vicinity of Northeast Geo, and FDNY was still staged in the area, awaiting another tremor, which would signal possible fires. The Bomb Squad and ESU, working with Northeast Geo, were finally beginning their careful excavation of the shafts.

Loose ends.

Now, as he looked up at the charts, yet one question arose in his thoughts and he instructed the phone to make a call.

'Hey, Linc. What's up?' Lon Sellitto sounded impatient.

'Just some follow-up on the case. When you came to see me the other day about that gas device that didn't go off, the one in that woman's basement? Claire Porter?'

'Yeah. What about it?'

'Had you been to the scene before you came over here? Think carefully. It's important.'

'What's to think? The answer is no. I was downtown and somebody called me. I was never at the scene. Why?'

'Loose ends.'

'Whatever. Anything else? We're *Walking Dead*.'

'What?'

'Night, Linc.'

Other questions floated to the surface.

But then he turned to the entryway to the parlor and the idea of trying to answer them was put on hold momentarily, while he focused on the immediate item on the agenda for this evening.

Dinner with his bride.

Amelia Sachs was walking into the room now. She was wearing a long, green dress, low-cut and sleeveless.

'You look beautiful,' he said.

She smiled. Then, it seemed, she couldn't help but reply with 'And you look thoughtful.'

'Nothing that can't wait for a bit. Thom! Time for dinner! Could we get the wine open, please and thank you?'

His eyes drifted back to Sachs. He really did like that dress.

V
BRILLIANTEERING

WEDNESDAY, MARCH 17

CHAPTER 68

As placid as ever, the Mexican attorney Antonio Carreras-López tugged at his vest and looked over at his client, sitting opposite him.

Eduardo Capilla – El Halcón, the Hawk – was the least avian-looking criminal who ever existed. (A more appropriate nickname for him would be La Tortuga.) Fat, balding, squint-eyed, with a broad, upturned nose. Still, he was one of the most dangerous men on earth. His hands and feet were shackled, and those shackles affixed to steel rings in the floor.

The interview room was in the federal courthouse for the Eastern District of New York, Cadman Plaza. The building was modern and stylish and only a little scuffed. Plenty of suspects from mean streets had passed through here but, as their offenses were federal, they tended to scrub up better than their counterparts in state court.

Both men here were in suits – even the defendant, as was customary, since a prisoner in a jumpsuit might prejudice the jury to think guilt and taint the Sixth Amendment's right to a fair and impartial trial.

The U.S. Constitution, the Mexican lawyer had reflected on occasion, was just so quaint, so charming . . .

Outside the room were two guards – both dedicated to making sure El Halcón didn't fly the coop, a witticism that Carreras-López couldn't resist.

Carreras-López's pen made whispering noises on the yellow pad before him. One would think that the notes he was jotting had to do with the appalling information that federal prosecutor Henry Bishop had just presented: that a new analysis of the evidence had proven, to a certainty, that his client was not hiding in the bathroom at the time of the shoot-out but was, in fact, armed and firing at the police.

That son of a bitch, Lincoln Rhyme, had set him up.

This was, of course, an irony in itself, because Carreras-López had himself contacted Rhyme with the express purpose of setting *him* up. The lawyer had come up with the absurd argument about tainted evidence solely to give himself a chance to meet Rhyme and look into his eyes. Carreras-López was a master of assessing men, and could tell in an instant if Rhyme suspected the plot had nothing to do with any diamond lodes in Brooklyn, but was about something else altogether, directly involving El Halcón. But no, the criminalist might be brilliant at analyzing fingerprints and trace evidence, but he was completely oblivious about what was really going on.

Which was that within the hour, El Halcón would be free. The plan to break him out of the courthouse here and spirit him away to a compound in Venezuela was proceeding perfectly.

There is a rumor that there is no extradition treaty between the United States and that troubled South American nation. That's not correct. The 1922 treaty between the two nations remains in effect, though the extraditable offenses are a bit bizarre – bigamy, for instance. There are rules about shipping fugitive murderers and drug dealers back to the U.S. but, of course, they are enforced only if the foreign authorities want to enforce them. And, depending on where the decimal point falls, the Venezuelans' motivation for enforcement can be a bit limp.

The escape plan had been long in the making – from the moment El Halcón had been taken into custody after the shoot-out at the warehouse on Long Island.

Carreras-López had known that a legal defense wouldn't work – El Halcón had in fact grabbed the pistol of the warehouse manager, Chris Cody, and shot Barry Sales, the cop on the tactical team. Escape was the only option. He'd called a troubleshooter whom the cartels in Mexico sometimes used, a man in Geneva, Switzerland, named François Letemps. Carreras-López had paid a million-dollar deposit against a three-million-dollar fee for Letemps to break the man out of custody.

Letemps had suggested staging the escape in some locale other than New York, which he viewed as problematic. But, no, that wouldn't work. There could be no change of venue; the Eastern District of New York had sole jurisdiction. And once he was convicted, as surely he would be, he would be in high-security lockdown until he was transferred by a government plane to the infamous Colorado super prison, from which escape was not possible.

No, New York was the only option. And since the federal courthouse in Brooklyn was the most vulnerable spot in the system, Letemps set to work on a plan to orchestrate a mass evacuation of the courthouse when El Halcón was present. In the chaos, it should be possible to take control of his armored transport van and escape.

But simply calling in a bomb threat, for instance, would have been far too suspicious and brought even more law enforcement down on El Halcón, Letemps reasoned.

He therefore decided to create a potentially deadly gas leak in the courthouse, for reasons that appeared to have nothing to do with any escape attempt. Specifically, Letemps's plan provided, a mercenary – hired to sabotage geothermal drilling nearby – would set gas bombs in the neighborhood.

Letemps had arranged for a shipment of diamond-rich kimberlite to be delivered to New York from Botswana. Carreras-López had some of his men, who'd accompanied him from Mexico, strew these rocks around the geothermal site and the waste dump where debris from the site was taken. One of the men also took some kimberlite to a famous diamond cutter – Jatin Patel – who had it analyzed and found that it was indeed diamond-rich stone. Whatever Patel thought of the stone was irrelevant. The plot merely depended on getting the kimberlite to him.

Letemps himself pretended to be the contractor representing New World Mining in Guatemala, which was not involved in any way. He hired Andrew Krueger to plant the bombs and kill Patel and the assayer Weintraub. Then that mad Russian had showed up, worried about the diamond find too, but in the end none of that mattered. The important thing was that the police were convinced there was a series of gas line devices planted throughout Brooklyn, near the courthouse.

Any other gas leaks would immediately be attributed to Krueger and his attempts to sabotage the drilling.

Poor Andrew Krueger – he was merely an oblivious pawn; he believed that he'd been hired by the Guatemalan company and had no idea that he'd been set up. And set up to fail: A key part of the plan was making sure the police figured out the diamond lode sabotage plot.

Lincoln Rhyme had, unwittingly, accommodated in this regard.

With a frown of concentration, Carreras-López jotted more notes on the pad before him. He shook his head, crossed off one entry. Added another. This was an important document: a grocery list for a dinner party he was planning to cook in Mexico City tomorrow night. His wife did not enjoy the kitchen; he did.

Chicken, poblano peppers, crème fraîche, cilantro, white Burgundy wine (Chablis?).

Now, as El Halcón pretended to read some court documents and fantasized about añejo tequila, the building shook with a faint tremor.

This was the result of a C4 charge planted not by Krueger but by one of Carreras-López's men at the geothermal site. This IED was not on a timer but had been detonated by radio signal, as the explosion had to coincide with El Halcón's presence in the courthouse.

The guards in the hallway outside looked briefly at each other, then returned to staring at nothing.

Carreras-López's mobile gave a brief tone. He looked at the text.

Your aunt has been discharged from hospital.

This meant that the lawyer's men were beginning to release the natural gas odorant – not the gas itself – into the courthouse HVAC system from outside the building.

Carreras-López switched his screen to the local news. A

breaking story reported yet another explosion, meant to mimic an earthquake. Residents in Brooklyn were urged to be on the lookout for gas leaks and to evacuate immediately if they were aware of any. Another text:

Her ride has arrived.

The helicopter had landed and was standing by at a construction site in Brooklyn, near the water – the craft that would spirit Carreras-López and El Halcón to an airstrip on Staten Island, where private jets would speed them to, respectively, Caracas and Mexico City.

Carreras-López prepared himself for what was coming next: the emergency evacuation of the courthouse. The guard detail would have Carreras-López leave and would usher El Halcón to his armored van in the loading dock on the ground floor for transport back to the detention center.

But El Halcón's evacuation wouldn't go quite as the federal marshals planned. The armored transport van would not be driven by the guards assigned to the vehicle. Carreras-López's men, dressed in guard uniforms, would have shot them with silenced weapons and taken over the van. It would drive up to the exit to await El Halcón and his two guards. Once they were in the van and the door closed, those guards would die too and the van would speed to the helicopter.

By tomorrow El Halcón would be enjoying life in his compound outside of Caracas. And Carreras-López – to whom no links to the plot could be proven – would be at home whipping up a Latin coq au vin, his own recipe.

And marveling at the plan.

Gracias, Monsieur François Letemps.

Or, *merci*.

Accompanying this thought was the first whiff of natural gas.

His eyes rose and met those of his client. El Halcón's brow furrowed only slightly. Carreras-López ripped the grocery list from his yellow pad and carefully folded and slipped it into his pocket.

Only sixty seconds later the door burst open and the guards streamed inside.

'The building's being evacuated.' To Carreras-López, one said, 'Out the main exit. Front.' Then turning to El Halcón. 'You're coming with us. Not a word. Keep your head down and walk where we tell you.'

Out of courtesy, or adherence to the rules, they repeated the statement in Spanish, and a guard undid the shackles from the floor rings. El Halcón rose to his feet.

With concern on his face, Carreras-López asked, 'But what's going on?'

'Gas leak. That asshole set the gas bombs? In the news? He planted one here or nearby. Move. Now!'

'*Dios mío!*' Carreras-López muttered and, blessing himself, walked to the doorway.

CHAPTER 69

He had asked for chaos and chaos had been delivered.

Antonio Carreras-López was across the street from the prisoner entrance loading dock of the federal courthouse. He was on the second floor of a coffee shop, where he had planned to observe the operation.

The streets were jammed with rescue workers – actually rescue *preparers* since no explosions or conflagrations had yet occurred. Fire trucks, police, ambulances. The press too, of course. And plenty of gawkers, arms lifted like saluting Fascists as they held high cell phones to record the anticipated carnage. Loudspeakers urged pedestrians and onlookers to back up behind the barricades. 'Immediately! There is a major fire and explosion risk! Move back!' The voices were stern. Nobody paid any attention to the warnings.

Behind this coffee shop Carreras-López's limo awaited. He had confidence in Letemps's scheme but, ever a practical man, the attorney was hedging bets. If the plan stumbled now, which was a possibility, of course, and the guards shot and killed his men and kept the Mexican drug lord in custody, the lawyer would hightail it from the country.

He had a family and a fortune and a cooking engagement awaiting at home. And he had a jet of his own all paid for.

Now he stiffened. He observed the armored transport van assigned to El Halcón pull forward. He had received another text.

Your aunt is on the way home.

Meaning that the prison guards in the van were dead and Carreras-López's men had taken over as driver and accompanying guard.

Now for the most critical moment.

The two guards from outside the interview room would soon appear, accompanying El Halcón as he walked to the van. Carreras-López could count three other guards, presently outside, armed with submachine guns, eyeing the crowd. It seemed to him that they were distracted, and understandably. Yes, they would not want their prisoner to escape, but they also would not want to burn to death when the gas blew; by now the scent should be overwhelming. And they would know, like the rest of the city, that the timer on the gas line was counting down – ten minutes from tremor to blast.

Then El Halcón and the two guards – only two – appeared from the doorway.

They hurried to the van as fast as they could – the crime boss's legs were still shackled – and the door opened. In they went. The door slammed shut.

Then, very faint, came several flashes of light from inside.

The silenced pistol killing the guards.

Pulling into the street, which had been cleared of traffic, the van accelerated away and turned the corner.

Another text.

She is doing well.

The last of the coded messages meant that the guards were dead and the van was proceeding to the rendezvous spot.

Carreras-López turned and hurried down the back stairs of the coffee shop to his limo. He climbed inside. The driver greeted him and they started off, the Caddie circling the blocked streets. Soon they hit the highway, about five minutes behind the van.

The security van would have GPS; its progress would be tracked. So Letemps had picked a rendezvous spot that was just off the highway on the way to the detention center. Anyone tracking the van would think that, when it pulled off, it was simply diverting briefly to avoid a traffic jam.

It would stop fast to let El Halcón and the other men out. The stop would eventually alarm the security people at detention.

But by the time they got reinforcements here, El Halcón and Carreras-López would be long gone.

Now the Cadillac in which Antonio Carreras-López sat was gaining on the van. He could see it about a hundred yards ahead. In sixty seconds they were at the turnoff, and the van, then Carreras-López's limo, turned into the empty, weed-filled parking lot that surrounded a dilapidated factory. The towering sign read only *H&R Fab icat s, I c*. These remaining letters, six feet high, would have been proudly red at one point but were now scarred and sickly pink.

The van and limo stopped near the helicopter, its rotors idling, and a van, in front of which the lawyer's men stood.

Carreras-López glanced back and saw no police vehicles. Nor any choppers overhead or boats in the choppy water where the East River met the harbor.

None of the authorities suspected a thing. They would have ten minutes before anyone at detention grew concerned about the van's absence and sent cars.

Carreras-López climbed from the limo. He said to the driver, 'Leave now.' He gave the man five hundred-dollar bills and shook his hand.

'Thank you, sir. I've enjoyed driving you. I'll see you when you're back.'

Which would never happen. But he said, 'I'll look forward to it.'

The Cadillac slowly bounded out of the broken, uneven parking lot.

Carreras-López waved to the van, where El Halcón was probably stripping the dead guards of their money and weapons. His client had once killed a man for his wallet – not for the money but because he liked the embossed leather . . . and the picture of the victim's wife and daughter. El Halcón had told Carreras-López that he'd kept the picture on his bedside table for years.

A thought that even now gave the lawyer a shiver. What a man I have for a client.

The door to the van opened.

'*Hola!*' Carreras-López called.

415

Then he froze. He whispered, '*Mierda*.'

Because it wasn't El Halcón climbing from the vehicle. But a redheaded policewoman, in full tactical gear and holding a machine gun. She was followed by three, no four, no six other officers, half with the letters *ESU* on their body armor. Half with *FBI*.

'No!' the lawyer cried.

Two of these officers ran to the helicopter and dragged out the pilot, and the others arrested the men by the van. The policewoman stepped quickly to the lawyer, with a younger, blond male officer. 'Hands!' she shouted. The lawyer sighed, licked his lips with a dry tongue and lifted his arms. He remembered seeing her in Lincoln Rhyme's apartment.

How? How had it happened?

A perfect plan.

So perfectly ruined.

How? The question looped through his mind.

As he was cuffed by the woman and patted down by the man, he tried to figure this out.

The texts were the right codes.

El Halcón had gotten into the van. I *saw* him.

I saw the flashes of the gunshots.

Or did I?

A clever man himself, he thought: No, no, no. They had learned of, or guessed, the plan and had located Carreras-López's men before they could murder the driver and guard. The police had offered them a plea bargain in exchange for the codes and the details of the escape.

The flashes from inside the vehicle weren't a gun but a cell phone or flashlight to convince anyone watching that the second set of guards had died. As soon as the van was out of sight, it had diverted and this one, with the tactical officers, had taken its place for the trip to the factory here.

But that didn't answer the bigger question of how: How had someone – Lincoln Rhyme, surely – come to suspect that an escape was in the works, in the first place?

The policewoman said, 'Sit down here. I'll help you.'

She eased him to the ground. 'Please. How did you figure it out? How did you possibly know what we were doing? I want to know. Will you tell me?'

She ignored him as her attention was drawn to an approaching black limo. It stopped and a tall, lean man got out.

Carreras-López sighed. It was Henry Bishop, the U.S. attorney.

The policewoman walked to the man and they had a conversation. Not surprisingly, as they spoke, they both kept their eyes on him.

Finally, Bishop nodded. They both began walking, in long strides, to the lawyer.

CHAPTER 70

Rhyme was in his accessible van, not far from the takedown site by the water's edge in Brooklyn.

He was presently watching though the window and listening to the staccato voice traffic on the police scanner.

Yes, he and Sachs had had a lovely dinner last night.

But they hadn't discussed movies or politics or the thousands of other topics grand and topics small that husbands and wives talked about over meals; they talked about the loose ends that had piqued Rhyme's interest about the Diamond District case.

'Anomalies, Sachs. Pieces don't fit quite right.'

'Such as?'

She had been enjoying quite the nice Burgundy. Chardonnay, of course. But not overly oaked, a subtlety that the French – unlike the Californians – had mastered. Rhyme took this on faith; he had swapped the Glenmorangie for a Cab. If one had to drink wine, it should be red and formidable.

He'd explained the loosest of the ends: 'How did Jatin Patel come into possession of the kimberlite in the first place?'

She'd cocked her head. 'Never thought about it. A good question.'

He'd asked with more than a dusting of irony, 'Somebody strolling past the geothermal site or the refuse dump *happens* to notice an unremarkable dark hunk of rock and takes it to a diamond merchant for assessment?'

'Doesn't make sense.'

'Another problem: Didn't the whole fake-earthquake thing, didn't it seem just a bit improbable? Almost as if we were supposed to figure out it was staged.'

'True. You get caught up in a fast-moving case, you don't step back.'

Rhyme had said, 'Say there's a Mr Y.'

'Is "X" taken?'

A smile. 'Remember? I used that before.'

'Okay, go ahead. Mr Y.'

'He has a plan too. Mr Y, or somebody working for him, calls Krueger – anonymously – and claims he's working for New World Mining. They're all in a frenzy because a drilling site in Brooklyn has dug up diamond-rich kimberlite. They hire Krueger to create fake earthquakes to shut down the drilling and kill Patel and anyone else who knows about it.'

'And,' Sachs had said, 'Mr Y ships some kimberlite from Africa and plants it at the geothermal site.'

'Exactly. Remember the trace we found? *Coleonema pulchellum* – the confetti bush – also from Africa.'

Rhyme had then enjoyed another piece of veal in a fennel cream sauce, laced with vermouth. Back in the day, for years after the accident, Thom had had to feed him. Of late, as long as someone cut up his food, or it arrived naturally in bite-sized form, he could handle the dining part on his own just fine.

She had said, 'Got it, so far. Mr Y sets up this elaborate plan for fake earthquakes apparently to stop diamond production . . . but he's got some other plan entirely. Which is . . . ?'

'I couldn't figure that out. Not at first. But then I asked myself, why Brooklyn, why the Northeast Geo site? Mr Y could've picked any construction site in the area. No, there was something special about Cadman Plaza. And what was unique there?'

'The government buildings. The courts.'

Rhyme had smiled once more. 'And was there any other piece of the puzzle that connected the dots?'

'I have a feeling,' Sachs had said, 'that is an extremely rhetorical question.'

'The other day Pulaski smelled gas in the town house. I assumed it was because Lon had just come from the scene at Claire Porter's apartment – where they recovered the *lehabah*, the gas bomb. It didn't go off but it did melt through the gas line, and there was a major leak. I figured he'd picked up the scent there. But I called him. And he hadn't been to the scene.'

'So where did the scent come from?'

'From the box of files on the El Halcón case. Delivered to me by Mr Y.'

'Mr Y!' Her eyes glowed. 'Carreras-López.'

'Exactly. One of his minders brought the case files to me. Wherever they'd been, it was also where they'd stored the odorant. Maybe they tested it, maybe it leaked. But some odorant got on the files. So. The gas bombs had some connection with El Halcón's attorney and, presumably, his trial.'

Sachs had mused, 'And that explains why Carreras-López came to you with that claim about somebody planting the gunshot residue evidence in the warehouse.'

'Yep. He wanted to get inside the Unsub Forty-Seven op. Keep tabs on us, make sure we weren't suspicious that the diamond plot was fake. If I hadn't given Bishop the capital murder lead, I think he would have been a regular guest – well, spy.'

She'd set down her fork. 'But, Jesus, Rhyme. He's going to try to break El Halcón out . . . tomorrow, maybe. We're just sitting here.'

He'd shrugged. 'Nothing can happen until then. I called my new friend Hank Bishop and found out El Halcón's arriving at ten a.m. Besides, we haven't finished our meal.'

She'd given him a coy look. 'And you've already called Lon, Ron, Fred Dellray and probably someone from ESU. When will they be here?'

'A half hour. Won't interfere with dessert. Thom! *Thom!* Weren't you going to flambé something special for Amelia?'

Then this morning Sellitto and Dellray had initiated the operation that had been put together the night before. They decided that Carreras-López probably would have his own men, dressed as guards, hijack the transport vehicle, so FBI agents and undercover detectives did a sweep of the guards in and around the courthouse. They found two men who were imposters – and armed with weapons equipped with silencers. Dellray – in his inimitable, and intimidating, style – convinced them to give up details of the plot in exchange for reduced charges. ('I'm triple-guaranteeing you, you will not be enjoying the par-*tic*-u-lar prison, not to mention the population, you will be going to, if you don't help. Are we all together on that?')

So far, so good.

Then had come the debate. Rhyme, Sachs, Dellray and Sellitto – and some senior NYPD brass, as well as City Hall.

They knew that there was no risk of an actual gas attack. Carreras-López's men would merely release the odorant, to start the evacuation; they couldn't risk burning up their client with a real gas leak. The federal marshals and NYPD could simply have ignored the release, and passed the word on that there was no danger. Open the windows, ventilate the place. And let the trial continue.

But, Rhyme believed, if they could nail Carreras-López, they could offer the lawyer a plea bargain in exchange for El Halcón's partner.

Which meant they had to let the escape plan go forward – but divert El Halcón's van and use a second one, filled with tactical officers, to proceed to the helicopter and take down the lawyer and his entire crew.

Exactly as had happened, without a glitch.

Rhyme's phone now hummed with a text.

FYI. Carreras-López has accepted plea offer. Identified his U.S. partner: Roger Whitney, Garden City, Long Island. Thx, Lincoln. – H. Bishop.

Rhyme now heard the sound of the Sprinter door opening behind him. He turned.

Sachs stood in the doorway, her machine gun slung, muzzle down, from her shoulder. Her helmet in her left hand. Rhyme reflected that she was nearly as appealing in this outfit as she had been in the green dress.

'Can I hitch a ride?' she asked.

'Think we can fit you in.'

Sachs climbed in and slammed the door. She sat, pulled the

magazine from her weapon and ejected the round in the chamber. Their eyes met.

'So,' she said. 'That's it.'

'That's it, Sachs.'

CHAPTER 71

Vimal Lahori had not seen his father yesterday.

After supper with his mother and brother, Vimal had gone to spend the evening with Adeela. He'd returned late and by the time he arrived home, he noted his father's car was in the drive but he had gone to bed.

Upon waking this morning, he learned that Papa was again out.

Whatever business the man was about, he hadn't shared it with his wife, much less his younger son. But then Papa never shared anything unless it was a pronouncement coming down from on high.

Vimal knew, without doubt, but with dread, what the man's mission was: finding Vimal another apprenticeship. But it wouldn't be easy, despite Vimal's skills. The young man was tainted. He was now associated with the worst thing that could happen in the diamond world – a robbery and murder. Oh, he wasn't guilty of anything himself, and the crimes had turned out to be something quite different, but diamantaires wouldn't dwell on those distinctions. They would forever link Vimal with the death of the genius Jatin Patel, one of their own.

Vimal Lahori had become a living reminder of the dark and perilous side of these miraculous gems, from blood diamonds in Africa, to slave labor in Siberia, to armed robberies in Belgium.

But his father would beg or bluster until someone signed Vimal on.

He was presently in his studio, looking over a two-pound piece of lapis lazuli. Vimal loved this intensely blue mineral. It was generally used for jewelry but one could find pieces large enough for sculpting, at reasonable prices. The metamorphic rock has a long history in both jewelry and art. Tutankhamun's funeral mask featured it, and Chinese artists would carve miniature mountainside villages into vertical pieces, just as they did with jade. Lapis was first discovered in Badakhshan province in Afghanistan and is now found there, as well as such exotic places stone Siberia, Angola, Burma, Pakistan and – where this particular stone had come from – Pleasant Gulch, Colorado.

He was turning the stone over and over in his hand, waiting for it to talk to him and explain what incarnation it wished to achieve through Vimal's eager hands. Yet at the moment it was silent.

Then footsteps on the stairs.

Vimal knew the tread falls. He set down the brilliant blue stone, layered with gold pyrite, and sat on the work chair.

'Son.'

Vimal nodded to the bleary-eyed man. He reflected: must be hard work trying to pimp a whore nobody wants.

Papa was carrying two envelopes, one large and one small. Vimal glanced at them, supposing they were contracts for cutting assignments. His eyes slipped back to his father.

The man said, 'I missed you last night. I was very tired. I went to bed. But your mother told me you were well. Unharmed after that incident with the man. The killer.'

Incident . . .

'Yes.'

'I was very grateful for that,' Papa said, then seemed to realize the absurdity of the words.

His father's eyes were on the lapis. 'Mr Patel's children and their families have come to town. They and his sister have held the funeral and cremation privately.' In the Hindu religion, cremation is the only acceptable way to treat the body. In India the funeral and the cremation occur at the same place – traditionally, of course, the body is burned on an open pyre. Here, the Hindu funeral rites, the Antyesti, are modified to allow for Western custom and laws.

His father added, 'But they are holding a memorial at his sister's house tonight. That's one reason I've been away. I was helping with that. You will come?'

'Sure. Yeah, of course.'

'You can say something if you like. But you don't have to.'

'I will.'

'Good. You'll do a good job.'

Silence.

One reason I've been away . . .

Now it was time to learn of the other reason. Who was to be his new master?

Well, Vimal Lahori decided. This was the end. He was going to say no to the man.

At last he would say no.

He took a deep breath to do so but his father handed him the smaller of the envelopes. The trembling of his hand was not so bad today. 'Here.'

Vimal held back on the monologue he was prepared to deliver and took the envelope. He glanced into his father's eyes.

The man's shrug said, Open it.

Vimal did. He looked at what was inside and his breath stopped momentarily. He looked to his father then back to the contents.

'This is – ' He actually choked.

'Yes, a check from Dev Nouri's company.'

Payable to Vimal Lahori. Only to him.

'Papa, it's almost one hundred thousand dollars.'

'You will have to pay tax on it. But you'll still keep about two-thirds.'

'But . . . '

'The rough that you cut for him. That parallelogram.' The word came awkwardly from his mouth. 'Dev sold it at private auction for three hundred thousand dollars. He was going to give you ten percent.'

A talented diamond cutter in the New York area could expect to make around fifty thousand dollars a year. The thirty that Mr Nouri had offered for a one-day job was very generous by any standard throughout the world.

'But I said no. He and I had some discussions. He agreed, as you can see, to thirty-three percent. It's less than an even one hundred, because he insisted on subtracting the money he'd already paid you. I thought we could not object to that.'

Vimal could not help but smile.

'Open an account, deposit it. It's your money. You can do with it as you like. Now, I will say something else. You will be getting many phone calls. There is not a single diamantaire in the New York area who does not want you to work for them. I have heard from a number of them who would want you to apprentice to them. They have all heard of the parallelogram. Some people are calling it the Vimal Cut.'

The news was interesting – he was not a pariah – but it was also disheartening. The pressure from his father was back. More subtle, but pressure nonetheless.

Papa muttered, 'You can get a job at any one of them and they will pay very well. But before you do that, think about this.' He offered the larger envelope.

Vimal removed from it a college catalog, for an accredited, four-year university on Long Island. A yellow Post-it was stuck in the middle. Vimal opened to the page, which described the MFA, master in fine arts, program. There was a track for sculpting, which included a semester abroad in Florence and Rome.

Feeling his heart stutter, he looked up to his father.

The man said, 'So. I have been the messenger. The rest is up to you. You may want a different school, of course. Though your mother and I were hoping that if you do, we would prefer you to become the Michelangelo of Jackson Heights, rather than of Los Angeles. But, as I say, it's up to you, son.'

Vimal had no intention of flinging his arms around his father but he couldn't help himself.

The awkwardness faded quickly, and the embrace lasted considerably longer than he and, he guessed, his father anticipated. Then they stepped away.

'We will leave for Mr Patel's sister's at five.' He turned and started for the stairs. 'Oh, and why don't you invite Adeela?'

Vimal stared. 'How did . . . ?'

The look on his father's face was cryptic but the message might very well have been: Never underestimate the intelligence – in both senses of the word – of one's parents.

His father left the studio and trooped upstairs. Vimal picked up the lapis lazuli and began turning it over and over and over in his hands once more, waiting for the stone to speak.

CHAPTER 72

'Barry.' Rhyme was in his parlor, on the speakerphone.

'Lincoln. I'm pissed off at you, you know that.'

'Yeah? Why?'

'I was a bottom-shelf kinda guy. You turned me on to *real* scotch. The pricey stuff. Actually, Joan is pissed at you. Me, not so much.'

A pause.

Then Rhyme said, 'We nailed him, Barry. He's going away forever. El Halcón.'

'Jesus. I thought the case was dicey.'

'It became undicey.'

More silence.

'And we got his partner. The American.'

Rhyme could hear the man breathing.

'You have anything to do with that?'

'Not much. A little.'

Sales laughed. 'Bullshit. I'm not believing that.'

'Well, believe what you want.'

'That's the Lincoln Rhyme I know and love.' Then, diverting from the edge of maudlin, Sales said, 'Hey. Talked to my sister? She had an idea. I'm getting a temporary prothesis. Just a hook, you know. She's going to bring the kids over and, guess, what? We'll do the Wolverine thing. They'll love it.'

'What thing?'

'The movie. You know.'

'There's a movie about wolverines?'

'You don't get out much, do you, Lincoln?'

'Well, I'm happy it's working out.'

'We'll get together soon. I'll buy the whisky.'

They disconnected and Rhyme was wheeling back to the

evidence table when his mobile hummed melodically with an incoming call.

He hit Answer.

'Lincoln,' came the voice through the phone, obscured by a cacophony of electric guitar licks.

Rhyme snapped in response, 'Rodney, for God's sake. Turn down the music.'

'You *do* know that's Jimmy Page.'

A sigh. Which the Computer Crimes expert couldn't possibly hear, owing to the raw decibels.

'All right. Just saying. Did you know that Led Zeppelin holds the number two record for most albums sold in the U.S.? Wait. Forget that. In *history*?' Szarnek dimmed the volume. Somewhat. You'd expect him to have shoulder-length curly hair, inked skin and body piercings and wear shirts open to the navel – if that's what heavy-metal band lead guitarists still looked like. The fact was he fit the image of the computer nerd he was.

Amelia Sachs walked into the parlor, bent down and kissed Rhyme.

Szarnek said, 'Found some things you'll want to know about the Kimberlite Affair.'

'That's what you're calling it?' Sachs asked. Her voice was amused.

'I kind of like it. Don't you? Nice ring. K, here's what I'm talking about. You sent me the number of that lawyer's burner phone, Carreras-López? I checked the log. A lot of calls were to the folks who got rounded up at the courthouse and helipad and in the hoosegow.'

'The what?'

'A jail. Like in old-time Westerns. The pokey.'

'Rodney. Get to the point.'

'But this's interesting. *Most* of the calls and texts were to and from somebody in Paris. In the Sixth Arrondissement. That means "district."'

'I know,' Sachs said.

'In and around the Jardin du Luxembourg. That's a garden. But you probably know that too.'

'That I didn't know.'

Szarnek added, 'Whoever it was, the lawyer called and texted a lot over the past few weeks. Almost like he was reporting in.'

'Maybe a consultant,' Sachs said. 'You thought the lawyer was Mr Y. Who planned it all out. Might have been this person.'

'Could be.'

'Rhyme,' Sachs said, lifting an evidence bag. It was Carreras-López's day planner. Pasted inside the cover was a Post-it note with the name *François Letemps*. A series of numbers was beside it. Account numbers maybe.

French name. Was he the man on the other end of the line in Paris?

Szarnek said, 'Now, here's the weird part.'

In an already weird case.

'The texts were encrypted with exactly the same algorithm you were asking about a few days ago. Duodenal. Using numbers zero through nine plus the upside-down two and three. Never rains but it pours.'

Jesus. Rhyme's eyes slowly eased to the evidence boards.

'And no chance of cracking it?'

'About the same as me appearing on *Dancing with the Stars*.'

'The hell is that?'

'Let's say impossible.'

'I've got to go.' Rhyme disconnected and shouted to Mel Cooper, 'That package we got from the Alternative Intelligence Service? The international delivery?'

It had arrived last night but Rhyme had been too preoccupied with the case to look at it.

Cooper sliced open the box. There was no letter, only a note from Daryl Mulbry.

Here you go. Any thoughts would be helpful.

Cooper lifted a small evidence envelope. Inside was the small crescent of metal that had tested positive for radiation, though not of any dangerous dosage. Rhyme now studied it.

He recalled that Mulbry was concerned that the bit of springy metal might be a timer in a dirty bomb – part of a mechanical detonator, intended to avoid the defenses to an electronic one.

This, Rhyme now knew, was not correct.

But the truth behind the bit of metal was, in a way, even more troubling.

Rhyme placed a call to Mulbry now.

'Lincoln! How are you?'

'Not much time here. Maybe have a situation. That bit of metal you sent me?'

'Yes.' The man's voice was sober.

'Let me ask a couple more questions.'

'Of course.'

'You found anything more about your suspect, the man who dropped it?'

'We finally found the café he was hanging out in when he made a lot of his calls. It was—'

'Near the Jardin du Luxembourg.'

'*Mon dieu*, Lincoln. Yes. How—'

'And what did the EVIDINT unit find?'

'Nothing No prints, no usable trace, no DNA. Just a description.'

'Which is?'

'White male, forties, fifties. Spoke perfect French but possibly with an American accent.'

Rhyme's head rested back against the leather pad. Thoughts swirled. 'It's not a bomb, Daryl. No terrorist issues.'

'No?'

'You don't have anything to worry about.' He paused. 'I do.'

'You? That's a bit cryptic.'

'I'll send you a detailed report,' Rhyme told him. They disconnected.

He was now looking over the charts. Impossible. But on the other hand . . .

'Rhyme, what is it?' Sachs asked. She'd be noting the frown.

He didn't answer but called Rodney Szarnek back and asked for the number of the phone that Carreras-López had called in Paris.

'It's a dead burner, Lincoln. We've pinged it a dozen times.'

'Just the number, if you would.'

Rodney dictated it.

'Thanks,' Rhyme muttered and stared at the digits as he disconnected.

He verbally commanded his phone to send a text to the French phone. It was a simple message:

Text or call this number. – Lincoln Rhyme.

After disconnecting he said to Sachs, 'Didn't we say this whole plot was complicated?'

'Yep.'

'And do you remember what the extra features of a watch are called? Like the date, phases of the moon, tides, different time zones.'

'They're called complications. Where's this going?'

'The encryption package that Mulbry's suspect in Paris was using – and the one Carreras-López and his contact used – was written in the duodecimal system. Twelve. Like the hours on a clock.'

He nodded at the bit of metal. 'It's not a detonator. It's a watch spring. And the radiation isn't from a dirty bomb. It'll be radium from the dial of a clock or watch. The man AIS was suspicious of . . . and the man hired to put together the El Halcón escape plot were one and the same. And he has a hobby. Building timepieces.'

'Rhyme, no!'

But the answer was yes, he believed.

The individual in question was none other than Charles Vespasian Hale, though he often used a favored pseudonym, Richard Logan, if he needed to be less obtrusive. Rhyme thought of him, though, exclusively by his nickname, the Watchmaker.

Rhyme closed his eyes briefly, recalling he'd been thinking of the Watchmaker just the other day, reflecting that Unsub 47's plot, while smart, didn't rise to the level of Hale's brilliance.

'Rhyme,' Sachs said, looking at the evidence bag containing Carreras-López's day planner. 'Letemps. French for "time."'

He gave a brief laugh. 'He's got Mexican connections. Remember that case a few years ago? The Watchmaker was hired by one of the cartels. It was an assassination, if I remember. So Carreras-López must have known about him, maybe from that job, and signed him on to break his client out of lockup.'

Sachs asked, 'Do you think you'll hear from him? As soon as he learned the operation failed, I'd imagine he pitched that phone in the Seine.'

But Rhyme knew the phone was alive and well. The Watchmaker had held on to it for one reason, and one reason only.

No more than ten minutes later Rhyme's own mobile chimed – several times – with a series of texts.

Hello, Lincoln. It's been some time. Doing well, from what I've heard. My, I was afraid this might happen. I tried to plan El Halcón's escape anywhere but New York, worried that you would leap into the fray. Sadly, there could be no change of venue – for El Halcón or for my plan. Brooklyn was the only weak link in security.

And so I created as smart a plan as I could, to keep you fooled, but we saw what happened. I have my down payment on the job but you cost me three million dollars for the rest of the fee. That, I don't care so much about. What troubles me is the damage to my reputation. Word will get around and people might think: Perhaps his timepieces are not ticking as accurately as in the past. After all, a clock that loses only a thousandth of a second a year is still a faulty clock. Time is absolute.

This cannot happen again. The next time we meet – and we will meet again, I promise you – will be the last. Farewell, for now, Lincoln. I'll leave you with this sentiment, which I hope you will ponder on sleepless nights: Quidam hostibus potest neglecta; aliis hostibus mori debent.

Yours, Charles Vespasian Hale

Rhyme was not a classics scholar but he could translate that line well enough:

Some enemies can be ignored; other enemies must die.

He read the text once more – to see if there were any clues as to where the Watchmaker was texting from or where he intended to go. Nothing. And by now the phone was, in fact, destroyed. He told Cooper to power down his phone, remove the battery and throw it out. Then call the server and cancel that number.

He then moved to the landline and spoke into the microphone attached to it.

'Call Daryl Mulbry. AIS.'

The numbers trilled by quickly as the dialer went to work.

Two rings. Then a woman's matter-of-fact voice: 'Yes?'

'Daryl Mulbry. Please.'

'I'm sorry. He's not available right now.'

'It's important.'

'I'll make sure he gets the message. If you—'

'Please tell him it's Lincoln Rhyme calling.'

A pause. 'Just a minute, sir. I'll get him.'

Acknowledgments

Many, many thanks to the team: Will and Tina Anderson, Cicely Aspinall, Sophie Baker, Felicity Blunt, Penelope Burns, Giovanna Canton, Francesca Cinelli, Luca Crovi, Jane Davis, Julie Deaver, Andy Dodd, Jenna Dolan, Jamie Hodder-Williams, Kerry Hood, Cathy Gleason, Emma Knight, Meriam Metoui, Carolyn Mays, Wes Miller, Claire Nozieres, Hazel Orme, Abby Parsons, Seba Pezzani, Michael Pietsch, Betsy Robbins, Katy Rouse, Lindsey Rose, Roberto and Cecilia Santachiara, Deborah Schneider, Vivienne Schuster, Kallie Shimek, Louise Swannell, Ruth Tross, Madelyn Warcholik.

About the Author

A former journalist, folksinger and attorney, Jeffery Deaver is an international number one bestselling author. His novels have appeared on bestseller lists around the world, including those of the *New York Times*, *The Times* of London, Italy's *Corriere della Sera*, the *Sydney Morning Herald* and the *Los Angeles Times*. His books are sold in 150 countries and translated into twenty-five languages.

He has served two terms as the president of the Mystery Writers of America.

The author of forty novels, three collections of short stories and a nonfiction law book, and a lyricist of a country-western album, he's received or been shortlisted for dozens of awards.

His *The Bodies Left Behind* was named Novel of the Year by the International Thriller Writers association, and his Lincoln Rhyme thriller *The Broken Window* and a stand-alone, *Edge*, were also nominated for that prize, as was a short story published recently. He has been awarded the Steel Dagger and the Short Story Dagger from the British Crime Writers' Association and the Nero Award, and he is a three-time recipient of the Ellery Queen Readers Award for Best Short Story of the Year and a winner of the British Thumping Good Read Award. *Solitude Creek* and *The Cold Moon* were both given the number one ranking by *Kono Misurteri Ga Sugoi* in Japan. *The Cold Moon* was also named the Book of the Year by the Mystery Writers Association of Japan. In addition, the Japanese Adventure Fiction Association awarded *The Cold Moon* and *Carte Blanche* their annual Grand Prix award. His book *The Kill Room* was awarded the Political Thriller of the Year by Killer Nashville. And his collection of short stories, *Trouble in Mind*, was nominated for best anthology by that organization, as well.

Deaver has been honored with the Lifetime Achievement Award by the Bouchercon World Mystery Convention and by the Raymond Chandler Lifetime Achievement Award in Italy. The *Strand Magazine* also has presented him with a Lifetime Achievement Award.

Deaver has been nominated for seven Edgar Awards from the Mystery Writers of America, an Anthony, a Shamus and a Gumshoe. He was shortlisted for the ITV3 Crime Thriller Award for Best International Author. *Roadside Crosses* was on the shortlist for the Prix Polar International 2013. He's also been shortlisted for a Shamus.

His *The Starling Project*, staring Alfred Molina and produced by Audible.com, won the Audie Award for best original audiobook of the year in 2015. A serial novel he created and contributed to, *The Chopin Manuscript*, also won this honor.

He contributed to the anthologies *In the Company of Sherlock* and *Books to Die For*, which won the Anthony. *Books to Die For* recently won the Agatha, as well.

His most recent novels are *The Burial Hour* and *The Steel Kiss*, both Lincoln Rhyme novels; *Solitude Creek*, a Kathryn Dance thriller; and *The October List*, a thriller told in reverse. For the Dance novel *XO* Deaver wrote an album of country-western songs, available on iTunes and as a CD; and before that, he wrote *Carte Blanche*, a James Bond continuation novel, a number one international bestseller.

His book *A Maiden's Grave* was made into an HBO movie starring James Garner and Marlee Matlin, and his novel *The Bone Collector* was a feature release from Universal Pictures, starring Denzel Washington and Angelina Jolie. Lifetime aired an adaptation of his *The Devil's Teardrop*. And, yes, the rumors are true: He did appear as a corrupt reporter on his favorite soap opera, *As the World Turns*. He was born outside Chicago and has a bachelor of journalism degree from the University of Missouri and a law degree from Fordham University.

Readers can visit his website at www.jefferydeaver.com or Facebook and Twitter.